HOMUNCULA

John Henri Nolette

Black Powder Press
&
C.A.L. Press

2016

First Printing: 2016

ISBN-10: 0692642552
ISBN-13: 978-0692642559

Published by

Black Powder Press
www.blackpowderpress.com

In collaboration with

C.A.L. Press
Post Office Box 3448
Berkeley, California 94703
www.anarchymag.org

Acknowledgements

This book never would have been possible without the help and guidance of Apio, Chris Weber, LJ and LD. Thanks also to the Horror Theory Crew, Erin, Matthew, and Salena, for going down the rabbit-hole of utmost horror nerdery with me, and to LJ for repeatedly (and with freakishly enhanced intuition) handing me exactly the books I needed, exactly when I needed them.

Dedicated to
ETHAN HABUDA
One of the brotherhood

HOMUNCULA

The problem that I set here is not what shall replace mankind in the order of living creatures but what type of man must be bred, must be willed, as being the most worthy of life, the most secure guarantee of the future. This more valuable type has appeared often enough in the past: but always as a happy accident, as an exception, never as deliberately willed. Very often it has been precisely the most feared; hitherto it has been almost the terror of terrors;— and out of that terror the contrary type has been willed, cultivated, and attained; the domestic animal, the herd animal, the sick brute-man, the Christian.

Friedrich Nietzsche

PROLOGUE

AS I SIT QUIETLY IN THIS CROWDED CAFÉ, ALONE WITH MY TEA AND MY notebook, an anonymous stranger among many, I am made forcibly aware of the fact that this will be the last time I shall be permitted to sit peaceably, shoulder to shoulder with my fellow man. By this time tomorrow my name and face will have appeared in all the major New England papers and associated with crimes so ghastly that I will be universally reviled, hunted down, and (if only they could find me) murdered like a mad dog. The meek-mannered and amiable citizens of York, Maine will have organized themselves into self-righteous vigilante mobs, eager to comb the hills in search of a most hated scapegoat, a fiend in human form, whose existence they will not abide. Some, having seen my face in the papers and on wanted posters may even recall that the day before the story broke they sat harmlessly near to me in this crowded café... and they will shudder at such intimate proximity. They may even recall seeing me scribbling this, my final letter, in which I shall attempt to elucidate the incredible circumstances of my imminent disappearance from the face of this green earth. This, therefore, shall necessarily be my last attempt to communicate my experiences to my own species.

Of the atrocities that will be found in the abandoned farmhouse on Arnold Lane, in Sudbury, Massachusetts, I can offer no earthly rationale. I know that I am objectively responsible for them and this I freely admit, knowing, as I do so, that I have precious little hope of explaining what has driven me to do such things, without sounding, to the great herds of humanity, like a depraved psychopath. What I hope to show to the thoughtful reader (if there be such a one) is that it was not merely "I" who committed those admittedly heinous brutalities but also... an incredible and indescribable Other... a being which first came to me in the early days of my youth, and slowly, by some unknown species of telepathy, found a way to insinuate Itself among my very thoughts, to govern and manipulate my mental faculties. The slaughter in the farmhouse is merely the most recent example of that which I was compelled to do in the course of my service to this being. It is only the aftermath of their peculiar manner of feeding that you will find there upon the farmhouse floor (and also in the tool shed, the cellar, and in the corner of the yard near the fence).

How may I hope to speak of such things to the uninitiated? How might I describe those painful "transmissions," which began as a mere melancholy, a simple depression in spirit, some 25 years ago, and have since grown into this all-consuming, mind-erasing obsession? How might the dead words on this page possibly convey the frightful things I have seen and heard and done? I realize that I cannot say whether I am insane or not. Were I mad, so I am told, I would not necessarily be cognizant of the fact. Nevertheless, I would very much like to know if what I've lived through has been real or is only some elaborate, self-organized delusion. I sincerely hope, for the sake of all the living things upon this earth, that it might be the latter and not the former. I fear that I shall have my answer soon enough. Perhaps, dear reader, you shall too.

There is just one more thing which I must say before I begin, a thing which haunts me with its pathetic sweetness and makes my heart ache as I write these words. Ever since my earliest boyhood I have suffered from a vivid, recurring nightmare, in which I die brutally at the hands of a lynch mob. And now, as this exact fate seems to be closing in around me, I am genuinely touched and heartbroken by the poetic possibility that I have, since early childhood, been dreaming vividly of my own death. The mind is a labyrinth in which we flatter ourselves to think that we are the 'captains of our soul.' The idiot who said that probably beat his children and dreamt of bloody murder.

I

MY NAME IS ROBERT HENRY PEARCE I WAS BORN ON NOVEMBER 29th, 1897 in the village of Southwick, in the hill country west of Springfield, Massachusetts. My father (who died in a sanitarium when I was four years old) was then just a traveling musician happily married to my mother, a girl of 16, who worked as a clerk. I was their only child (or so they said) and apparently without cousins, aunts, uncles, or grandparents on either side. It seemed improbable to me that I had no living relatives and yet I accepted these declarations without question and tried to believe them in earnest.

I received what I would call a liberal education, was given the usual moral instruction, immersed in the various mores, codes, and taboos of my people. I recall that I was taught to care a great deal about "being good" and was prompted to concern myself with such things as "the Greater Good," "the Truth," and "the condition of my eternal soul." I was encouraged to do things that were for "the benefit of humanity," to study Medicine, or Law, or to create some artistic masterpiece. However, I sensed that this was not for me. Right from the start, it was evident that something was absent. Something was not quite right.

I am told that from earliest childhood I was "chronically morose" and "awkward" and I do recall quite distinctly, from as early as four and five years of age, that even my own mother seemed to find my presence repulsive and unnerving. Those who knew me generally spoke ill of me and even the neighbors remained aloof. To them, it must have seemed that I was nothing more than the half-wit son of a man who had gone mad, and one of my earliest memories was the painful realization that I was regarded by my own people as a kind of living tragedy. I did not "belong," the children at school used to say, and in my heart, I knew they were right. I was always hungry, always restless, always daydreaming. I was unaccountably dissatisfied with the society of human beings and it made me nervous and irritable. I remember a strange and desperate feeling that there was somewhere else I was supposed to be, some other life that I was supposed to be living... though I could not have described it even if I had been asked to do so. There was something inside of me, some appetite or craving that I could not name or identify, which seemed to haunt me and set me apart.

To all this there was the added problem of certain anatomical abnormalities which seemed to underscore my strangeness. First, there was curious discoloration upon the iris of my left eye, a brownish stain which covered the area directly above my pupil, so that my mostly blue eyes were not so much dissimilar to each other, as they were noticeably mismatched. Second, there had been some sort of trouble with my mouth, something oddly amiss with the size, shape, and arrangement of my teeth. They had grown in too long and thick for my mouth and with a curious tendency to twist, sometimes even curling around each other. This deformity was so serious as to require corrective surgery, though the memory of this is dim as I was still quite young. Furthermore, my head was unusually large for my body and I walked with a noticeable stoop, my head thrust forward at an angle which most people seemed to find brutish and uncouth.

In addition to these minor deformities, I also suffered peculiar physical symptoms which seemed to correspond oddly with certain mental impressions I had. My stomach, though full, would frequently cramp as if from a tremendous hunger, as if my body were being deprived of some vital nutrient or mineral which it desperately needed. At these times I also suffered mild auditory and visual hallucinations, as well as recurring bouts of insomnia. These frequent physical ailments robbed me of any sociability I may have otherwise possessed and, since they also prevented me from participating in any form of youthful play, my fate as a recluse was sealed.

I do not wish to convey that I made no friends; rather the few friends I did make along the way dwindled significantly as I entered my adolescence. They seemed to me increasingly frustrated or annoyed by a growing contrariness in my character and put off by my generally critical perspective towards life. They told me time and again how I thought "too much and too deeply about everything," that I took things "too personally" and that I should "try to be more optimistic about society," so that in time, tensions mounted and we would invariably drift apart. Early on, I resolved to keep my true thoughts and feelings to myself, while feigning a generalized interest in my peers, most of whom seemed content to speak endlessly about themselves and to rarely, if ever, actually ask me anything about myself. This faux curiosity proved to be the very best way to remain relatively unnoticed and undisturbed by the people around me.

The doctors to whom my mother took me were universally baffled by my symptoms and yet, like some laboratory rat, I was made to ingest all manner of pills, powders, and awful tasting draughts, all designed to correct my numerous aberrations. Once properly dosed, I was routinely interrogated, cross-examined, and made to describe the confusing and eerie side effects of said drugs. I recall that these experiences frightened me terribly and I withdrew inside myself, becoming less and less cooperative as I entered adolescence. As guarded as I already was, I grew even more disingenuous toward my mother, my many doctors, and towards the society that silently condoned these medical procedures. I constructed a mask, a disguise which I hid behind and I learned quickly how to lie, placate, and hide my symptoms from the world.

I engaged in this subterfuge for several years, until eventually the visits to the doctors became less and less frequent and I was, in due time, left to myself. This was my coming of age, seventeen pitiful and lonely years, made all the worse by the fact that I continued to be plagued by that gnawing hunger in my guts (though I remained mercifully ignorant of what I hungered for).

Outwardly, my disguise was complete. I did what I was told. I finished school, graduated alongside my peers and sought employment in the nearby port city of Plymouth. Day after day, I went into the great belching factories along the wharf until at last I found employment at the Plymouth Cordage factory, feeding bales of hemp into a machine at nine dollars a week. I was lucky to have found such work at this time, for unemployment was then at epidemic proportions. The streets were crowded with immigrants fresh off the boats from Italy, Russia and elsewhere, hungry and desperate for any kind of work and willing to work for almost nothing. With the money I earned at the Cordage, I was able to move out of my childhood home in Southwick and rent a small room in Plymouth, a picturesque nook in a boarding house, with a tiny circular window overlooking an adjacent park. For a period of about eight months my various symptoms seemed to go into a kind of remission and for the first time in my life I began to experience what others might call true joy and contentment.

*   *   *   *

THIS CONTENTMENT, HOWEVER, WAS SHORT-LIVED AS I SOON BEGAN to notice an increasing sense of social unrest in the factory where I worked and in the streets outside my window. The Great War in Europe was, at this time, just getting underway and all over America "Preparedness" was the watchword of the day. Newspaper accounts of the spectacular (and ongoing) Zeppelin attacks against London had so shocked the sensibilities of the man-in-the-street that many had slipped into an eerie state of submissive, flag-waving stupefaction. In the weeks and months that followed, the government organized Patriot Parades and Preparedness demonstrations designed to instill in the youth a thirst for German blood and a desire to go to war.

But while jingoism appeared to be at a fever pitch, I was surprised to learn that many of the people with whom I worked were actually against the war, even against the entire economic system that it represented. Occasionally, in smoky gin joints and rented halls, I attended lectures and listened to speakers who brought to light the true nature of the capitalist system.

"America is going to shed oceans of blood and heap mountains of human sacrifices!" I heard one anti-war orator shout. "Europe is in a blaze with twelve million men engaged in the most frightful butchery the world has ever known... and why? For what? To fatten the wallets of a few already rich men!"

They called the war a "millionaire's game," "a power struggle of the imperialist powers," with workers serving as cannon fodder, so that it was absurd to favor one side over the other. This war was not (as many seemed to think) evidence of some tragic flaw in human nature, nor some unintentional mismanagement of foreign affairs (as the politicians implied)... but rather an integral part of every government's reason for existing; ever-expanding systematic domination. War, in fact, is the very health of the state, they said, so that it was quite incoherent to oppose the war without also opposing the entire political machine, of which it is a mere extension. "It's not just the war that must be stopped," they said, "but the entire economic system which rewards greed, exploitation and cruelty, appealing to and rewarding the very worst of human tendencies. The entire class structure that enables such calculated waste of life and limb must be razed to the ground! Not just on the battlefield but in the mines and in the factories and on the farms!" To the anarchists (for that is what these people called themselves), the politicians and the millionaires they represented were "a race of parasites," a "reptile brood" who would never stop trying to expand their own wealth and power. They want a hive-like slave world where the great masses of impoverished humanity are slowly worked to death in the name of Industry, profits, and something they called Progress.

And these words had the ring of truth to my ears, for all over Massachusetts workers were striking. In Plymouth, Milford, Hopedale, Lawrence, and countless other cities, striking workers, fighting for a living wage, were being beaten back by police batons and jailed or deported without so much as a trial. New laws were being passed every day it seemed: imposing curfews, forbidding large public gatherings, and criminalizing any person who spoke out against the war or was critical of the government. Regularly we heard stories of government agents and police rounding up

4

"radicals," beating them with clubs, smashing their printing presses, and shipping them off to Russia… all for the crime of printing a newspaper which laid their system bare. Peaceful unarmed May Day marchers were being clubbed in the streets by company militias in plain-clothes while nearby policemen stood around and did nothing. And all of this was being overseen and enforced by strange new government ministries and offices, agencies which none of us had ever heard of before. I recall that at a nearby factory in Hopedale several outspoken persons had mysteriously vanished while in police custody. This sort of thing only added fuel to the fire that was already raging.

I was, at first, rather amazed to hear such things said aloud but I quickly understood that I was surrounded by a very different class of people than I'd ever been permitted to mingle with. With growing interest, I sought to learn all that I could from the many disparate people around me, reading newspapers with names like *The Blast*, *Alarm!*, *Lucifer*, and *Nihil*.

These ideas impressed me deeply, reflecting back to me in a clarified way, many of my own private conclusions. I had long felt that society (and perhaps civilization as well) was organized in such a way as to bring out the very worst in man and that the war was just an obvious example of the stupidity and cruelty that was more or less everywhere, at all levels of society. Standing in a mass of four to five thousand angry working people, listening to these fiery speeches, it was not hard to imagine that someday soon our numbers might become sufficient to successfully attack the many government buildings and company headquarters located throughout the city, and burn them to the ground. Such an event, I must admit, would not have been objectionable to me in the least. On the contrary, after eighteen years of being bullied, lied to, and experimented on by countless agents of control, I rather looked forward to such an opportunity.

So, I suppose, in some embarrassing way, I finally felt as though I had found my people though I remained on the edges of this milieu, necessarily, mostly as an observer. For even among the radical people who attended these lectures there was vehement disagreement on almost every point imaginable. Speakers were often shouted down and replaced by their detractors. For example, some were morally opposed to the use of violence while others said it was "the only way." Some said the system could be reformed while others said there was no sane reason why it should exist at all. These discussions fascinated me. At the time I remember agreeing with the more militant point of view. What better way to strike at the arrogant money-men than to bring the very carnage they inflicted so willfully onto others right to their own doorsteps? The pacifist argument simply didn't make sense to me as I could not see it leading to anything but total extermination, sooner or later.

The vicious and deadly process of weeding out subversives had already begun. To this end, the cops employed guns, billyclubs, paddywagons and hired mobs. They used guile and subterfuge when dealing with us. It seemed obvious to me that we would need to be comparably set up.

At this time, several bombings at the homes of prominent industrialists in New York and Boston had already occurred, and by the spring of 1915 they showed no signs of abating. Along with these bombing campaigns, great efforts were made to inform people through propaganda of the true nature of the American caste system, cloaked as it is, in this so-called democracy.

"We were not born to toil as automatons…" as one flyer put it, "but to live free, to destroy this world of crime and misery that has been built around us and to rebuild with its freed atoms a new civilization, as yet undreamed of."

All of this thrilled and terrified me. The anarchists impressed me strangely with their fearless, unflinching assessment of the workers' predicament and throughout my time in Plymouth I would see much to bring me around to their point of view.

*   *   *   *

LIVING IN SOUTHWICK ALL MY LIFE, I HAD BEEN PROFOUNDLY (IF NOT deliberately) insulated from just this sort of talk and it angered me to think I had been kept in the dark. In Southwick, the turbulence of the times had barely been permitted to touch my life. It was all a dim nightmare occurring somewhere beyond the horizon. During my last year of high school my schoolteachers had spoken in an ominous way of the "German Threat" and this had formed my principle understanding of the matter. The Polite Society to which my mother belonged would barely speak of the war at all and they had all discouraged my inquiries so entirely that I had soon stopped asking questions altogether. But on the streets of Plymouth, Massachusetts I received a condensed education on the war between the classes in America. The headlines of all the major newspapers endlessly stated and restated the rich man's point of view but the growing frustration and disgust of the man in the street provided a jarring counterpoint. Thus, I soon found myself in a boiling cauldron of bitter animosities between those who called themselves Marxians, Wobblies, Nihilists, Egoists, Christians, foreign Nationalists and a few plain old-fashioned crazy people. And there, in the center of this maelstrom, was that small but determined anarchist minority with whom I worked.

For myself, I bit my tongue, though I remained a keen observer of the events happening around me. By and large, I agreed with those people who

6

called themselves anarchists and saw in their uncompromised position a ray of hope unlike anything I had previously encountered in my fellow man. As a small boy I had once had a terrible vision of the world as a gigantic processing machine, a harvester of human souls comprised of smokestacks, schools, churches, and workhouses. I longed to see it all demolished and the people trapped within it set free and yet I was afraid. I had always been afraid, and so I had never spoken of this vision to anyone. These were my private thoughts and I could think of no good reason to display them publicly. Doing so could only attract unwanted attention from the plain-clothes coppers and the company spies I knew must be lurking nearby. I kept to myself, feigning mere curiosity when confronted, reading and attending lectures with varying degrees of interest and attempting to remain reasonably well-informed.

*   *   *   *

THROUGHOUT THIS TURBULENT PERIOD (AND DUE IN LARGE PART TO my improved physical health) my sociability towards my fellows improved considerably and soon enough, at the factory where I worked, one of the pretty young secretaries developed a crush and began to court me. She was a thoughtful, talkative girl and (perhaps more from a sense of amazed disbelief than anything else) I responded to her in kind and we began to see each other. (I will omit her name, since she showed me great kindness and should in no way be associated with the horrible things I must soon describe.) Before I knew what was happening we were engaged to be married and making all sorts of wild plans. Her wish, and mine too, was to build a cabin in the woods and perhaps raise some children. The city was fast becoming a place to escape from, and many times she came to me and begged me to flee with her into the unknown countryside. She would regale me with breathless descriptions of a life which sounded like heaven; on many happy evenings I would sit smoking at the window sill and listen to her elucidate the details of our happy ever after.

And so at the ripe age of 18, in a city that seemed, at times, poised on the brink of revolution, my life was finally beginning to resemble the kind of life that I could actually be proud of. My fiancée was an open-minded and adventurous woman and those precious seven months I lived with her, symptom-free, are the one bright spot in a life otherwise darkened with dread, confusion, and horror. My sweetheart was, among other things, a tireless animal lover who, in her spare time, took in stray and wounded animals and nursed them back to health. It occurs to me now that it was in a like manner that she took me in, into her heart and her home. And I, an absolute stranger to this sort of treatment, greedily devoured all the love and compassion that she willingly gave to me.

For a time we were quite happy and had even begun to talk about having a child, when there came that fateful day when, to my profound disappointment, the headaches, the stomach pains, and the nightmares returned (only now with a renewed and bracing intensity). Along with these symptoms, there also came the acute foulness of mood which had heretofore spoiled my prospects for real human intimacy. But even this was not the worst of it, for it was at this time of mounting fear and uncertainty about my future that I made that most incredible and horrendous discovery, a discovery which firmly placed me on the road to madness.

Walking home from work one evening, along the sloping meadows at the edge of town, the sound of an explosion reached my ears. The automobile was an increasingly common sight on the lesser turnpikes of New England, though in these desperate times motorists often avoided back roads for fear of bandits. Running at my top speed in the direction of the sound, I came upon the scene of a terrible motor-crash. An automobile had hopped the embankment and tumbled down a considerable slope, rolling over many, many times before landing, right side up, at the bottom of the ravine. Without hesitation I scrambled down the grassy incline, calling out to whatever survivors might still be conscious. My hopes were dashed however when, upon arriving alongside the crumpled hulk, I saw through the shattered windscreen the sole occupant of the vehicle whose tremendous injuries left no chance for survival. The interior of the vehicle was covered with blood and the driver, a young woman no more than 25 years of age, was draped over the steering wheel, the many impacts and subsequent explosion having placed her beyond all possible human aid. The angle of her neck indicated in no uncertain terms that it was broken and her head, shattered across its backmost portion, was broken open from scalp to neck leaving the protuberant brain profoundly exposed.

Dumbstruck, I turned to leave with a plan to fetch help at one of the country houses I had spied earlier along the turnpike, but, having gone just a few steps, I found my feet strangely rooted to the spot. A feeling of elation swept over me and, for a moment, my body swayed drunkenly in the still air. Then, with a lump in my throat, and without conscious effort on my part, I moved back toward the wreck again, with something like a dimly formed plan to inspect the mangled form of the woman more closely.

It was then that a sensation I can scarcely describe overwhelmed me. My stomach began to heave and to twist inside of me with such violence that I collapsed in the grass, where I lay doubled up and in terrible pain for several minutes. I recall a tremendous feeling of terror descending upon me and then, as I lay there helplessly immobile, I became senseless. The grass around me seemed to come alive with hissing and swishing sounds and ugly shapes and shadows danced at the edges of my vision. The spasms in my gut were now profoundly painful, being noticeably worse than ever before. Within minutes the convulsions had settled into a rhythmic cramping and I realized that the inexplicable hunger had returned, bringing with it a keen awareness of the object of my desire.

Weak with horror and confusion, I felt myself crawl up inside the wreck, crouching oddly upon the passenger seat beside the corpse, my mind lost in a vortex of indescribable longing and hunger. A disembodied urge to touch the corpse overcame my repulsion and I watched, in helpless wonder, as my own trembling hand (now imbued with a queer alien grace) reached out and caressed the warm, wet brain, returning to smear the shiny effluvium across my lips and tongue. This simple act sent waves of grotesque pleasure throughout my entire being. My hands and mouth seemed to be responding to commands entirely separate from, yet utterly embedded within, my own conscious mind. Seconds later I had pulled the brain out of its gelatinous sac and devoured it, at which time I was overwhelmed by a fit of ecstatic trembling unlike anything I have ever felt before or since. I huddled there for several minutes feeling my muscles writhing, as if rearranging themselves upon my bones, and listening to the sound of my teeth chattering as wave upon wave of pleasure coursed over my body.

Quite suddenly, my senses came rushing back to me and, terrified that I might be discovered in this pitiable state, I ran as far as my tottering legs would carry me, stumbling headlong into the tall grass some 50 yards away from the wreck. There I wavered on the edge of consciousness for an unknown span of minutes.

It was then that I had a poignant nightmare-vision, a dream of breathtaking vividness which I immediately recognized as the culmination of (and source material for) a thousand lesser nightmares which I had suffered since youth. Of this vision I will say simply this: it was all the more horrifying because it had about it the glamour of a prophecy. I will describe here, as simply as I can, the basic contents of that dream.

I dreamt that I was standing on the verge of a vast stone courtyard adjoining a windswept temple, hideously constructed atop a massive pinnacle of jagged black stone. Many thousands of feet below was an endless sea of roiling mist, out of which there rose a legion or more of similar colossal peaks, hovering, like islands or oddly shaped planets, raising their split and broken heads into the black vault above. The sheer alien immensity of this scenery conjured strange thoughts of some antediluvian cemetery of banished gods, abandoned eons ago, and rotting in some cold and desolate hollow in the floor of the universe. Something about those towering stone peaks reminded me of enormous tombstones, or altars, or perhaps the clawed and crumbling perches of some inconceivably gigantic flying beings. Surely, no such place existed on the earth that I knew.

I had just resolved to cross the courtyard and explore the temple when, looking up, I became aware of a faint red glare on the uppermost portions of the masonry, emanating from some point behind and below me. Turning myself completely around I walked several paces back till I found myself standing on the brink of a cliff, representing a dizzying drop of several hundred feet into a red-litten abyss, in the center of which, illuminated in the vaporous darkness, there lay a most incredible construction.

On a low ridge that connected my peak to its nearest neighbor, I could see with astonishing, almost telescopic, clarity the torch-lit dimensions of a stone palace. A fantastically intricate complex of scalloped terraces and megalithic buildings had been carved directly into the ridge of the mountain, interconnected by a swerving web-work of narrow avenues, walkways, and staircases. The doorways and porticoes were of trapezoidal design and the walls had curious niches built into them where the strange red torches burned with an almost supernatural brilliance. And there, beneath that eerie crimson glow, filing swiftly along the many passageways and converging upon the main plaza from all quarters, I saw the robed and hooded inhabitants of the palace gather in a throng, in the vicinity of one of the city's rear gates. They seemed to be making preparations for some sort of religious ritual; standing in rows that formed curious geometrical configurations, swinging and convulsing their bodies in a manner most unpleasant to look upon, and every few minutes, raising up their voices in an eerie, flute-like howling which the blasting wind never quite succeeded in carrying off.

Then, from a curtained portal in the central edifice, a procession of ten red-robed women appeared wearing frightful wicker helmets bearing symbols of something which could have been interpreted variously as a sun, an octopus, or a spider. Furthermore, these women were carrying nine long, white bundles which seemed to writhe and wiggle in the torchlight. These bundles were ceremoniously anointed with a dark liquid and then, after a series of ghastly vocalizations from the crowd, thrown, one after another, over the top of the massive gate.

The crowd fell silent and for several minutes they stood in an attitude of intense listening, staring all the while at the gate. My vantage point from the cliff afforded me the best possible view of the scene below.

Following the direction of their gaze, I attempted to peer into that inky blackness immediately outside the gate, the area bordering (but not quite within) the radiant glow of the torches. Here, where any hopeful recipient of this gruesome offering must eventually appear to collect it, I searched for any signs of movement. Then, as my eyes adjusted to the murky red glare, I observed twenty or thirty pale forms slowly divorcing themselves from the line of trees. From beneath the canopy of leaves there now emerged a group of humanoid beings absolutely incredible to look upon and creeping very swiftly over to where the white bundles lay in a tumbled heap, perfectly still.

These strange white beings were in every essential way the twin of man, though noticeably taller and hideously ugly. Their faces, when they actually had them, were grotesque caricatures of the human countenance with toothy mouths almost twice their usual size. Their loping, swinging gait called to mind the gigantic Orangutans of Borneo; deceptively ungainly when upright yet capable of moving at blinding, bone-crushing speeds. So far as I could tell, these beings appeared to be hermaphroditic, with a large number of them possessing both sets of genitalia, one above the other. Others had no genitalia whatsoever. Most of them appeared to be savagely, incomprehensibly injured, mutilated, or otherwise disfigured. Well over half of them were actually headless, with eyes and large mouth-like orifices appearing on their chests, shoulders, and arms. Still others (and these worst of all) were only partially headless, having inconceivable remnants when decapitation would have seemed a foregone conclusion. In most cases the head was merely thrust forward to a point entirely below the shoulders, the flesh scalded and scarred around these deformities as if by some tremendous heat. Others seemed to have had their heads and faces melted or fused directly into their shoulders. Some lacked hands, feet or entire limbs, yet it was clear from their movements that they were in no way hindered by these mutilations. They seemed, on the contrary, quite accustomed to their various injuries, as if they had long ago learned to move with a deadly swiftness despite them. These nightmarish beings were eager to collect their prizes and go, a thing they did with devilish quickness, snatching up the lifeless bundles and vanishing into the trees.

The dream ended abruptly there, and when I next opened my eyes I saw only the purple clouds of evening above me. I do not know how long I lay there dreaming, but when I awoke the sun had set and the infinite peril of my situation came upon me again with an awful suddenness. Sitting up, I could see the meandering beams of spotlights nearby and hear the voices of several policemen busy in their attempts to drag the wrecked vehicle back up the embankment by way of a truck with a winch. Keeping low to the ground I managed to creep away unseen and, moving parallel with the roadway at a safe distance, I resumed my journey southward under cover of darkness.

The rest of the walk home was a blur of confusion. I vaguely recall washing my face and hands in a stream and burying my shirt in the woods.

Then I must have stumbled home, for that is where I awoke, two days later, to the sound of my sweetheart begging me, with tears streaming down her cheeks, to explain where I had been and why I had come home incoherent and "stinking like a butcher shop." Apparently, I had stumbled in at about 9:00 p.m. on the prior Thursday, muttering nonsense and passing out on the bed after which she had been unable to wake me for over forty-eight hours. Feeling that she deserved some reassuring explanation to ease her mind, I fabricated a story about inhaling dangerous vapors at work and then pleaded with her to please allow me to recuperate without the added strain of having to account for myself. My need for rest must have been apparent for she agreed to let me sleep, with a promise to hear the full story as soon as I felt capable of telling it. This stalling tactic afforded me exactly two days' time to re-organize my thoughts and to decide what I might do next. In the relative peace and sanctuary of that sickbed, I tried to make sense of what had occurred.

How might I hope to convey the utter chaos of my thoughts now? First and foremost, why had I done what I had done? Why, in heavens name, had I eaten that woman's brain? It was nauseating, detestable, gruesome beyond all comparison! And yet, could I not also feel the muscles of my body warming at the recollection of it, longing for more of that delicious intoxication? I was not simply repulsed by my foul deed. That would have been easy. I was also, with each passing hour, more and more fiendishly eager to repeat it. Already I could feel the beginnings of a craving welling up inside of me, a craving which, if not mitigated in the proscribed manner, I felt horribly certain would explode into some horrific climax of uncontrollable violence and bloodshed. This revelation, useful though it was, at last robbed me of whatever shred of hope might have remained in me. A thousand dreadful questions assailed my mind. Where could I go? What could I do? Was I completely insane? Had I contracted some grotesquely enhanced strain of vampirism? Should I throw myself into the Housatonic River and be done with it? What if there was a way out of it? What if it was only a sickness? If it was a disease, could there be hope of a cure? What if I could find an adequate substitute? If I could successfully raid mortician's waste bins, for example, could I continue to lead an otherwise normal life? There was so much I still needed to understand and yet, in my delicate circumstances, I had no idea where I might possibly begin.

Finding nothing useful in a diagnosis of mere insanity, I put to myself two very simple questions. First, what physiological or nutritional deficiency could possibly cause a man to need to consume the brain of one of his own species? Second, what had been the meaning of that vivid and unforgettable dream which had followed? These two questions became my own private obsession, functioning as a roadmap for me over the next eleven years, as I did all within my power to answer them each to my own satisfaction.

Having learned the object of my lifelong craving I was a changed man. I can scarcely imagine how I made it through those last two days recovering but when I did return fully to my senses I knew that my quaint and ordinary life was at an end. Realizing that I could not risk implicating my sweetheart in any of my gruesome misdeeds and seeing that my now-blossoming illness would render me absurdly incapable of returning to her the love which she most assuredly deserved, I determined to leave her. Thus, with the sickness growing rapidly inside of me, I packed some bare essentials into a backpack and fled. One day I told her that I was going to the corner market for a loaf of bread and I never returned.

"Coward" you might say (and perhaps you are correct), but I left her because I could feel that the hunger, grotesquely invigorated by that single taste, was now growing, day by day, hour by hour, into something which I knew must soon consume me entirely. And so, with a knapsack full of clothing and blankets, I hopped a train to Springfield where I procured several days' worth of food and then walked to the northern edge of town. There I entered the Berkshire Mountain wilderness at the Charleston road. I can still recall how a light rain fell that first night out, so that I was forced to sleep in one of the abandoned mines just north of Wilton. There, curled up in a tight ball beneath a flimsy blanket, I cried myself to sleep like the naive sheltered child I was.

For the next few years I roamed about the countryside, something like a common vagabond. Not merely a common vagabond, but rather one whose seemingly erratic wanderings actually took him to every single country cemetery and potter's field that appeared on his map, wherein he nocturnally violated whatever fresh graves he might be lucky enough to encounter and engorged himself on human brains.

II

MY TRAVELS TOOK ME ALL OVER NEW ENGLAND. I WENT everywhere. The year was 1915 and it was the season of the May Day Festivals. With the many wandering tent shows and caravans of revelers traveling the byways of the countryside, I was able to move on the margins of these large processions with near complete anonymity. In this way I roamed, mostly at night, moving from one end of New England to the other, making a thorough investigation of the place that had birthed me. I had never felt the urge to travel much before but now I was unexpectedly eager to explore the entire region and especially those deep wilderness areas which had not yet been invaded by civilization.

Time does not permit me to tell the full tale of all that I saw and did on this eleven year tramp. Suffice it to say, there is hardly a town or village in New England which I have not walked through at twilight, no river I have not crossed, no mountain I have not slept under. I have bathed in Round Pond, Sumner's Pond and Walden Pond, swum across Candlewood Lake and climbed the slopes Mt. Greylock. I have floated down the Pawtuxet River on a wooden raft and camped on her many islands and shoals. I have slept in the queer soapstone caves near Monkton, Vermont, and I have walked the Berkshires by moonlight with only the owls to listen to my idiotic raving. I even spent several weeks in the cave reputed to have been the home of Sarah Bishop, the famous hermitess of Ridgefield, Connecticut who, a century before, turned her back on human habitation and finished her years in the wooded hills west of that city.

For the first few weeks of my wandering, I skirted the edges of civilization, entering small rural towns only occasionally, for supplies and other amenities. When it rained I sought out the wealthier country estates and secreted myself in people's barns, tool sheds, and carriage houses. This arrangement worked so well that I repeated it whenever bad weather caught me unawares, without money for a proper room. I never stayed in one spot longer than was absolutely necessary, attaching myself to larger processions only when it served me to do so.

Sometimes, for my own peace of mind, I spent weeks, and even months, in the wild hills. Other times I moved among the teeming crowds, sleeping in the shrubbery of the city parks when loneliness or other concerns demanded human proximity. On occasion I traveled with the caravans purely for the relief of human closeness; there were times, dreadful to remember, when, alone in a darkened wood, I sometimes became convinced that I was being followed and observed by an unseen, inhuman presence. I would become so frightened that I would run to whatever crowded places I could find, where the lights and the music and the bustling crowds would dispel this terrifying and persistent impression. Luckily, this happened only very rarely. Most of the time the forest served as my refuge.

The spring and summer months were easier in some ways but harder in others. When I was out in the countryside during the warmer months, I simply scavenged in the orchards and fished in the rivers. When the desire for solitude coincided with favorable weather, I was able to remain in the deep wilderness for weeks at a time, camping in caves or else constructing crude structures from pine boughs and logs. Securing food, shelter (when necessary) and a steady supply of brains became my sole concern and, mastering this fairly early on, I was surprised at how easy it was for me to scratch out a meager existence, tramping from place to place and living by my wits.

Truth be told, as frightened and confused as I felt, I adapted remarkably well to this bizarre existence and, as I was on the outside of civilization looking in, I began to notice certain curious alterations in my general perspective. Having removed myself entirely from the routines of the ordinary world, I felt free to think my own thoughts, dream my own dreams, and to move about entirely as I pleased. For the first time in my life, my days truly belonged to me and I answered to none but myself.

When passing through larger cities or towns I had often sought out anarchist events and lectures where I would collect books to read during the long solitary spells in the wilderness. In Milford, among the anonymous crowd, I listened to speakers discussing the importance of the general strike as a crucial weapon in the conflicts that lay ahead. At one of the literature tables, I met a steely eyed Italian bookseller, a thoughtful, well-spoken fellow with a kind face and a heavy accent, from whom I purchased such forbidden literature as *The Anti-Christ* and *Beyond Good and Evil* by Friedrich Nietzsche and that shunned masterpiece of anti-philosophy, *The Ego and his Own* by Max Stirner, which I re-read several times.

I learned quickly that I needed to consume one human brain roughly every two weeks. I could eat more but not less than this. The pain, when I failed to maintain this schedule, were so abominable that I immediately adopted a kind of system, sometimes securing my sources weeks ahead of time. Early experimentation revealed that, curiously, animal brains did not constitute an adequate replacement and so I was initially thrust into the role of grave-robber. Modern embalming practices made it so that I had much better odds at the potter's fields than at the cemeteries (although, thankfully, many of the deeper rural villages still buried their dead in the old-fashioned way). Occasionally, and whenever possible, I also sought temporary employment with my predilection in mind. For a time I worked as a night janitor at a surgical clinic and once as groundskeeper at a potter's field in Springfield, these positions providing me with obvious benefits.

After leaving Plymouth, I followed the mountains north for five days before encountering one of the aforementioned nomadic tent shows. I traveled on with them for several days, to the outskirts of Boston, slipping away from the group once to visit potter's fields along the way. Outwardly I was friendly, making several acquaintances, two of whom where artists on the tramp, with whom I struck up a warm, though short-lived, friendship. In the towns and villages I passed through I sometimes met up with hospitable strangers who, upon learning of my transience, simply invited me into their homes to stay for as long as I liked. These kindly interactions did much to instill a feeling of hope in my own humanity and renewed my resolve to investigate, with all the resources at my disposal, all possible causes and cures for my condition.

Outwardly I must have made a pretty good show of it, but inwardly, I seethed like a man possessed. My thoughts frequently raced in pursuit of strange emotions and lingered on ghoulish imaginings. I also continued to be haunted by curious and inexplicable alterations of mind and body. With each new feeding I relived that initial shock, alternating waves of pleasure and pain followed by that same dream of the ritual in the red-litten palace as seen from the wind-swept portico. Often on feeding days I was barely able to raise my voice above a whisper, so intense was the feeling of strangeness and terror upon me. I would, at times, be horrified by the very simplest interactions of human life. Briefly exchanging pleasantries with a stranger on a country lane, for example, could sometimes make me weep pathetically. Other times the mere sight of another person would inspire loathing and overwhelming disgust with the entire civilized mode of existence.

Throughout the first three months of my traveling I had been distinctly nervous to remain in (or near) those cities and towns where I had robbed graves, frightened that I might, at any moment, be recognized by a policeman or seized by an angry mob. I did all that I could to alter or disguise my appearance from day to day but, alas, after six or seven weeks of haunting the graveyards of central Massachusetts, my nerves failed me and (convinced that I was being watched and followed) I fled to the peace and security of the woods. Truth be told, I was not yet in danger, for, at this time, my exploits still numbered few. Yet I had no way of knowing for certain whether I had been seen by some random passerby who might have come unexpectedly upon me feasting in one of the many burial grounds I had visited. Who would have blamed them for running immediately to the police? Those early feasts, so clumsy and desperate, would have been a mighty unpleasant sight to a harmless soul out on an evening ramble.

Three months after my departure autumn arrived, bringing with it the knowledge that it was becoming increasingly difficult to dig up graves. The horror and difficulty of procuring brains in this way had already begun to wear on me and, eager for a cleaner, simpler method, I was able to secure employment perfectly suited to my needs. Upon arriving in Bolton, a factory town just outside of Boston, a group of other vagrants and I were approached on the street by a somewhat frantic-looking fellow and offered a job working as a night janitor at the surgical clinic of one Dr. Herbert West and Associate on Pond Street. I had expected stiff competition for so rare and coveted an opportunity as paid work but upon hearing the name of the doctor the other vagrants became taciturn and even turned their backs to the man, with strange glances passing between them. Baffled by this, I stepped forward and gladly accepted the offer and was instantly employed, no questions asked.

I worked strictly off the books, for cash. The good doctor never asked me my name. I arrived at 11 pm every weeknight, as instructed, and let myself in at the back. Often I heard the voices of Dr. West and others, raised up in animated debate, emanating from the stairwell that lead to the locked cellar, but I never disturbed them. It was truly appalling work, by anyone's definition, but I never once complained. I went about my work diligently (covertly gathering what I could from the surprisingly abundant refuse bins) and then went on my way, collecting my money from an envelope which Dr. West was kind enough to leave on the counter for me every night. In this way I was able to sustain myself (financially and nutritionally) through the autumn and winter months while I explored the legend-haunted city of Boston, with regular forays into Cambridge, Medford, and Somerville. It was the first time since fleeing Plymouth that I was gainfully employed. The first thing I did was to buy a new suit and to get a room where I could clean myself up a bit before setting out to explore the city.

*   *   *   *

IT WAS ABOUT THIS TIME THAT IT FIRST OCCURRED TO ME THAT I might learn something useful by doing some research on cannibalism. Making myself presentable to the general public, I entered the teeming maze that is Boston and made my way to the Public Library. In this discreet manner, I eventually visited all the major libraries. There is one in each of the larger New England cities and I have been to them all; Boston, Stamford, New Haven, Cambridge, Salem, and Providence. The Yale and Brown University libraries proved the best, though specific information on my area of interest was, at first, hard to come by. I started in Boston, where, over a period of weeks, I researched all I could on my particular form of cannibalism.

There was much on the subject generally, but very little on the topic of brain-eating, and I lost several days researching all the major world religions in vain for cannibalistic rites that included anything resembling my particular practice (the Christian practice of eating Christ's flesh and drinking his blood at the Eucharist notwithstanding). Certainly I was not the first to develop such an appetite? Far from it, but an initial perusal of the primary psychology texts proved not so much fruitless as banal and uninspiring. I quickly determined that no good would come of wasting my time with the new fangled ideas of modern psychology (which seemed strangely preoccupied with blaming everything upon the mother). Perhaps, I reasoned, an extensive study of the many documented cannibal societies would offer something more useful and so I began with the basic reference books.

Here I learned of the Cheddar man of Somerset, England (the oldest complete human skeleton in Britain) whose bones, found in 1903, reveal unmistakable gnaw-marks of a distinctly human type. I read of the African Zulus and the countless cannibal tribes reputed to inhabit the Amazon River region in South America. I learned of the Aztecs of Mexico and Central America who reportedly sacrificed and ate some 1500 persons per year (though the preferred organ was said to have been the heart rather than the brain). I read of the famous Greek physician, Galen, who lived in the first century and in whose compendium of medicinal remedies he often included such ingredients as human brains, liver, and even raw flesh. Finally, and closest of all to my own inclinations, I read of the brain-eating tribes of New Guinea who ritualistically consumed the brains of their deceased relatives, a practice which eventually resulted in the rare and deadly Kuru virus which has nearly wiped them out in the modern era.

This was, as one may well imagine, all very fascinating to me and for many continuous days I spent whole afternoons in the library, absolutely transfixed, pouring over volume after volume of obscure anthropological tomes and digging through mountains of research journals and academic letters. I absorbed it all and I daresay I became something of an expert on cannibalism, though there were certain things which continued to elude me. For example, I had, on several occasions, encountered obscure and baffling references to a "Corpse-eating Cult of Leng" though these references seemed strangely more anecdotal than factual and always lacked the proper footnotes and citations to enable further investigation.

* * * *

ONE DAY THERE OCCURRED THAT REMARKABLE COINCIDENCE WHOSE mystery amazes me even still — a chance discovery which saved me from countless hours of researching in the dark. I was sitting at a table in the rare and antique book section when, pausing to rest my weary eyes, I looked up at a large framed photograph several feet wide hanging on the wall directly across from me. It was a somewhat hazy black and white photograph depicting a lofty ridge crowned with stone ruins long since reclaimed by the surrounding jungle. Absentmindedly I stood up, stretching my legs and arms, and wandered over for a closer look. Here and there one could see, just beneath the creeping vines, a system of interlocking, labyrinthine walls spanning several hundred feet across and almost as wide. Something in the architecture seemed oddly familiar to me, when suddenly a bolt of nauseous panic rinsed over me as I recognized what I was looking at.

On trembling legs I moved along the corridor where a series of pictures of these same ruins hung. The interlocking buttressed stonework, the many scalloped, curving terraces, the trapezoidal doorways, windows and niches built into the walls; there could be no mistaking it. It was the megalithic palace from my dreams. With my best efforts to compose myself, I inquired of the librarian the name and location of the ruins in the pictures. He informed me in a bland, Bostonian monotone that it was "Machu Picchu; The Lost City of the Incas" discovered by Yale professor Hiram Bingham five years prior, on a university funded expedition to the Peruvian highlands. He handed me a pamphlet which stated a few basic facts about the discovery of the "ancient city" and "the enduring mystery of its abandonment."

As horrifying as it was to receive photographic proof of that nightmare palace, this clue was also like a gift from the Fates. I read all the literature I could find on the ruins at Machu Picchu including the highly censored and candy coated article Bingham wrote for *Harpers Monthly*. Later, I was also able to read large sections of his private journals, transcribed and archived in the New Haven Public Library. It was from these that I learned the particulars of the discovery of Machu Picchu and of the frightening local legends connected with it.

According to Bingham's article, the Yale expedition of 1911 had had a devil of a time persuading the reticent natives to show them the ruins at Machu Picchu and Huyanu Picchu, owing largely to a local taboo. For years, anthropologists had been hearing rumors of an abandoned megalithic site north of Cuzco but Bingham had been the first to locate it (though the obstacles had been numerous). Twice they set out from the walled fortress at Salapunco with native guides, but both times they had become hopelessly lost, returning frustrated and empty-handed. According to Bingham's private journals, their progress was further slowed by three curious and disruptive visitors who intercepted the party at different points along the way. Evidently, word of the Yale expedition had spread quickly through the jungle tribes and as the group made its way to the interior of the Urabamba River Valley, they encountered several Indio messengers, representatives from nearby tribes, who attempted to dissuade them from continuing their search for the ruins.

A few miles north of La Maquina, they encountered a wild-eyed young savage who informed their native guides in Queche that he had been sent by the elders of the Tupinamba tribe to relay a warning. He called the "ruined palace" a forbidden place, warning that the white man's violation was sure to incur the wrath of the Yurupari, legendary man-eating ogres said to inhabit hidden ruins in that region. On the following day another young man arrived, having traveled from the land of the Araucanian peoples, a three day walk to the south. According to Bingham, the man was in a state of near-exhaustion, having run the entire way. The Araucanian youth similarly warned the party that they were marching straight into the hunting grounds of creatures his people called the Chivato, a race of deformed man-eating monsters long associated with that particular valley. Two days later, near Mandor Pampa, they were accosted by a third and final Indio emissary, this one from the Tukano tribe, who implored the Yale expedition to turn back, lest they be devoured by the Boraro, enormous white-skinned cannibals who hunted and ate any who dared enter their valley. The Boraro, the Tukano man claimed, were responsible for the disappearance of several previous expeditions of white men who had ignored the warnings of the local Indios.

The native guides Bingham had hired (who also served as translators) seemed to grow increasingly agitated with each new visitant, some abandoning the expedition suddenly, unpaid and without explanation. Their obvious terror appeared to center around the ruins on Huyana Picchu specifically though Bingham was unable to learn much beyond this. Furious, he returned once again to Salapunco where he fired the remaining native guide.

At last, it appears that he succeeded in bribing a young Indian boy in one of the nearby fishing villages to lead the party directly to the ruins. While on the strenuous hike up the mountain, Bingham describes encountering several massive blocks of granite (some weighing an estimated 15 tons) strewn along the road. When he asked the boy where they had come from he was told that the great stones had originally been destined for the stone palace but that

20

some of them had "grown tired, wept blood, and refused to move." Two hours later they reached the peak where the boy led him into a courtyard of stone buildings overgrown with jungle vines. Bingham immediately set up his camera, while the others in his party sought to uncover, as best they could, the stone structures around them. The rest is history. Most of the photographs that hung along the corridor had been taken by Bingham himself.

Despite this remarkable discovery, there were many things in Bingham's account that seemed strangely incomplete: the reticent, circuitous natives, the unwillingness of the local people to reveal the ruins on Machu Picchu and the desperate, almost frantic efforts of certain Indios to conceal the ruins on Huayna Picchu. It all seemed to mask some larger mystery which Bingham had failed to uncover. The accounts of the Yale expedition had been informative up to a point, but in the end I was left with the impression that Bingham and the others had been lied to by natives who resented their intrusion and that the explorers, in fact, had no idea what they had actually found.

*   *   *   *

STARTING FROM THE APPARENT DEAD END OF BINGHAM'S account, I began a study of ancient Peru that lasted several weeks. Learning that the ruins were of Incan origin, I redirected my investigations in that general direction, beginning with an examination of the related cultures which had preceded them in prior centuries. I began to research the history of that region of Peru that falls roughly within a two hundred mile radius of the ruined palace. Nothing I found provided me with anything I could call conclusive, and yet I had barely made a beginning when I immediately began to encounter certain frightening and familiar themes.

The landscape surrounding the ruins at Machu Picchu is an odd collision of three or four very different sorts of terrain. To the west there is the incredibly vast Nazca plain; to the north the Andes rise up to massive stony peaks, from which flows the Urabamba River, one of the many tributaries of the Amazon; to the south lies Lake Titicaca, overshadowed on its southern side by the looming bulk of the Bolivian Plateau.

I read Reiss and Stubel's "Land of the Incas" and various works by Molina, Markham, and Garcilaso De La Vega. I learned much from Prescott's now-famous report and also the collected writings of Max Uhle which describe a series of succeeding and sometimes overlapping civilizations, beginning in the first half of the first millennium BC, starting with the Chavin and Paracas Necropolis Culture (so-named for the extensive underground tombs they left behind). There followed the overlapping Nazca, Mochica, and

21

Recauy cultures, all lasting, more or less, from the first through the sixth centuries. These cultures were succeeded by the tremendously successful Tiwanaku culture whose mysterious collapse (circa 1000 AD) has been the topic of much speculation and academic debate. Also beginning around 700 AD, certain areas were under the control of the Huari and Chancay Empires, both of which appear to have gone into decline by 1000 AD. At the peripheries of these various empires, there has always existed an indeterminate population of unconquerable tribal savages, still extant today, and with whom these different civilizations were forced to contend and co-exist.

Of these civilizations which preceded the Incas, a fair amount is known. The peoples of the Paracan culture were said to have been potters and weavers of the highest type, the fabric of their tunics and tapestries being up to ten times more durable than the finest Victorian equivalent. Paracan tapestries and statuary reveal religious themes typical of that region: a blending of human and animal imagery, human figures with the mouths of wildcats overhung with large curving fangs, and with great staring eyes on the chests and arms. Depictions of sacrifices, supernatural beings, trophy heads, and fanged monster gods comprised the dominant themes.

Perhaps the most well known (because of the hoards of pottery they left behind) are the Nazca of the Plain, who were said to have also been gifted astronomers and surgeons. Of especial interest to me was the evidence that certain prehistoric Nazca Indians had developed a mastery of numerous surgical procedures, unprecedented among any other ancient peoples of the known world. These accomplishments include amputations, bone transplantion and excisions, as well as a gruesome and mysterious form of brain surgery. Among the skeletons found throughout this region there is evidence of a curious, systematic surgical violence done to people's heads. A vast quantity of strangely misshapen human skulls, unearthed in burial mounds, reveal that the still-living owners underwent (and recovered from) some kind of primitive trepanning operation, wherein obsidian chisels were used to make holes in the forehead, granting direct access to the living brain. No convincing explanation for this practice has been put forward.

The Paracas, the Recauy, and the Mochica were all remarkably skilled in metallurgy, pottery, and pyramid-building, traits that would persist (in one form or another) into the time of the Inca. The Tiwanaku, well known for their massive stone portals and statuary, also left behind curious evidence of a particularly grotesque sort of human sacrifice. Bones found at Tiwanaku sites indicate that violent sacrifices were made upon the roofs of stone temples where (according to paintings on the temple walls) prisoners were ritually slaughtered, flayed with obsidian knives, and had their entrails scattered to amuse (and assuage) a certain unidentified sky god. Furthermore, the disquieting creation myth of the Tiwanaku (also later adopted by the Inca royalty) continues to permeate the beliefs of the countless savage tribes who occupy the Amazon River region from Peru to Brazil to Bolivia and beyond.

It is believed by some that the Inca are the descendants of wanderers from the Nazca Plain who settled in the Andean foothills circa 1200 AD, building a stone metropolis on what is now the site of the modern city of Cuzco. It was some time around 1230 that the first dynasty of the Incas arose, a curious composite of disparate and far-flung remnants of these preceding civilizations.

Like all civilizations, the Inca Empire (or Tahuantinsuyu) did all it could to expand, conquering and absorbing many of the surrounding people, imposing laws, Inti worship, and work taxes on those they colonized. The Inca, while similar in many ways to their predecessors, also differed in certain crucial ways. For one, the Inca detested cannibalism and even attempted to ban it throughout the region, a ban which most scholars agree was the cause of a great many of the violent popular uprisings which plagued them throughout their reign. The vast majority of these uprisings originated among the hordes of tribal savages (many of whom were known cannibals) and who were so numerous and obscure that even the diligent Spanish priests (ordered by Pizarro to chronicle and catalogue them) soon gave up in vain. Some of the larger tribes, such as the Chancay, the Alcaviza, and the Araucanians had conducted successful raids against the Inca and were well known to the Spanish. But the vast majority resisted all efforts to be documented, let alone civilized, and so have remained obscure, even into the modern era. The Inca elite who passed laws that forbade cannibalism also shunned, at least initially, ritual human sacrifice and do not appear to have practiced it much at all prior to a certain date (the large numbers of sacrificed female skeletons later found at Machu Picchu being a curious exception).

In 1230 AD, Manco Capoc became the first Sapa (or Emperor) of the Kingdom of Cuzco, the first Inca Dynasty, followed by five others, each ruling for thirty years. There were thirteen Incan Emperors in the era prior to the arrival of the Spanish, each with his own legends, legacies, failures, and accomplishments. Sapa Inca Lloque Yupanqui, the third Sapa, established the first market in Cuzco while Capac Yupanqui, the fifth Sapa, is credited with vastly improving the city of Cuzco, adding extensive roads, bridges, and aqueducts. Sapa Inca Yahar Huacac defeated the Chancas, long-standing (and much feared) enemies of the Inca, while the ninth Emperor Patchacuti (meaning Earth-Shaker) is remembered as a war hero, said to have possessed the ability to call enormous stones to life with a movement of his hand and even to make them participate in campaigns against his enemies. Many believe that it was Patchacuti who ordered the construction of Machu Picchu. Huayna Capac, the eleventh Sapa, was also considered a war hero for his violent suppression of native uprisings. There is a legend that tells of how, after almost being killed in a raid by the Cayambi, he led a campaign to hunt down and kill every member of that tribe. In this, he very nearly succeeded, throwing thousands of their corpses into a lake which to this day, bears the name Yahuarcocha, the Lake of Blood.

At the peak of their influence, the Inca Empire, under the leadership of Huayna Capac stretched from northern Ecuador to present-day Santiago, Chile, nearly three thousand miles from end to end. The Inca worshipped Inti the sun god; temples, shrines, and depictions of this deity are omnipresent throughout Inca art, textiles, and architecture.

But while Inti remained the official deity of the Inca religion, numerous shrines have been found that were built for another, much older, deity who appears, surreptitiously, in much of their later artifacts. It was a commonly held belief among the Inca that each of the Sapas had been possessed by an obscure deity they called the Viracocha, an ancient shape-shifting creator god whom the Inca had expropriated from among the many prehistoric jungle tribes they had conquered. This was that same creator god from the earlier Tiwanaku creation myth, whose worship, as I have mentioned, had spread throughout the savage regions.

According to some scholars, there is evidence of a secret Viracocha cult developing within the Inca royalty during Inca Roca's reign sometime around 1350. Sapa Inca Hatun Tupac, for example, was believed to have been so entirely possessed by this creator god that, after a dream in which he was visited by the Viracocha, he changed his name to Sapa Inca Viracocha and, for the remainder of his reign, he was regarded as it's living incarnation. His successor, Sapa Inca Pachacuti was also said to be in this cult, as evidenced by the fact that he later set up yearly holidays where children were sacrificed to the Viracocha. On the surface, Inti remained the god of the Incas, the sun that gave life, but in secret temples on remote peaks, the cult worshipped this older, darker god, who possessed them, gave them visions, and demanded human sacrifices.

*   *   *   *

UPON HEARING OF THE SECRET WORSHIP OF THE VIRACOCHA, I endeavored to learn all I could about this ancient god and of his alleged creation of the world and its inhabitants. This led me directly to the Tiwanaku creation myth, a legend which can be found in countless books, essays, and articles concerning primeval deities of the New World. It is a legend which remains widespread in Amazonia to this very day; I daresay there are academies of learning where schoolchildren are taught the legend of the Viracocha as part of their studies of the ancient world. The legend is, in many ways, comprised of typical themes. There is a god who created the world (and the human race itself) out of nothingness. There is a catastrophic flood and also an explanation for most natural phenomena. Yet it was the utter simplicity of the tale that filled me with a creeping dread which sickened me and made my skin crawl. Here, at the culmination of my Inca researches, I caught my first glimpse of the ageless horror which I had been pursuing.

Thus far my researches had opened up incredible vistas on an ancient and mysterious world, yet, somehow, it had all seemed like so much harmless and remote hyperbole. But upon reading the Tiwanaku creation myth, I was seized with the impossible conviction that what I was reading was not allegory but was somehow, literally, factually true. I began to sweat and tremble, until at last I slammed the book upon the table and fled from it as one would flee from a lit stick of dynamite. As written, the legend was several pages long, yet I never made it past the first four or five paragraphs. The relevant portion of this legend runs as follows…

In the beginning, Lord Viracocha, the Prince of the Void and Creator of all things, emerged from the great blackness and made the earth and sky. After he had finished molding the mountains and valleys of the earth he dug an enormous pit and filled it with water. This was Lake Titicaca and, swimming down to the bottom, he made his home there.

Returning to the surface, Lord Viracocha created, out of mud, many strange and incredible animals to inhabit this new world and to keep him company in the endless darkness, for the sun had not yet been created. For a time he was amused by these creatures but soon he grew weary of them. He wished to create a better race of beings that might worship him and chant his name aloud. And so he set about to invent the first people. He decided to make this new superior race of beings out of better materials than mud, choosing instead great white stones from the bottom of the lake. Setting these white boulders upon the southern shore of Lake Titicaca he proceeded to sculpt them, one by one, into a race of gigantic human beings, upon whose pale white skin he drew strange symbols which brought them to life. Then, just as these beings were beginning to stir and to move about, the Viracocha slid back into Lake Titicaca, where he remained hidden, in order to secretly observe his new creations. His boneless, formless body being more liquid than solid, he made himself perfectly flat upon the surface of the water, with only his many bulging, and bubble-like, eyes showing. It is from this that he got his name, Viracocha, a Queche word meaning "the skin (or foam) of the water."

At first things seemed to go well but soon the white giants began to behave violently, frightening the other animals of the forest and fighting brutally amongst themselves, sometimes even engaging in cannibalism. This enraged Lord Viracocha and he devised cruel tortures to try and break their spirits and to make them behave. Some legends say he punished them with a terrible liquid fire from the sky, which burned their heads and melted their stone flesh, their screams of agony being so loud that they caused great thunderstorms and earthquakes. Other versions say he smashed and disfigured them, even tearing off their limbs, but still they would not obey him. Fearing that their minds had become poisoned, he even removed their brains but, in the end, all of these actions, far from helping, seemed to make them more deranged and rebellious. Disgusted by the giants' cannibalistic habits and mutilated appearance, Lord Viracocha, at last, decided to destroy them and so he caused a great flood which covered the land, drowning the giants and sweeping them into the bowels of the earth.

He then retreated to a dark cave where he set about creating a second race of human beings, which he made smaller, weaker and gentler. This second race of homunculi was a success and he sent them out of the cave in small groups to inhabit the land, sending with each group a walking, talking piece of himself in the shape of a man. These "men" were also called Viracocha and served as teachers and leaders to the various groups of human beings. Each Viracocha gave their group a language, a food to cultivate, told them how to dress, and taught them how to survive. He even built a stone city and taught them the secret of stone-melting, so that the stones in their walls would be perfectly fitted against each other. He instructed them to populate the area and to worship him by chanting his name aloud and worshiping those among them who were his representatives. These mysterious beings, who were his Helpers in Creation, became the Emperors (or Sapa Inca which is Queche for 'Unique One'). They were considered to be Viracocha's special children.

The legend goes on to describe how Viracocha returned several times to walk among people and to teach them increasingly better ways of surviving. Taking the form of a black man in rags, the god traveled through the mountains (on what would later be called the Inca Road), visiting the cities his children had created, observing them and thinking of ways to help them improve their lot. Usually he went disguised as a filthy beggar so that he would not be noticed, other times he is said to have enchanted and then impregnated certain women who later bore him demi-god children. Later, the Inca aristocracy would claim these demi-gods as their ancestors. In this way, the Tiwanaku creation myth established the divine origins of the Tiwanaku and Inca royalty and provided a rationale for their superiority over all others.

*   *   *   *

HERE I STOPPED MY RESEARCH. I WAS, AS I HAVE STATED, powerfully, hideously, affected by what I had read and I needed time to contemplate all this bizarre new information. Why should I feel so troubled by an ancient Amazon legend? I, who was not Peruvian, had never even been to Peru? Why should I be so affected by a myth which had no conceivable connection to me or my life? All I can offer is this. It was as if I had known this story once, long, long ago and done all that I could to forget it, only to have it reappear before me, suddenly and unexpectedly, in all its terrible vividness, like the illuminated face of a fiend in an otherwise darkened room.

I cannot know, dear reader, how this odd agglomeration of facts and myths may strike you but, for myself, a dim and hideous notion was beginning to take shape in the back of my mind. It was an idea so ludicrous that I could barely bring myself to spell it out, yet, like a newborn creature slowly, painstakingly, emerging from its amniotic sac, a hypothesis was forming which seemed to connect me, however tenuously, to all that I had just absorbed.

Reading the Tiwanaku creation myth filled me with a nameless, formless terror, and as I closed the book and fled the library (as calmly as my shattered nerves would permit), I felt the cold blank weight of the eons bearing down upon me. My body was bathed in sweat, despite the chilly November air, and my skull throbbed as I made my bleary way through the dim Boston streets towards the terminal where I caught the next bus to Bolton. Arriving two hours later in my empty room, I collapsed on the bed and fell into a deep sleep. The nightmares where unusually horrendous that night, grotesque beyond all description, but, terrible as they were, they were but a picturesque preview of the horror to follow.

*   *   *   *

TOWARD THE END OF NOVEMBER 1915, I HAD DONE MY BEST TO prolong my employment as a night janitor at the clinic of Dr. Herbert West but I was soon laid off; the good doctor abruptly closed his practice and enlisted (along with his colleague) in a Canadian regiment to serve as a field surgeon in Flanders. One night I showed up for work and found the place deserted. The placard on the door was gone and, peering in at the window, I saw that not even a stick of furniture remained. The doors were chained and padlocked. With a sinking heart, I understood that my perfect job had come to an end. Being cut off unexpectedly in this way from my supply of fresh brains (and nearing the end of the interval when another would be needed) I suddenly found myself in a rather precarious predicament.

I was sitting in a churchyard cemetery outside of Walpole, Massachusetts, sometime after midnight. I had just spent several hours quietly exhuming a fresh grave whose occupant I had been led to believe (incorrectly as it turned out) had not been embalmed. The hunger sickness was already upon me and my symptoms were growing worse with each passing minute. Knowing that I possessed neither the strength nor the will to dig any more graves that night, I sat down beside a tombstone, with my head in my hands, overcome with self-pity and pathetic despair. I could already feel a painful twisting in my entrails and I had just lain myself down in the cool grass to await what I knew would be an agonizing end when suddenly, from the darkness, I heard a loud click and the soft jingle of keys.

Looking up, I saw a heavy-set middle-aged man in dark robes coming out of the rectory and carefully locking the doors behind him. Crawling sideways into a shadow, I hid myself, watching him, as if in a dream, for several minutes. He circled the building once, checking to see that the lower windows were all locked, and, having satisfied himself on this account, he turned to leave the church grounds by way of a gravel footpath. The footpath through the cemetery was bordered by rows of large stones and snatching up one of these I fell in behind him, stepping lightly on the grass to avoid being heard.

I followed him for several hundred feet to a place where six or seven large trees blocked out all the moonlight, and there, in the brooding shadows, animated by some ghastly primeval instinct, I moved in for the kill.

He never even turned as I came up behind him, striking him, several times, with every ounce of strength I had, in the back of the head. He fell limply, gasping and wheezing at my feet. Seeing his collar and robe, I had confirmation that he was, in fact, a clergyman (an archbishop no less, as I later learned). He let out a long low moan which startled me, at which time I dealt him the final, life-extinguishing blow which split his skull into three large pieces. These pieces I extracted with a minimum of difficulty and carefully picking out the bone fragments with trembling fingers, I removed the still-warm brain. Carrying this to a nearby wooded hillside, I devoured it, whereupon I experienced that heightened feeling of intoxication which I have elsewhere described.

Having failed, in my carelessness and overconfidence, to secure a secondary source, I graduated from mere necrophagist to actual murdering cannibal. I could no longer tolerate anything but the very freshest of brains. When the need arose, I would kill in order to obtain the brains I required.

III

I WOULD LIKE TO STATE CLEARLY THAT I DID NOT KILL indiscriminately or at random. On this particular point I drew inspiration from the more militant class-war anarchists, initially choosing for my victims those persons whom I felt contributed most to the general imprisonment, subjugation, and exploitation of good, kind people. Police chiefs, priests, military recruiters, schoolteachers, headmasters, judges, politicians, and millionaires all met (and often exceeded) these criteria. If I now needed to kill to live, then I would select my victims (whenever possible) from among the privileged classes that occupied the uppermost echelons of New England society, as well as those who worked to keep them there. Over time my views on this began to change, for example, as much as I hated priests, it was difficult to feel that they deserved to be killed for their spreading of Christian values, poisonous though I felt them to be. The same held true for schoolteachers and cops generally. Most cops and schoolteachers, even though they served the ends of the bourgeoisie, were of the poorer classes. This complicated matters. I was not opposed to killing cops and priests and schoolteachers, but I found, over time, that I could not feel entirely right about these killings and soon pressed myself to avoid, whenever possible, killing people of the lower classes. Judges, on the other hand, were an entirely different story; while I could make a good case for the possible existence of a redeemable schoolteacher, I could think of no good reason to spare a judge, even a supposedly benevolent one.

The same was true for sheriffs, Pinkertons, military officers and prison wardens, yet I still tried to keep an open mind about the matter. A short time later, after observing their methods at a traveling circus in eastern Massachusetts, I temporarily added lion tamers, as well as bear, ape, and elephant trainers to this list. And, after reading an illuminating pamphlet in a Tarrytown bookstore, I added vivisectors as well. Some jobs were so reprehensible that there could be no mitigating circumstances. But I am getting ahead of myself.

In the days and weeks that followed the initial murder of the archbishop, I immediately became aware of certain curious "enhancements" (I don't know

29

what else to call them) developing among my sensory perceptions. I have since come to believe that some mineral or enzyme present in the still-warm brain matter must have triggered, in some inexplicable way, a string of mutations that had lain dormant in my bloodstream, enabling the marvelous improvements I am about to describe.

My ability to see, smell, and taste underwent shocking amplifications, the most remarkable of which were in the area of sight. My vision, for example, improved so suddenly and to such a startling degree, that, at first, I thought I was suffering hallucinations. Just days after consuming my first fresh brain, I found I could set my sights on distant objects or locations and bring them into focus with an almost telescopic clarity, resulting in an eerie and manifold intensification of my sense of location. My ability to detect and track subtle noises and movements increased substantially. My sense of smell became almost distractingly acute; in a startling way, odors which previously would have gone unnoticed, now refined my understanding of who and what was around me.

At first, these sporadic enhancements had seemed random to me, but looking back now, I can see a definite progression or onset, the systemic commencement of some cumulative biological effect. I developed an acute semi-visual sensitivity to the heat produced by nearly all living bodies within a hundred feet and so became aware, as never before, of the nocturnal movements of rodents, birds, snakes, insects, and human beings. Incredibly, within a few weeks, this heightened awareness seemed to surpass even that of the many wild animals around me, so that I found I could sometimes sneak up on birds, rodents and even deer and actually catch them unawares. I never ate these animals, nor felt any desire to do so, continuing to get my chosen meat exclusively from human beings and adopting an otherwise vegetarian diet. In time I found that I also lost my taste for milk, cheese, and butter, feeling, now, increasingly repulsed by the quasi-vampiric circumstances under which these substances are collected.

These sensory improvements I noticed most when in the forest at night; after the loss of employment in Bolton (and the subsequent murder of the archbishop), I had once again loaded up my knapsack with supplies and, wanting to put distance between myself and the scene of my crime, I entered the wooded hills outside of Somerville. For a period of several weeks, I traveled west, alone and on foot, avoiding even the most rural vestiges of civilization.

When walking in an uninhabited wilderness valley, I now found that I could, in some strange way, "feel" the towns and cities that lay beyond the horizon, almost "see" them through the hills and mountains that lay between us, even when they were still several miles away. Hereafter, whenever I desired the solitude of the woods, I would walk for days through hidden valleys, avoiding the towns entirely, without ever needing to consult my map to do it. These abilities were continuously improving; I was not sure where it all would end.

At some point, I had developed the ability, more or less, to see in the dark. On moonless nights in the deep woods, beneath a thick canopy of maple boughs, I was amazed to find that I could still see well enough to read Stirner without the aid of a candle. When I got up to explore the darkness I discovered, to my utter astonishment that, though I knew I walked through pitch blackness, I never once stumbled or bumped into anything.

In the weeks that followed, I had occasion to familiarize myself with these new abilities and to learn their limits. Even with a total absence of light, such as a cave, or an unlit root cellar at night, I found I could easily see the basic contours of my environment and move swiftly, even soundlessly, through it. On a quiet country lane, I could hear (and feel) a person approaching me from about a hundred yards off, even in almost total darkness, giving me ample time to step behind a tree and let them pass. It was not long after this that I had an opportunity to put these incredible abilities to the ultimate test.

*   *   *   *

AT ONE POINT, SOME MONTHS LATER, I HAD OCCASION TO CROSS the border into New York State and, in the hills north of Tarrytown, I thought to go and have a look at Kykuit, the famous Rockefeller estate in Pocantico hills. I had heard a disturbing story which had made Rockefeller of particular interest to me.

A dreadful massacre had occurred a year earlier in the coalfields of southern Colorado, at a place called Ludlow. A group of striking coal miners (along with their wives and children) had been mercilessly slaughtered and burned alive by thugs hired by the company that owned the mines. Conditions in these mines were so dangerous that, in 1913 alone, newspapers reported over four hundred men had been killed or crippled in accidents. The coal miners (mostly immigrants who did not speak English) breathed soot from coke ovens all day long and slept in filthy cramped company houses with their families. The strikers' demands (contrary to Rockefeller's statements) had not been unreasonable. The men were developing painful lung infections from the soot and demanded, among other things, proper ventilation shafts. They wanted to adhere to an eight-hour workday and to have recognition of the Miner's Union as a bargaining agent. But the company had stubbornly refused to acknowledge these demands, responding instead by sending hired thugs to terrorize and shoot at the strikers, evicting them from the company houses, and then riding through their tent camps in an armored vehicle outfitted with machine guns. Several strikers had been killed during these raids and local authorities had done nothing to end it. On the contrary, the police had participated (as they usually do), on the side of power and property. Then the massacre had happened. At dawn on April 20th 1914, deputies and company gunmen sworn in as soldiers opened fire on the encampment at Ludlow, afterwards riding through and setting fire to the tents with oil-soaked torches, killing altogether nearly fifty people, eleven of whom had been children.

The company that bankrolled this vile slaughter was the hugely successful Colorado Fuel and Iron Company, owned and controlled by the multi-millionaire John D. Rockefeller, Senior, now the object of a particularly intense public outrage. His public image had taken a beating in the press and he had been vociferously denounced by such persons as Mother Jones, Emma Goldman, Upton Sinclair, and Ida Tarbell, as well as countless reporters of the associated press. "The charred bodies of two dozen women and children show that Rockefeller knows how to WIN!" as one headline put it. Even Helen Keller, who had once been helped and befriended by Rockefeller, told the newspaper "Mr. Rockefeller is a monster of capitalism. He gives charity and in the same breath he orders the helpless workmen, their wives and children to be shot down." Even President Wilson had been unable to persuade the multi-millionaire to face down this tragedy, nor even to issue a public statement.

To all of this, Rockefeller had responded in a remarkably pathetic way. Thrusting out his well-heeled, inheritance-hungry son and heir, John D. Rockefeller, Junior, as a spokesman, to answer to his many accusers. Meanwhile, Rockefeller Senior had hidden himself away like a coward at his heavily patrolled Tarrytown mansion. It was the identical response he'd had seven years earlier when his Standard Oil Corporation had been inundated with charges of corporate monopoly. The man whom the newspapers called "a ravening monopolist" had simply hidden from his detractors, refusing to let himself be found. He had remained so elusive, in fact, that he had even avoided being present for the death of his own wife and the birth of his grandson, just to avoid the possibility of being ambushed by one of a growing number of dangerous enemies.

Rightfully fearing violent reprisals over the Ludlow massacre, Rockefeller Senior had sequestered himself behind the locked gates of his castle-like mansion with a private militia patrolling the walled perimeter day and night. Agitators had gone up to Tarrytown to hold a rally and to discuss the situation publicly, but they were ambushed by police, clubbed, arrested, and run out of town. The subsequent murder trials for the Ludlow killers had been a farce; radicals everywhere were calling for a general strike to bring the enemy to terms. The police, the courts, the entire judicial mechanism had rolled over like a puppy before Rockefeller's millions and so the only real hope lay in the outrage of the working people themselves. As the weeks passed, huge numbers of angry protesters showed up at Rockefeller's Tarrytown mansion, as well as his office at 26 Broadway in Manhattan, only to be beaten back by police and soaked with water hoses by the local fire department. At one point, Emma Goldman (whom I had once heard speak in Plymouth) showed up outside the gates of Kykuit, demanding to speak with Rockefeller, but she too was attacked by police and forced at gunpoint back onto the train to New York City. Such is the judicial system, built, owned, and maintained by the ruling class and used as a shield by the wealthy against the rage of the exploited masses.

But all of this had been many months ago. The rallies outside Kykuit had, after so much police violence, tapered to almost nothing. A few people had successfully gained entrance to the walled estate, throwing rocks through windows, but all had been routed successfully and chased off.

What can I say, dear reader? With my heightened senses and my newfound ability to creep about undetected, the idea of infiltrating Kykuit seemed the ideal testing ground. And, should I be able to successfully gain entrance, who knows, maybe I would strangle the greedy bastard myself and eat his brain, in vengeance for all his horrendous and heartless deeds. The bullies who, from the safety of their fortified mansions, casually exterminate ordinary, decent people must be made to understand that such things as the Ludlow massacre would not be tolerated. They must be deprived of the feeling of invincibility that enables them to do such things.

* * * *

THE STRINGS OF RECENTLY STRUNG BARBED WIRE GLEAMED IN THE moonlight the night I first laid eyes on Kykuit. The riflemen I saw loitering near its entrance and wandering its grounds had the unmistakable look of Pinkertons: dim-witted, and unspeakably ruthless, the cold, dead-eyed look of the hired killer. Kykuit is located atop a massive hill overlooking the Hudson River Valley. There are extensive terraced gardens, tree parks and links that lay all around the place. With my enhanced senses, not only was I able to scale the wire-topped wall and cross the heavily patrolled gardens unseen, but to clamber, spider-like, onto Rockefeller's own bedroom terrace where, positioning myself in the shadow of a large potted cypress, I watched him preparing for bed.

As I peered in on him, I tried to recall all that I had heard of the man. He was a slight fellow, smaller than I had imagined, piebald and almost feeble in his movements. His Valusian face, curiously immobile, betrayed a strange, leathery impassivity; there was something almost reptilian in his bearing. He had the pursed, frowning lips of a prudish old church-lady, offset by the vindictive eyes of a wounded viper. Furthermore, it was also painfully evident that something terrible was happening inside Rockefeller's body. It appeared as though he was being eaten alive from within, as if by some horrible, unnamed, wasting disease. He was noticeably thinner than the pictures I recalled seeing in the papers a few years earlier. He had lost substantial bone-mass and looked oddly reduced beyond what mere aging could explain. Once tall and well-built, he now had the appearance of a wizened corpse. He could not have weighed 100 pounds, giving him a spooky, cadaverous appearance. Seeing him there, just beyond the glass door, I did not see Rockefeller, the Titan of legend, but a trembling, sad-eyed miser, wretchedly alone and old before his time.

Upon seeing his diseased state, I knew I would never consume his brain, feeling distinctly unwilling to imbibe what I knew must be a poisonous concentration of avarice, depravity, malice, and hypocrisy. This was a man whose fearful, tight-lipped grimace revealed a heart haunted and possessed by a monstrous self-doubt. This was a man so uncertain of his own goodness that he spent his days making little deals with his Christian god, playing mind-games with himself, to ease the sting of his guilty conscience.

I had read in the papers that this strange little man had once claimed God Almighty would show the world just how much he loved John D Rockefeller by allowing him to live to 100. But even this ridiculous boast only betrayed his eagerness to put off the question of judgment, as well as revealing his preoccupation with his own mortality. It was written all across his face that thoughts of his own demise haunted him without mercy. Hence, I supposed, his need to edify himself endlessly with all these ridiculous externalities, the countless grandiose monuments of a dubious existence. Gazing in on this pitiful man, alone in his mansion, I could feel his claustrophobia, his terror at the knowledge that so many people wanted to see him swinging from a lamppost. As if to emphasize this, I watched for nearly two hours as he played pathetically with a system of electric lights whereby he could illuminate any portion of his wooded estate with the press of a button. This had been installed no doubt to assuage his fears about anarchist assassins and other intruders from without. Yet somehow it only seemed to make things worse for him. Many times he wandered away from the picture window to busy himself with other things but, obsessed, his face would grow pale again and he would return to the window, fingering the buttons methodically and squinting fearfully out into the night.

I don't know what came over me as I squatted among the cypress boughs. A spirit of perverse hatred at the ludicrous wealth of this pampered idiot inspired in me an intense desire to hurt him and his people — to shatter forever his ridiculous fantasy of superiority. Sometime after midnight he finally retired, at which time I very quietly opened the patio doors and slowly, cautiously, entered his bedchamber. Pulling up a chair, I seated myself beside his bed. For a long time I just sat there, watching him sleep, listening to his troubled, uneven breathing and slowing my respiration until it matched his own. After several minutes, feeling entirely calm, I got up and explored the three adjoining chambers, one of which was his office. I sat at his desk, studying the portraits that hung upon the wall and perusing his papers in the moonlight. Some of these were memos from his cohorts at Standard Oil, asking for his approval on this and that expenditure. One letter, from his son, requested that he make some kind of public statement of contrition regarding Ludlow, though the whole tone of the letter sounded pleading and hopeless.

Recalling Rockefeller Senior's few public remarks, made through the medium of his son, it was evident that he actually believed himself to be the victim in the Ludlow situation. Always it was some other persons fault, never his own. On the one hand, he whined and griped that he was "being portrayed as a frightful ogre" in the papers and on the other, that he was being pressed to answer for "decisions he had not made." Claiming he had not worked in ten years, he had made his son feign ownership of Standard Oil and then pawned off the presidential title on his friend and protégé John D. Archbold (hoping that this would magically absolve him of all legal culpability). Secretly, from within his stronghold, avoiding anything that contradicted his delusions of victimhood, he had resumed his usual work-related tasks. Returning thoughtfully to his bedside, I asked myself, "Was there anyone more pitifully ruthless than this man? Could anyone make an argument for someone more deserving of a vicious, violent death?" He was everything that is wrong with the human animal, an utterly deranged and heartless specimen, enshrined, untouchable, and beyond all reproach — or so he had hoped.

As I sat there listening to him snore, I realized that the public would eventually be made to forget all about the Ludlow massacre and were, in fact, already being made to forget about it. Fifteen other catastrophes vied for their attentions, not the least of which was American entry into the War. Public outrage was being postponed indefinitely on this account and it seemed less and less likely that any meaningful change in society would occur at all. Besides, did anyone really believe that denunciations and exposes like Upton Sinclair's and Ida Turbell's were, in and of themselves, enough to stop men like Rockefeller? And so, the question remained. How might men like Rockefeller be stopped? The much-feared general strike had not materialized in any meaningful or sustained way. In Ludlow the miners had gone on a rampage, destroying the mine headquarters of Colorado Fuel and Iron, but even this had lately been crushed by federal marshals who had stepped in to defend the mines. What then could common people do to stop such destroyers of life, such monopolizers of everything?

Again I got up from the chair, no longer making an effort to be quiet, and stepped up onto the bed. Straddling Rockefeller, I lowered myself onto his chest, my knees pinning his arms at his sides, and laying my gloved hands across his snoring mouth in one fluid movement. His eyes flicked open suddenly and peering about the room he attempted to scream, wriggling uselessly against my weight, his legs pinioned beneath the blankets. Forcing his mouth shut, I crushed his head backwards into the pillow until, at last, he fell quiet. For an instant his right arm lunged violently against my thigh and, following the direction of his gaze, I spied a small alarm button built into the bedframe just beside the pillow. Seeing that I had noticed this button he went into another awful spasm and began to weep, though in a sad muted way. Then, realizing that he was perfectly immobilized, he finally went limp and shivered beneath me.

"If you make a sound...." I whispered, "...I will break your neck." Then, bringing my face within a few inches of his, I said, "Nod your head if you understand me, John." He nodded.

After some minutes of us looking at each other, I slowly took my hand away from his mouth. The house around us was empty. I could detect no living presence in any of the nearby rooms and so, having no fear of interruption, I began to contemplate how best to make a lasting impression upon this most stubborn of men. He interrupted my musings, however, with a sadly predictable and insulting attempt to purchase my mercy.

"I'll give you money, young man, more money than you could ever dream of," he said in a low whisper, his eyes momentarily agleam with the thought of his bountiful riches. Somehow I found this display both shamefully degrading and highly amusing and was moved to actual laughter, until, looking down and seeing that my laughter had affected him awfully, I stopped. A foul smell informed me that he had soiled himself.

I wanted to ask him a thousand questions. "How many people have you killed? How many lives have you ruined? How many miles of beautiful green earth have you gouged and spoiled and poisoned, beyond all hope of recovery, with your mines?" I wanted to present him with all the many pointed questions which he had, until now, so deftly evaded. But I said nothing. I just stared into those strange, watery, reptilian eyes and waited to see what else he might say for himself. I began to grow impatient with his silence and, in an effort to prompt him, I said, "So, this is the wealthiest, most powerful man in the world."

Hearing verbal acknowledgment of his millions had a curious effect on him. Imagine my amazement when, after gazing into space, he seemed to come back to himself and, discovering some reservoir of dignity within, a look of anger slowly passed over his face, so that he seemed to frown at me. Then, in an attempt to intimidate me, he asked, voice brazen and indignant, "What is your name, young man?"

Something in his tone made my decision clear and I resolved, then and there to kill him. "My name is Ludlow," I growled and then gripping him suddenly around the neck with both hands and staring hatefully into his eyes, I began to squeeze the life out of him. Here I would do, with my own two hands, what no Labor Reform laws, no Supreme Court Judges, no angry Presidential memos, no peaceful protests, no international manhunt had been able to do, namely, to show this arrogant piece of human garbage that he was answerable for his deeds, that he was not untouchable. But I had been strangling him for nearly a full minute, had even felt him go limp in my hands, when a stray thought made me slacken my grip.

Looking down at that sad, contorted face, lit by the glow of the newly risen moon, I saw a man who had made a monster of himself, a destroyer and enslaver of his fellow men, a man who had wrung the blood, sweat, and life force from his victims and utilized them for his own hideous sustenance. I saw a man who had been swept away by momentums much more powerful than himself, and who had grown more than a little frightened of the thing he had permitted himself to become. I suppose, in that moment, in some faint way, he reminded me of myself. I let him go. I released him and, though he still breathed, his eyes remained shut. He lay still upon the bed, apparently in a dead swoon. Looking down at him, my thoughts began to grow confused and every argument I'd ever heard for (and against) violence came suddenly pouring into my mind.

Every legal measure had failed to rouse this man from his stupor of greed. Perhaps it was true what the militants had said, that men like Rockefeller were not to be negotiated with, but to be exterminated to the last, without mercy. Their money placed them above the law. Ludlow, if nothing else, proved this. To pretend that the Rockefellers and the Carnegies and the J.P. Morgans of the world could be reasoned with, in any truly meaningful way, was to engage in a most dangerous fantasy. Yet something inside me cringed at the idea that the only thing left to do was to kill them all. Soon, news reports of the Russian revolution would describe hundreds of thousands of angry peasants storming the Winter Palace, beheading every aristocrat they encountered. Was this really the only way for a people to rid themselves of their oppressors? To infiltrate their palaces and strangle them in their beds?

Furthermore, unlike Russia, I was only one individual, tacitly allied with, at best, a tiny militant minority. I was not so dense as to imagine that it would not require, at least, several thousand furious ex-citizens to topple the entire social order (and many thousands more to keep it toppled). I could have killed Rockefeller easily enough, but what would it have changed? Tomorrow he would be replaced by a similarly deplorable specimen, who had already been selected. John D. Archbold had already taken his position at the helm as the new president of Standard Oil and was thus far showing every intention of adhering faithfully to the same heartless creed as his forbear. Like Rockefeller, Archbold also had that curious habit of whining, speaking as if he were the victim and bemoaning all attempts to curtail and regulate the company's brutal monopoly. "Darkest Abyssinia never saw anything like the course of treatment we received at the hands of the administration," he would later complain. This, from the same man who had lent a hand in orchestrating the Ludlow Massacre. It was positively nauseating.

This gave rise to yet another bizarre question and I wondered; could being strangled within an inch of his life, in his very own bed, by an outraged commoner turned-assassin, cause this cold, unfeeling man to reconsider his path in life? Would being spared by a committed enemy with a soft spot, awaken any humanity in this arrogant maniac? Or was he beyond all possible hope? It seemed worth a try.

In the spirit of a scientific experiment, I decided to spare him (though I suppose there will always be a part of me that will wonder if I should have). Letting him dream the dreams of a man who thought he had been murdered, I climbed off him, leaving him unconscious, but still very much alive. The following day he would awaken with nothing more serious than a pounding headache and a severely bruised throat. Slipping back out the way I had come in, I lowered myself down the brickwork and, within a few minutes, had crossed the lawn undetected, and secreted myself in a large hedge, near a wooden barn by the fence. Entering this barn I found a pick, not unlike the ones used by miners, and using it, I scratched the word "Ludlow" in three foot long letters into the smooth packed ground just outside the barn doors. Then, after quietly releasing the dozen or so frightened horses into a nearby field, I doused the barn with a can of kerosene I found inside and torched it, fleeing back into the hills. Half an hour later, from the safety of the woods, I watched the barn, still burning in the distance, illuminating the surrounding hillside with brilliant cataracts of flame that rose and boiled furiously, like some colossal, hundred-foot-high demon dancing beneath a billowing cape of thick black smoke.

For ten days I hid out in the hills north of Tarrytown, venturing down each morning to collect a newspaper, to see if Rockefeller had made any grand, Scrooge-like declarations regarding a change of heart or reversal of policy towards the striking miners. Finding none, I deemed my experiment a failure, and cursing my naiveté, planned a second visit to Kykuit. Ten days later, however, I returned to find the place so well-lit and thoroughly patrolled, that even with my enhancements, I was entirely unable to penetrate it. The hired guns were on high alert and in addition to the forty or so men I saw standing around in the open, I could detect, all over the estate, as many men hidden in the shrubbery. Furthermore, it was long after dark, and the windows in Rockefeller's bedroom were unmanned and unlit, strongly suggesting that the rabbit had fled the burrow. Thus, I decided to settle for John D. Archbold, his protégé, instead.

* * * *

AS I HAD LEARNED FROM A MEMO ON ROCKEFELLER'S DESK, Archbold was recovering from a mild stroke at Cedar Cliffs mansion, also in Tarrytown, and conveniently located a mere three miles from Kykuit. There was a private, unlit country lane which connected the two estates. Utilizing this, I made the journey in just over a half hour, savoring the moonlight and the bucolic scenery as I went. Cedar Cliffs was infinitely easier to penetrate, though security was formidable enough, on account of a recent bomb plot. Evidently, at the end of the previous year, someone had placed high-powered explosives on the long winding driveway, hoping to blow the new president of Standard Oil to Kingdom Come when his car tire passed over it. It was widely understood that this had been done to avenge the murder of Joe Hill, a miner, songwriter, and labor agitator who had been framed and executed in Salt Lake City, Utah. The bomb plot had failed when a gardener had discovered the device. Despite the heightened security measures, I had no trouble entering Cedar Cliffs undetected. Scaling the wall of the mansion, I found a second story window that was unlocked and, entering the bedroom, I wasted no time.

Killing the man had been a simple act, accomplished in a matter of minutes. John D. Archbold was lying in bed snoring when I woke him gently singing one of Joe Hill's songs (the only one I knew from memory). "Work and pray and live on hay… you'll get pie in the sky when you die." He stared at me for several seconds and then I crushed his face with a pillow, relieved him of his brain, and let myself out through the service door.

* * * *

IMMEDIATELY FOLLOWING THE SMOTHERING OF ARCHBOLD, I knew that I must not tarry too much longer in Tarrytown. The police, undoubtedly driven to a trigger-happy frenzy by my outrages, had stepped up their efforts to clear the streets of all persons not submissively engaged in his patriotic duties, which is to say working (non-union of course) or preparing to go to war. As a result of this, the streets of Tarrytown had fast become a very unsafe place for me (or anyone else) to be. The parks were crawling with cops, Pinkertons, and recruiters eager to get every man and boy, citizen or not, conscripted with a rifle in his hands. It is a pathetic truth, of which I took full advantage, that a crippled beggar is nearly invisible, not just to the recruiter, but to many of his fellow creatures generally. I affected to exaggerate slightly the defects of my posture and thus remained practically unseen by more than half of the population. Sometimes I spread a big foolish grin across my face and muttered softly to myself for a similar effect.

Feeling distinctly unwelcome on the cop-infested streets of Tarrytown, I headed northeast, walking back across the border into Connecticut. Circumventing several small cities, I traversed the wild countryside on foot, moving toward Salem, stopping off in those towns which are like little islands of civilization in an otherwise wild land. This meandering journey took me several months. When I could find no work in the towns along the way I would sleep in train stations or on park benches and get my food at the soup kitchens with the rest of the tramps.

I continued to maintain a rigid brain-eating schedule. On the outskirts of Litchfield, I lured a lion tamer out to the woods (on the pretense of showing him an unusual specimen) whereupon I brained him, fed, and threw his corpse into a deep ravine. Two weeks later I ate a deputy sheriff outside of Capetown, and two weeks after that I ambushed a retired Supreme Court Judge on his wooded estate near Stafford Springs, sinking his brainless corpse into a lovely frog pond which he had just had installed in his immense garden.

*　*　*　*

AS I PASSED THROUGH MILFORD, THERE WAS A MASSIVE STRIKE underway and here I was lucky enough to attend a lecture by the infamous Luigi Galleani (editor of the newspaper, *Cronaca Sovversiva*), whose fiery speeches drew huge crowds of angry working men and women. Before Galleani took the stage, I made a point to purchase more radical literature, including such titles as *God and the State*, by Mikhael Bakunin, *Catechism of a Revolutionist*, by Sergey Nechayev, *Twilight of the Idols*, by Nietzsche, as well as numerous back issues of Emma Goldman's *Mother Earth* magazine.

For my more light-hearted reading I selected *The Flowers of Evil*, by Baudelaire and *Melmoth the Wanderer*, by Maturin. Making my way over to the bookseller, I was startled to see that I recognized his face from other anarchist events I'd attended. It was the steely-eyed Italian bookseller with the kind smile and the gentle face — the same fellow who had sold me *The Antichrist* and Stirner the last time I'd been in Milford. It seemed to me he traveled with Galleani, selling books to raise funds while his friend spoke out against the coming war, imploring his listeners not to register. Occasionally, he too would take a turn at the podium.

Exchanging a few kind words, he gave me a meaningful smile as I paid him, afterward lingering for a moment as I inserted the books into my satchel. As I did this, the amplified voice of Galleani rang across the plaza and I heard the great orator say, "There will have to be destruction! We will destroy to rid the world of these tyrannical institutions which strangle us to death!" at which, a great roar went up from the crowd. I glanced back at the bookseller, who was still grinning, with all the joy of life in his eyes.

"He is good," I said.

He nodded and replied softly, "I believe he was born to do it." His accent was thick and guttural, so that I guessed he was from somewhere in the south of Italy.

"Will you be getting up there today?" I asked, trying to prolong the conversation, but he shook his head modestly and said "Not today, my friend, not today. Please, enjoy your books."

Taking up my pack I made my way over to the lectern, listening for nearly an hour as Galleani enumerated the nightmares of class society, doing his best to awaken in his listeners that hunger for freedom which separates the truly thoughtful being from the mindless brute, the living, breathing animal from the automaton.

For, sadly, the automatons comprised the vast majority. From the mining towns south of Danbury, to the crowded streets of Marlborough and Milford, to the cluttered shores of the Woonasquatucket and Connecticut Rivers, and finally onto the bustling streets of Salem itself, I saw the same unfortunate situation unfolding. Everywhere I was confronted with the pathetic plight of a degraded humanity. In the larger cities the omnipresent smokestacks of industrialization were spreading like a plague of gigantic poison mushrooms against the sky, exuding great suffocating clouds of black smoke and an almost ceaseless drizzle of charred metallic ash. In city after city, I saw nameless fear in the eyes of the people, a despair that seemed to suggest something worse than the effects of poverty and war-time anxiety.

These dingy, overcrowded cities and ever-expanding townships had been the common scenes of my upbringing, scenes which I had looked upon all my life with a dull complacency. They should have been as familiar to me as my own two hands, yet something was wrong, had always been wrong, with everyone and everything. Of the people I encountered, I was increasingly aware of a fearful vacancy behind their eyes, as of minds disordered by some all-consuming terror, thinly covered over by ritualized clichés and half-hearted formalities.

And I knew these formalities only too well, for these were the same formalities that had, since birth, dictated the parameters of my own thoughts, words, and deeds. Somehow, year after year, I had not seen through them. Now, however, it was unavoidable. The cities and towns were diseased and monstrous places to me now, and more and more it seemed as if all of civilization was the deranged and cancerous outgrowth of some abominably warped and malevolent consciousness.

To make matters worse, there appeared to be a disturbingly large number of people who were simply rabid patriots, mad as March hares about what American democracy symbolized to them, eager to inflict it on each other and the rest of the world. Even amid the friendly hustle-bustle of a warm Sunday afternoon in the park, an accusatory furtiveness seemed to emanate from the crowd. The increasing numbers of policemen one saw here and there exuded suspicion, poisoning every interaction, tainting every exchange with their scrutiny.

*　*　*　*

MEANWHILE, UPON THE QUESTION OF MY OWN GENERAL MENTAL state, I continued to think much. There was something about killing the archbishop, especially the archbishop that had affected me deeply. It was not just that I had killed and eaten one of god's humble servants, but that, in my heart of hearts, I did not feel that badly about it. A voice in my head continued to assert that I had done the unthinkable, the unforgivable. I had blasphemed against the Holy Spirit! I was a cannibal fiend now, a nursery bogey, a walking, talking abomination, dressed up like a human being. It was all too grotesque, too hideous to be real.

And yet... increasingly, as I traversed those wild hills and lost valleys, I was haunted by a feeling of profound and incredible forces converging upon me. It was as though some vast and ancient intelligence dogged my every step, a being whose very nearness sometimes made me freeze in my tracks like a statue, trembling and breathless beneath a starry sky, afraid to look up lest I see a trillion winking eyes where the stars should be. A feeling of transformation and transcendence seemed to follow me wherever I went. I recall, at times, that I felt as though I might actually be inventing some new religion, or was perhaps reviving a very, very old one, the likes of which had not been seen upon the earth for many hundreds of thousands of years. I had the sense that some unseen force was guiding my movements and that I was being initiated into some secret understanding so incredible that I could not assimilate it except in little pieces.

Moreover, it was increasingly clear to me that I had always known, as if by instinct, that the ordinary world of men would conspire against me. Had I not intuitively held myself apart from them? Without understanding exactly why or how... I had allowed myself to fall completely out of step with my own civilization. Like the famed Ethan Brand, or William Wilson before him, I had turned my attentions to the pursuit of a hideous darkness, a profound negativity, renouncing all morality as I went. I beheld before me a path without signposts or guidelines of any kind. Of course, there were others who saw as I saw. They were called anarchists, everywhere the subject of a hysterical fear campaign, hunted down, beaten, arrested, deported, banished.

Despite these very real dangers, however, I felt strangely emboldened and unafraid. Why should I be afraid? The human world was against me now, yes, most undoubtedly, but what of it? The universe and all of wild nature, it seemed, were on my side. Every bird and insect, every leaf on every tree seemed to whisper a wordless encouragement. As I studied the examples of the plants and animals around me I began to feel my mind drifting further and further away from the realm of human conceptions and morality, and ever more into the world of my own unfiltered senses. I watched ravens devouring an animal carcass in a field and felt a sense of kinship that calmed and assured me. Once, while tramping through a marsh near Danbury, I knelt down and watched as one enormous grey leech drained and devoured another in a cesspool. Later, in an abandoned barn outside Fairfield where I had passed the night, I had the rare good fortune to witness an enormous black widow spider trap and devour one of her own kind in her web, draining it of all fluids and then discarding the hollow corpse.

As strange as it may sound, these things encouraged me and inspired in me a strange sensation of reassurance, as well as an increasing curiosity about my own predilections. I continued to wander, a rapidly distorting shadow of the man I had once been. All that remained of the mind I had come to know over a lifetime had begun to alter and to reconfigure itself, until at long last, I was an entirely new creature to myself.

"Let us say... I am repugnant to myself; I have a horror and loathing of myself, I am a horror to myself... From such feelings springs self-dissolution or self-criticism. I am possessed and want to get rid of the evil spirit. How do I set about it? I fearlessly commit the sin that seems to the Christian the direst, to sin and blaspheme against the Holy Spirit. 'He who blasphemes the Holy Spirit has no forgiveness forever, but is liable to the Eternal Judgment.' (Mark 3.29) But, for myself, I want no forgiveness, and am not afraid of the judgment... for I shall be the enemy of every higher power."
—Max Stirner

IV

DURING 1917, WHILE I HAD BEEN OUT EXPLORING MY NATIVE LAND, the United States government had entered the European war and remained busy trying to stifle the unrest I have earlier described. When I had passed through Plymouth, there was a massive strike underway and I heard of similar situations in Hopedale, Boston, and Milford, where a radical by the name of Carlo Tresca, arrested on a fabricated murder charge, had narrowly avoided being lynched. The recently passed Espionage Act of 1917 (which outlawed all anti-draft radicalism), had done its job a little too well, sowing the seeds of hatred toward "anarchist conspirators" as well as immigrants in general, and causing widespread paranoia among the general population. Mandatory military conscription (from which my obvious deformities exempted me at a glance) only confirmed the idea that the poorer classes were disposable in the eyes of the State. On the overcrowded streets of Salem, people on soapboxes spoke with increasing anger at the way impoverished young men were being rounded up and shipped off to death and dismemberment in the hellholes of Belgium and France. Enforcing the "work or fight" law seemed to be the new priority of the police, and harsher provisions for the deportation of political dissidents made it so that people were afraid to say the word "anarchist" aloud, or even to allow themselves to be handed a pamphlet or flyer without looking nervously over their shoulder.

This, of course, was the desired effect of a government that wished to continue the bloody harvesting of its most vulnerable citizens uninterrupted and uncriticized. The newspapers kept up a steady supply of blood-curdling articles designed to crush any arguments against entering the war and the Patriot Parades drew sizable crowds. Labor agitators and striking workers were depicted as treasonous scum, foreigners out to destroy America. The anarchists, as one paper ludicrously claimed, were funded by the Kaiser of Germany himself.

It was a source of great annoyance to me that, while the everyday violence of the police, the Army generals, private militias, and men like Rockefeller were always framed as regrettable inevitabilities, the incomparably lesser anarchist counter-violence against the wealthy elites continued to be described as nothing short of demonic. Anarchist violence had, in truth, killed far fewer people than a single month in a typical Rockefeller coal mine and yet this vilification continued under a cloud of non-comprehension. Expressions of hatred for the anarchists, on the other hand, served almost as a test of one's patriotism (and a lack of it was likely to be interpreted as a tendency towards treason).

Furthermore, despite the outward show of patriotism, the parades and the propaganda were not having their desired effect upon most young men. There was, amongst the youth of all classes, a tremendous apathy and ambivalence about the war, hence the necessity of passing the Conscription Act (just six weeks after U.S. involvement) which required every male, citizen or not, between the ages of twenty-one and thirty, to register with the draft board.

The press mostly sang the praises of this new legislation, promising "better days ahead" (with considerable hand-wringing and head-shaking on account of what they called "a growing disregard for the established forces of law and order"). One conservative journal, fairly typical of its kind, cautioned workers against "following the noxious example of the sub-human Russian rabble" and warning against "long-haired anarchists preaching a social upheaval which will mean nothing less than a reversion to savagery or Medieval barbarism." By equating the anarchists (and the Labor movement in general) with Bolshevism they hoped to undermine it completely. This was a decidedly aristocratic point of view, though I encountered it most often, oddly enough, among people who were themselves not members of the bourgeoisie, but who seemed to cherish a curious fantasy that they were of that class. Workers who struck for better wages or improved working conditions were accused of being "unpatriotic" and of "exhibiting the symptoms of a herd on the verge of stampeding." Meanwhile, politicians and professors who spoke out against the war were jailed and made to pay enormous fines. The offices of anti-war newspapers like *Mother Earth, The Blast* and several others were raided, people were beaten and arrested, printing presses smashed, subscription lists seized, lives ruined. The people who envisioned a radically altered social order were "deluded," they said, because American Democracy was "the product of the natural development and improvement of all human relations" and therefore absolutely inevitable. Since this was "the best of all possible worlds," desiring something else was not only "backwards" but almost anti-human, political and social heresy. "American Democracy is the greatest system in the world!" one writer boldly declared. But in one bustling New England city after another the haunted faces of the poorer inhabitants told a very different story.

In the midst of all this was Red Emma, the Queen of Chaos herself, a Brueghelesque villain come to usher in the apocalypse. Emma Goldman,

46

whose *Mother Earth* journal espoused such satanic philosophies as free love, marriage refusal, draft-dodging, and political assassination; Red Emma, whom the newspapermen fell over themselves in their efforts to ridicule and discredit. Goldman had come to America to awaken the sleeping giant, and therefore had to be neutralized at all costs. It was truly pathetic to see how the well-heeled reporters sneered and denounced her from afar (never once daring to interview her, knowing how she would put them to shame), she who had no terror of their puny, mealy-mouthed authority. How the rich and powerful must have feared Emma Goldman's message to sic their dogs upon her with such ruthlessness. They spared her no indignity and drove her from town to town, raining insults, lies, and distortions upon her, so that I was at times put in mind of the witch hunts of old. It was (and still is) fashionable for New Englanders to smugly denounce the Salem Witch hunts of the 1690s as some anomaly of history, yet here I watched a comparable (albeit greatly updated) social mechanism worked upon Red Emma and her comrades. They did all but incite the mob to hang her from a lamppost (though the implications that they hoped somebody would do so seemed clear enough to me).

Despite these ongoing distortions and misrepresentations of her character in the press, everywhere she went, Emma Goldman packed lecture halls to overflowing, filling them with the scathing wisdom of her words. It was, in fact, from one of her lectures that I had learned the ugly details of the Ludlow massacre and the ensuing charade that had gone on in the courtroom. It was also there that I learned how Ludlow was only one of many similar incidents and that other fatal attacks on striking workers had occurred in Chicago, Milwaukee, Cleveland, Homestead, and Lattimer, just to name a few.

What was I to make of this hysteria against the anarchists in particular? Why this witch hunt for Emma? What anarchists asked was actually rather simple (if not too much to the point). Why do we of the working class complacently slave our lives away for a vampiric, bureaucratic leisure class? The anarchists located the problem in the very organization of society itself, exposing institutions as a vast system of control imposed upon the masses by the elite, instilling and ingraining capitalist values, myths, and morality and normalizing, day after day, the hierarchies of class. Schools and factories, utilizing techniques taken from the ruthless Prussian military model, were quite literally designed to produce docile, unthinking beasts of burden. The heresy was that the anarchists exposed these methods and even advocated that working people join together, rise up, and go on the offensive against the dominant class. When the capitalists committed atrocities such as the Ludlow Massacre, the more militant anarchists, not content to write angry diatribes, actually attacked them in return. They placed dynamite outside the mansions of millionaires and politicians and mailed incendiary devices to their homes.

It was from *Mother Earth* that I also learned of numerous episodes where mobs of apparently ordinary citizens had organized attacks against various poor and disenfranchised peoples. These attacks included the horrendous slaughter of nearly two hundred Black men, women, children, and babies in St. Louis, by an angry white mob, egged on by racist union officials who told them that job scarcity in that city was just a case of "too many niggers, not enough jobs." Other mob violence included the November 5th massacre of several Free Speech fighters in Seattle, done to death by patriotic vigilantes, as well as the stoning of Free Speech advocates in Tarrytown. Further incidents also included the near-lynching of anarchist Ben Reitman in San Diego, California. Reitman had gone there to lecture and to publicly expose the divisive methods employed by the local capitalist class, but the public had been so poisoned against anarchists by the local press (and by the paid provocateurs planted among them) that they had mobbed up and tried to lynch him.

Of these many victims of vigilante lynch mobs, I wondered if this was to be my fate as well. Had my youthful nightmares been a prophecy, or simply a product of my fears? I had no answer to this question and yet as I read these accounts I could not repress a shudder. It chilled my blood to think that such things were not only possible, but increasingly put into practice against persons who looked, thought, and acted differently from the patriotic herd. After being tarred and feathered, Reitman had, for whatever reason, been permitted to escape, though the experience had shaken him badly. Such is the effect of a good smear campaign upon a frustrated populace, not dissimilar from the one inflicted upon Red Emma and her friends in New England.

I must add here that I remained skeptical regarding the true nature of these so-called patriotic vigilante mobs. On the one hand, rebels, whores, negroes, uppity workers, and poor people in general were so routinely scapegoated and misrepresented in the public imagination that it seemed entirely possible that ordinary folks had mobbed up against them. On the other hand, Ben Reitman made a pretty good case that these apparently spontaneous lynch mobs were in fact being organized and financed by union leaders, politicians, and wealthy industrialists like Rockefeller. During Reitman's ordeal in San Diego, for example, police had been present before the mob appeared, overseeing throughout the attack and never once intervening until the very end. It remained an open question in my mind, yet I could see how even this confusion played to the interests of the wealthy elite. I could also see how rented mobs represented the weapon of choice for the millionaire, a weapon which they could utilize to great effect in their very public conflict with the forces of Labor and dissent in general. Mobs always come off so curiously in the papers. When angry mobs attack the sacred structures of government they are described as "subhuman rabble" but when they lynch an anarchist, or a bunch of poor negroes in St. Louis, people shrug their shoulders and say, "Well five hundred people can't be wrong." In this way rented mobs remain the perfect weapon for the wealthy minority, resembling as they do the "Will of the People."

These lynchings disgusted and enraged me. That such horrors as these could be permitted by the placid, unrebellious majority sickened me to my bones. How could they fail to see what was being done to them? How could they fail to be outraged by the system of domination being imposed upon them? As I walked among them on the streets of Salem, I was oddly inclined to study them, to see if I could learn their reasons for not rebelling. It baffled me how they permitted themselves to be herded like cattle to the slaughter, even arguing passionately in defense of the circumstances that enslaved them. Where had all their dignity gone? In what precise manner had all the fight been taken out of them? Were fancy-looking newspapers and the threat of police batons really all that was required to keep them in line? Or was it, as the anarchists argued, the very structure of American society that had made them so cowed, so crestfallen before the Almighty Rich? I hated them all for allowing ignorance and petty differences to break them up into warring factions, to be played endlessly and repeatedly against each other instead of banding together to overthrow the rotten system that enslaved them all. I could see how mentally lazy they were being, how they clung to their naïve notions of fair play and gradual reform. The power elite would make meaningless capitulations, very publicly, as a way to maintain the illusion of negotiation, but it was all a show, and I hated the masses for not seeing through it. The American people seemed sadly inclined to have all their thinking done for them, as if to retain some foolish notion of child-like, unworldly innocence, to make a virtue of their smug, privileged naiveté.

I continued to be impressed by the determined, no-nonsense sincerity of anarchists like Emma Goldman and Ben Reitman; when I saw the way they were treated by my fellow New Englanders I was disgusted to count myself among them. I saw too many people who shared their plight, the countless refugees of industrial society, endlessly slandered, blamed, and attacked, driven from place to place, on the run from authority. This legion of the dispossessed, it seemed to me, was growing every year and I feared where it was all headed. Thousands arrived by boat every day, only to find poverty, treachery, and violence worse than what they had fled. The broken promises of America's opportunity had made fugitives of us all. Everywhere I went, I met people who felt as I did, angry and lied to, tricked and trapped, with nothing to lose.

My apprehensions of being hunted by a large group of people continued to haunt me. By this time, Rockefeller was sure to have drawn the obvious conclusion that Archbold's killer and the fiend who had accosted him in his bedroom were one and the same man. It was only logical to assume that he had, by now, dispatched his own private lynch mob (the best, most bloodthirsty brigands his money could buy) to hunt me down and either kill me, or else collar me and bring me before the man himself, to receive his personal vengeance face to face. Frightened as I was by this possibility, I was also much consoled by the thought that my enhanced abilities would make me a most formidable and elusive quarry, and that any hunting party hoping to corner me would, in all likelihood, never get within five hundred yards of me without my having knowledge of their presence and using it to its greatest possible advantage.

* * * *

WITH REGARD TO SOME OF THE SIDE EFFECTS OF MY STRANGE NEW abilities, I must now mention that period of intensely lucid dreaming which came upon me in the final weeks of the summer of 1917. Immediately following my departure from Salem, I headed northwest, traversing many miles of wild mountain countryside as I made my way into the endless pine forests of New Hampshire and Vermont. It was during this time that I first began to dream of those horrific Beings who (as I now understand) have, since time immemorial, been visiting, studying, and steering the development of terrestrial life. These dreams came as an awful revelation to me, confirming certain nagging suspicions which had begun, through the long weeks of contemplative solitude, to creep into my thoughts. I took it on faith that the frightening things I saw in these dreams were indicative of actual events, representing a fairly accurate (albeit fragmented) history of the covert visitation of earth by the denizens of some unimagined Outer Darkness.

Almost nightly for nearly eight weeks in a row, the dreams were often so disturbing, so incredible, that I frequently awoke bathed in sweat and panting, with a throat strangely raw, as if from breathing tainted or rarefied air. Over time I became somewhat inured to the incredible insights these dreams yielded, though it all came at a terrible cost; afterwards, I could never feel anything even approaching the relative safety and comfort I had taken for granted all my life.

I saw monstrous, blasphemous things of every conceivable size and shape (and some with neither size nor shape). Always the background was mundane, familiar, pastoral. Sometimes it was an earthy New England scene I had recently tramped through, other times it was entirely unknown country (and always with me observing from some shifting, disembodied vantage point). In the first few dreams I observed a fleet of hulking, ugly grey things (each the size of a two-story house) lumbering forth upon the moonlit hills of my native Southwick and even passing through the high green meadows where I had played as a child.

In another, similar, dream I drifted down a deserted country lane at sunset and watched, in breathless terror, as things I had taken to be enormous, lichen-encrusted boulders in a field suddenly rose up on thick, odd-numbered limbs, gave forth deep, thunder-like vocalizations, then proceeded, crabwise, to congregate in a hollow between two low hills. When an approaching automobile appeared upon the horizon, I watched in awe as these boulder-things returned, with a blood-chilling swiftness, to their prior positions upon the landscape, hunkering down until the automobile had passed on, at which time they returned, cautiously, to the circle formation and resumed their mysterious activities.

On another occasion, I dreamed of several enormous wraith-like entities (which casual observation would have dismissed as mere low-lying fog) gliding with hideous, purposeful slowness into a furrow in a hill beside a frozen swamp. Two nights later, I dreamed of a thing that looked like a great black morass, situated at the bottom of a grassy ravine, yet which rose up into the air (somewhat in the manner of a great black manta ray) to observe its surroundings and to prey upon a group of people picnicking on a neighboring moor.

In yet another dream I saw a great earthen mound in a grassy meadow, beside a footpath where a group of schoolchildren in Puritan garb soon appeared, marching along two by two. When the children were present, this hummock appeared in every way as a commonplace earthen mound, but when the children had passed on over the hill, I watched in horror as numerous great yellow eyes (each the size of a dinner-plate) bloomed forth upon its bulk. It sent forth a wavering tentacle to examine a scarf, dropped by one of the children. When, several minutes later, a solitary schoolboy came running back to recover the dropped article, without the saving presence of his companions, the mound suddenly rose up like a great silent pillar and dropped itself upon him, instantly absorbing him into its loamy bulk.

I dreamt once of another monstrosity who appeared as nothing more than a dead and fallen pine tree, rotting among the ferns and saplings of the forest floor. Upon finding itself alone with an unsuspecting hunter (dressed in Elizabethan attire) it reared up, centipede-like and, paralyzing its prey with sheer terror, quickly seized upon the hunter and swallowed him whole, musket and all. More horrible still was the way this many legged horror, upon hearing the approach of the man's companions seconds later, had suddenly bolted back to its prior position upon the forest floor, leaving no detectable clue of what had transpired save a barely visible bulge near the center of its massive trunk.

So it was through these dreams that I learned the precise ways in which these covert visitors had, for centuries, masked their presence by insinuating themselves perfectly into the natural landscape. Always they bore the semblance of familiar, earthly phenomena, resembling trees, boulders, bogs, meteorites, wind, lightning, fog, piles of dead leaves, even the fleeting shadow of a cloud gliding across the face of a hill. I marveled at their incredible camouflage and was made to wonder what other dreadful powers such beings might possess.

With my newfound knowledge of alien visitation, I now cast a suspicious eye upon even the most homey country scenery and increasingly felt that I was the subject of a malignant and clandestine scrutiny. The dreams inspired a heretofore unknown vigilance, so that I became more reflectively sensitive to my surroundings than I would have thought humanly possible. Every boulder, every tree, every harmless morning mist was now suspect, and I scanned with unprecedented skepticism for any peculiarities of form, tone, or movement.

Finally, and to my undying horror, I soon discovered that, though they did not permit me to see them, I could *hear* those hidden Things from my dreams, chirping and whistling beautifully to each other across deserted hillsides and lonely meadows, utilizing a language that so closely resembled the chanting of crickets, the creaking of a windblown tree, or the chirping of birds, that any hapless hiker passing through those places would have detected nothing out of the ordinary. My ears, however, could distinguish the difference now, and many nights I lay listening to their eerie voices before drifting off to sleep. The sound itself was pleasant enough; without knowing its true source, one might have even found it soothing. But to me it was like the whistling of demons, a sound as mesmerizing as it was dreadful.

In this watchful manner, I traversed, first the White Mountains of New Hampshire, then the Green Mountains in Vermont, arriving seven weeks later at the Soapstone caves near Monkton, where I spent several nights camping in the winding passages of that remarkable formation.

*　*　*　*

THAT THE DREAMS OF VISITATION WERE SO INTENSE THAT THEY WERE sometimes accompanied by a painful secondary symptomatology all their own. Often, upon waking, I was assailed by strange, short-lived fevers, curious shooting and stabbing pains, odd migrating bruises of unknown origin and that strangely raw throat, as if I had suffered prolonged exposure to some poisonous emission.

By now it was early autumn and, searching out adequate quarters for the cold months ahead, I was lucky enough to have gained access to a large rural residence in the hills west of Monkton, which perfectly suited my needs. The cellar of this rambling house contained an enormous coal furnace which the wealthy inhabitants kept burning all night long, maintaining the entire place at a very pleasant temperature, even on the coldest and wettest of nights. I slept there six or seven times, letting myself in after midnight through a small window entirely obscured by shrubs and waking and leaving before dawn each morning. It was an admirable spot (while it lasted) and there, beneath the floorboards of that mighty edifice, as I lay listening to the nocturnal comings and goings of the large family above me, I read Bakunin, slept, and was protected from the increasingly harsh outer elements. This ideal situation, however, lasted less than a week before the dreams I have earlier mentioned culminated, unexpectedly, into that final nightmare which was by far the worst.

I dreamed that I was in yet another bucolic New England scene, watching (as usual, from my oddly elevated vantage point) as a Boulder Thing, roughly the size of an elephant, crouched by the side of the road, with all of its attention fixed upon a solitary, unsuspecting human figure who was slowly walking toward it up the road. When this figure had passed it by, the thing rose up on its elongated legs and scurried up and over the ridge, where I saw it vaulting ahead, as if to intercept the walker at a point farther up the road. A car appeared over the crest of a nearby hill and, crouching by the roadside, it waited, like a gigantic grey spider, until the car came within striking distance, at which time it threw itself with tremendous violence against the front fender, causing the vehicle to leap the embankment and to tumble sideways down the gully. The Boulder Thing then returned swiftly to its spot upon the hill just as the figure came running up the road. Dashing down the slope (as if to rescue persons trapped inside the vehicle) the man scrambled into the gully, shouting with great concern as he went. It was then that I recognized the running figure by his clothing and his voice; it was none other than myself — four years earlier and upon that fateful day in the hills above Plymouth.

From this final dream I awoke screaming, recognizing, too late, the tremendous peril I had placed myself in by doing so. There was a frantic tramping of feet on the floorboards just over my head and before I could even get my bearings I heard a voice, trembling with rage and fear, calling out to me, "Who the hell is down there! Answer me, damn you! I have a Remington and I'm going to shoot you on sight!"

His terror was understandably great, having been awakened in the dead of night by what must have been a truly blood-curdling scream, issuing from directly beneath the floorboards of his own front room! The cellar door flew open with a crash. A blinding light poured down into the darkness as I scrambled, dazed and half-asleep, toward the window. Looking back only once over my shoulder I saw a man in a red bathrobe descending the stairs with an enormous gun thrust out in front of him, swinging it angrily from side to side. There were two wide-eyed teenage boys behind him, each with a lantern held high over their heads. Suddenly there was a deafening boom and a great rush of air along the left side of my body. Seconds later, I was just able to squeeze myself out the tiny window, narrowly avoiding the second round of buckshot that shattered the plaster casement mere inches from my foot.

* * * *

THIS MARKED THE END OF THAT PERIOD WHEREIN I COULD SAFELY sleep in the basements and tool sheds of private estates. No more could I trust myself not to scream out at the frightening dreams that sometimes came to me in the small hours. Leaving Monkton that night, I began to make my way south again over a period of several months, train-hopping, hitch-hiking, sometimes riding on buses, zigzagging southward through Vermont, Connecticut, New York, Pennsylvania, and even into Maryland. During the colder months, to avoid trouble, I stayed at the only places I could — cheap motels, gambling saloons, whorehouses, and any other place where strange cries in the night were, if not expected, then at least tolerantly ignored.

Throughout this time of rapid travel and low-living, I also had the honor of killing several persons of high social standing. In January of 1918, I crept into the home of James Henry Brady, the US Senator and former Governor of Idaho, dispatching him quietly with a pillow to the face and then de-braining him on the spot. On April 6, I killed and ate the brain of John Q. A. Brackett, former governor of Massachusetts, at his absurdly huge mansion in Arlington. Three months later, while passing through Windham County, Connecticut, I dropped in to visit with Major General George Whitefield Davis of the US Army, former puppet-dictator of Puerto Rico and military overseer of the Panama Canal Zone. Later that same July, while visiting Syracuse, New York, I similarly rid the world of Charles Andrews, a Chief Judge of the New York Court of Appeals.

I should mention that, at the time, killing these professional overlords and casual exterminators of men did not trouble me one bit. I found their legacies so disgusting and so entirely wrong-headed, that my conscience acquitted me entirely. I remained, in truth, rather sentimentally proud of these

54

killings, considering them to be among my finer contributions to the class war (though I no longer harbored illusions that they could trigger a social revolution). Such overpaid stooges as these are far too easily replaced for their deaths to be of much consequence and yet, on account of the sheer vengeful satisfaction it afforded me, I would have liked to have killed more than I did. Alas, I was beholden to the limitations which time and circumstance imposed upon me.

An interesting footnote: in all of the newspaper articles which concerned these high-profile killings, no mention was ever made of the fact that they had been murdered and that their brains had been removed, a thing I found both gratifying (since it spared me the headache of a widespread panic) and suspicious (why suppress the fact?). This was a mystery I was never able to solve.

* * * *

ONE DAY, AS I WAS WALKING IN THE HILLY MARSHLANDS EAST OF Sudbury, Massachusetts, I came upon a wild, green glade, in the center of which there stood a two-story farmhouse, obviously uninhabited and in a woeful state of neglect. In the side yard there was a large, partially collapsed barn as well as a squat, stone pump house located around back. A low hemlock hedge surrounded and enclosed the main buildings, which were overgrown with weeds, unpruned fruit trees, and wildflowers. This house, located at the end of Arnold Lane, had at one time been a solid clapboard affair, though time and the elements had left it little more than a decaying wreck. There were four modest bedrooms, as well as a kitchen, dining, and living rooms all located on the main floor, with a spacious, half-subterranean basement of equal dimensions, whose damp stone walls formed the foundation of the house. Another unique feature of this structure was a laundry chute, a vertical, chimney-like passage which communicated between all three floors of the building.

The kitchen was semi-detached, connected to the larger structure only through the medium of the dining room, which was slightly higher, a single step separated one room from the other. In the dining room there was a great dry sink, full of filthy but otherwise intact whiskey tumblers, as well as several full bottles of four or five different kinds of whiskey. Beneath this dry sink I discovered the perfectly intact skeleton of a housecat, whose pure white bones had, evidently, been picked clean by insects. A small bullet-shaped hole in the top of the skull indicated that the cat had been shot. In the kitchen, great timber rafters crossed the ceiling and the western wall was lined with cabinets, a large sink, butcher block counters and a rusty stove, now home to a number of small rodents. Above a massive oaken kitchen table hung a wagon wheel, suspended from three nearly horizontal chains which met in the center, where a heavy iron ring was bolted to the rafter. At various points around the rim of this wheel, the stubs of several usable candles stood in empty tins. These candles I lit with no trouble and soon the room was bathed in a warm golden light. Beginning in the kitchen, I started removing all of the various broken, rotten or useless items from around the house and tossing them into a large heap, forming a barricade, against the backside of the front door.

This decomposing house was oddly, I must add conspicuously, well-furnished and decorated, giving the strong impression of having been abandoned quite suddenly by its prior tenants, who didn't even take the time to pack up and remove their many possessions. Lamps still stood upon tables, decaying tatters hung from curtain rods, and pictures adorned the walls, including an oil painting of the whaleship *Charles W. Morgan*, badly overgrown with black fungus. I found this troubling. Why had nobody come to scavenge the many valuables I found lying about the place? Surely these woods contained numerous vagrant populations, squatters, gypsies, and the like, yet something had caused even these penniless vagrants to shun it entirely, leaving its many treasures to rot.

Regardless of these unsettling mysteries, I took up residence in this place, moving in sometime in August of 1918 and remaining there, more or less, for a period of roughly six months. The kitchen cabinets were stocked with numerous canned vegetables, as well as soup broths, peaches, and condensed milk; I was spared the nuisance (and the danger) of too many trips to town. Taking one of the smaller ground floor bedrooms as my own, I constructed a crude mattress out of some old woolen bedding, which I laid over a skeletal boxspring I'd found half-buried in the tall grass beside the barn.

Shortly after the housecleaning was completed, I began to set about accomplishing certain other, admittedly curious and seemingly inexplicable, tasks. Without knowing precisely why, for example, I was seized with the urge to collect large stones from the surrounding fields and to assemble them into a large ring on the dirt floor of the basement. I also blacked out the basement windows by smearing handfuls of mud upon the inner panes and, utilizing random objects from around the house, I successfully barricaded every door in the place from the inside, wedging shut every ground floor window, with the exception of the one located in my bedroom which I used to come and go.

I was not without the occasional human visitors at my new home, though they were visitors of a most unwelcome kind. Several times I looked out the front window on a sunny weekend afternoon and saw invaders from civilization poised at the garden gate, old Studebakers loaded up with red-cheeked, white people in sun hats who had come puttering down Arnold Lane (the wildlife fleeing madly at their approach) in search of a quaint place to picnic and get drunk on a Sunday afternoon. I would hear the rattle of the engine coming down the road and a thrill of fear would go through me as it inevitably came to a slow, squeaky standstill just outside the old picket fence that bordered the front yard. Moony faces would press against the windows with stupidly awed expressions as I stood flattened against the wall, holding my breath until they passed on. Picnickers in this region, as I soon learned, tended to favor such locations as old cemeteries, hidden ponds, and abandoned houses for their activities and apparently, my picturesque farmhouse (overgrown with wildflowers as it was) proved an irresistible setting for more than a few of these peculiar events. Several times I spent a fearful afternoon crouching beneath the window sill as they frolicked and fucked, drank, and made sick in the orchards across the road, or else set up easels on which to paint the sky, the hills, or the house itself. All the while with me peering out at them through a slit in the curtain, studying their movements, trying to anticipate whether or not one of the damned fools would get the bright idea to try and enter the house.

For they had only to step down out of their poisonous, stinking automobiles and to hurtle a low fence and they would be ten steps from my very doorstep. They'd need only toss aside the large branches which I had thrown across the path and walk up that narrow, flower-lined lane. If they mounted the stairs and dared to peer into any one of the ground floor windows, what would I have done? What else could I have done if one of them caught a glimpse of me and my barricades, and was aroused to suspicion?

Thankfully, this never happened, and as the weather turned colder and the leaves fell from the trees, the puttering, cloud-spewing automobiles soon dwindled away. The sky grew dark and grey and the wind brought a chill which discouraged outdoor activities and made one long for a blazing hearth.

*　*　*　*

IN MID-SEPTEMBER, I WAS STRUCK DOWN WITH A CURIOUS ILNESS which prostrated me for several days. This strange period of fever lasted exactly three days, during which time I elected to stay down in the cellar, lying myself out on the cool moist earthen floor, drinking large amounts of water but unable to eat. On the third day, I awoke to a violent trembling of my limbs and after several hours of lying there, breathless, I rose up on my hands and knees and vomited forth a thick mass of grayish slime, which I took to be

57

bile. Dragging myself back up the cellar steps, I crawled into my makeshift bed where I slept for an unknown period of hours, after which I awoke feeling entirely better.

The next day, I went back down into the cellar to clean up the floor and was stunned to find that the slime I had regurgitated had somehow coalesced into a cloudy, egg-shaped globule several inches long, whose hazy edges my eyes were oddly unable to define. On account of the fact that it was pulsating slightly, I was unwilling to examine this thing too closely, though I puzzled over it at a distance for the better part of an entire day.

Returning on the morning of the second day, I was unnerved to find the thing gone entirely, and (despite my enhanced vision), even after a fairly thorough search of the cellar I remained unable to locate the globule directly. Unnerved and confused, I sat down upon the cellar stairs haunted by the feeling that I was not alone. I must have been sitting there for an hour, stock still and quiet as a mouse, when my patience was at last rewarded and I heard something moving clumsily among the rusty tools and old milk bottles which lay in piles along the cellar walls. Still I saw nothing yet I was certain that I was not alone. On the morning of the fourth day, the globule finally came out in plain sight and I observed it actually moving of its own accord, oozing along very much after the manner of an enormous sea slug. Shortly thereafter it improved upon its rudimentary mobility and began foraging about on the cellar floor, attaining an increasingly pinkish hue which quickly darkened into a deep burgundy red.

Regarding the incredible texture, mobility, and general absorptive powers of this apparently living substance, a short description is warranted. From a distance of a few feet it most frequently appeared as a lumpy, gelatinous puddle of bloody syrup, but with endlessly varying degrees of hardness and pliability. Its surface was subject to a host of fascinating, ever-changing instabilities, sometimes appearing entirely fluid, other times hard like glass, with a brittle, shell-like exterior, something akin to the carapace of a beetle or trilobite. Detailed inspection (which I was eventually fortified enough to perform) revealed its surface to be, most often, something akin to an infinitely dense coat of tiny reddish black filaments, each no more than a tenth of an inch in length, which stretched and reached, like a sea anemone, whenever I put my face near to it. If one were to envision some hideously mobile patch of thick, crimson lichen, growing on the surface of a bloody pool, one would not be too far from the mark. At other times, these filaments lay down smoothly so that it had a kind of sheen, not unlike mink fur or the velvety skin of a seal. I noted that it was entirely dry, leaving no trace of moisture on the surfaces over which it flowed, so that I was reminded of the peculiar properties of mercury. At other times it appeared as though it was in a state of cellular disintegration along its outermost borders, as if the molecules themselves were in rebellion against the noxiousness of it's form. At these moments, it had the appearance of a great heap of heavy red dust, several inches deep.

This thing traversed the cellar floor like a living liquid, extending leg-like projections as it explored its strange new home. Moving uninjured, for example, through the prongs of an old pitchfork or the shards of a shattered milk bottle, it switched effortlessly, back and forth between several independent streams and one unified mass. In this amoeba-like manner it would later flow up walls, along ridgepoles and rafters, lingering puddle-like on the ceiling, for hours at a time, or else retreating to the deeper shadows of the cluttered cellar floor.

On the evening of the ninth day I received directions, through the medium of several unforgettably explicit and instructive daydreams, to go and fetch sustenance (in the form of fresh human brains) for my little companion, which I promptly did, culling these brains in the aforementioned way (and according to my usual criteria) from the surrounding cities and towns. The brains so collected, I arranged in pieces upon a metal tray which I then placed at the foot of the cellar stairs, repeating this offering roughly once every ten days. Upon returning several hours later, I would invariably find the metal platter empty, with the appearance of having been scoured clean, as if by fine metal brushes or steel wool. Entering the cellar one fine September morning, I was rather touched to find the red blob waiting at the foot of the stairs for its meal. Subsequent to this, I was pleased to see it emerge, at each feeding, to greet the coming of the tray.

At times, I must admit, I was shocked and rather repulsed to think that I had served as incubator and sustenance provider to this seemingly extra-dimensional entity who had nested in my very own digestive tract. And yet, curiously enough, this feeling never lasted. In time, I would come to cherish the fact that I had been selected for so important a task and I embraced the peculiar way of life into which I'd been drawn.

V

REGARDING THE PARTICULAR EVENTS THAT WENT ON IN THE farmhouse after the arrival of the red thing, I am reluctant to go into too much unnecessary detail. It will be enough to say that neither I nor my little companion ever wanted for fresh brains. If I had been a gifted assassin before, I now became masterful, luring my chosen victims, on false pretenses, to various remote locations (usually at a safe remove from the farmhouse itself) whereupon I attacked, killed, de-brained, and then buried them, returning home with the spoils which I divided equally between myself and the red slime. I mostly killed far away from the farmhouse, but with some notable exceptions. Several times I lured policemen back to that horrible farmhouse, telling them fabulous lies which I adapted to suit the preoccupations of the blossoming police state. Then, after de-braining them, I tossed their corpses into an unused upstairs bedroom.

Meanwhile, with each new feeding, the red thing grew noticeably in size; I came to feel that I was feeding a newborn thing not yet able to hunt for itself, but which I was convinced would eventually grow into something quite gigantic (and in direct proportion to the amount I fed it). This eerie impression of parentage became even more startling when the thing started to follow me around the cellar, lingering, for as long as possible, near my feet and emitting a mournful, flute-like trilling sound each time I left the cellar.

It was beginning to get quite cold by late September and, fearing that chimney smoke might alert others to my presence in the farmhouse, I only ever set fires in the hearth very late at night or else in the early mornings, when a nearby river caused the entire valley to fill with a dense morning mist. Luckily, throughout the autumn months, this mist did not usually burn off until several hours after sunrise.

There came a day when the Red Thing seemed to discover (and to immediately begin cultivating) its remarkable shape-shifting abilities, imitating (crudely at first, but with steadily increasing proficiency) the various spiders, snakes, centipedes, and pill-bugs it encountered on the cellar floor. At such times, I was amazed to observe it ambling slowly and clumsily about on spindly, misshapen legs or stumps. There were times when, search as I might,

I could not find the red blob at all, though I was always made aware of its presence by a unique odor which it emitted. It gave off a strangely cold, hollow smell, an aroma which made me think of nothing so much as the icy, airless voids of outer space itself; a smell of dead molecules and cold, motionless atoms.

Once, several weeks after the Red Things arrival, as I sat upon the steps watching it eat from the tray of brains, I absentmindedly pointed to a hunk of half-melted brain that had fallen off the edge of the tray. I watched in utter amazement as the Red Thing became strangely still and, rising up in the manner of a snake, seemed to actually regard me, sending forth from its back a shiny red appendage which instantly took the shape of a life-sized, pointing human hand! Such were its ongoing and increasingly sophisticated attempts to mimic other nearby organisms.

Meanwhile, having learned to negotiate the cellar stairs, the Red Thing adopted the slightly unnerving habit of following me around the entire house, accompanying me into the various rooms and lingering nearby. We were careful never to touch each other, maintaining, at all times, a distance of at least six or seven inches. For my part, I did not mind this closeness as much as one might expect, and over time, I found that I rather liked it, mostly on account of the fact that as the autumn air grew colder, I noticed that the thing emitted a noticeable heat, generating a necessary and much-appreciated warmth in an otherwise chilly house.

* * * *

ONE DAY, WHEN IT WAS STILL NO LARGER THAN A MANHOLE COVER, I turned to observe it following me down the cellar stairs and noticed that within its liquid mass there seemed to be a cluster of small spheroid organs which appeared to swim and dart about within the liquid body. I worried that they might be eggs, and for several days I was haunted by terrible visions of my beloved farmhouse sanctuary overcome by a whole brood of similar, hungry globules, yearning for fresh brains and with only myself in the role of provider. My fears were, however, if not precisely allayed, then transformed into a queasy relief, when, one sunny afternoon, the spheroid organs broke through the surface and I saw, to my profound discomfort, that they were eyes, bulbous, staring, red eyes with enormous black pupils that dilated and shrunk with a quickness that implied an eager, almost frantic examination of the farmhouse and me. These eyes (which migrated with utter fluidity through the mostly liquescent skin) were approximately twenty in number and, though they mostly remained interior, I was occasionally horrified to look up from my reading and to find myself the subject of a decidedly unnerving scrutiny. More and more, I would catch it staring at me, almost expectantly.

There were days, indeed whole weeks, where I simply lingered near the farmhouse reading my books, cleaning, and sleeping, always with my bizarre little companion following close at my heels. Initially, the Red Thing had not permitted me to leave its vicinity. It had, from the very start, possessed an uncanny ability to send my thoughts and emotions into a painful, vertigo-inducing chaos, which it would deploy whenever I tried to leave on anything but a hunt for food. By the fifth or sixth week, however, the Red Thing had become more and more inclined to leave me alone for hours or even whole days. I soon surmised, while on these bi-monthly hunting expeditions, that the Red Thing had devised a way to come with me, inside my head, like some bizarre guardian angel, whose enigmatic scrutiny and promptings I could subtly detect among my thoughts. Whether it achieved this utilizing methods purely psychic or by sending some small piece of itself directly into my body, (or both) I was never able to determine.

* * * *

OUR HOUSEHOLD SOON ACCUMULATED A SUBSTANTIAL AND PROBLEMATIC number of rotting and brainless human heads as well as several whole corpses. From the start, I had been treating the upper bedrooms as my own personal mortuary. Having laid out the corpses and severed heads in the two larger rooms, I left the windows wide open and the doors shut tight to reduce the smell. I had selected these particular rooms with the vague idea of drying out the corpses, these rooms being the ones that received, by far, the greatest amount of sunlight and wind. I was unnerved by the possible effect long spells of warm, windy weather might have upon the corpses, concerned that the smell might drift across the fields to the highway or, worse still, to the little town of Sudbury that lay just beyond. I was anxious for the advent of winter   (knowing that a frozen corpse would give off almost no smell) and distinctly nervous that it had not yet come. By mid-October the temperature had still not dipped below freezing. I was, therefore, grateful when I soon received rather startling, and not wholly unwelcome assistance in disposing of my ever-expanding corpse-pile.

One morning I awoke terror-stricken at the sound of a curiously forceful tapping and semi-rhythmic knocking, coming from somewhere inside the house. My first thought was that someone was rapping lightly upon the outer windows (or doors) and my mind leapt at the myriad of unpleasant possibilities: Rockefeller's thugs or the police, or some bold and curious person from the highway who had caught the stench and sought its source. A quick survey of my bedroom revealed that the Red Thing was nowhere to be seen and, snatching up a .38 special I'd taken off a deputy sheriff (now headless in the upstairs room), I crept quietly over to my closed bedroom door, lowering my head and peering underneath it to determine if anyone was lurking in any of the ground-floor rooms. After the momentary silence that followed, I heard the sound again, coming from directly overhead, a series of oddly grouped clicks and knocks accompanied by vocalizations of a most repellent sort. Looking up, my enhanced senses informed me of a strangely shaped cluster of warm, living matter in the upstairs bedroom, though it was so oddly shaped, covering the floor (and the level surfaces of the furniture) and flickered so quickly here and there, that I could make no guess as to what manner of creature, or creatures, it might be.

Suddenly, from the rooms above me, there came an outburst of hideously garbled cackling which made my blood run cold and the hair on my arms stand up. On trembling legs I stepped into the empty kitchen to steady myself and, making sure that my gun was in full working order, I made a swift investigation of the ground floor before tracing the garbled muttering up to the two corpse-strewn bedrooms in the upper story.

Moving very cautiously, gun held out in front of me, I mounted the stairs, listening with terror and disgust to the sounds of uncouth muttering and throaty, guttural syllables emanating from behind the two closed bedroom doors. Upon reaching the top, I promptly kicked open the first bedroom door, an act which created such a frantic exodus of bodies out the window that the air was soon filled with deafening shrieks and a hurricane of swirling winged blackness which poured, like a feathery liquid, out the square portal of the window. The brief glimpse I had of the room revealed to me the very un-magical fact that the smell of my corpse-piles had attracted a small legion of hungry ravens. I had, after all, left the bedroom windows open. The other bedroom revealed a similar scene, with the vast majority of body parts having been eaten almost down to the bone (a fact for which I was mightily grateful).

Helpful though this was, it was not the most remarkable part of the episode. After the last of the ravens had fled the chamber and all became quiet again, an odd thumping sound caused me to turn and look into that portion of the room which the open door had kept hidden from me. Peering cautiously around it, I saw the Red Thing, stumbling awkwardly to and fro, tottering on two spindly legs which ended in a pair of frightfully elongated, hooked talons. In a clear attempt to imitate the noisy black birds whom it had been observing, it was only able to do so in a gruesomely imperfect (though shockingly enlarged) way. Its face and chest, bisected into two curving, sword-like beaks (which opened and closed like some huge, fiendishly flexible pair of scissors) festooned with several shifting rows of darting, blinking red eyes, which peered out, like a school of strangely disembodied, cyclopean fish. Stumbling forward quite suddenly, it waved two shiny, red triangles at me, resembling nothing so much as a great malformed, crimson penguin.

I counted myself lucky that the Red Thing did not immediately pursue its attempts to mimic the ravens and for a time seemed content to abandon the notion of flight altogether. Having learned the basics of mammalian, reptilian, and arthropodal perambulation, it still seemed to prefer to move as one, oozing, tongue-like mass, pouring quickly and quietly over anything that happened to be in its way. This came as a great relief to me, as I could only imagine the difficulty of keeping track of the Red Thing should it develop the ability to fly.

After the arrival of winter and the cessation of the annoying Sunday picnickers, I moved operations out into the backyard to better facilitate the scavenging of the ravens, who, to my great relief, continued to leave nothing but (relatively) clean white bones, which I promptly threw into the attic of the barricaded house.

As the winter of 1918 set in and the nearby creeks and river froze solid, the heavy morning mist I had come to rely upon ceased. With nothing to hide my chimney smoke, I set out to discover a way that I might maintain my presence in the farmhouse while avoiding the unpleasant fate of freezing to death in my sleep. By the middle of November I had begun to notice that the cellar seemed to remain at something like an even sixty degrees despite the increasing outside chill which I initially accredited to the fact that the cellar, being half underground, would have the benefit of certain insulatory effects. But as the winter weather grew colder and more severe, and the temperature inside the cellar (and to a lesser extent the ground floor) actually began to rise, I concluded that the Red Thing was now generating an increasingly compensatory heat inside its body which it radiated outward. It was for this reason that I would later theorize that the creature had come from a place of tremendous, polar, if not stellar, frigidity. Whatever the reason, I promptly relocated my bed to the cellar and thereafter enjoyed deep and restful sleep from which I consistently awoke refreshed and enlivened.

*　*　*　*

AFTER A SHORT TIME, I WAS ABLE TO RESUME MY TRAVELS. IF I loaded up the tray with six or seven brains at a time, I could sometimes go wandering for several days before the Red Thing called me back to the farmhouse on Arnold Lane. Additionally the surprisingly large sums of money I'd found in the wallets and purses of my victims was sizable enough to cover the costs of several short journeys by train to neighboring cities where I was able to resume my researches and to feed and shelter myself adequately. Toward the middle of November 1918, for example, I was able to slip away for two days to Providence, and the Brown University Library, where I endeavored to learn all that I could about the ongoing excavations at Machu Picchu and also the Corpse-Eating Cult of Leng. Cities like Providence, by this time, had become cacophonous, almost unbearable places for me, yet I forced myself to enter these overcrowded, idiocy-inducing mazes only because I needed to continue to do my research at the best libraries available.

It was not, however, from the Dewey Decimal System (efficient though it is) that I received the most useful guidance into the world of outré mythology. My chief source of information was actually a highly unique and intelligent individual whom I was lucky enough to encounter in the library at Brown; it was only with the assistance of this most remarkable young man that I was able to make several more fascinating and crucial discoveries.

While sitting in the Brown Library reading about those tribes who inhabit the jungle valley that lies between the Bolivian plateau and the Paraguay River, I came upon a passing reference to the Lengua Indians, a cannibal tribe said to have inhabited that region since prehistoric times. Having come across, yet again, that odd word "Leng," I spent the better part of three hours focusing my researches on tracking down this one reference. All my efforts had come to naught, and I was on the verge of giving up.

As I stood up to return several volumes to the cart, I caught an unusual-looking gentleman staring at me. He was sitting in an armchair in the common area, pretending to read a newspaper. He was a pasty, moon-faced man, definitely of the local stock, though dressed in the fashion of the previous decade. Normally I would have taken him for a policeman, except that no plainclothes copper with half a brain would be so foolish as to appear in public in that absurd garb. Returning to my table, I twice more caught him gazing at my profile and scarcely making any effort to hide his evident interest. He was a queer looking fellow to be certain. His thin, pursed lips and slender hands, his overly round face with eager, child-like eyes that bulged ever so slightly in their sockets, all combined to give him a curiously androgynous aspect which I found strangely compelling.

Deciding that he could not possibly be a policeman, I considered another equally unpleasant possibility, one which I had heretofore managed to avoid. In those strange days, it was not unusual for the occasional passerby (perhaps one in every five hundred) suddenly to stop cold in their tracks at the sight of me and to stare in wordless terror. This curious thing had happened often enough that, over time, I had developed a theory that certain sensitive persons could, in some unknown way, perceive me for the ghoulish thing that I was. It seemed as though some people, including at times, very small children, could somehow glimpse my abnormality with a kind of second sight, a thing which caused them to recoil from me in utter horror, but without the benefit of knowing precisely why. I would occasionally catch these rare souls flinching in stark terror at me, eyes wide with fear. Within a few seconds, however, these bewildered gawkers would invariably collect themselves, rubbing their eyes and seeming to shrug it off as a illusion. And yet I could not help but wonder; just how much could they see of me and my curious passenger.

This moon-faced fellow in the library struck me as yet another of these eerie gawkers, though I noticed that his expression conveyed more of a pleasant wonder than the usual loathing. This intrigued me, and, obeying a sudden impulse to interview such a person, I walked straight over to where he was sitting and introduced myself, pretending that he looked familiar. As he rose to greet me I saw that his cranium was remarkably massive so that I could only wonder at the dimensions of the brain it contained. Standing up to his full height, he resembled a somewhat pigeon-chested giant, with an unusual slenderness so totally at odds with his overly large head, that I was made to wonder for a moment at the mating habits of those New England families for whom genetic purity remains a lingering obsession.

I recall that his first name was Howard but, sadly, I have forgotten his last name (though I remember that it was unusual). None of the bare facts of his life, as he gave them to me during our introduction, gave a clue as to his interest in me. He was the editor of a conservative political magazine and was actively involved in the amateur writer's movement. Born and bred in Providence (and rather fiercely proud of it), he was full of curious historical facts and bizarre local anecdotes. He was also interested in astronomy and spoke passionately on the subject of stargazing. He had, for several years, made a hobby out of chronicling any astral anomalies he might be lucky enough to observe, describing his observations in a monthly column which appeared in yet another local journal. When I asked what an "astral anomaly" might be, he mentioned (somewhat conspiratorially I thought) the recent disappearance of a star from the Pleiades constellation.

Noticing the ponderous books I carried, he enquired after my interests, to which I confessed a lifelong fascination (entirely untrue) with primitive mythology. Unfortunately, this had the opposite effect of what I had intended and instead of deterring him, he launched into a half-comprehensible laundry list of his favorite mythographers, past and present, articulating himself with a flowery, poetic style of speaking, which I found utterly charming. We chatted in a friendly way for several minutes when at last there was a sufficient pause and I brought the discussion back, as casually as I could, to the matter at hand.

"If you don't mind my asking, Howard, why were you staring at me?"

"Please forgive me, I meant no disrespect," he blurted and then, leaning back in his chair, he regarded me doubtfully.

"I'm sure this will sound bizarre," he resumed in a low voice, "but something in your appearance seems to have awakened in me a dim memory. I was just wondering where it was that I might have seen you before."

Again my fear of having been seen during one of my nocturnal feasts rose up in my mind; I felt my pulse quicken as I waited to see if his friendly smile would melt into a grimace of horror. I watched and waited in vain.

Suddenly, he looked at me wide-eyed. "That's it! I know where I have seen you before. Oh but it's quite marvelous, ridiculous even! I saw you in a dream last night."

"Did you?" I replied, doing my damnable best to sound nonplussed.

"Yes! Yes I did. I was so moved by it that I awoke this morning and wrote it into my commonplace book."

"That is rather astounding," I said nervously. "What happened in this dream of yours?" Before answering, he glanced furtively about the room and a small frown came over his face. Then, taking me by the elbow, he led me over to a private alcove, and, after he had satisfied himself that none were watching us, he turned to face me.

"It was dark. I was running for my very life, up through a dense and frightfully steep forest, being pursued by an enormous, white ghoul-thing — a great hairless, malformed giant, grotesquely hunchbacked — so that its face almost emerged from its chest rather than growing out the top of it, and with skin as white as moonlit marble."

I was thunderstruck. It took all I had not to grab him by the lapels and shake him. "Do go on." I said as calmly as possible.

"Suddenly," he continued, "I burst from out the trees, stumbling onto a wide, flat courtyard, where I tripped and fell violently upon the paving stones, curling myself up into a defensive ball and awaiting the emergence of my terrible pursuer.

"Huddling there, I looked back at the tree line behind me, fully expecting to see the loping, headless monstrosity explode out of the foliage. But, merciful fate, it never came. The next thing I knew I was being lifted up by a man with your face and carried into a small stone temple on the other side of the plaza. I was made to lie down there in total darkness. I awoke seconds later in my own bed, breathless and soaked with sweat."

"How bizarre," I shrugged, uncertain how to interpret this most fabulous and unnerving enigma.

"Are you feeling alright, just now?" he asked suddenly. "You're as white as a sheet!"

"Yes, I'll be fine." I said, "Tell me more about this thing that was chasing you."

Clearly puzzled by my blanched features, Howard continued, "Upon waking, I recognized the dream creature as matching a similar description to a race of legendary beings known to folklore as the Blemmyes, described by Pliny the Elder in his *Naturalis Historia*, which documents similar monsters, allegedly living near Nubia and Ethiopia, circa 75-79 AD."

"I'm afraid I have not read that particular book," I replied somewhat sheepishly.

"Acephalos, he called them, meaning 'headless' or 'brainless.' *'Blemmyes traduntur capita abesse, ore et oculis pectore adfixis...* 'It is said that the Blemmyes have no heads, and that their mouth and eyes are put in their chests.' Descriptions of similar beings occur in the *Nuremburg Chronicles of 1493* as well as Sir Walter Raleigh's accounts of his explorations in South America. Disparate legends of such beings are known all over the world. They are known as Blemmyes in Austria-Germany, Ewampanoma in Amazonia, and in Greece they call them Acephalos. Later during the reign of Henry the First," he continued, "the term Acephalos became the casual term for untitled, un-landed peoples who were without a 'head,' as in 'kingless,' people we might nowadays call anarchists, but in its original usage it referred to the headless giants of legend."

"Amazing." I said, finding it increasingly difficult to conceal my astonishment, "Where in South America did Walter Raleigh claim to have seen them?"

"I think it was Guyana, along the Caora and Orinoco Rivers but I cannot be certain."

Here he paused and I had the sensation that he was appraising me, sizing me up, for some unknown purpose. His searching gaze ended at my face where it stayed for several seconds.

"I'm sorry, I don't believe I caught your name. You're not, by any chance, related to the Pickman clan are you?" He was practically leering at me now.

"Sorry to disappoint you," I said, quickly scanning the shelf directly behind him for a suitable moniker, "but my name is... Hoffman." His eyebrows rose up in quiet alarm then dropped again, lower than before. "Edward... Thomas... Andrew... Hoffman," I continued rather unconvincingly, "and I'm afraid I don't know much about my ancestry."

"Really?" he smiled. "Your initials are E.T.A Hoffman? How astounding."

Then, following the direction of my glance, he turned his head and looked directly at the shelf behind him where a thick volume clearly bore the name E.T.A Hoffman.

"Too bad," he replied turning back to me, more amused than anything. "Still I cannot help but wonder if you don't share a common ancestor with the Pickman clan. There is a subtle but unmistakable resemblance in the arrangement of your features." He said this last bit with such dramatic emphasis that I could only infer sinister things about this Pickman clan, whoever they might be. Furthermore, I felt distinctly uncomfortable, for I was beginning to think that his odd remarks were just his clumsy and unconscious way of saying that he could see the ghoul in me.

"Who are the Pickmans?" I asked, determined to keep him talking.

"A very old Boston family. I would even say prominent, though the family line ended in gruesome tragedy." Here, he leaned in and bulged his eyes for emphasis, "People talked of a tainted bloodline."

At this I recalled my earlier thoughts on his visibly pure stock and thought I was about to receive confirmation along those lines. But I was wrong.

"Well, I suppose that depends on what you mean by 'tainted bloodline'?" I countered, "Do you mean that they mixed interracially? You can't honestly believe that racial cross-breeding weakens or in any way harms the bloodline. If anything it strengthens it, makes it more..." But here I stopped, seeing how he was looking at me very doubtfully, as though I had disappointed him immensely.

"I did not mean to imply," he said, "that the bloodline was tainted by the blood of another human race, ruinous though I know that can sometimes be..."

Just then he looked off into the distance as if this subject had brought up some disturbing memory that pained him greatly.

"Well, then what sort of tainted blood are you referring to?" I asked pointedly.

"I am referring," he said severely, looking about and lowering his voice to a grave whisper, "to the blood of a servant of Tsathoggua... in Red-Litten Yoth."

"Excuse me?" I asked, certain that I had misheard him.

"A cannibal, a man-eating ghoul of prodigious size, like the one from my dream, a brainless monster who survives by eating brains... our old friend Acephalos."

I nodded, mesmerized and somewhat nauseated by the cosmic look that had come into his eyes. His pupils seemed to expand like pools of ink spilling into his irises, until at last he blinked and the illusion disappeared.

"Mr... (ahem)... 'Hoffman'," he said, "I believe we may have more in common than a fascination with primitive legends. How much do you know about your family tree?"

"As I said, I know almost nothing of my family history. My father died in an asylum when I was three. In fact, it is a rather painful subject for me so, if you don't mind, perhaps we could change the topic."

"Ah, the son of a widow. Fascinating." He nodded, bowing his enormous head in deference to my wishes, "Alas, you were about to change the subject."

"I am here today in pursuit of a particularly obscure legend," I said, "which has eluded my best efforts for the last two and a half hours. I was just thinking perhaps you, with your extensive knowledge of mythology and folklore, might know something about it."

"Please," he said, beaming with the pride of expertise, "if there is any way that I could be of assistance to you in your quest, I am at your disposal."

"I seek information on the "Corpse-Eating Cult of Leng..." I began though I stopped short at the sudden change that came over him. At the mention of that name his face had gone ash-white and glancing down at his feet, he yanked me, with considerable force, sideways into the stacks.

"My dear man!" he hissed, glaring at me. "What do you mean by all this? First I meet you in a terrifying dream. Then I find you in the Library displaying that unmistakable stoop. Now you inquire about the Corpse-Eating Cult of Leng? Who has sent you? I want the truth! Was it the Freemasons? The Golden Dawn? The Illuminati?"

Recognizing none of these names, I stared blankly at him. My apparent ignorance seemed to please him, and he collected himself with a thoughtful sigh.

"Never mind, it doesn't matter. The important thing is that you wish to learn about Leng. Lucky for you, that knowledge lies rather close at hand just now. I will take you to the secret room where the books you seek are kept."

"But how will we get in if they are kept in a secret room?" I asked, to which he replied with a proud smile.

"They know me here," he said.

Then this excitable young man led me to the information desk where he obtained permission for us both to peruse certain rare and ancient books which are kept under lock and key, but which the average citizen is sometimes permitted to view during certain hours if he can feign a sort of generalized, superficial, and harmless curiosity. In a high, windowless, book-filled room we spent several hours examining such books as the *Necronomicon* by the insane

Arab poet, Abdul Alhazred, as well as the Yothic and Pnakotic Manuscripts transcribed in 138 BC by scribes of the Greek King Abacus, whose mathematical demonology so frightened his subjects that he was lynched, burned, and forever expunged from all historical documents. These ancient books describe events, entire epochs of history, which have been kept secret from uninitiated humankind for many thousands of years. It is a history known only to certain secret societies, crypto-mythographers, and the serious (and well-connected) occult scholar.

Of Leng itself there were numerous descriptive passages, most of which assumed a certain prior knowledge of the subject, which I did not possess. Still, it was consistently described as a stone monastery upon a high plateau and rumored to be inhabited by an ancient order of horribly disfigured cannibal priests alternately referred to as the Almost Humans, the Corpse-Eating (or Face-Eating) Cult of Leng or the Ghouls of Neb. In several places these books referred to these Almost Humans as the straggling survivors of a once-mighty race who, having offended their creator, were wiped out in a catastrophic flood, leaving only a handful of survivors dwelling in an obscure cave on a remote peak, somewhere in an unnamed mountain range. These beings were regarded with extreme terror by all who lived in their vicinity and though the exact nature of their worship was never described, it clearly involved frequent human sacrifices and ritualized cannibalism.

Some descriptions of the Monastery at Leng also made references to a stone house, hidden by jungle growth on an adjacent peak, where a High Priest Not To Be Described was reputed to dwell. It was said of this terrifying being that he took human form merely as a courtesy and to avoid driving his devotees mad with terror. He was said to keep himself hidden at all times beneath a veiled cloak of golden silk and that he was, in some unexplained way, ragged in appearance. This peculiar personage, was sometimes referred to as the High Priest, Inkari Kuri, the Yellow King, or else El Dorado, the Gilded Man. The books hinted that this shape-shifting being was of that same gelloid race as Ubbo Sathla and a cousin to that entity. The Voorakookla, as it was sometimes called, was said to be the dreaded offspring of Tsathoggua, the liquescent god of various Hyperborean peoples, whose lore and general description, in many ways, parallel that of the High Priest.

Lacking the proper organs for vocalizations, the High Priest was said to communicate by using a curious flute-like instrument, conveying his prophecies (by some unknown species of musical telepathy) to those rare shamans who dared to visit the high stone house. All three authors were in agreement that the cannibal priests in the nearby monastery revered this High Priest as a God in human form, worshiping him and making regular bloody sacrifices at his altar.

71

Superficial efforts to learn the location of the Leng Plateau, however, revealed to me glaring discrepancies within each of the three ancient texts. One set of statements placed Leng in the frozen steppes of Asia, while others indicated it was in Antarctica, still others placed it somewhere in the southern hemisphere. All three documents contained these contradictory statements both internally and cross-referenced against each other. I was eventually led to the conclusion that either there was more than one Leng Plateau or else the authors had all separately deemed it prudent to keep its true location shrouded in secrecy. At no time did it occur to me that the plateau might be, in some way, movable.

This inconsistency, which Howard was unable (or unwilling) to account for, frustrated me immensely, implying as it did that I was chasing after fairy tales. At some point shortly hereafter, an elderly gentleman entered and announced that the library would be closing in fifteen minutes; returning the aforementioned books to their proper places, we made our hasty exit out into the dim maze of windswept Providence.

It was roughly sunset by this time and, having spent the entire afternoon in the library, we were quite famished. Finding a relatively inexpensive Italian restaurant, we dined on soup, pasta, salad, and garlic bread until at last we were so full we could barely speak. During dinner the conversation had turned to somewhat more philosophical themes and we discussed, in a general way, the direction of industrial civilization. I told him of my great trepidation for the future and my instinctive distaste for our increasingly poisonous and massified Machine Age.

"Yes," he replied woefully, "I too worry about the way things are headed." Here he gazed thoughtfully out the window, staring with an almost parental concern, at the many bundled figures darting this way and that in the darkened street. "The general tension is quite horrible. To this season of political and social upheaval there seems an added sense of brooding apprehension, an underlying fear of some hideous physical danger. It's as if there is a monstrous guilt upon the land."

"I think there is. This war has made idiots of us all," I said.

But Howard and I, as I soon learned, could not have been further apart on the political spectrum. Indeed, on the subject of politics, he even struck me as one of those peculiar folks who fancy themselves a member of the ruling elite when, in fact, they are nothing of the kind. That said, there were several places where our perspectives were curiously similar. We both agreed that western civilization was now a victim of its own hideous momentum, with nothing more concrete to guide it than the myth of progress and the apparently inexhaustible urge toward total separation from (and subjugation of) the natural world, with the bulk of humanity and animal life in the role of dumb, brute laborers. We agreed that there seemed to be a generalized sense of underlying, generalized fright, a mass hypnosis which strongly suggested that the experiment of urban industrial civilization had, in fact, been a dismal failure, that it was a model to be abandoned with haste. We went on this way for nearly an hour and could have gone on further still, but at last the lights dimmed and we saw that the restaurant was closing for the night.

When the bill arrived I paid for both of us, and gathering up our coats and hats, my guest thanked me profusely as we made our way to the door.

*　*　*　*

STEPPING OUTSIDE, I TURNED TO MY NEW FRIEND AND ASKED IF HE was headed home for the night, to which he replied by gazing up appraisingly at the starry sky and then shaking his mighty head emphatically.

"Oh no," he said with a grin. "On a night like this I like to go walking in the old cemeteries."

"Really?" I asked with a playful chuckle, though this amusement was entirely an act, for by this time I was beginning to harbor a suspicion that my friend, knowing far more than he should about me, had somehow observed me in the act of feasting. Now, having finally built up his nerve to actually make my acquaintance, was he toying with me, taunting me with hints designed to unnerve me, perhaps with the ultimate plan of blackmailing me?

Furthermore, despite the fact that he seemed to know too many intimate details of my inner life, I could not deny that his oddly insightful comments might just as easily have been innocent coincidence. More difficult to explain was the fact that he had dreamed of me in connection with a legendary headless giant. A part of me refused the supernatural explanation and I clung defiantly to the more prosaic notion that he might be a blackmailer. However unlikely this may have seemed to me at the time, I kept my voice and my demeanor light, cheerful, and unsuspicious.

"So you like to hang around cemeteries in the dead of night," I said with a grin. "What an amazing coincidence. So do I."

"Well if such things interest you, you're more than welcome to accompany me. I will be taking a nocturnal perambulation of some of the more ancient graveyards in and around the College Hill neighborhood, with many other points of interest along the way."

"That is a very tempting offer," I said, "but I really should try and find a room for the night before it gets any later."

"I see," he mused. Then, after brief consideration, he said, "You could stay at my house if you like. It would no trouble at all. We have plenty of room."

"If you're sure it wouldn't be a bother," I said, moved and disarmed by this gesture of hospitality.

"Not at all. I would not have offered it if it were," he replied. Accepting his offer, I thanked him.

"If you don't mind my asking," I mused as we pulled on our gloves and turned up our collars to the cold, "why cemeteries?"

"Actually," he said, "I am composing a narrative involving a graveyard scene and I have been exploring the local burying grounds in search of one which might serve as a model."

With this pronouncement, my companion and I disembarked from Delapore Square at about 7 p.m., walking and talking for nearly five hours as we roamed his beloved city. During this time, we covered a truly startling amount of ground both conversationally and geographically. Following crooked alleyways which opened onto hidden, oddly shaped courtyards overgrown and mysterious, I followed as Howard lead me up tottering old staircases, past shunned and abandoned houses, through steep overgrown lots and narrow pedestrian thoroughfares. I could not have asked for a better guide, for his knowledge of local history was near encyclopedic and his storytelling abilities were nothing short of literary. I recall passing through several ancient and impressive parks which overlooked Providence at various and precipitous angles, as well as stargazing at one terraced, hillside cemetery that was so steeply pitched in some places it almost seemed to lean out into the starry darkness of the night, so that I actually lay down and half-jokingly clung to a tombstone, lest I slip and plunge into the steepled darkness below.

Threading this seemingly endless grid of curving side streets and downward sloping avenues, we discussed a myriad of overlapping topics, all of which pertained, however tangentially, to my researches (which in certain eerie, unstated ways, seemed to parallel some of Howard's own). At Prospect Point, while sitting on a bench with yet another astounding panoramic view of the city, the conversation turned to the subject of dreams and, with a fair bit of prompting from Howard, I told him about my Machu Picchu dream. He listened with a deadly earnestness that impressed me, afterwards stroking his chin and staring at the stars for several minutes.

"The Inca were astronomers, you know," he said thoughtfully. "As research continues at Machu Picchu, they are discovering what appear to be enormous astronomical observation decks. Similarly, many of the windows and doorways in the central temples actually frame and indicate various aspects of the scenery. The neighboring peak, which is called Huyanu Picchu, is frequently highlighted in this manner, and also, at certain times of the year, various constellations, specifically that cluster of stars known as the Pleiades."

"Yes, I've learned quite a bit about the Inca these past few years," I said. "They were a strange and fascinating people."

"Are," he corrected "*are* a strange and fascinating people. For while it is true that Pizarro exterminated or enslaved most of the Inca royalty and soldiery, the majority of the Inca people fled into the mountains, or were merely dispersed into neighboring regions. I mention it because I was just yesterday reading about the Inca in Fraser's *The Golden Bough*. You have heard of this book, yes?"

I nodded but said nothing.

"It is quite fascinating. Did you know that once a year, during certain festivals, the Inca priests would select various special children, born to women under allegedly divine circumstances, and bleed them for ceremonial purposes?"

"I did not," I replied.

"Evidently, they would make a small but deep incision in the place where the eyebrows meet, collecting the unusually thick blood that poured forth into vases shaped like human heads. They would knead this brain blood into the dough of a sacred bread which they ate as a protection against certain hostile spirits. Similarly, the remaining bloody dough was smeared upon the face and arms as a further protection against certain malevolent entities."

"Amazing," I said hiding my discomfort. "Did they say anything else about the significance of imbibing brain matter?"

"Some anthropologists say it had a psychotropic effect. It gave them visions. Others say it was a form of god-impersonation, though precisely which god they were impersonating is not known."

"Fascinating," I replied with false non-chalance, searching his face for any hint that he was intentionally playing games with me.

"Well," he continued, "this sort of decadence is probably what led to the Incas' downfall. Decadence of this type is usually one of the symptoms of a civilization in decline. Most civilizations tend to start eating themselves from within sooner or later. It usually starts in the higher religious cults and then spreads outward from there."

"I don't know about that," I said. "There are numerous brain-eating tribes who have survived quite successfully into the modern era, though most have been hunted to extinction by colonists of one kind or another, most of whom used exaggerated accounts of their cannibalism as a pretense for extermination. But the Tolaki of central Celebes, the Efugaos tribe in the Philippines, and the Kai of German New Guinea have all survived quite well into our modern era, despite numerous attempts to wipe them out."

As this statement set my companion thinking, I stood up and suggested we resume our walk. The temperature was, by this time, dropping rapidly, making sustained and vigorous movement the only remedy against the increasingly chill sea air. Moving south down a series of deserted streets and alleyways we soon came upon yet another overgrown lot with an incredible view, where we stopped to catch our breath and to watch as a thick cloud of mist began to invade the city from the seaward side, enveloping it street by street, block by block, until at last, the entire harbor district was lost to view.

Just then, as I leaned forward to re-tie one of my boots, my well-worn copy of *Flowers of Evil* fell out of my inside coat pocket and tumbled onto the ground at his feet. Taking up the Baudelaire with obvious recognition, Howard smiled and, closing his eyes, he recited,

At my side the Demon writhes forever,
Swimming around me like impalpable air;
As I breathe, he burns my lungs like fever
And fills me with an eternal, unlawful desire.

"Speaking of decadence…" I said with a chuckle, though I couldn't help but interpret his choice of that particular quotation as yet another of his subtle taunts.

"I haven't finished that book just yet," I continued. "I can never seem to get past the bit about the 'Vampires' and 'The Fountains of Blood' without going back and rereading it several times." at which my friend laughed heartily.

"That reminds me," he replied "of an anecdote I heard the other day about Baudelaire, which I think you would especially enjoy."

"Do tell," I replied.

"Baudelaire, the story goes, once asked an amusing aspiring decadent poet who had copied — and even exceeded — his own colorful Satanism without reflecting to any dangerous extent his genius, a rather amusing question. A trifle exasperated by the ostentatious 'shockingness' of the young man, Baudelaire 'went him one better' by asking very gravely, 'Have you ever tasted young children's brains? They're quite delightful, and taste exactly like walnuts!'"

With this he threw his head back in one of the most demoniacal displays of human mirth I have ever witnessed while I, stunned and unnerved, sat silently, gazing at his massive profile, silhouetted against the glow of a nearby streetlamp. This little joke of his, this harmless anecdote, was the last straw, and I could no longer rationally dismiss the notion that this man (whomever or whatever he might be) was, if not a common blackmailer, then some kind of seer, telepath, or mindreader at the very least.

While I ceased to dispute this fact within myself, I continued to be of two minds about what it meant. On the one hand, if he was a mere blackmailer, then what precisely was he waiting for? What was the point of dragging out the proceedings with clues and casual banter? Certainly, he might be a madman who was savoring the power he had over me and yet this had seemed somehow, less and less probable as the night wore on, owing to the affinity that had immediately developed between us. If, on the other hand, he knew me (either from surreptitious observance, or from some innate, supernatural sensitivity) to be the brain-eating cannibal killer that I was, then why did he not recoil in horror at my very nearness? Why, for example, when he had seen me in the library, had he not grimaced (as all the other gawkers had), but actually smiled? Could it be, I wondered, that he was, despite his evidently detailed knowledge of my atrocious deeds, somehow sympathetic toward me? Was he, like me, an eater of abominable things, a secret fiend, dressed up in the guise of an ordinary human being? Were his cryptic comments some kind of ongoing shibboleth, designed to function both as casual banter and secret code? He certainly seemed human enough and yet, was there not something else, shining out at me from those strange dark eyes?

Despite these many questions, I held my tongue. I wanted very much to ask him why he thought I, of all people, should especially enjoy an anecdote about brain-eating. But I didn't. I simply laughed along with him and then waited to see where the discussion would next lead.

Leaving the overgrown lot behind us, we descended at last into the maze of foggy streets directly below, at which time Howard (utilizing both street signs and those constellations still visible overhead) endeavored to lead us back to central Providence where he lived. It was nearly 1 a.m. when the house at 598 Angell Street came into view and, looking up at the lovely three-story townhouse before us, I noticed lights on in several of the upper windows.

"Will we wake anyone if we enter?" I asked.

"No, no," he laughed, "I come and go at all hours throughout the night. We are a family of either deep sleepers or else insomniacs! My mother is often up late as well."

"You live with your mother and father?" I asked.

"No it's just my mother, my Aunt Annie and myself. Father died many years ago in a madhouse."

Placing his hand haltingly upon the knob he moved to enter, but stopped, turning back toward me.

"I should warn you that my mother Susie, is... not well. The doctors have instructed us to confine her to the upper floor but we simply don't have the heart to do it. I assure you she is quite harmless. There is a chance that she is already asleep in bed but, in the event that she is awake…" Here he seemed to struggle for the right words, "…please keep conversation to a minimum and, by all means please refrain from, touching her. Not even a friendly handshake if you please, I'm afraid she's become what you might call a 'touch-me-not' ever since Father passed away."

"Please," I said, "think nothing of it, my friend. I am your humble guest and I will conform myself entirely to the rules of the house."

With an expression that was something between a cramped smile and a wince, Howard turned, opened the door with a single key and we stepped into the darkened portal of the house.

VI

THE ATMOSPHERE INSIDE THIS STRANGE HOUSE WAS POSITIVELY electrifying. The air seemed oppressively dense, almost pressurized, as if this three-story townhouse had suddenly been transported to the bottom of some great coral-encrusted chasm in the floor of the Pacific Ocean. Silently, I followed my friend through the entry hall and up the stairs to a guest room at the top of the landing. Sitting down in a small wicker chair beside the nightstand, he slid open the drawer and invited me to place my personal effects there for safe keeping. Turning on the small bedside lamp for me and giving directions to the nearest bathroom, he seemed just about to rise and make his exit when a creaking floorboard outside the door caused us both to turn in that direction.

There was a soft but rapid knocking at the door and my friend seemed to stiffen, looking nervously from the door to me and back again, laying his finger upon his lips as if to silence me. When the insistent knocking resumed, he stood up, eyed me significantly and then went to the door. In the brief instant between the opening of the door and Howard placing himself in the threshold, I caught a fleeting glimpse of a thin pale female face staring in at me with a visible eagerness. Our eyes locked for an instant and then she was promptly eclipsed by his shoulder.

"Howard, I need to speak with you," I heard her say.

"Yes Mother, what is it?" Howard said, stepping into the corridor and closing the door behind him.

With my enhanced senses I easily heard every word they said, though they spoke in the faintest of whispers.

"Howard," the little woman said severely, "I want to know who that man is."

"He's a man I met at the library. Why are you so upset?"

Upon hearing this I stood up, not wishing to remain in a house where I was not wanted. I was just pulling on my backpack when I heard Howard say, "He was looking for information on the Corpse-Eating Cult of Leng, Mother." after which there was a long pause.

"What did you do, Howard?" she said accusingly.

"I showed him!" he replied, almost defiantly.

There was another heavy silence that followed, as if my being initiated into the secrets of Leng were a matter most profound.

"Did you show him the Yothic Manuscript?"

"Yes I did. And the Pnakotic as well."

"Let me speak with him, Howard," she demanded.

"No, mother! You are in your nightshirt and besides, my guest is very tired. Tomorrow we shall all have a lengthy chat over breakfast."

I heard my friend say these words and yet I knew that he would do all within his power not to let this happen.

"He has brought… something with him into our home," she whispered "Can you not feel it, Howard?"

"Yes," I heard him say, "of course I can feel it. But it appears to be asleep. Everything will be fine, Mother. Please go to sleep. We will discuss it in the morning."

"But Howard," she retorted.

"Go to sleep, Mother. We will discuss it in the morning."

There was the sound of a kiss and then soft padding steps retreating down the corridor. Then the door opened and Howard returned looking exasperated.

Apologizing for the interruption, he made a hopeless gesture in the direction of the door. Again he wished me good night and after asking me yet again if I needed anything, which I did not, he departed the chamber. Minutes later I had stripped off my clothes and was crawling into the fresh clean sheets, relishing the warmth they offered to my cold and tired body.

Two hours later I was aroused from sleep by a curious sound in the hallway directly outside my door. Looking at the clock on the mantel I saw that it was a few minutes before 4 a.m. I heard a soft click and watched, astonished, as the doorknob rotated and the door to my bedroom swung silently open, revealing an empty threshold and the equally empty hallway beyond it. Then a series of shuffling, rubbery thumps informed me that something had entered my room and was now crawling, low and clumsy, across the carpet toward the side of the bed. Even through the oaken footboard I could make out the warm glow of the hunched living thing as it drew nearer. Peering cautiously over the edge of the mattress, I was suddenly staring into the big brown eyes of Howard's mother, Susie.

"Um…ma'am?" I stammered. "Can I, perhaps... help you with something?"

The creature beside my bed only cocked its head and emitted a series of sharp, low clicks.

I repeated the question and for my efforts received several low grunts accompanied by a series of unnerving facial contortions which I will not to describe, except to say that each ended with a brief but horrible stretching open (to their farthest possible extent) of both eyes and mouth. Appalled by this oddly terrifying display, I leaned away from her only to see her pull herself, with unusual quickness, onto my bed. That's when I saw that she was, like me, entirely undressed.

"You have brought something with you into my home," she stated, unequivocally. "A little visitor from the Outer Darkness."

It was my intention to respond to this statement but, on account of my shock, I found that I was momentarily robbed of the power of speech.

"How do you know?" I finally managed to whisper.

"I can always smell them," she said, glancing at the ceiling. Then she closed her eyes, inhaled and swallowed hard. "My husband had one, and now, I'm afraid poor Howard may have one as well."

"What about you?" I asked.

"Heavens no!" she snapped. "Unlike most of these fools and degenerates, I know enough not to give in to those... dark impulses. Therefore they cannot enter me."

She peered about the room hatefully, her eyes probing the shadows that pooled beneath the various pieces of furniture.

"Lord knows, I tried to protect Howard, for as long as I could but..." Here she trailed off, her eyes closed tightly, as if in prayer.

"I kept him out of the war, you know," she said proudly. "I wasn't going to lose my boy to that Supreme Idiocy. Oh, the things they would have made my sweet boy do. They would have destroyed everything that is beautiful in him. They would have turned him into a machine, a marching, faceless automaton." Here she paused, sighing, mostly to herself, "Oh, the horrors that such men inflict upon the world... they inflict also upon themselves."

Something about the heartbroken, world-weary manner in which she made these statements caused my eyes to well up with tears. I nodded and we stared sympathetically into each other's eyes for a time.

"I see in your eyes that you are a parent, as am I," she said confidentially. "We must protect our little ones from this wicked world, yes? That is a parent's primary duty."

Again I nodded but said nothing, terrified by the obvious implication that this woman, like her son, had access to information which I had not provided.

All at once, Susie seemed to retreat into herself. Her eyes rolled up into her head and she began to sway softly from side to side, emitting a low, melodic humming sound. She grimaced strangely at the darkness around her as though it had begun to cause her physical pain. "You must stay close to your little one until it is grown. When it reaches maturity, it will leave you to find the nearest portal. It is where they come from, and whence they must return. It is a doorway to their world, and countless other worlds besides. But you should not let your offspring out of your sight until then. "

"Where is this portal?" I asked, but she fell silent, eyes shut tight, an oddly pained expression on her face. Several times I tried to prompt her but, after repeating her name several times, found that I could elicit no response whatsoever.

Growing desperate to rouse this woman from her trance, I disobeyed Howard's dictum, and stretching out a solitary finger, I touched her softly upon her upper arm.

The reaction was instantaneous and profound. Her eyes flicked open and she inhaled sharply. Gazing about the room in fright, she turned to me, with eyes wide, as though seeing me for the first time.

"Excuse me!" she hissed. "Who are you? And where am I?"

"I am Robert," I stammered, making every effort to sound reassuring, "a guest of your son, Howard. You are safe in your home in Providence, Rhode Island." Hearing Howard's name seemed to have an instant calming effect on her, and she hid her face in her hands for a moment before looking up at me.

"Young man," she asked softly, "do you know who... I am?"

"You are a widow named Susie, living in a townhouse on Angell Street in Providence, Rhode Island with your son Howard and your sister Annie."

"What is today's date?" she asked.

"It is December 11, 1918."

"Excellent. Thank you," she said, looking down for the first time and noticing her nudity. "I... I should go back to bed now. Please forgive my intrusion. Goodnight, Robert."

"Wait, Susie. You mentioned a portal..." I said, but she slipped out so quickly, shutting the door behind her, that I knew our discussion was over.

Unable to sleep, I lay awake and thinking for a while, finally dropping off to sleep some time just before dawn.

Some hours later, I awoke to an oddly urgent feeling that the Red Thing needed me, and that I should get back to the farmhouse as soon as humanly possible.

I dressed and went downstairs, finding Howard sitting at the breakfast table reading a newspaper and sipping a cup of coffee. He offered to make me some toast with jam but I politely declined, explaining that I had somewhere I needed to be. Having no other means of showing my gratitude for his hospitality, I handed him my copies of *The Antichrist* and *Beyond Good and Evil*.

"Please, accept these as a gift." I told him, "I have read them both twice. I have a feeling you may enjoy them."

Looking down, he accepted them saying, "That's so odd. I was thinking just yesterday how I really need to read this man's works."

"These should make a fine beginning." I said with a smile.

With that, we shook hands warmly, both of us insisting that I come and visit him again soon. I departed, making my way to the Providence Station, where I caught the next northbound train.

*   *   *   *

ON THE TRAIN RIDE BACK TO SUDBURY I HAD PLENTY OF TIME TO think. Having spoken with Howard and his mother, I finally began to glimpse, for the first time, the desolate truth of my situation. I was on my own now, completely disconnected (in any meaningful way) from all community. I was an agent of the Outer Ones, a human being who, like countless others since the advent of humanity, had been made aware of (and pressed into a secret alliance with) those ancient entities who visit, observe, and manipulate us. What is more, my days and nights were now spent helping raise up one of their spawn which I had conceived in my own gut, feeding and nurturing it as if it were my very own offspring. I was now as detached from ordinary humanity as any misanthrope could ever hope to be. Yet, as much as I would have liked to deny it, I understood for the first time that I almost missed some of them. Having met such unique and likable specimens as Howard and Susie made me comprehend how lonely I was for decent human companionship. As the train sped through the frozen fields of Dunwich, my thoughts drifted back to the only other person I had ever known who had inspired such feelings in me — the fiancée I had abandoned in Plymouth.

I began to torture myself with certain unanswerable questions: Would I ever be able to see her again? Would I ever have another chance to speak with her? I knew it was sheer stupidity to even think of it but I could not help myself. I knew that I could never return and yet I nearly succeeded several times in persuading myself to get off the train at the next station and catch a southbound train for Plymouth. Would she still be there? Had she moved away? Four years had flown by. It would have been the height of arrogance to expect that she would even acknowledge me and so... I banished these thoughts, cursing myself, as I drifted in and out of sleep. Two hours later I disembarked in Sudbury. An hour after that I was wriggling in through the one window I'd left slightly ajar.

Upon my return to Arnold Lane, the farmhouse felt unusually hollow and tomb-like. The Red Thing was nowhere to be seen. I tried not to speculate on its whereabouts, as it could only upset me to imagine such things. Despite my immense concerns about attracting attention to the farmhouse, I was forced, in its absence, to light a fire in the fireplace, dragging my box spring back upstairs and placing it alongside the hearth.

Staring into the fire, I could think of nothing but the Red Thing and where it could be. As I tossed and turned in the firelight, Susie's odd comment about protecting the little ones from the wicked world echoed like an admonition. A feeling of utter desolation came over me when I considered that I might never see it again. I cursed myself for ever having left the Red Thing alone. I was also beginning to entertain fearful speculations about what might have happened to my offspring, wandering, lost and hungry, alone in a strange and dangerous place. My mind reeled at the grim possibilities. What might happen if it were to meet up with a troop of hungry Tree Things or Boulder Things? Would they prey upon my smaller and weaker offspring? Would they fight bloody territorial battles to the death? Perhaps, like the many ants, spiders, and beetles of the earth, they would simply pass each other by with utter indifference.

I tried to focus my thoughts to see if I could locate the Red Thing with my mind, and soon received a startlingly strong impression that, although it was presently very far away, it would be returning soon, perhaps as early as the next morning. I tried to envision where it might be, what it might be doing, but of its present location I could form no picture whatsoever. I saw only the blackness of a whirling void, which seemed instantly crowded with lurking shadows that pressed close and stared back at me. I flicked open my eyes and stoked the fire, feeling suddenly terrified of all the little sounds that came to me out of the darkness of the house. I longed for the Red Thing to return, if only to have another sentient being there to keep me company, to distract me and to help me to detect the approach of any overly inquisitive travelers who might have been attracted by my chimney smoke. Eventually, exhaustion overtook me and I fell asleep for a period of several hours.

All night, I'd suffered cruel, tormenting dreams, in which I was back in Plymouth with my fiancée, welcomed, forgiven, loved, and adored as before. You may therefore understand my emotions when I say that, when I awoke to a thin, lank arm draped across me, I rejoiced and actually believed, for one heart-rending instance, that I was somehow back in Plymouth and in the arms of my long-gone sweetheart, my whole horrible ordeal nothing more than a vivid nightmare. Imagine my horror, then, when, upon opening my eyes and seeing where I was, I leapt out from under that oddly pliable arm and spun round just in time to see a branch-like appendage retract into the heaving mass of the Red Thing (which was no longer actually red, but a deep, shimmering, purplish black) while a bouquet of blinking red eyes peered up at me, startled, confused, and perhaps even a little hurt.

It wasn't until the following day that I noticed the myriad of tiny pin-hole burns all down the right sleeve and breast-pocket of the shirt I'd been wearing. I threw it away and, for several nights, took to sleeping in the bath tub where the thing, unable to press close to me, contented itself to sleep on the floor beside the tub. Soon enough however, at the palpably psychic insistence of the Black Thing, I dragged my box spring back down into the cellar and my strange existence at the farmhouse resumed; an existence comprised of hunting, eating, sleeping, reading, and inventing little games for the Black Thing.

There were so many bizarre incidents during this period that it's difficult to know which will convey the utter strangeness of this incredible co-habitation. Shall I tell you how, over a period of days, I actually taught it to play hide-and-go-seek? How its favorite places to hide were invariably the laundry chute or else the bathtub on the second floor? Shall I mention how I soon took to tossing its allotted portion of brain across the room, so that it could lunge and splash itself grotesquely through the air and catch it on the fly? Shall I explain to you how I taught it "stay" or to follow close at my heels, to move in swift, lilting circles at my whispered cue? Should I mention that, after spending so much time with it, I began to notice certain behavioral patterns which seemed to imply a kind of personality? For example, when, in the course of its feeding, it invariably came in contact with a human corpse, it was always careful to avoid the hands and feet, as though it regarded these appendages as too revolting to be touched? Or should I describe how it frequently played with its food, leaving the corpses it fed upon curiously melted, fusing tissue and bone, merging and reconfiguring (so that I was reminded of the deformations of the white giants and of the punishments they were said to have received from the Viracocha)? Shall I mention its crazed, frenetic fear of lightning? How, twice, it hid in the cellar emitting pathetic chirps when thunder and lightning storms passed through the valley. I learned all these things, and more, as I watched it learn and grow and mature, developing its many peculiar abilities and forming a curious rapport between us. It continued to grow daily, increasing so steadily in size that it quickly became obvious that, very soon, its appetite was going to outgrow my ability to hunt for it. The implication was clearly that at some point I was going to have to let it start hunting for itself.

One of the first things I did upon returning to my housebound existence was to attempt to teach the Black Thing that it must not kill randomly, but only such victims as were indicated by me as "edible." To this end, I immediately made each meal a lesson in which I attempted to teach it the difference between a worthy target and ordinary folks. For its part, the Black Thing seemed genuinely interested in my attempts to communicate with it, giving me its undivided attention during said lessons and deciphering my cues almost immediately. Nevertheless, lacking anything approaching a common language, I could never feel certain that I had actually been understood and so remained apprehensive about taking it out for its first hunt. Although I was never able to teach it to hunt exclusively for politicians, cops, and businessmen (as I would have liked) I did succeed in training it to associate feeding time with the cue phrase "Viva l'anarchia," taken straight from the literature I was reading at the time, which it soon came to recognize as the prompt for "eat now."

The ongoing experiments in shape-mimicry continued to shock and amaze me. One day, I was coming downstairs with a tray of fresh brain and, upon seeing a gigantic human shape coming up at me out of the darkness, I panicked, dropping the tray and scrambling backward up the stairs and into the kitchen. Snatching my .38 special off the counter, I fell back against the kitchen wall, watching as the huge thing slowly emerged from the black rectangle of the doorway, steadying itself awkwardly against the threshold with furry, paw-like hands. Somehow, seeing this thing mold itself to the oversized and slightly exaggerated dimensions of my own body seemed a particularly monstrous violation of my individuality. I knew I was gazing upon that timeless, ageless Being whom the Inca had called the Con Tiki Viracocha, the Inkari Kuri, that legend-haunted being whom the Spaniards had dubbed El Dorado, the incarnation of the shimmering Black One, molded into the form of an oversized man in a golden cloak. I was, at last, face to face with that One known in the elder books as The High Priest Not To Be Described (only without the benefit of the golden cloak and veil to spare me the sight of its mind-blasting abnormality).

The likeness was uncanny, right down to the shape of my curly, unkempt hair and the bulging of my ill-fitting sweater (though the color was of the deepest tar black… just as it had been described in the old books). Human enough in its general contours, the manner in which it moved, however, instantly revealed the ruse. Its gait and carriage were utterly, grotesquely wrong. It had a lurching, swinging lope, at once too fast and too stilted, with a gruesomely boneless flexibility almost nauseating to behold. I did all I could to take in that awful, shimmering silhouette as it advanced toward me, but it seemed to waver in and out of sight, vanishing into folds of thin air; I seemed to see it through a mist. I must have screamed again, and then the gun in my hand went off. At this, the Black Thing immediately melted into an oily black puddle which retreated soundlessly down the cellar steps, even pulling the door violently shut behind it as it went.

After this episode, things became somewhat strained between us.

ON THE MORNING OF JANUARY 15TH 1919, WHEN THE THING WAS AT last grown to a sufficient size and had mastered its peculiar form of locomotion, it departed. It was the day after a particularly voracious meal of four adult brains, after which the Black Thing had reared up at me frightfully on the cellar steps, a thing which it had never done before, and I was forced to flee up the staircase in terror for my life. Minutes later, I watched in horror from the front window as it flowed, like an enormous black wyrm, from beneath the front porch and meandered away into the woods. When the tail end of the liquid monster finally appeared (a thing which took entirely too long) I simply could not resist the overwhelming urge to follow it at a safe distance. I dragged out an old bicycle I had found in the barn onto the lawn and launched myself in the direction the thing had gone. After several minutes of furious pedaling, I finally caught up with it, slithering along, like some gigantic black anaconda, through the cold, wet meadows of Arnold Lane. The bicycle proved invaluable and I was able to keep pace with the thing for several miles as it made its way swiftly across the wild terrain of the winter countryside, moving always due east, toward Boston. It had been an unusually warm morning (up from somewhere near freezing the night before, it was now a comparatively mild 40 degrees); I was thankful for the minimal snow on the ground, which made the journey that much easier.

In the course of this strange pursuit, I was at last able to see, more clearly than ever before, the true extent of the thing's unbelievable, and at times highly disturbing, shape-shifting abilities. I saw it utilize several different types of movement, sometimes pouring along the grassy meadows as little more than a dusty shadow, other times attaining a density that pressed the grass down flat as it went, leaving a clear trail for me to pedal along when the terrain caused me to fall behind. Twice it ran alongside me in a shape that was somewhere between a galloping hound and a very large spider, and at one point it even rose up in a liquefied impersonation of myself and the bicycle. Most of the time, however, it resembled nothing so much as a small dark pond which had somehow overrun its borders and was now precariously on the move.

At all times the Thing took great care not to let itself be seen by any of the people we passed along the way. Twice, when it came to densely populated areas, it simply liquefied, and vanished into the frozen ground, resurfacing twenty, or even fifty feet away, though always along that same trajectory and maintaining that same speed, so that recovering its trail was never overly difficult.

There was a terrible fear inside of me (and also a mighty curiosity) to see what would happen when the thing reached a densely populated urban center. Would the Black Thing make an appearance on the streets of Boston? Would it dare to take the shape of a man and actually walk the streets, or might it slip covertly, undetected, through the sewers? My intuition was that it longed to reach the sea and that it would traverse all obstacles to attain this goal. Might it simply pass beneath the great city of Boston, as a whale might pass beneath a vast fleet of ships? It had, after all, seemed intent upon hiding itself throughout our journey over the countryside. Would this change, however, once the creature came within range of so many helpless human beings, each with a warm pulsating brain ripe for the eating?

I had a great trepidation; if it did run amok on the streets of Boston, it might hurt ordinary working people, a tragedy which I knew would eventually attract the attention of the authorities and then, who could say what might happen? Certainly bullets and billyclubs would not hurt it, yet I still worried, feeling oddly protective of the Black Thing. Who could say what might happen if the Army were called in? What if they caught it off guard with a well-placed hand grenade? Could it even be injured by such terrestrial devices? (It's fear of lightning seemed to confirm the idea that it was perhaps not as impervious as I had originally assumed). Worse still, what if the Army found some way to capture and contain a small piece of it? Would they torture it to death in the name of scientific curiosity? Or, as was more likely, might they find some way to use it as a weapon, harassing it into a frenzy, for example, and then drop it on the trenches of some future enemy of the American Empire? Filled with something like fatherly worry, I pedaled along, unnerved by the many possible reactions a bigoted world might have to my unusual offspring. At one point, true to my prediction, it dropped into a dangerously steep creek bed which I knew must eventually empty into the Charles River. Shortly afterwards, I lost sight of it as it plunged down a hill and vanished into the trees near the river's edge, moving always due east.

The bicycle performed much better on the stone streets of Boston and, some minutes later, I was maneuvering with tremendous facility, riding downhill toward the sea and continuing due east at something approximating the creature's chosen speed. Some twenty minutes later, having traveled overland in the precise direction I believed the Black Thing to have gone, the streets ended and, just as I had feared, came to the crowded riverfront of industrial northern Boston.

With all the aforementioned concerns foremost in my mind, I leaned the bicycle against a railing and stepped into North End Park, scanning the wide dark waters of the Charles River for any discolorations or odd disturbances upon its surface. Above the city itself, as far as the eye could see, a low grey ceiling of clouds hung, stretching from north to south. The sky above the ocean was smooth and cloudless, pouring its golden light evenly upon the sea, and illuminating, in a startling way, the endless waves as they rushed headlong into a forest of barnacle-encrusted piers. Massive ships were coming and going, steamers bound for points further up and down the coast, old iron ships arriving from distant ports with bleary-eyed captains and crews of grimy, overworked sailors. Here I stood for several minutes, watching as a particularly degraded ocean-steamer with the unusual name "Yorikke" steamed past, displaying a more deranged and dilapidated looking crew than I would have thought possible in this century. It was noon and behind me, all along the wharfs, clusters of workmen sat here and there, eating sandwiches and hailing the vendors who sold hot peanuts for three cents a bag.

Turning right onto Cooper Road, I continued east toward the intersection of Cooper and Commercial Street. On my left was a hotel with what appeared to be a brothel in the back, while on the opposite side of the street were a tavern and several warehouses whose front windows looked out to the river. As I turned northeast onto Commercial Street, passing under the elevated train tracks, I kept my head downward, nervously scrutinizing every drain hole and rain gutter, half-expecting, at any moment, for a great ravening black blob to come boiling up from one of the many steel grates, transforming this noisy North End neighborhood into a human abattoir.

One can, therefore, imagine my horror when I was suddenly thrown against a wall by the force of a huge shockwave that seemed to rock the entire neighborhood, sending a shudder through the very sidewalk beneath my feet. I leapt into the road and gazed, stupefied, in the direction from which the sound had come. All pedestrian movement in the street had ceased and I recall an eerie moment of impending catastrophe as we pedestrians looked about, exchanging dazed uncomprehending looks.

Suddenly, from out of the front wall of the large white industrial building at the top of the street there came the awful shriek of bending metal, as a towering wave of purplish black liquid issued forth from the now buckling facade. I would say it was over sixteen feet high, and as wide as the street itself. The wave came thundering down Commercial Street, engulfing women, children, man and beast, sweeping trucks and pushcarts along like so many children's toys and laying waste to the storefronts on both sides. Some ran to escape the deluge and were overtaken and drowned, others were hurled against collapsing buildings which, having had their foundations ripped away, were now falling to pieces.

I did not think. I did not wonder. I did not hypothesize. I simply turned and ran, as fast as my legs would carry me, across Commercial Street and into the first upward sloping alleyway I came to. More horrendous explosions boomed forth from the street below as the great wave struck the elevated train tracks I had so lately passed under, bending their steel girders and knocking the train that was parked overhead completely out of its tracks with the force of its impact.

Looking west down Cooper Street, I watched in horror as the deadly purplish wave swept up everything in its path, racing toward the harbor, dragging with it huge pieces of shattered timber, sheet metal, plaster, masonry, and any other debris from the numerous buildings it had defaced along the way. Among the detritus, one could discern, here and there, the struggling bodies of humans and horses alike, all thrashing in vain to free themselves from the suffocating syrup that held them in its awful tide, pinning them to the ground, or else dragging them down over the docks and into the dark, freezing waters of the Charles River.

Horrified, I ran back down the alley and surveyed a scene of carnage as bizarre as it was dreadful. Here and there I could see battered human forms crawling about on hands and knees, weeping and screaming and vomiting up the thick dark liquid. I ran to help as many as I could to free themselves from the tar-like grip of the strange fluid. It had left behind several massive puddles, in which I could see a great scattering of lifeless, broken human beings. Wading in up to my knees, I pulled several struggling persons up, getting first their heads above the surface of the ooze and then pulling them to their feet. Noting the strange texture of the mysterious liquid, I immediately ruled out my initial impression. While I had at first assumed it was my own hideously overgrown progeny run amok, I now realized it was something more along the lines of honey or maple syrup. Noticing the sickly sweet smell in the air and overhearing the shouts of those other persons engaged in rescue attempts, I soon learned that the wave had been nothing less than several tons of molasses which had flooded the street when it's container in a factory at the top of the avenue had burst. I spent the remainder of that afternoon helping to search the damaged buildings for survivors. I found only corpses, which I carried out on a stretcher with the help of a sturdy Irishman named Murphy, who was helping out with the rescue.

Some weeks later I learned from a newspaper that the industrial accident I had witnessed had claimed the lives of some twenty-one people and that it had been the result of a rupture in a poorly maintained container. Tellingly, the management had tried to blame the disaster on "anarchist saboteurs," but large numbers of people from the neighborhood had come forward to say that the molasses container had been cracked for years and that this had been common knowledge. Everyone who couldn't afford molasses went there to fill their jars. All the employees had known about the crack as well, but since management had told them repeatedly not to worry about it, they had not given it a second thought. Years later I learned that the company had settled out of court with all the plaintiffs and that all official charges had been dropped. Fantastically, this tragedy went down in history as an act of God; most accounts relate how it was due to an increase in temperature. Twenty-one people and three horses dead, over one hundred others seriously injured, and they blamed the weather. Evidently judges and businessmen share a common understanding in such matters.

After this awful tragedy, I fled the Boston area. I had had far too many bizarre and unpleasant experiences thereabouts and, feeling that I had spent too much time in that part of the state, I had an overwhelming urge to get as far away from Boston as possible. The Black Thing, wherever it might have gone, had made no obvious attempt to find me; I resolved to carry on as I pleased, confident that if it needed me, my offspring would find me. The following morning, after a shower and a decent enough sleep in a cheap motel, I bought another new suit (to replace the one that had been ruined in the molasses flood) and caught the next train to New York City. I dozed for most of the ride there. Upon waking, as I saw the ominous spires of that great city appear on the southern horizon, I balked and changed my mind. Exiting the train in Hastings-on-the-Hudson, I caught a northbound train up the Hudson River Line, and headed toward upstate New York.

VII

I WAS NOW 22 YEARS OLD. EVERYTHING I POSSESSED WAS HANGING on my back. Hidden in my left boot was all the capital I owned in the world, a sizable $114.27, culled from the purses and wallets of my victims as well as the pawned jewelry I had stripped from their fingers and necks. Alone at last, and free, for the first time in many months, of my immediate obligations to the Black Thing, I felt like an indentured servant tentatively set free. It was still winter and, needing to spend my nights indoors, I realized that I had nothing to fear on this count, for I was growing inured to my many recurring nightmares (disturbingly prophetic though they sometimes were). The dreams had, in short, gradually ceased to frighten me, so that I now awoke from them not with shrieks of terror, but with growing interest and morbid fascination. This odd shift in perspective I associated somehow with the departure of the Black Thing, though I remain unable to explain precisely why or how. I passed the remainder of that winter traversing the hilly countryside of northern Westchester county.

I soon learned that my separation from the Black Thing had had another effect, which altered my entire mode of existence. My craving for brain meat simply and mysteriously vanished, thereby ending the nightmarish cannibal existence to which I'd slowly and resolutely grown accustomed. For the very first time in my life, my diet became one of utterly ordinary cravings, though I did retain a distinctly potent revulsion toward flesh and other by-products of enslaved livestock.

With the cessation of my cannibalism, I also could not help but consider, once again, the (admittedly slim) possibility of somehow returning to an ordinary human life, such as the one I'd had ripped away in Plymouth. The thought of this, appealing though it was at the time, also struck me as utterly implausible. Despite the fact that I had never once been ambushed, chased, or even, to my knowledge, followed, I could not say with absolute certainty that I might not suddenly find myself surrounded by some lynch mob, hell-bent on my destruction (and anyone else perceived as being an associate). So my solitude remained an absolute necessity, despite the fact that it was beginning to wear upon me. As one who was most certainly the object of several overlapping manhunts, ongoing association with anyone I actually cared about was simply out of the question.

My alienation from my own species was now most profound, and the thought that I could never again assume a civilized mode of survival saddened me. A deep melancholy came over me, which lasted many weeks and at times reduced me to something little more than a somnambulist. Stumbling through the frozen forests of northern Westchester, I wondered, after all that I had seen and done and become, if I would ever be able to relate to ordinary civilized human beings again?

When the spring of 1919 finally arrived, and the weather became warm enough for me to sleep outdoors, I loaded up on food and supplies and headed into the Taconic mountains. I drifted northeast, barely aware of where I was at any given time, floating between two worlds yet belonging to neither. I was alone, free from the unusual companionship of the Black Thing, and this was apparently true. Yet as I traversed the landscape, I consistently sensed that the thing was somewhere nearby. I dreamt of it almost nightly, and I came to believe that it was following me (perhaps, I suspected, even visiting me as I lay sleeping). At the very least, I felt certain it was keeping me within range, while maintaining a sufficient distance to avoid detection. On two separate occasions, I thought I even glimpsed it on a distant hilltop.

*   *   *   *

IT WAS ALSO AT THIS TIME THAT I CAME TO BELIEVE THAT I WAS, IN fact, carrying a piece of the Black Thing inside of me (or else was, myself, transmuting into something not entirely human). How else could I explain the dreadful fact that the unseen extra-terrestrial horrors that had always taken pains to hide themselves from my sight, the many Tree and Boulder Things, no longer hid themselves no more... deeming it no longer necessary to spare me the terrifying knowledge of their presence. Amongst the hills of Westchester and Putnam counties, I observed horrendous migrations and monstrous happenings. Things I would have much preferred to remain ignorant of, now played themselves out right in front of me and in broad daylight.

Once, in a green valley north of Mt. Kisco, I watched dumbfounded from a nearby ridge as several hundred Boulder Things, of every conceivable size and shape, filed awkwardly through a deserted gully and up into the thick hilly forest that bordered that town on three sides. Another time, I observed some fifty or sixty shrub-like creatures, ambling along the edge of a great pine forest near Yorktown Heights. Still another time, in the tiny lakefront village of Shenorock, in a clearing known locally as Nine Acres, I had the grave misfortune to observe two gigantic Tree Things, each a hundred feet tall or more, conversing in the moonlight, at one point taking up stone slabs from a nearby rock wall, and, with their branch-like hands, scratching crude pictograms in the dirt.

Some of these beings ignored my presence entirely, while others paused to take note of me as I passed, falling silent and pointing their weirdly shaped heads at me as I went. Though they never once menaced me or displayed anything but a passing curiosity, it always send a chill of terror straight through me, knowing as I did that humanity was to them, first and foremost, a source of food. Despite my apprehensions, these encounters remained highly educational.

There was, however, one particular episode which very nearly unhinged me. One warm, windless March evening, while hiking along Route 202, eager only for a room to let and a decent meal, I came upon a vast lowland marsh which bordered the road. The miasma of this bog had congealed into a thick fog which was now descending upon the green vale like a lowering ceiling, blotting out the stars with its silvery vapors. As I walked along the road near the edge of this bog, I could not shake the feeling that I was being stealthily watched; suddenly I dropped to one knee, drew my revolver, and crouched beside the skunk cabbage, peering about and listening.

I must have been there just a minute or two when, from out of the swamp on my right, there came awful sucking and squirting noises, steadily increasing in volume, as if numerous unseen persons were lurching through the muck, converging upon me through the mist. About forty feet away on the road, ahead as well as behind me, something like ten or twenty large, white shapes flit, one after another, across the empty darkness, disappearing into the wall of trees on the other side of the road. Had it not been for the drum-like pounding of running feet upon the road, I might have mistook them for fleeting wisps of fog. Running in a crouch, I crossed to the other side of the road and, stepping through the thick carpet of dewy grass, I made for a huge azalea bush that lay twenty feet away up a small hill, near a stand of trees.

As I approached my intended cover, however, I made a shocking discovery: namely, that while I was moving swiftly toward the shrubbery, the shrubbery was also moving swiftly toward me! All at once, there was a great confusion of brambles, inches from my face, which, upon contact with my out-thrust fingertips, suddenly withdrew entirely and with shocking speed, back into the line of trees. Stopping immediately, I turned full circle, my weapon held out in front of me, scanning the darkness for any trace of movement.

I was soon enclosed in an ever-shrinking ring of approaching monsters. My pursuers had swung round behind me, maintaining a formation of containment which assured that I could not escape. Seeing these deliberate efforts to contain my movements, I was overcome with terror, and, standing up in the wet grass on trembling legs, I placed the barrel of the .38 special in my mouth and drew back the hammer with my thumb.

My intention had been simply to spare myself any conscious awareness of the gory fate which was at hand. But as I stood there, breathless, gun in mouth, my heart pounding in my chest, I noticed the sudden change which my self-destructive gesture had effected upon the advancing shadows. Seeing this suicidal pose (and perhaps in response to the implied threat to the brain meat they so coveted) the things suddenly ceased their advance, stopping along the very edges of that curiously thick fogbank, which they seemed to bring with them from the deeps of the swamp.

Here and there, I caught incomplete glimpses of their fiendish outlines against the glowing vapors behind them, an army of swaying, staring hulks looming up out of the grey mist. Having converged upon me at the very edges of visibility, these indistinct silhouettes formalized the frightful ring they had made around me; every gap was soon filled in with a lurching, hunched shadow. They fell silent, as though waiting to see what I would do next. The local wildlife had long since evacuated the region; the silence that fell was unnatural and breathtakingly absolute.

While I could not see these creatures overly well (a limb here, a shoulder there) these odd glimpses seemed to confirm my suspicion that they were not Tree Things or Boulder Things but something smaller and bulkier, with pale grey skin. My enhanced vision simply did not work upon these curious beings. I was left to suppose that, being made from solid stone and animated by some inconceivable alien alchemy, they were not actually "alive" in the usual sense, and emitted no body heat whatsoever.

Nevertheless, in the glow of the moonlit mist, I saw that they were essentially humanoid in shape, though nearly nine feet tall, and perversely asymmetrical. When the fog momentarily parted, I could see, for example, that one of them leaned upon a mighty branch, which it utilized in the manner of a crutch, having a great gnarled stump where its right leg should have been. Several others were not so much headless as profoundly hunchbacked, with heads that slumped so far forward that they merged into their breastplates. Recalling the words of Shakespeare, I whispered aloud the passage from Othello's first act — "the Cannibals that each other eat, the Anthropophagi... men whose heads do grow beneath their shoulders." The only part of them which was not primarily in silhouette were their strangely placed, silvery eyes, oddly shark-like, which I occasionally saw flash and flicker in the moonlight.

To my unending terror, from out of that strangely thick fog, one of the Things actually spoke to me, and in such a deep, wet, bass tone that I felt my bones turn to jelly and the skin upon my scalp to prickle and itch. Issuing forth from a throat as wide as a cannon barrel, from behind a veil of churning mist, one great swaying shadow seemed to address me directly. It spoke one phrase, several times, which the others echoed in eerily perfect unison. This appellation they repeated again and again, so that I began to feel that they were telling me their name... or perhaps the name of their god. The syllables, spelled phonetically, can best be rendered as "Gog... Magog," a phrase which was, at the time, unknown to me, though oddly familiar. And that second, awful choir of lion-like voices was of such a profound resonance that it seemed to act directly upon my nervous system, causing curious aches in my skin and a lethargic paralysis in my muscles. I was suddenly clammy, my skin crawling dreadfully and my legs leaden and immovable. My arms, despite considerable efforts to control them, began to twitch, awkwardly curling and uncurling with a gruesome alien slowness. I had dropped my gun onto the grass by the roadside; it was as if my body had become a dumb, disobedient thing in the presence of these monsters, whose predatory minds were so vast, yet so powerfully focused, that I soon felt them impinging upon my very thoughts, as if searching about for a point of entry.

All at once, my thoughts were flooded with blurry images which quickly coalesced into a series of terrible visions, depicting a mercilessly detailed panoramic of what I can only describe as a full-scale alien assault. Horrendous scenes played out: a bloodbath of unspeakable scope and violence. Closing my eyes, I watched as an enormous Boulder Thing galloped at full speed into the side of a great white farmhouse, trampling underfoot the shrieking inhabitants and sweeping them up into its horrible beak-like mouths. In the distance I could see similar monsters afoot nearby, making similar attacks upon neighboring houses, decapitating, in one bite, whatever luckless persons they found hiding inside.

So far, I have only spoken of one general type of Boulder Thing, as if they all resembled each other more or less. I should say that, in fact, there were several quite distinct types and these tended to travel with others of their similar shape. Some were great oozing spikes of stone, wide at the bottom but rising to great jagged peaks which were anywhere from ten to thirty feet high, so that it was especially frightening to watch them emerge from a stand of trees, or from out of a river or lake, as they were wont to do. Other Boulder Things were relatively oval in shape but of every conceivable size and with anywhere from three to six "legs." During one particularly violent siege upon a church (barricaded from within by refugees from the nearby town, which I could see burning in the distance) I watched as one great big Boulder Thing tore off one side off the building and dumped the people out, the way a child might capsize a box of dolls, catching up several at a time, biting off their heads and discarding the spurting bodies.

In this particular vision, the Boulder Thing displayed a peculiar mutative ability as well, when, in the course of chasing the rest of the fleeing villagers down a grassy hillside, the hungry Boulder Thing suddenly dropped onto its belly, crumbling into numerous, considerably smaller Boulder Things, each of which split off to chase down its own individual prey, so that after several minutes, there was not one human survivor left uncrushed or uneaten. After this gory feast these smaller Boulder Things regrouped, merging, like drops of mercury, back into one massive Thing which continued on its quest to demolish numerous other buildings in the neighborhood.

In the wake of these noticeably larger Boulder Things, I saw numerous frightful others; each stone juggernaut seemed to lead an entourage of lesser monstrosities, a wave of secondary scavengers, some of whom were to be classed amongst the Boulder Things, some with the Tree Things, and several unprecedented specimens who were beyond all classification. I saw, for example, tiny rolling hills of multi-colored jelly, who seemed to hunt in packs, overwhelming their human prey with a detestably eager quickness. Digging through the wreckage of the many demolished buildings, I also saw terrible shaggy quadrupeds with great humped heads, which feasted (by means of oddly triangular mouths) on whatever human portions had been left uneaten. As the minutes passed, these hallucinations seemed to intensify, so that I was soon privy to scenes of carnage so pitiful and brutal that I cannot bring myself to describe them.

Here, in the ruthlessly bright moonlight, on the verge of that lonely swamp, surrounded by those bellowing hulks, I am certain I would have gone stark raving mad, had it not been for the fact that my experiences with the Black Thing had, in a curious way, almost prepared me for this frightening eventuality. As my captors (quite possibly the Gog and Magog of ancient legend) forced upon me those awful premonitions of the holocaust to come, it took all that I had in me to remain calm, composed, and upright.

As the pictures in my head began to fade away, another hunched Thing addressed me in a voice so weirdly layered that I knew it must be speaking not just from the mouth upon its head, but from multiple mouths. It spoke for nearly a minute, in a detestable crescendo of cackling grunts which I dare not call sentences, though they seemed a sort of explanation for the scenes of carnage I had just seen.

Although I have never heard such terrible sounds issue forth from a living thing, I was immediately made to understand (through some apparently incipient telepathic ability) this bizarre message, in no uncertain terms. Its message was simply this: barring a sudden worldwide revolutionary uprising of the enslaved masses against any and all human overlords, in some not too distant future, our failing, hamstrung human civilization would be wiped from the face of the earth, cleared off, to make room for yet another, less egregious race of beings who, with any luck, would be able to avoid falling into the habit of constructing the kind of all-consuming authoritarian social structures which are so horribly stunting the present human race. The implication was quite clear. If we, domesticated humanity, the homunculoid children of a frustrated creator, cannot find a way to outgrow this latent tendency to submit to being ruled by a deranged minority of our own kind, then we will be considered a failure as a species and duly exterminated.

As insane as all of this may sound to you, patient reader, it was, to me, all of a piece with the Tiwanaku Creation myth. I was inclined to interpret this message (and its accompanying imagery) as a kind of final warning. In the moment however, the apocalyptic implications of this communication caused me to go into a kind of swoon. When I regained my wits, I was once again alone by the roadside, my visitors having withdrawn into the misty darkness.

Taking several minutes to collect myself, I resumed my journey, which is to say, I ran the rest of the way to the nearby village of Somers, where I was able to procure the meal and the room that I so desperately needed. That night, as I lay in my hotel bed staring up at the ceiling, I tried to imagine what it meant that the deformed cannibal giants were here in New England and interested enough in me to have sought me out. These questions were so hopelessly huge and unfathomable however, that I despaired of ever knowing the entire picture, and soon fell into a deep but fitful sleep.

*　　*　　*　　*

ENCOUNTERS LIKE THIS ONE FORMED THE FINAL PHASE OF MY ongoing edification and enlightenment. Primarily through the medium of vivid daydreams, I came to understand that the aforementioned mass migrations and relocations I was observing in the hills of New York represented only the local manifestations of a furtive re-positioning that was occurring worldwide. I soon discovered that on every continent of the earth, in dark, secluded valleys and unpopulated areas, the alien watchers were growing restless, surreptitiously migrating in vast numbers to the very edges of large settled areas, or else congregating in secret places deep inside the earth, to articulate strategies in anticipation of the inevitable day when they would be let loose upon the unsuspecting humans, whose flawed and broken civilization they longed to eradicate.

Meanwhile, as the foreshadowing of this apocalypse became more and more apparent, I felt less and less capable of interacting with anyone or anything, be they man, mob, or monster. I continued to make my way through New York State, avoiding all but the most necessary human interactions. When involved communication was unavoidable, I kept my head down and spoke in minimal grunts; I was considered dim-witted and left to myself.

I moved in patterns so random that even the most diligent tracker would be unable to follow me. I took trains, buses and trolley cars haphazardly, moving aimlessly across the countryside. Once I took a steamboat all the way up the Connecticut River. On another occasion I floated on a crude raft down the Pawtuxet River for nearly ten days, camping in the woods along the way. Whenever I came to the ocean, I rode the ferry, so that I traveled up and down the coast several times, from Milford, Connecticut to the Pemaquid Peninsula in Maine and, once, over to Sag Harbor in Southampton across the Long Island Sound. On those occasions I encountered numerous kind-hearted individuals who, seeing that I was unwell and indigent, gave me bread, apples, and wine. These generous folks often invited me into their homes to eat and bathe, or to sleep in their barns, sometimes in exchange for work, sometimes just out of old-fashioned human kindness. During these exchanges, I could barely muster the will to speak except to express my gratitude, for I was so deeply saddened by all that I had been made to understand, that I was constantly on the verge of tears.

I did not succumb entirely to the malaise that was consuming me. In an attempt to cheer myself I engaged in several different sorts of activities to force myself into a better humor. On several occasions I crept into zoos, farms, circus menageries, and pony shows where, utilizing my enhanced abilities, I freed as many of the animals as I thought stood a decent chance of survival in the wilds of New England. At a traveling zoo near Danbury, Connecticut, I released an entire family of brown bears, as well as some unknown species of black badger, into the wild hills east of that town. At a fur farm in Bedford I freed several hundred minks, stoats, and rabbits from their hutches. At a circus outside of the town of Barrett, I liberated numerous hawks, eagles, owls and falcons into the foothills of Mt. Greylock.

It is perhaps not so difficult to imagine how this cheered me. Some newly developed part of me could no longer abide the confinement and degradation of such magnificent creatures and, obeying the urge to free them, I could not help but feel that I was also freeing some buried part of myself that had also been caged. Despite the apparent futility of such acts, it lifted my spirits considerably. Furthermore, I found myself wondering what sort of people could actually sit down and take pleasure in the spectacle of imprisoned wildlife, or of whipped and tortured animals being made to perform inane tricks for their amusement. Once, through a slit in the tent, I saw great hordes of thoughtless gibbering people, applauding and laughing as stoic apes juggled multi-colored balls while casting fearful glances at a tall, stern-faced man, holding some sort of hooked club, standing by a column near the exit. It amazed and saddened me that such a shamelessly barbaric event was considered, by most present, to be jolly fine entertainment.

* * * *

ONE NIGHT, WHILE I WAS LURKING BEHIND THE SCENES AT A traveling circus near Lynn, Massachusetts, I stumbled upon a comparably unsettling scenario which yielded even more unsettling knowledge. I was moving through the shadows towards a group of caged bears behind a closed gate, when I passed by a series of wooden partitions where a small placard informed me that, for ten cents, I could step behind a tattered curtain and observe a Human Freakshow, a sideshow which boasted such abominations as Alligator Boy; Jen and Jan, the Double Girl; Johannus Bimbo, the Fish Boy Who Cannot Be Drowned; Goliath, the Human Leviathan; and someone they simply called Monster Man. At first I thought the sign a relic, since such sideshows had supposedly been outlawed in the mid-1880s. But with my enhanced vision, I could easily see through the flimsy canvas tent to the curious silhouettes, now shambling to and fro in their dismal stalls, just beyond a row of benches where a small crowd had assembled. I stepped out of the shadows and dropped two nickels into the hand of a dangerously inebriated man propped up on a stool, who bade me enter with an out-thrust arm.

The tent was a low, dark, cave-like room, ripe with the smell of unclean flesh, alcohol, and perspiration. I was instantly drawn to several bent and twisted figures, arranged dramatically upon a row of small enclosed stages, where spotlights and grotesque costumes emphasized and accentuated their various deformities. Standing in a huddled group near the edge of the stage, whole families of wide-eyed country folk (who had come from the neighboring villages) looked on aghast, crossing themselves and, not infrequently, muttering odd little prayers of astonishment. From somewhere in the crowd, a child started weeping as an announcer intoned the name and supposed origins of each "freak." As I stood there observing this bizarre scene, I could not shake the feeling that beneath the surface of this macabre display, something extraordinary was being enacted and, pushing my way towards the stage, I chanced to gaze into the eyes of the first exhibit I came to, the giant whom they called Goliath. He was just about to turn his enormously scarred and misshapen, back to the crowd when my movements attracted his attention. For an instant our eyes locked; I was only slightly surprised to see his large pupils flicker and dance suddenly outwards, like tiny, black wings, and to feel my own eyes tickle and itch, as if in response. I had to rub them with my knuckles until the itching passed.

When I looked up again the Goliath was grinning at me, having turned himself fully around to face me, so that the quivering lamplight shone down upon his gigantic anatomy. His proportions were massive and in all his anatomical particulars he was easily three, maybe even four times as large as I. He towered over all the other freaks, his enormous fingers, nearly as thick as my wrists, dangling at the ends of his mighty hands. Aside from his giantism, however, one thing set him apart. Except for his loincloth, he was naked, and beginning at his groin, I could see a cavernous pink scar, several inches deep, which ran vertical up towards his sternum, and nearly obscured by the huge flaps of skin which hung down thickly on either side of it. It was as if, long ago, some enormous animal had taken a huge bite out of his once-massive belly, leaving a great cleft in the flesh which had healed very strangely. Something about the size and location of the wound reminded me of a Cesarean scar, except that it was nearly two feet in length and more in the nature of a rip than a cut. Looking back at his eyes, I saw that he was still staring at me. After several seconds of sizing each other up, I began to feel slightly dizzy so that, when he beckoned to me with his massive finger, I went without hesitation. It was as if he was drawing me in on a string, closer and closer, until I was just two or three feet from him and could smell the whiskey on his breath.

"Hello, old friend," he said. "We meet again."

I understood these words, not by the painfully slurred voice, but because I could actually hear his voice in my head. I understood all at once that we were utilizing that same curious thought-reading ability which had enabled me to understand the Things in the swamp.

"Old friend?" I replied. "But I have never seen you before."

"You do not recognize me?" he asked with a smirk, eyebrows raised.

I looked very closely at his face now, searching for any trace of familiarity but, not finding any, I shrugged, very much at sea.

"So, it is just as I predicted," he said appraisingly. "I see you are becoming a monster after all, just as I always knew you would."

"I have no idea what you are talking about," I said, which was true enough. I was uncomfortably aware that the Goliath seemed to know exactly who and what I was. I continued to stare at his unnerving physique.

"Do you find my appearance startling, young man?" he asked.

"Nothing startles me anymore," I replied in a low voice, at which he smiled approvingly.

"I was not always this way, you know," he said arching his massive back and spreading his arms out in a mighty stretch. "I was once like you. I could pass as an ordinary man, living an ordinary life." And here he chuckled heartily to himself, as though the very concept of an "ordinary life" was the punch line of an excellent and well-timed joke.

"Ahhh... but that was a long, long time ago..." Looking down, he continued. "I am too far along in my development now. But, once upon a time, I was considered handsome, like you..." he said, though I must have looked skeptical because he added, with unnerving emphasis, "Well... handsome enough to seduce a beautiful young woman."

"I do not doubt it for a minute," I said, sensing the intense emotion this subject had evoked in him. Intuiting that this drunken titan had a somewhat explosive temperament, I quickly changed the topic.

"What do you know about the strange creatures in the forest?" I asked.

"You have nothing to fear from the likes of them. The rest of these people..." and here he made a broad gesture indicating, not just the small crowd behind me, but the entire surrounding countryside. "...I cannot say as much for them, but you will be fine."

Here he reached underneath his bench and, stealthily drawing out an enormous jar of cheap-smelling whiskey, he unscrewed the lid and took several large pulls; his slur was not just the result of a deformity, but also of extreme intoxication. Nevertheless, listening with my mind as well as my ears, I continued to understand him perfectly, and, though the idea of interacting with this mad giant when he was in his cups was beginning to alarm me, I steadied myself, resolved to take full advantage of any insights he had to offer.

"I still don't know what you're talking about," I lied, at which he leaned down to me and, bulging his enormous bloodshot eyes, he whispered dreadfully, "Can it be that you still do not understand what is going to happen if we do not rise up and overthrow this civilization?"

"I have caught fleeting glimpses of it, I think," I said, unnerved by his proximity, "but they were more than enough for me."

"You are pregnant," he muttered, his nostrils flared, "and far enough along in your development that they will not harm you. Still, when the day arrives... if I were you, all the same, I would keep my distance."

"I am pregnant, AGAIN?" In dream-like disbelief, I watched him nod his massive head. "I am cursed!" I said, loud enough that several people looked over at me and frowned.

"Listen to me," he sneered. "You must not attempt to hide yourself from them. And do not, under any circumstances, run away from them. If you behave like prey, they will most certainly hunt you. When that glorious day comes, just get yourself to a wide open space, like a field or a rooftop, and sit it out."

"How much more time do we have?" I asked.

"There is no way of knowing," he replied. "It could be weeks, it could be decades. They do not communicate such things to me."

"I have been approached, several times, by those... Things," I told him. "Once they even spoke to me, though I could understand it only dimly. They seem to regard me as though I am one of them."

"Well then I am happy for your good fortune," he said reservedly, "but consider yourself lucky. When they become overly hungry, they are not always so discerning. Nor do they always care if you are gestating." He looked down at his oddly-cloven belly, gulping once again at his whiskey and muttering strange words which I could not understand. Suddenly, he looked up at me again, quite disdainfully it seemed to me.

"Listen," he said, lowering his voice and speaking through his teeth, "You are going to have to smarten up if you expect to survive what is coming. You are arrogant and thoughtless. You don't pay attention to what is going on around you. How do you expect to survive the end of civilization when you are so... distracted?"

"Well, I've managed pretty well so far," I said somewhat defensively. He laughed.

"You have no idea what lies ahead, do you?" he replied, shaking his head.

"What about you?" I shot back, "You don't look like you're in the best shape either. This can't be much of a life for you, sitting around on this bench getting drunk."

It was a stupid thing to say but before I could retract it, he chuckled at me.

"Oh, there are far worse fates than this, my friend," he said looking down at himself, "far, far worse. Believe me, I have seen them."

Then the Goliath leaned back and took another mighty swig of whiskey, emptying the half-full jar in something like three gulps. When his eyes looked back into mine, they were bright red and full of hellish glee. "Yes, I am quite content to watch the collapse of industrial civilization from right here on my cozy little iron-reinforced bench. I don't know about you, but I intend to drink my way through the apocalypse!" Here, he inhaled deeply and then, closing his eyes, he raised his face toward the sky and said, mostly to himself, "I have almost outlived my usefulness here on this earth. I am only waiting for the Ragged Ones to come and take me home."

Then, just as I was getting ready to ask him who the "Ragged Ones" might be, as if on cue, I saw the dangerously inebriated man enter at the far side of the tent, asking everyone to please move to the exits and make room for the next group of curiosity seekers.

"If I may ask you just one more question," I said. "Where is it that you know me from?"

"The show is over, sir. Kindly make your way to the exit," was his only reply. Standing up, he began moving back to the rear of the stage. When he reached the curtain he looked back at me, his face an odd blend of pity and irritation.

"By the way," he said reluctantly, as if against his better judgment, "the One you seek is in the foothills east of the Catskill mountain range, about 180 miles due west of here." He frowned. "The entire region is in a panic. It seems your offspring has failed to conduct itself in a covert manner. The Dark Ones are not amused. If you cannot control your unruly progeny... they will exterminate it. The Overlords will not tolerate such a nuisance to their agenda."

I opened my mouth to speak, but he raised his hand to silence me, and pulling aside the thick red curtain, he said goodnight.

"At least tell me your name," I implored and, at this, he paused and an enormous grin stole across his reluctant face. It was as if my ignorance of his name was a thing most ironic to him, and smiling back at me over his massive, pock-marked shoulder, he said, "I am Legion: for we are many."

Then he winked at me and, cautiously stepping through the curtain, he disappeared from view. I am not certain how long I stood there wide-eyed with my mouth hanging open, but the voice of the barker pulled me from my daze and, seeing that a fresh crowd was preparing to enter the tent, I moved slowly and reluctantly to the exit.

Walking down the row of stalls, I passed each of the other freaks one by one, and had a brief opportunity (for better or for worse) to view their deformities up close. In the glare of those spotlights, I glimpsed the Alligator Boy, Stella the Goat-Faced Girl, Jen and Jan, the Fish-Boy, and the Monster Man.

As I lingered before the stall of the Monster Man, I was struck with a terrifying thought, a hypothesis so obvious that in retrospect, it seemed incredible that I had not thought of it before. Looking back down the line of freaks, I saw numerous things which seemed to lend credence to the idea that these deformed persons on display were not, in fact, victims of random biological abnormality, but were actually half-breeds, the miraculous by-products of a union between human and non-human entity. Could it be that what the barker had called abnormal deformities were, in fact, the awkward and incomplete manifestations of an entirely different set of anatomical priorities (introduced into the blood-line in some unknown manner), now attempting to assert themselves upon the human physique? In the leathery hide of the Alligator Boy I thought I saw the rough, bark-like skin of the Tree Things. In the great misshapen head of Stella the Goat-Faced Girl, I thought I recognized the lineaments of the shaggy horrors I had observed in my vision at the swamp. And there were other eerie resemblances.

The one they called Monster Man, whose head resembled nothing so much as an enormous stone with a face on it, also had a tremendous shelf of protruding grayish bone that ran across his shoulders and down his chest; I thought immediately of the Boulder Things I had seen upon the meadows, and wondered at the circumstances that must have created this incredible hybrid. The so-called Double Girl, Jen and Jan, were conjoined twin sisters, rather like Siamese Twins except that Jen's "sister" seemed, in my estimation, only tenuously human. Rather "Jan" was a semi-sentient, hairless, eyeless, canine-looking creature, with a muzzle like a dog and long rubbery fingers that did not move.

Later, I was able to do some reading on the history of other conjoined and subsumed twins and, after wading through a sea of medicalized jargon (which sadly relegated everything to the category of disease and aberration), I reached the unsettling conclusion that generation after generation of pathologists and scientists had overlooked and/or misconstrued most of what they had seen, creating a whole system of terms, phrases, and categories which obscured far more than they illuminated. In various medical journals, I found numerous photographs of incredibly misshapen persons, including several conjoined twins, some of whom were two fully formed siblings joined at the hip, and others where one of the twins was either profoundly under-developed, or else (as I was inclined to believe) a separate species altogether grafted awkwardly onto, or else emerging out of, a recognizably human being.

These deformed and conjoined beings filled me with a strange blend of awe and dread, as I was forced to reflect upon the question of whether I was not, myself, a hybrid. Moreover, looking at these old photographs, I wondered: what would have happened if, when the Black Thing had decided to depart from my body, it had decided to burrow out the front of my chest, or back, rather than courteously utilizing a pre-existing passageway. How different would my life have been had the Black Thing remained attached to me rather than oozing off into the shadows?

What did it mean that a part of it had stayed behind, inhabiting my body like a wandering bacterium? Would it (as the giant had said) eventually begin to gestate in my gut, thereby reviving my strange and terrible cravings? In "Anomalies and Curiosities of Medicine," by Drs George M. Gould and Walter L. Pyle, I read about two different men who, like me, had given birth to things that had resembled, if not fetuses, then curious masses of embryonic tissue, including "fetal bones." The authors describe the little-known case of a twenty-seven year old German man who went to the hospital to have a tumor surgically removed from his abdomen, only to find that this "tumor" was a lump of flesh which contained hair, teeth and bones. I also learned of the fascinating case of a fatherless baby, surgically removed from the belly of a two-and-a-half year old French girl, and who lived for nearly a year on its own. Despite considerable research, however, I remained entirely unable to discover one single case in which a middle-aged man had regurgitated a carnivorous, multi-eyed blob.

These vaguely analogous case studies, oddly reassuring though they were, also raised still broader questions. Had the Black Thing been living inside me since birth? Was it perhaps my sibling, rather than my offspring? Whatever it was, had it lain dormant until the eating of my first brain, whereby I had triggered the onset of its gestation? Or was it the reverse? Had the onset of gestation caused me to start craving the brain meat? Finally, who (or what?) had my father been? I was not so foolish as to think I would ever get satisfactory answers to these questions, yet, as I made my exit from the sideshow, I was filled with such wonder and confusion that I trembled at the sheer strangeness of it all.

*   *   *   *

HOW HAD OUR BELOVED, FORWARD-THINKING CIVILIZATION displayed its fear and wonder towards these unique individuals whom they had designated "freaks?" Initially, they were poked and prodded by the curious Men of Science — and then, after the novelty had worn off, they were relegated to the circus sideshow where they often lived in filth and rags and poverty, gawked at, day after day, by wide-eyed children and their wide-eyed parents who joked and snickered or else shook their heads in anger and disgust. I could not help but think that in another time, in another place, such individuals might be regarded as divine beings, marvels of nature, ordinary human beings who also had the attributes of curious, unknown gods. But in this land where money is the one true god, the great wounded giant was forced to play the role of biblical monstrosity to earn his meals, and the incredible offspring of the Boulder Things are no more than a macabre thrill for the curious and unkind. I recalled once hearing a story about Joseph Merrick, the Elephant Man of London, an intensely deformed young man who, while traversing the Liverpool Street railway station one day, had nearly been done in by a hysterical mob who pushed him down and spat upon him before he was rescued by a policeman and brought to a hospital.

Leaving the freakshow behind, I continued to travel in my irregular fashion throughout May and June of 1919, savoring the relative solitude of the backwoods (despite the occasional encounters with migrating monsters, who seemed to frighten me less and less with the passing of time). Making my way up and then down the coast of Maine and Massachusetts, I entered the cities of men only rarely.

VIII

ONE COOL JUNE EVENING, AS I WAS WALKING THROUGH THE DEEP woods of eastern Massachusetts, I spied the illuminated windows of a large, barn-like building almost hidden amongst a stand of oak trees. This building stood in the lee of a mighty hill which overlooked the twinkling lights of a small town far below. I had not expected to see human habitation in such desolate country but, relieved at the idea of human contact, I resolved to knock upon the door and offer my labors in exchange for a warm place to sleep. Several times on my long walks, when I'd come upon houses in the wilderness, I had done exactly that and been much renewed by the experience. Lights were visible in in each of the windows, despite efforts to black them out with blankets. As I started up the driveway, I could detect seven or eight persons moving about inside the barn, their movements strangely furtive, as if slowed by exaggerated caution.

I stopped walking, coming to a halt halfway up the gravel driveway. Still at a distance of about forty feet from the barn, I saw that there was a watchman posted: a stocky fellow with a rifle across his lap, leaning backward in a chair propped against the outer door of the barn, throwing occasional glances in all directions. I froze, but it was too late. The man's head jerked suddenly in my direction as he slowly and carefully lifted the rifle off his lap. Rising to his feet, he took several steps forward, moving towards cover, as though in preparation for a gunfight, and never once taking his eyes off me. It occurred to me that this fellow had probably been posted there in anticipation of some approaching enemy, and that now, mistaking me for that enemy, he intended to kill me. Being too far away for talking and yet too close to run for it, I did the only thing I could think to do which was to wave my arms in the air and to break the ominous silence that was between us.

"Excuse me, sir," I shouted in a friendly way, "does this turnpike go through to Aylesbury?" The man made no response, and I began to sweat despite the cold, repeating myself in as disarming a manner as possible.

As I stood staring at this man in the moonlight, I suddenly realized that I recognized this man. Upon closer inspection, I saw that it was none other than the steely-eyed Italian bookseller himself, though his hair and mustache were in an entirely new style so that he looked like a completely different man.

"You?" he said, eyes wide with recognition.

"I'll be damned!" I said laughing, though I stopped myself. There was no trace of a smile on his face. "I was just looking for a place to stay for the night. I was going to knock…"

"You should go, my friend," he said significantly. "Now. This is not a good time for visitors." He said this last part with a mirthless chuckle, as though this were a colossal, almost ludicrous, understatement.

Then it hit me. The wind must have changed direction, for I caught the unmistakable odors of nitroglycerin and gasoline, with a faint whiff of gunpowder. I understood, all at once, that I had stumbled upon a bomb-making laboratory.

Before I had a chance to notice the sudden silence that had come over the figures within the barn, the door pushed open and out stepped a man whom I immediately recognized from the lectures I'd attended. It was the notorious orator himself, Luigi Galleani. I held my breath as he looked me over.

In addition to having heard him speak, I'd overheard numerous anecdotes about this man in the lecture halls; over time, I had learned a fair bit about him. Here was the man who had been kicked out of every country he had ever lived in. Born in 1861, Luigi Galleani had begun life as an extremely promising middle-class student of law in Turin, Italy. But after studying the legal system inside and out for three years, he dropped out in disgust and, while still in his late teens, dedicated his life to rousing the masses to overthrow all authority. Imprisoned on a small island off the coast of Tunisia, under police supervision, he escaped and fled to France, where he was eventually hunted down, beaten, and exiled by the authorities. He had lived in London before coming to the United States in 1901. Everywhere it was the same: Inciting large groups of working people to take up arms against the cops and soldiers paid to suppress them, he participated in whatever labor struggles he found in these places, trying to expose the lie of bureaucratic union solutions and to foment a revolt against capitalist civilization itself. Living for a time in Paterson, New Jersey, he later took refuge in one of the oldest anarchist communities in the United States, in Barre, Vermont, amongst a group of marbleworkers and stonecutters, a brotherhood of anarchists transplanted from their hometown in northern Italy.

Since the spring of 1919 however, Galleani had been implicated in several unsuccessful assassination attempts, via mail bombs, against such persons as J.P. Morgan, Senator Lee S. Overman, Thomas W. Hardwick, and even my old friend John D. Rockefeller. Galleani was also the publisher of "Cronaca Sovversiva," the most well-known Italian anarchist newspaper in

America, and a speaker of considerable force when placed before a crowd. Some claimed he was the mouthpiece of a secret society of anarchist assassins, whose bombs had demolished the mansions of several prominent men of power, including Senator Mitchell Palmer and State Representative Leland Powers.

All this flashed through my mind as I stood there, frozen, like a man caught in a searchlight. I cursed my stupidity for having blundered so thoughtlessly into such a delicate and deadly situation as this. From my minimal grasp of the Italian language, I was able to follow their comments in a general way.

"Who is your friend?" Galleani asked the bookseller in Italian, eyeing me suspiciously through the smoke of the cigar he held in his teeth. Both his hands were thrust into his coat pockets and with my enhanced vision I could easily discern the two pistols he held leveled at my chest and groin, respectively. Looking out past me, into the darkness beyond, he asked, calmly and in English, "You traveling alone tonight, kid?"

"Yes, I am," I replied, looking gravely at him.

"Can you vouch for him?" Galleani asked the bookseller in Italian, without taking his eyes off me.

"No, not really," was his reply. "I have only sold him some books. Though he says he found this place by accident and I believe him."

"Where are you headed?" Galleani asked me in English.

I truly had been walking at random and so had no quick reply to this, a circumstance which gave me the appearance of one fumbling about for an answer.

"My friend here was just leaving," the bookseller interrupted, "weren't you?"

"Yes, I'd best be off," I said with hollow cheerfulness, gazing into the night.

"Hey..." the bookseller stopped me. "This barn does not exist, eh comrade?"

"What barn?" I replied, and we shared yet another utterly mirthless chuckle.

As I turned and walked away I could hear Galleani whispering in Italian to the bookseller.

"Are you certain he isn't a cop?" he asked pointedly.

"I cannot say for certain," came the reply, "But, when I look into his eyes, Luigi, I can see that he is one of us."

I heard the older man laugh and then, with an involuntary cringe, I braced myself. Every step I took felt like my last as I walked slowly down the gravel driveway, waiting for the crack of a pistol shot and the ripping force of a bullet in my back. But it never came.

The next thing I heard was Galleani calling me back. I headed back up the driveway, cold sweat running down my ribs. The blankets that had been hung in the upper windows now trembled and shifted to accommodate the myriad eyes (and guns) that now peeped out at me, tracking me as I trudged back toward the two men standing by the barn door. When I arrived it was Galleani who spoke first.

"My friend here, whose instincts I trust implicitly, tells me that he believes you are one of us."

"If you are asking if I am an anarchist," I said as boldly as possible, "the answer is yes," at which, Galleani took his fists out of his pockets and taking several steps towards me, stared directly into my eyes with an intensity that made me take a step away from him. At first, he almost unnerved me, and I got to thinking that somehow I had offended him deeply. After several seconds, however, our eyes locked strangely, and my fear of this imposing man turned into something else. There was a familiar blackness flickering in the depths of his eyes, a hungry shadow which seemed to reach straight into me; Moreover, I felt certain that we were about to have a fistfight. My eyesight sharpened and my limbs became light and loose. My heart began to pound in my chest and I heard a dim roaring in my ears. Stepping even closer, so that he was only a few inches from my face, his eyes burned into mine with a fierceness that was almost supernatural. Yet I did all that I could to match this intensity, and even surpass it. Staring into the blacks of his eyes, I saw his pupils waver oddly, losing their roundness for an instant and becoming ragged; I was reminded of Howard's eyes and the eyes of the giant named Legion. Suddenly, my pupils began to itch and to tickle, just as they had in the freak tent, and I could not help but rub them vigorously against the palms of my hands. At this, Galleani exploded into peels of booming laughter which were echoed by the other men.

"Bartolo is right again! He is one of us!" Then placing a hand on each shoulder, he smiled at me. "So, what should we do with him, boys?" he asked.

"Kill him anyway, for being so stupid!" someone shouted from the window above and the others laughed in a chorus. When the laughter subsided, the bookseller, whom the others called Bartolo, looked at me appraisingly.

"Well," he said, "if we are not going to kill you, then you must come with us on our little adventure. We will have to give you a job which no undercover copper in his right mind could ever do. That is the only way we can be sure of you."

I nodded, a knot of terror tightening in my guts again. I really needed to keep moving towards the Catskills, and yet I knew that Bartolo and the others would not (and could not) let me go until I too had implicated myself.

"Of course," I said, trying to sound as calm as possible, "What do you want me to do?"

The two men exchanged a sinister smile.

"You," the bookseller said, "are going to plant the poof."

"The what?" I asked. The others snickered and shook their heads.

"You, my friend," Galleani said with a grin, "are going to unleash the Ragged One."

*   *   *   *

DURING THE THREE DAYS I SPENT WITH THE GALLEANI GANG, I was treated as an honorary member of the brotherhood. The first thing I noticed about these men was that each fellow, in his own peculiar way, was sensitive to the brooding strangeness that had come upon the land. They, too, felt the shifting currents of rebellion in the world, the mass uprisings of domesticated humanity against their overlords. Perhaps they had noticed certain other changes too, the changes in the earth, the wind, and the rain, which revealed subtle abominations and anomalies. One thing was clear: each of these men (whether he actually understood it or not) was attuned to the fact that, one way or another, it would not be long before the world-eating civilizations men have built will be reduced to smashed and smoldering ruins. Further, each man seemed to understand that he was destined to play a central role in the coming destruction which seemed, every moment, to be drawing nearer.

Taking me into the barn that first night, I met all the fellows, one by one. Emilio was a rude man, smart and dedicated, but arrogant and hot tempered. Another lad, whom they called Crowbar Joe, was a stonecutter from Needham and a poet of no small talent. There was Fernando, or "Freddy" as they called him, a quiet, thoughtful chap, a teetotaler who never swore. I recall three (or was it four?) men named Bartolo, one of whom, as I said, was my friend the bookseller who, as it turned out, also happened to be the best bombmaker of the bunch. These were not peaceful anarchists, like the ones I'd met on the streets of Boston. These men were soldiers in a war — the oldest, dirtiest war of them all, the class war — and they were buried deep behind enemy lines.

I did not assume, of course, that these were their real names and was later rather shocked to learn that, in fact, they were. Galleani was the undisputed leader, though this leadership had nothing in common with the artificially imposed and enforced leadership we all know so well. This was a leadership

Galleani *earned*, minute by minute, through consistently clear-thinking, brilliant insights, and affinity of perspective. This sort of leader needs no hierarchy to hold the loyalty of his comrades, for he was not at all fearful of losing his status as leader. He was, quite simply, remarkably full of excellent ideas, and the other men, recognizing this natural talent in their friend, simply helped him to realize the dream (which was also their own) which Galleani seemed best equipped to articulate and embody. The moment his ideas ceased to amaze would be the moment he stopped being the leader, and they all knew it. These men had lived together for years, on the run in the forests of New England, having recently traveled to Mexico together to avoid the draft. They knew each other intimately, a brotherhood sharing the dream of a world without authority. Having discussed these things many times over the years, they were in full agreement about certain basic principles and spoke up bluntly when they felt these principles were being violated. The others did not wince at such criticism, or seek to silence it; rather they encouraged them, listening closely to their concerns and giving these matters careful attention.

Had I met these men on the street, I would have passed them by without a second thought. Who would have dreamed that these seven *paesanos* had been quietly amassing an arsenal, in preparation for nothing less than the opening blasts of a general uprising which they hoped would end with the toppling of the American industrial machine (an event which they anticipated to be somewhat on par with those recent uprisings of the Russian and Mexican peasants and workers)?

In the room at the top of the stairs, the weapons were being assembled for the next assault on the power elite, wherein these determined men would send a series of shockwaves ripping through the corridors of the New England aristocracy and jumpstart the exhausted, and overworked population of exploited and impoverished workers into one semi-unified, self-directing uprising of the dispossessed. During this time I learned, in no uncertain terms, what set these men apart from the anarchist folks I'd met elsewhere.

On that first night, Bartolo, Galleani and I stayed up talking for several hours in the yard, after the other men had gone to sleep. It was then that I came to understand their particular school of anarchism.

At one point, we had made our way to the subject of the unions. Bartolo was expressing his rejection of that model on account of it being hierarchical and fundamentally accomodationist, and therefore non-revolutionary. I'll admit I was rather drunk and feeling like playing Devil's Advocate (a thing to which I am especially prone when drunk).

"The workers," Bartolo had declared "must emancipate themselves. There can be no elite vanguard, no formal leadership at all."

113

"Yes, yes," I replied, "what you say is true enough... ideally. But don't you think you are asking a bit much, under the present circumstances? I don't know about you fellows, but when I walk through the cities and towns, I am painfully aware of what I have come to think of as the irretrievable defects of a degraded humankind."

"What do you mean?" Bartolo asked.

"I mean that most people are broken-spirited, crestfallen, and submissive toward authority, people who have been trained since birth to accept their place in the hierarchy, beneath whatever rulers present themselves. Their rebellions are incoherent and poorly planned at best. Do not misunderstand me. There have been victories in this class war, certainly. But, on the whole, you must admit, they are incremental, tentative, and temporary. I'm afraid the vast majority of working people are impervious to the lessons of history. They *want* leaders to tell them what to do and what to think because, frankly, most of them are stupid and lazy. Countless failed revolutions notwithstanding, the masses mostly seem to take it for granted that they are to be ruled, policed, and exploited. I'm beginning to believe they prefer it this way."

Bartolo and Galleani had listened quietly to all of this, staring into the distance, as if carefully absorbing the meaning of each word. Uncertain whether or not I had made my point clearly, I continued.

"Honestly gentlemen, look at all that they endure... a life of servitude and exploitation, day after day, year after year, without ever rebelling in any sustained or significant way. They are strangely timid and cowed, despite the fact that they vastly outnumber their exploiters! And, saddest of all, when they do rise up, as they have in Russia, Spain, and Mexico, it appears that they reclaim the territory only to recreate some new hierarchy, only with themselves at the top and their perceived enemies at the bottom. I'm afraid I have no faith in your masses. Most of them are opportunists who can be bought for a song. They only care about their short-term comfort. They are flocking like sheep to the union leaders even now, to beg the master class for little favors, as if that will save them. They are not worthy of your honorable philosophy."

There was another long pause, just long enough for me to regret my little speech, which had become progressively louder. After a moment, Bartolo spoke, in a low, sympathetic voice.

"I gather from your dim view of humanity, Robert, that you have suffered greatly at the hands of your people."

This pronouncement caught me off guard, and I was suddenly flooded with a thousand ugly recollections, the flickering overview of an admittedly pitiful and awkward life. I turned my face and shoulders away from them both. Now it was my turn to stare into the distance.

"I have no people, Bartolo," I corrected him, "and no family either. I am entirely on my own. You, on the other hand, are part of a brotherhood, with a worthy cause. You have comrades who know you, love you, hug you, and kiss you. I have not been so lucky; it has been quite the opposite with me. The life I've had could make even a decent, kind-hearted man into a hermit. Or a fiend."

"Robert," Bartolo said, "I understand your frustration. The cruelty and coldness that men inflict upon one another can be a pathetic and disheartening thing to observe and endure. But I think, if you take a few steps back, you will see that it is, perhaps, you who is being lazy."

I looked up at him and he met my gaze squarely, with a humility that inspired me to hear him out.

"One must never be so careless as to imagine that the degraded state of humanity is a result of some inevitable human nature."

"Well, what else, if not that?" I asked, looking over at Galleani, who, having perked up, was lighting up a cigar. It was he who answered me.

"Have you considered the possibility, Robert, that the general social malaise, to which you correctly refer, derives from the fundamental monopoly of the fields, the mines, the factories and forges, the railroads and ships, the very earth beneath our feet? That the general malaise is merely the frustration of a thwarted humanity, cleverly ensnared, from birth till death, in an economic stranglehold which the privileged minority maintains with impunity? It is the desperation of living in this stranglehold which compels men to regard their fellows as competitors, obstacles, enemies. Every day of his life, everywhere he goes, the worker sees the social structure validated and sanctioned, so that he comes to accept it as part of his world. The church consecrates these usurpations of the bourgeoisie as a special blessing of god. The state legitimizes it in parliaments, codes, tribunals, it is protected by the laws, police, and armies..."

Bartolo and I looked at each other and smiled.

"It is quite true what you say, Robert," Galleani continued, "but it is not the whole truth. This civilization brings out the absolute worst in everyone. That is just one of the reasons why it must be destroyed."

"Yes," I replied, "but would the anarchist society you are proposing really be much different?"

"Humankind is currently quite stunted in its development," he continued. "We are presently breeding for a race of weaklings and slaves. In the society I am proposing, people would develop themselves to their full potential, outgrow the ugly limitations of capitalism, christianity, poverty, and a life of wage slavery."

"Of course," I said, skeptically, "but how?"

115

"The essence of anarchism," he said, "within the evolution of thought and society, is the total image of man, his integration, his needs, his unexplored energies, his infinite capacity for development, his sociability, his many relations with his fellow man, and with the creatures and beings of the outer world. We do not even know what we are all capable of because we have not yet escaped the holding pen that moulds us to its dimensions. It is for this reason that we must overthrow the social machinery."

This idea that human beings possessed an infinite capacity for development — that we all carried unexplored energies within us — fascinated me. Concealing this from my hosts, however, I continued to play the pragmatist.

"Pardon me for being, perhaps, too specific, but how exactly will destroying the current civilized order translate into a new kind of man, this 'total man' as you call him?"

Galleani laughed, as if he had expected this question and, crushing out his cigar, he counted off on three fingers. "First, through the economic integration of the civilized man, who is at present fragmentary or incomplete, either master or slave, mind or muscle. By combining the qualities of inventor, artist, producer, and consumer in every single person, by making the tools and means of invention and production available to everyone. Second, through the intellectual integration of the working people by uniting material and intellectual work, industrial and agricultural work, by means of a variety of occupations, so that all the human faculties, and not just some, may be activated and expanded, freeing us for the intensive cultivation of the total human being." He looked over at Bartolo, who was listening intently.

"And finally, through the moral integration of man; satisfaction of all his moral and material needs. Giving all men liberty, freeing them from coercive authority in all its forms, to experience the complete development of a self-directed life, for himself and for all human beings." Here he paused, looking deep into my eyes. "When we demolish the social order that is reducing human beings to a race of stunted, submissive, overworked drones, only then will we evolve. Only then will humanity be free to grow into all that we were meant to be."

"And what is it you think we were meant to be?" I asked, trying to hide my intense curiosity.

"We shall have to see, Robert," he said with a smile. "At this point... who can say?"

"I should tell you that I am strongly inclined to agree with you," I replied. "The question is, how do we awaken the sleepwalkers? How do we alert the masses to this higher destiny, inundated as they are with slave morality and capitalist propaganda? Well over half of them will immediately dismiss you as a lunatic. If you persist, you are likely to be misunderstood, hounded, imprisoned, perhaps even tortured and killed. Some of the workers are deadly loyal to their overlords. They cling to the master's leg. They love the whip, and are the first to cry 'Crucify!' the moment a protesting voice is raised..." Before I was done speaking Galleani was already nodding his head emphatically.

"The American proletariat is currently a mass, not a class. If it were a class, if it had a clear, full consciousness of its own formidable strength, the revolution would have happened long ago, my friend, freeing us from these melancholy and bitter musings."

"Melancholy and bitter musings," I echoed with a cynical laugh. "Are there any other kind?" This was intended as a joke, but since neither man laughed, I followed it immediately with, "So, where do we go from here?"

Galleani was quick to reply.

"The first step towards the future society will be revolution, inevitable because the ruling class will yield only to force. The working man must make his revolution, take back what has been taken from him, repossess everything which he has produced and his bosses have seized. In short, expropriate the owners and the capitalists! The American ruling class will never surrender their power and privilege, except symbolically, and they are, in fact, already fighting a very dirty fight to retain and expand it. The only solution is for the workers to give up these shell games and pipedreams of a unionized America and to arm themselves for a mass uprising."

"But don't you think some good could be accomplished by the unions, a few steps forward taken, by participating in the elections with formal candidates? Perhaps as part of an intermediary phase?"

"No!" he said emphatically. "We know for certain that workers are cheated in elections. They will never be able to vote them into positions of power. Even if the government were infiltrated by members of the working class, they would be unable to do anything meaningful in the larger sense."

"Well, perhaps not," I said, "but participating in elections could help the workers in certain ways. It would give them a voice to speak to those in power, for example."

"Only to beg for scraps and crumbs from the master's table," he said with a frown. "Instead of helping the workers, engaging in these reformist measures damages their cause. Once elected to office, even the more active and intelligent among their comrades become idlers and renegades. History is full of these cautionary tales. The people are led to believe that salvation will come from the government, from the unions, and they cease to fight for themselves."

"But do you really think the revolution you describe is possible in America?" I asked.

"Regardless of whether or not it is possible," Galleani said, with considerable impatience, "it is necessary."

Here I caught my first glimpse of the strange tension that existed between these men and me. It was clear that they would have preferred that I drop everything I was doing to dedicate myself to the cause of the Worker's Revolution. I knew that, in a certain sense, they were absolutely correct. What on earth was more important than the liberation of the enslaved masses? Had I been able, I might have asked them if I could join their gang. However, my situation was complicated, to say the least. I knew I had too many Things that I needed to take care of.

"The class war is already underway, Robert," Bartolo chimed in. "It is also true that masses of angry workers are being taken in by the unions, which are already proving themselves to be a pacifying influence. That is why we make newspapers and give lectures. Right now we need to spread the idea that the unions will not save workers from exploitation, not just because they are top-down, bureaucracies, but because the unions are intrinsically accomodationist with regard to the current ruling order. Striking workers are being clubbed and shot down in the street and the unions won't even organize an effective, ongoing general strike. This is why armed revolution is necessary."

"But," I said, "the question remains. What precisely is stopping the exploited mass from doing this for themselves? Why do they seem to regard their own exploitation as an inevitability? Their precious Labor movement is currently being crushed, dismantled, and absorbed by the capitalist machine. The big unions are no longer a threat to the class structure, but integrated extensions of it. Surely the workers must see how this is being done. Surely they must see that their cause is being betrayed. Yet they do not seem to have noticed."

"Here in America, the great mass is bourgeois," Galleani replied, "not by birth but by custom, not by origin, but by habit, superstition, prejudice. And by a sort of confused self-interest too, because it feels that its own interests are tied to, and dependent upon, the masters. In this confusion, the monopolist becomes providence itself, paternalistically providing jobs, wages, bread, life itself for father, mother, and child. So the problem is more complicated than it may have initially appeared."

"You know you still haven't told us what you think of the unions, Robert," Bartolo said with a wink.

"I think big business is already figuring out ways to commandeer the unions and to use them to steer worker dissent into forums where it can be more easily managed from above. That is why I can't get excited about the unions. They are very strong right now but what has come of it? The eight-hour workday, they say. Go tell that to the Colorado coalminers or the Boston fisherman. These Marxians who think the unions are the answer to all our problems are fooling themselves. This whole civilization is rotten to the core, and that includes the communists."

The two men looked at each other, smiled approvingly, and then Bartolo, as if to turn my answer into a toast, raised up the last bottle of homemade wine, sipped it, and then passed it to me with a smile. We continued to talk on these and related topics for a little while longer, until, at last, exhaustion, drunkenness, or some combination of the two, finally intervened. My hosts excused themselves and went inside to sleep, while I, unpacking my blankets, made my bed in an adjacent field, under the stars.

* * * *

I LAY AWAKE FOR A LONG TIME, GAZING UP INTO THE NIGHT SKY, thinking. These arguments had stirred up my imagination tremendously; speculations of a post-civilized society (not to mention a new and improved, post-civilized human being) filled my head with images that were simultaneously thrilling and terrifying. I could imagine a world where people were able to develop themselves in incredible new ways, expanding beyond mere personality and discovering, as I had, hidden mental powers, gaining access to knowledge and insights and abilities they never knew they had. Even though such a world was also bound to be quite dangerous, I knew I would gladly accept the risks to see it through, just for the pleasure of watching it unfold and unravel around me. What did the veneer of civilization hide? How differently would people think, feel, and behave without the landlords, the police, the taxman? I thought of Nietzsche and Stirner and could not help but wonder who (or what) we might permit ourselves to become once the shackles of civilization were removed.

Thrilling as all this was, the question remained: could such an idea truly take hold among such a poverty-stricken, war-torn, and heavily policed population as the American working class? The anarchist position seemed to presuppose a certain will to power on the part of the masses which seemed unlikely. Mentally and socially disfigured by a thousand conflicting nationalisms, divisive racialist attitudes, and mandatory patriotic poses, it was becoming increasingly difficult to imagine people setting aside their various differences and behaving as a unified legion of rebels against their oppressors. Far too many people were directing their frustrations, not at the power elite who exploited them, but at their fellow workers with whom they were forced to compete, cultivating and refining their hatred and suspicion of one another to the point of segregationism, destroying any possibility of collaboration.

It was true what Galleani had said at the end. For a great many people whom I'd met and spoken with, the raw struggle for survival, for one's daily bread, precluded all philosophical considerations. Sticking with their own kind and generally engaging (when they engaged at all) in reformist measures through their unions, they mostly confined their rage at the class system to the neat little channels provided for them, never comprehending that this was precisely how they were being neutralized and drawn into the system that was the cause of their woes. To truck with the bureaucratic machine on its own terms was to already lose. All opposition was absorbed into its endless procedures and processes. The reformist unions would be permitted to grow, but only to the extent that they could be brought under state control. All others, like the IWW for example, would have to be eliminated. Hence the beatings, the mass arrests, and the very public execution of Wobblies like Joseph Mikolash and Joe Hill.

*　　*　　*　　*

THE FOLLOWING DAY WE DRAFTED A LEAFLET WHICH WAS TO BE scattered at the numerous bombing sites. I can do no better than to quote the portions which were written by Bartolo himself, which I have kept folded in my breast pocket ever since.

"*It is the history of yesterday that your gunmen were shooting and murdering unarmed masses by the wholesale. It has been the history of every day in your regime; and now our prospects are even worse... Do not say that we are acting cowardly because we keep in hiding, do not say it is abominable. It is war, class war, and you were the first to wage it under cover of the powerful institutions you call order, in the darkness of your laws, behind the guns of your bone-headed slave. We are not many, perhaps more than you dream of, but we are all determined to fight to the last...*"

We stayed at the barn for three days. On the evening of the third day, about an hour after dinner, Galleani called all the men out onto the hilltop above the barn. Below us the lights of Lynn, Massachusetts, twinkled in the misty darkness and a warm breeze blew softly up out of the valley, bringing with it the smell of honeysuckle and the chanting of a trillion crickets.

"Gentlemen, we find ourselves within a crucible," he said. "The time has come. The kind, hard-working people can no longer abide the rule of these maniacs in uniform. They said 'Come to America and live as free men' and so we came... and found only poverty and rampant despotism. When we speak out about the rampant despotism of America they pass laws to silence us, to imprison us, to destroy our presses, and to remove us. We who spent every lira we had to get here, we who have worked so hard, day after day, year after year, to help build America, and they dare to throw us out! The American people have been put to sleep and we have tried to wake them. For this, the forces of power and privilege have loosed their fiercest bloodhounds upon us. But they will never catch us all. Look up at the stars, my friends. We are at the end of history. It is time to unleash the Ragged One."

This little speech he directed at no one in particular, and yet I could not help but feel that it had been primarily for my benefit. We ceremoniously passed around a bottle of red wine (just a few sips, to steady the nerves) and the next thing I knew, Bartolo the bookseller and I were climbing into a jet black Model T parked beside the barn. With Bartolo behind the wheel, we drove all the way to the Roxbury district in northern Boston, a journey which took us approximately one hour and a half (on account of the fact that we took back roads the entire way and drove quite slowly). In the trunk of the car, wrapped up in several thick blankets, was the nitroglycerin bomb which Bartolo had constructed. Knowledge of its presence made it so that every little bump in the road took my breath away, every pothole put my heart in my throat, but, thankfully, Bartolo the bookseller was also a driver of extraordinary skill and finesse.

During this hour-long journey, Bartolo filled me in on (as he put it) "how the class war was coming along" — and it was not good. He told me of the Palmer Raids and of several new laws which had heavy implications for immigrant radicals. The Sedition Act and the Anarchist Exclusion Act were laws which did away with any pretense of due process and enabled "radical undesirables" (very loosely defined) to be deported instantly and without a trial. He told me of the latest outrages committed by the power elite, working, as usual, in concert with the state and through the medium of hired mobs. He told me the story of the recent May Day riots in Cleveland, New York, and Boston wherein unarmed marchers were savagely attacked by mobs of patriotic vigilantes, including many soldiers and sailors in uniform. In Cleveland, soldiers, policemen, and gangs of club-wielding civilians had attacked an unarmed parade of workers, inflicting shockingly brutal (and in some cases crippling) injuries. In the end 106 demonstrators were rounded up, arrested, and charged with instigating the riot. Not one soldier, cop, or vigilante was arrested. In New York City, a similar situation had occurred when a massive detachment of soldiers and sailors stormed the offices of several radical newspapers and worker gatherings, smashing furniture, destroying books and pamphlets, and beating everyone in sight. On East Fifteenth street, at the Russian People's House, people who had come to sip tea and read books were suddenly assaulted and held hostage by vigilante

121

mobs who forced them, on threat of being clubbed, to sing the "Star-Spangled Banner," as they demolished the last of their equipment.

But the most violent of these May Day episodes had happened in nearby Boston. A parade of demonstrators passing through Roxbury had been suddenly set upon by large numbers of unidentified persons who ran through the crowd punching, kicking, and trampling demonstrators while police officers stood by and did nothing. Bartolo himself had been present at this riot and he described, in bitter detail, how the Boston police officers had eventually joined in the melee, dragging perceived labor leaders into their vans and inflicting frightful injuries upon them. But, in Boston, one of the protesters, anticipating just such an ambush, had brought along his firearm. A minor gunfight had ensued, during which, four men (including two policemen) were struck by bullets. There was, however, only one bizarre fatality (though it was entirely unintentional). A police captain was found dead in the street, near a large open sewer drain, his face twisted into a hideous grimace but with no apparent injuries. It was later determined that he had died of fright… a fact which unnerved me strangely.

Once again, over a hundred May Day celebrants (many of whom were suffering from broken bones) were arrested, including several prominent Americans like William Sidis, the son of Boris Sidis, a well-known Harvard Professor, and a grandson of the poet Henry Wadsworth Longfellow. Despite these and many other US citizens who had attended the parades, newspapers denounced those attending these gatherings as "backwards Red foreigners." As had been the case in Cleveland and New York, the protesters themselves were found guilty of disturbing the peace, while not one of the club-wielding attackers had been detained. Before passing the unusually heavy sentence, the Honorable Judge Albert F. Hayden chastised "these foreigners who think they can get away with their doctrines in this country… If I could have my way I would send them and their families back to the country from which they came." For the crime of peacefully protesting the appalling working conditions prevalent throughout the poorest areas of Boston, Judge Hayden sentenced numerous demonstrators to prison terms of up to eighteen months. Thus, once again, the hired mobs, working in concert with local police and judges, had achieved together what they could never have accomplished separately, namely the further demonization of radical foreigners (primarily Italians, Irish, Russians, and Jews) and the terrifying and brutal discouragement of labor agitation generally. By maintaining an artificial scarcity of jobs (carefully managed from above) the ruling class holds in reserve that vast pool of desperately poor workers, whom they can play endlessly and repeatedly against each other. I thought of railroad baron J.

Gould's famous boast, "I can always hire one half of the working class to kill off the other," and felt a familiar hatred welling up inside me.

"Disgusting," I said when he had finished. "It makes me sick."

"Yes, me too," replied the bookseller. "Lucky for us we are in an ideal position to do something about it."

"Where are we going?" I asked.

"We are not going anywhere," he began, pulling the car to the side of the road and cutting the lights and the engine. "We are already here."

"Where is here?" I whispered.

"That," he replied, pointing to an enormous, well-lit house barely visible through the trees. "That is the home of Judge Albert Hayden."

Exiting the vehicle, we fell silent, communicating only through simple hand gestures. He had already showed me how to activate the device, so that all that remained was to get to the house and back again in as short a time as possible. Retrieving the iron cylinder from the trunk, I began the long walk toward the house.

Looking down at this strange device in my hands, I was unnerved. Hadn't many of the anarchist bombers blown themselves up? Was this bomb going to go off when it was supposed to? Would I be blown to smithereens? What if, heaven help me, I should stumble and drop the damned thing? All these thoughts raced through my mind as I walked slowly and carefully through the darkened forest and into the shadowy side yard of the enormous mansion. Once I activated the device, I would have no more than three minutes to get away. We had calculated that it would take me approximately one minute to cross the lawn running at the top of my speed. Then about five seconds to get into the car parked forty feet away, leaving us just under two minutes to drive as far as possible (no less than three hundred yards) from the blast zone. This left us absolutely no margin for error.

As if in a strange dream, I stepped cautiously up to the impressive front door. A large mounted floodlight bathed the approach and the gardens with a misty golden glow. On either side of the door stood mammoth white pillars which rose up to the second story and supported that portion of the upper floor which overhung the entryway. Peering in through the glass panes and into the foyer, I spied a clock which informed me that it was approximately two minutes to midnight. Moreover, I perceived that the mansion was empty. Scanning the interior, I could detect no trace of body heat anywhere. Lights had been left on in several of the rooms, but not a soul was home. Learning this calmed me considerably so that, as I inserted the bomb into the narrow space between the massive column and the outer wall of the house, I breathed a sigh of relief. Then I lit the fuse and ran faster than I have ever run in my entire life.

Just as I cleared the yard, and was closing the distance to the waiting automobile, a sudden intuition made me stop in the middle of the street and turn around. Walking up the street from the opposite direction was a human figure, a young man, barely out of his teens, plodding through the darkness and moving straight toward the Hayden mansion. Precious seconds were ticking in my ears as I tried calmly to assess the young man's distance from the house. He seemed to be about a hundred yards from the front door, but was closing fast. How much longer till the bomb went off? Involuntarily, I did something which made me a candidate for the world's worst terrorist bomber in the history of class society. I let out a short blood-curdling shriek, like the cry of a startled animal, which cut through the silence of the neighborhood so strangely that even I was unnerved by it. The boy stopped dead in his tracks and, peering about cautiously, he stood frozen in time for several seconds. His eyes must have found me in the darkness; he looked directly up the street toward me, and did not look away.

I was just standing there stupidly, cursing myself for my sentimentality, when suddenly a dazzling brightness erased everything. The flow of time itself seemed to come to a sudden halt. There was a bloom of unearthly colors to my right, a piercing white light which poured skyward, vanishing into the upper air about forty feet above the roof of the mansion. As several hundred bolts of multi-colored lightning flew at the center, there was a tremendous implosion, and I saw an enormous shimmering animal rising up out of a hole in the air, throwing four massive ragged wings outwards against (and through) the façade of the mansion. This animal resembled, more or less, the great saurian birds, recalling to mind speculative sketches I'd once seen of a Rhamphorincus, a huge winged reptile of the late Jurassic period. The appearance of this creature was instantly followed by a ripping force that shook me to my bones and a blast of heat that knocked me to the ground, stunned and deafened. There I lay, my mind wiped clean of all thought, a man in a silent void. When I looked again, the creature was gone, having launched itself horrifically, incomprehensibly, into the night sky.

Immediately sitting up, I saw that the boy, who had been a good eighty yards or so further from the blast than I, was unharmed, though he was clearly beside himself over the astonishing spectacle before him. And what a spectacle it was! Where, seconds before, there had stood the great, pretentious, many-pillared mansion of Judge Albert Hayden, there now stood a gigantic doll's house, ripped open across the front, with a charming view of nearly every bedroom, some of which were still lit from within by crooked fixtures and swinging chandeliers. I was so dazed by this unreal scene that I barely noticed the headlights that immediately engulfed me, nor the strong arms of Bartolo as he pulled me to my feet, shoved me into the vehicle and sped away down the dark, winding streets.

It was lucky for me that I was currently unable to hear, for my occasional sideways glances confirmed that I was being admonished most severely and in no uncertain terms, no doubt for my foolhardy attempt to scare away the boy. I very much wanted to ask Bartolo what the hell kind of bomb has a gigantic winged monstrosity inside of it; instead, I let him rage at me. It was only his way of letting off steam and so I did not take it personal. Part of me regretted that I could not hear this diatribe. Had I been a better lip-reader I might have learned several choice Italian curses.

IX

AFTER DRIVING THROUGH A MAZE OF BACK ROADS, BARTOLO AND I finally arrived back at the barn. It had been our plan, before splitting up and going our separate ways, to meet back up with the Galleani gang one last time. I stood like a fixture against the back wall, barely aware enough to listen, as Bartolo recounted our little adventure to the others, mercifully omitting the part where I had shrieked. At one point during this brief reunion, two other men entered the barn and were greeted warmly by the others. There was an older man of about fifty-five, along with a much younger man, maybe twenty, and judging from the resemblance, father and son. After these greetings, we all took our seats around a small wooden table, the elder man calmly informing us of several places where we could expect to find refuge from the manhunt that was sure to come. Handing out maps to each one of us, he pointed out the three or four anarchist safe-houses which had been set up weeks before.

Overcome by a splitting headache and chewing on the leaves of the feverfew plant from the garden, I half-listened to the voices of the Galleanists as they talked among themselves and put questions to the mapmaker.

"What about that squatter camp near Leffert's Corners?" Galleani asked.

"I just came from there, Luigi," the newcomer replied gravely. "You don't want to go there just now."

"Has something happened?" Bartolo asked. The map maker looked nervously from face to face.

"Strange things are going on up there just now. You should steer clear of the place. Surprised you haven't heard about it." The man was clearly reluctant to elaborate.

"We've been a bit sequestered here." Crowbar Joe said with a smirk.

"What kind of strange things are going on?" Galleani asked, shooting an enigmatic look at the bookseller.

"People are going missing is what's going on. Nobody knows if it's a police dragnet or patriotic vigilantes or what, but folks go out walking and they are never seen again. Or, if their bodies are found…" Here he trailed off, looking over his shoulder.

"Or what?" Emile snapped. "What's the matter with the bodies they found?"

"Well..." he began, reluctantly, "they are in a very bad way — all torn to shreds. Turned insides out you might say, and always..." here he lowered his eyes as if ashamed to say this last part out loud "... always with their skulls broke open and their brains missing."

A stunned silence fell over the entire party.

Then the younger fellow spoke up.

"I've passed through the squatter camp near Leffert's Corners several times over the past few years. I got a cousin who lives there with his wife and two daughters."

"Speak your piece, boy." Galleani said.

"Not much more to tell, sir," he stammered, "other than folks going missing and the occasional shredded, brainless body found in the woods. It's been going on for years up there. Seems to come and go with the seasons. All through the winter months, despite woodcutters and hunters entering the forest in droves, none ever seem to go missing. But then, come springtime, there's always hell to pay. With the coming of the first thunder storms, the whole nightmare starts right up again."

"It's got folks talking crazy," the older visitor interrupted. "Saying there's some kind of devil in the forest that's doing it. I don't know if the well water's gone bad, and it's got folks hallucinating or what."

A feeling of icy dread rinsed over me as visions of my Black Thing, devouring harmless, decent squatter folks, danced through my head. The walls of the barn began to close in on me and I was overcome with a sudden and profound need to be alone, out in the fresh air and far, far away from any and all human beings. My mouth went dry and in the silence that followed I swallowed audibly, so that several people, including Galleani, looked over at me. Noticing the strange look on my face, he narrowed his eyes.

"Hey, you don't look so good, my friend. If you know something about all this, I would like to hear it."

"Maybe I do, and maybe I don't," I replied. "But I can tell you this: it isn't the local sheriff turning people inside out and removing their brains. Where did you say this place was?"

"It's up in the Catskills a ways, mister. But I just got through telling you it ain't a good place to be right now."

"Can you to show me on this map?" I asked.

"Surely," he said with a shrug, and as he unfolded the map on the table and placed a finger on Leffert's Corners, I could see that his hands were shaking.

"I need to go now," I said.

Looking around the room, I saw that all eyes were on me. From their expressions, I could see that I was now being regarded by my new friends with something akin to fear and revulsion, oddly mingled.

"Do as you must, my strange friend," Bartolo said. "We shall not meet again." Looking into his eyes I knew that he was right.

"Goodbye and good luck," I said. We embraced and, tipping my hat to the others, I stepped into the warm night air.

*   *   *   *

IT WAS WELL AFTER 3:00 A.M., AS I TRUDGED THROUGH THE moonlight, following the ridge back toward the train depot in the nearby town of Lynn. I was, at this time, totally exhausted and in pain. My bones ached badly from the blast, my muscles were honeycombed with bruises and stabbing pains, and there was a painful throbbing headache developing behind, and above, each of my eyes. Knowing that I was in no condition to dash off to Leffert's Corners, I reconsidered my impulse to get to the Catskills as quickly as possible. I decided to return to the one place where I knew I could hide out for a few days in uninterrupted solitude — the barricaded farmhouse in nearby Sudbury. Once there, I could recuperate from the lingering effects of the bomb blast, rest my aching body, and formulate some kind of theory regarding the situation at the squatter camp. Perhaps, once I was feeling like my old self again, I could pay a visit to the Harvard Library in Cambridge to research recent history and folklore of the Catskill Mountain region and to see if I could discover anything which might provide a context for the awful killings the mapmaker and his son had described.

But as I walked through moonlit fields and forest, my troubled thoughts kept returning to the bomb I had just detonated in Roxbury. I began to consider it from a variety of perspectives, none of which did anything to alleviate the disturbance of my thoughts and the trembling ache in my bones. I had passed some threshold, and no amount of philosophy could ease my thoughts. On the one hand, I had, for a long time, been frustrated with the ineffectual movements of organized labor. All attempts at a sustained General Strike had failed and I could not help but think that it was the result of some intrinsic defect in the movement as a whole. Battling for incremental improvements on an ever-shifting battlefield slanted entirely against them, the reformers exhausted themselves in the endless machinery of legislation. The unionists wanted to conduct negotiations. They took it for granted that a bureaucracy which would alleviate the mounting tension between the workers and the bosses was a good thing. But since no ruling elite has ever peaceably relinquished its power over the rabble, in a potentially revolutionary situation such as this, there could be no compromise between the two classes; nor could there be reconciliation. Advocating such a thing seemed foolhardy at best, a catastrophic, ahistorical misreading of the situation. It was time for the beleaguered workers of the world to stop negotiating and start taking back their cities and their lives. The capitalist class was already on the attack, killing thousands in coal fields, working millions to death every day in poisonous factories, shooting and clubbing unarmed workers openly in the streets, to show the others what happens to those who dared to rebel. And this death toll does not include those uncounted numbers that had been rounded up in police raids and were never heard from again, or else died strangely, hideously, in police custody. I knew that the papers would be howling for my blood and yet the question remained: did anyone really expect the working people to endure this steadily increasing brutality without ever striking back? The arguments put forward by the pacifists seemed to imply a sort of suspension of disbelief, as if somehow things weren't quite bad enough to justify such measures. But how much worse did it need to get before retaliation was justified?

There was a lump in my throat that would not go away, and a feeling of nausea so debilitating it sometimes threatened to overwhelm me. Despite my initial impressions, it was not guilt or moral outrage, it was terror, a vast and endless terror, not just for myself but for all of us, and from which, I now knew, there could be no escape. I knew that this terror was something I had felt since my early youth. I had done my best to ignore it, to hide myself from its implications. Now, at long last, it had found me. I too was a soldier in the war now — a monster on a battlefield with other monsters, some of whom were infinitely more frightening than I.

In this context, there was something I did not understand. Why had the Galleanists of Boston felt the need to reveal themselves as such, so publicly. Had they avoided propaganda altogether and focused on staying hidden, concealing themselves entirely, how much more effective and numerous could their bomb attacks have been? Had they maintained utter secrecy, like a Black Hand Gang (ordinary patriotic citizens by day... secret terrorist society by night), how many more assassinations might they have pulled off? The authorities would have been powerless to stop them. But this would have been antithetical to the ethos of the New England anarchists. They were fiercely proud of their beliefs. At times they seemed almost quaintly naïve, printing their actual names on the many books, newspapers, and pamphlets they produced, and regularly attending public meetings where they openly preached the destruction of the bourgeoisie within earshot of the coppers.

In sharp contrast to me, the Galleanists of Boston were acting in incredibly good faith. The fact that they had never once actually killed their intended targets seemed to imply an attitude of ominous warning rather than actual murderous intent. They stood in stark contrast to the increasingly fatal violence of the lynch mobs, the police, and the judicial system with whom they had to contend. These bombings merely revealed the extent of the class war; without their own independent press, how else could the anarchists and the Wobblies hope to counter the demonized and decontextualized interpretations of their deeds? They had hoped that their choice of targets (senators, millionaires, immigration bureaucrats) would make the philosophy of the assassins obvious, but leaving it to reporters, editors, and others loyal to the bourgeoisie to interpret these events would have been unthinkable. Carefully thought-out explanations would be necessary.

As much as I whole-heartedly agreed with their wish to destroy bourgeois civilization, I felt the need to distance myself and to end all contact with the anarchists; I knew they would never approve of my methods nor comprehend my numerous and various abominations. Theirs was a righteous struggle which I did not wish to stain with my gory deeds. The anarchists cherished a kind of belief in humanity; they were ready to see the best in people, while I felt myself moving in the very opposite direction, slipping toward misanthropy and generalized disgust. The anarchists dreamed of a better human world; I dreamed only of escape, to find some way to shrug off the last vestiges of my humanity. Unlike myself, the anarchists were not hateful people. On the contrary, they loved life, loved themselves, and loved each other. Moreover, they loved humanity and were willing to fight to the death to free us all. This is what had fascinated me most about the anarchist idea, for in it (more than any other) I heard, not a call for some new and better way of negotiating with authority, but the rejection of authority itself. Considered from this perspective, the people who refused this possibility only betrayed their own hopelessness and passivity. I wanted nothing to do with any of them.

Finally, the way in which the unrebellious masses (paid or unpaid) had turned upon the striking workers also seemed instructive, a cautionary tale of sorts, whose implications were not lost on me. The defenders of civilization were prepared, trained, and ready to engage them violently. Until the oppressed classes were prepared to meet them in kind, their defeat was assured.

*   *   *   *

TWO HOURS LATER I ARRIVED AT THE DEPOT IN LYNN WHERE, catching the first southbound train, I was soon dozing in my seat, bathed in the glow of the rising sun.

Rocked gently by the rhythmic motion of the train, I tried once more to reach out with my thoughts to see if I could detect the presence of the Black Thing nearby. Closing my eyes and slowing my breathing, I brought my thoughts into a sharp focus and attempted to project, or expand, my awareness toward the western horizon and to feel about with my mind for the slightest inkling of the Black Thing in the surrounding region. But just as before, the only impression I received was that it was, somehow gone from this world. I recalled Susie's words once again, and wondered if there were some sort of portal or gateway nearby, perhaps in Boston — a hidden passageway which connected this pastoral New England landscape to some fiendish alternate dimension.

One hour later, I disembarked at Sudbury, where, trudging through green marsh and meadow, with the sun high in the sky, I made my way overland to Arnold Lane. I was pleased to find everything just as I had left it; barricaded, sealed, and undisturbed. I spent the night there, sleeping, thinking, and savoring its eerie stillness.

My return to the farmhouse was not an altogether calming experience, however. These last few days had so altered my perspective that I was increasingly oppressed by sharply conflicted and contradictory feelings of dread and wonder about the Thing I was becoming. Stranger still, I was sometimes haunted by the sensation that I was not alone in the house; I was convinced at certain times, there were other, silent Beings close at hand (though I could not detect their exact locations). These Beings appeared to me as little more than flickering shadows seen from the corner of my eye, though they always managed to vanish before my gaze could fully discern them. These unseen Things occasionally succeeded in unnerving me as they apparently possessed enough density to bump tables and chairs, extinguish candles, and even cast ghoulish shadows upon walls.

The most noteworthy experience at the farmhouse came about noon on the second day, I ventured into the basement where I was immediately struck by an oddly sweet, musty odor which was so overpowering that I slid open several of the mud-smeared windows to let in some fresh air and sunlight. Peering about the dingy cellar, I beheld a peculiar and alarming sight. The hard-packed earth within the borders of the stone circle I had built was now most curiously disturbed, as if by a strange, and suspiciously localized, upheaval. At first I was afraid to approach it, but as I could detect no trace of abnormal lurking things anywhere nearby, my caution quickly gave way to morbid curiosity. Reaching down, I found this disturbed earth inexplicably soft and brittle, and, overcome by an odd inspiration, I went to the barn for a shovel. Upon returning, I began to dig.

I had barely begun my excavations when my foot went straight through the thin crust of earth. I fell about seven or eight feet down, into a wide, dark tunnel, rather like a rodent's burrow, but large enough to accommodate several grown men standing at their full height. For several moments I lay still, assessing my injuries and trying to discover what, exactly, I had fallen into. From the tiny bit of light which filtered in through the hole I had made, I appeared to be in a large subterranean chamber, vaguely spheroid, with two horizontal tunnels leading off into the chilly darkness. As I collected my wits on the cool, moist soil, my eyes began to adjust to the darkness; I could soon discern the dimensions of this strange underground hollow.

The first thing I noticed was a low but steady rumbling coming from somewhere far, far below me and emerging from the tunnel to my left. It was as if, elsewhere in this apparently vast system of passageways, a mighty torrent of water were plunging from the rim of some lightless chasm, thundering down through endless voids of black air before exploding on whatever rocks lay below. I guessed from the faintness of this sound that this mighty cataract was at a great distance from my present location. I was unaccountably afraid of that sound. Even after I stood up and wiped my hands on my pants, something in me refused to take a single step toward that leftmost tunnel. As the seconds passed, I was overcome by a dreadful presentiment of extreme danger, though I could detect no immediate cause for it.

Then I heard it — a strange grating sound, coming from the tunnel to my right. There was series of odd thumping sounds, followed by a sliding noise, then a pause, followed by more thumping and sliding, so that I was impressed with the distinct mental image of some huge creature dragging itself down the tunnel toward me. I turned to that part of the wall directly beneath the hole I'd made, where I attempted to grab hold of the dirt and pull myself up. The dirt, far from supporting me, simply broke off in my hands, crumbling uselessly between my fingers. Further groping movements eventually created a tiny cave-in which very nearly buried my feet, and momentarily filling the chamber with the soft sounds of falling earth and tumbling stones. I noticed that the approaching thumps had suddenly ceased, as if the Thing had actually paused, the better to listen to the sounds my fumbling had made. To my horror, the thumping and sliding resumed, only with a devilish, almost frantic, quickness, advancing without pause, and I knew that my presence had not only been detected, but that the unseen creature had quickened its pace frightfully, in order to come upon me all the more rapidly.

My terror gave me a hideous, almost supernatural, strength. No sooner had I heard the feverishly quickened shuffling of the approaching Thing, than I launched myself upward and caught hold of a great wedge-shaped stone which jutted out from the wall about two feet. Upon this thin ledge I managed to pull myself up and, spying another jutting boulder just a few inches further up, I reached out and caught hold of it. Dragging myself up onto this second boulder, I turned to check the progress of my pursuer only to discover that the great pale Thing had stopped just inside the mouth of the tunnel, on the very brink of shadow, as if reluctant to emerge into the pale golden light which was streaming in from above. Despite my enhanced vision, I was unable to make out the size or shape of this approaching horror.

I lingered on this perch just long enough to see that the walls and floor of this tunnel where minutely covered with the deep impressions of a great multitude of hand and footprints, some of which were of normal human dimensions, others which would best be described as grotesque parodies of the former. One handprint must have been twelve inches from wrist to fingertip. This imprint was quite distinct, clearly displaying the imprint of seven massive digits, each of which ended in a surprisingly deep and tapered slash mark, of the sort which could only be made by a hooked talon or overhanging claw.

From the corner of my eye, I saw that the Thing was overcoming its fear of the light, and making its first tentative moves into the dimly lit chamber. Turning my gaze back to the hole, I came to the awful realization that, once my body was inside the opening, the chamber would again be thrown into darkness, freeing my heliophobic pursuer to resume the chase with all speed! In a moment of pure dread, I understood that I might not be able to pull myself clear of the hole in time; paralyzed by the image of myself being dragged backward by my feet into that abominable pit inspired in me an inhuman quickness. In less time than it takes me to write the words, I had wriggled headfirst through the aperture and, seconds later, rolled onto the basement floor with my legs drawn up against my chest, breathless, pouring sweat, my hands gripped tightly, protectively, around my feet. Terrified beyond words, I scrambled away from the stone circle, fully expecting to see its surface explode with some hungry, many-legged denizen of the Abyss. To my amazed relief, whatever had rushed me in the darkness of the tunnel did not venture to pursue me into the light of day.

I managed to get myself upstairs where, sitting on the edge of my makeshift bed, I wept at the nightmare, within a nightmare, within a nightmare, that my life had become. Falling back, I wept for all the horrors I had seen and for the infinitely worse horrors which I knew must lay ahead of me. As I curled up into a ball beneath the tattered blankets, I grieved for the ordinary life I had left behind, and for the increasingly grotesque and monstrous reality which now stood in its place. It took me almost two hours to stop crying and another hour after that before my hands finally stopped shaking.

*   *   *   *

THE REVELATION OF THE GIGANTIC BURROW IN THE BASEMENT frightened me so much that, cured of all curiosity, I fled the house that very afternoon, heading off in a westerly direction. Still too delirious to conduct proper research, and deprived of the sanctuary of the farmhouse, I wandered off into the hills in a daze.

I contemplated catching a train directly to Leffert's Corners but, feeling further unnerved by my experience in the cellar, and being in even more desperate need of rest and solitude than before, I resolved, yet again, to postpone the trip until such time as I could find myself a new safe haven in which to compose myself and formulate a plan.

There was a part of me that felt obliged to find out, as soon as humanly possible, if my offspring was responsible for the squatter deaths and, if so, to put a stop to it at once. Yet there was another part of me that, to be perfectly honest, was simply afraid to go. To this end, I found myself constructing arguments (and not entirely fallacious ones) for postponing, or even canceling, the trip to Leffert's Corners.

First and foremost among these was the fact that the mapmaker had said that the brain-eating attacks had been going on for several years. This weighed heavily against the idea that my Black Thing was responsible. Having departed from my company only five months earlier, and being not quite one year old, it could not possibly be responsible for attacks which had been going on for several years. What if I made the 180 mile journey to Leffert's Corners, only to discover that it was not my offspring that was committing these atrocities, but some other brain-eating monstrosity, something older, bigger, and infinitely more dangerous than my Black Thing? Wouldn't my investigations inevitably lead me to a direct confrontation with this unknown Being? And, if so, did I have any compelling reason to believe that I would survive the encounter?

It finally occurred to me that there were others like me, people who had gestated and given birth to monstrous offspring similar to my own. The more I thought about it, the more plausible it seemed. Surely I wasn't the only person in the history of the world who had had this experience, and surely mine was not the only monstrous offspring lurking on the edges of civilization and feeding upon its unsuspecting inhabitants.

So, once again, I set out in search of some other sanctuary which I could temporarily call my home. My initial wanderings turned up nothing; as the days turned to weeks, and the weeks into months, I continued to wander the green hills of New England, crossing and re-crossing the landscape in winding, nonsensical peregrinations. Everywhere I went I remained constantly watchful for any hint of the Black Thing, but never did any come to me. Now and again, when exhaustion and despair threatened to overwhelm me, I reminded myself of Rockefeller's well-paid henchmen who, by now, must have made some headway in their efforts to trace my movements. I knew it was just a matter of time before these professional man-hunters found me and inflicted upon me whatever gruesome fate their master had decreed. Yet I had no real way of knowing whether or not I had, in fact, successfully evaded my pursuers, or if I was merely deluding myself on this count, wandering in blissful ignorance as they were, every second, closing in on me. For all I knew, they had already found me and were merely holding their positions, tracking me at a distance, watching and waiting for the ideal moment to strike me down.

* * * *

AS I MADE MY WAY THROUGH THE HAUNTED AUTUMN wilderness, there was another new and terrifying development with regard to the no-longer-hidden monstrosities insinuated into the landscape. Earlier, I said that I could sometimes hear the various Hidden Ones, conversing incomprehensibly across the deserted hills and pastures, with voices disguised as birds, frogs, crickets, and wind. It was during this segment of my journey that I became aware that I was not just overhearing, but actually beginning to *comprehend* their ghostly, vaguely symphonic, language.

At first I only caught random words and phrases, barely audible fragments of conversations which I heard and understood. Some previously inactive part of my mind, or else some dim and inexplicable familiarity with this bizarre language, surfaced within me like a memory, endowing me, over a period of weeks, with this new and terrifying interpretive ability. Recalling how, back at the Freak Show, I had been able to comprehend the Goliath's garbled mutterings, I tried to reassure myself that this frightening new development was merely an expansion of these same thought-reading abilities, only now extended to include extra-terrestrial, as well as earthly life-forms. This was cold comfort indeed, and, in the end, all attempts at reassuring explanations fell flat. One morning I simply awoke and the previously incomprehensible, monosyllabic utterances which I had been hearing for the last two and a half years suddenly yielded, and I was somehow able to draw actual meaning from them, deciphering these noises without any conscious effort, organizing them into the crudely equivalent phrases in English.

How, dear reader, might I hope to convey the mind-twisting horror of this most frightful eavesdropping? I will not attempt to transcribe all that I heard as I trudged through the wild autumn landscape; the things I overheard terrified me beyond all semblance of sanity and reason. Through this unintentional eavesdropping, I received confirmation, in no uncertain terms, that what we cherish to call our glorious modern civilization has always been, and is now, essentially, a farm and a laboratory.

I suppose it would be least shocking to say that the camouflaged monstrosities spoke of us in a way that was roughly analogous to the way in which the average man might speak of a cow or a pig, with a presumption of ownership, a master's unconcerned arrogance. Most often they spoke of us in purely clinical terms, discussing and assessing us (either individually, or as a whole) in terms of our relative capabilities and weaknesses. Most terrifying of all was the gruesomely casual way they spoke of our guided development; as if their surreptitious cultivation of humanity were a commonplace, banal, endeavor, an obvious necessity, barely worth a second thought. Some nights, as I lay half-asleep, listening to them murmur back and forth in the darkness, I imagined them as a group of scientists, eagerly, yet impatiently, tracking the progress of some experimental hybrid, the once-promising brainchild of a thousand failed attempts, whose viability had become an abstract uncertainty.

Additionally, I noticed that many of the hidden monstrosities seemed to nurse a curious grudge against humanity in general, looking upon us with impatience, disappointment and even, at times, a thinly veiled disgust. Now that I was able to understand the content of these conversations, I learned that the majority of them actually had elaborate theories and criticisms of us, positing strange and convoluted hypotheses that explained (or else excused) our herd-like stupidity, often elucidating to one another the ways in which they found our various cultures bizarre or quaint, depraved or pathetic, stultifying or decadent. One misty spring night, I lay in the tall grass listening as two great rolling hills of red jelly, sitting on the crest of a nearby hill, discussed at length how the dominant trait in human beings appeared to be extreme gullibility. On another occasion, two massive Tree Things expounded, in the most derisive terms imaginable, upon the pitiful betrayal and failure of every modern human revolution. At times, the implicit condescension of these remarks approached noxious hyperbole. I heard far more than I ever cared to about cowardly, crestfallen humanity; obedient, craven humanity, interesting certainly, in our way, but sadly and imminently doomed to regimentation, authoritarianism, and industrial suicide.

Some monsters spoke more derisively than others (often with outright malice) while others spoke of us with pure, undisguised pity, which was somehow worse. Still others found us so patently absurd that they performed mocking impersonations of us to each other, finding, in our various anatomical and intellectual characteristics, an endless source of jokes and snickering parody. Listening to this latter group (as I was forced to do on several occasions) was a particularly degrading experience; hearing such things said about one's own race, one could not help but to feel a certain loss of basic dignity — a kind of debased self-loathing which one intuitively extended to include the entire human tribe. Overhearing such commentary, one could easily get the impression that humanity was the laughing stock of the universe.

Everything I learned from these conversations only deepened my despair. They confirmed that the hidden watchers were not unlike the soldiers in a colonial army; restless, bored, impatiently awaiting the command to exterminate the natives.

The details of this period remain hazy and painful. I recall that, as autumn descended upon the landscape, I soon fell ill, eating almost twice my usual portions at mealtime, and sleeping for abnormally long periods. I became increasingly aware of a persistent, low-grade fever which quickened my pulse and caused me to sweat profusely. At one point, when these symptoms threatened to overwhelm me, I spent several days sleeping in a crawlspace beneath a gigantic house-sized boulder on the southern slope of Mt. Greylock. Another curious side effect of this fever was that I was able to walk for exceptionally long periods through frigid windstorms (and even driving rain) experiencing none of the discomfort one would expect under such circumstances. Nevertheless, I was also hallucinating badly at this time, slipping in and out of delirium and still quite thunderstruck by the things I had overheard.

Thou ancient oak! Whose myriad leaves are loud
with unintelligible speech,
Sounds as of surges on a shingly beach,
Or multitudinous murmurs of a crowd ;
With some mysterious gift of tongues endowed,
Thou speakest a different dialect to each ;
To me a language that no man can teach,
Of a lost race, long vanished like a cloud...

Henry Wadsworth Longfellow

X

IT MUST HAVE BEEN SOMETIME IN EARLY OCTOBER THAT I finally stumbled, lean and hungry, out of the woods west of Cambridge, Massachusetts and, composing myself as best I could, I entered the city on foot, with a plan to visit the library at Harvard. In the center of town, I procure a cheap room on the third floor of a rundown motel where, collapsing immediately upon the bed, I slept for nearly 24 hours. Upon waking, I felt surprisingly refreshed and, strangely eager to be among ordinary human beings. I walked, in a kind of fascination, to the nearby market where I purchased several days' worth of food. With this portable feast of fresh vegetables, bread, dried fruits, and assorted nuts, I returned to my room and carefully stowed these items into my backpack. After a quick meal, I set out for the Harvard campus.

As I entered Cambridge, I was increasingly struck by the obvious wealth and pretensions of the college town inhabitants. One can always tell when one has entered the wealthy part of any city. The general tidiness, the complete absence of bums, the increasingly grandiose structures, the arrogant, self-important bearing of the passersby... These things looked a thousand times more ludicrous to me now, when measured against what I knew to be the likely outcome of human civilization and, if not for the disastrous calamities which frequently resulted from their dubious academic achievements, I could almost have pitied their naiveté.

Threading past, I made my way through the famous College-yard (where, in 1701, angry students burned copies of Cotton *Mather's Wonders of the Invisible World*) and, entering the library through a side door, went to the newspaper archives. My initial motivation here had been to research the recent history and folklore of the Catskill Range, with the hopes of finding some clues which might confirm my suspicions.

Inquiries along these lines however, while tantalizingly suggestive, remained ultimately inconclusive. The recent history of the Catskills, as documented by the local newspapers, proved unenlightening and, aside from a few references to missing persons and mentions of the frequent and unusually intense lightning storms, I discovered nothing of use. I pressed on, redirecting my search towards the older Indian legends, as collected by such people as Washington Irving and the Dutch settlers of the previous century.

Most of these legends, while quaint and not without a certain old-world charm, were clearly of the fantastic type, Henry Hudson's description of an encounter with a race of stunted, waist-high pygmies, in the mountains near Albany, being a classic example of the more whimsical type. But there were certain other stories (or episodes within these stories) which were eerily reminiscent of the larger nightmare which was unfolding before me.

In the journal of one Mrs. Rutherford, written in the last century, the author chronicles a curious set of legends pertaining to that vast marshland in the Catskills which early Dutch settlers called the Gröt Vly (meaning Great Flat). This expanse was reputed to be the home of an ancient Indian Demon, whose glowing eyes were sometimes glimpsed floating by the water's edge. It was said to feed exclusively upon the flesh of females, reaching its long, flexible arm up out of the bog and snatching its unwary victims into the water. Mrs Rutherford wrote, in the spirit of a helpful warning, "On certain nights of the year (the Demon) was wont to rise up from his watery bed, and woe to the luckless woman, beloved of man, who might be wandering nearby."

In a similar document entitled "The Land of Rip Van Winkle" by A.E.P. Searling, the author transcribed the frightful legend of the unfortunate Iroquois sisters who, having wandered too far from their village one night, became hopelessly lost in the vicinity of Overlook Mountain. Having laid down to sleep alongside her elder sister in the forest, the younger girl was awakened a short time later by the sounds of chewing and crunching. Slowly turning her head, she was horrified to see her sister being devoured by what she would later describe as a strange vampyre-like being, a large cannibalistic humanoid who had torn open the elder sister's face and chest and hungrily devoured their contents. The Iroquois, as I soon learned, have long considered Overlook Mountain (as well as several of its neighbors) to be "infested with Vampyres" and taboos against visiting these places after dark are common.

Similarly suggestive amongst these Catskill legends were the stories told to the Dutch settlers by the Iroquois and Seneca tribes, stories of the wandering stone giants whom they called Jokao (or Stonecoats), man-eating trolls who haunted the mountains of central New York. These ghoulish descriptions find their counterpart in certain stories told by the Inuit of Hudson Bay, Canada, who tell similar tales of lurking monsters known to them as the brain-eating Tammatuyuq. Simultaneously intrigued and unnerved by these anecdotes, I decided to expand the scope of my researches and to make a more generalized inquiry along these lines.

Sequestering myself in an alcove with the appropriate books and papers, I spent a total of six hours scanning everything from textbooks, reference books, and historical documents, to numerous local and foreign periodicals. Among the countless articles I read, four or five stories in particular seemed to speak directly to my developing theory of what was happening to me.

*   *   *   *

AFTER LEARNING ALL I COULD ABOUT THE MYTHS AND LEGENDS OF THE Catskills, I resumed my earlier search for cannibal-giant legends in the various bestiaries and encyclopedias of anthropology. I was not disappointed. In fact, due to the ponderous number of legends I found which involved a hidden race of deformed cannibalistic giants, I was strongly encouraged to infer the very worst. In Venezuela they were called Ewaipanoma, headless men with eyes and mouths on their chests. The ancient Greeks, having encountered them in the desert wastes of Libya, called them Acephalos, just as Howard had said. In China they are known as Hsing-T'ien, ancient humanoids who had risen up against the gods in the legendary Battle of Mu, only to be decapitated and made to roam forever the waste places of the earth. English folklore is similarly rife with stories of the Anthropophagi, the Eaters of Men, pale-skinned ogres who lurk in swamps and bogs.

The largest concentration of these corresponding myths occurred in Central and South America. From the smallest cannibal tribes up to the highest echelons of the Inca and Mayan Empires, legends of this same type can be found. Ancient mythographers (as well as modern anthropologists) have done fascinating work in documenting the many interweaving myth-cycles of the countless Amazon tribes, many of whom they claim are practitioners of ritualized cannibalism. I immersed myself in these many diverse sets of legends for several hours. Without repeating those I have already mentioned, I would direct my readers to research the legends of the Brazilian Tupari tribe, which describe the dreaded Aunyaina, or else, the folk beliefs throughout Argentina and Chile, which detail the origins and hunting techniques of the awful, man-eating Cherufe.

I discovered another uncanny pattern in these legends: many of these cannibal creatures known throughout Amazonia were also associated with a certain water-dwelling creature of indeterminate shape, but with a pronounced appetite for human meat. These water creatures included the legendary Glyryvilu, the Vulpangue, and the Hide (or Manta), all of them shape-shifting aquatic monsters known throughout Chile, Peru, and Brazil. So great is the terror inspired by these creatures that, in areas where they are suspected to exist, local people will not wash, bathe, or even permit their fingers to break the surface of the water.

The most frighteningly complete of all these overlapping Amazon myths was the surprisingly gory legends of the Araucanian tribes in northern Chile. More than any other legend, these seemed to touch upon the hideous totality implied by my patchwork understanding. The Chivato, or more commonly, the Encerrados (meaning recluses or prisoners) were a race of beings who, while directly associated with both the cannibal-giants and the man-eating river blobs, remained distinct from them in several key ways. These remarkable beings are mentioned in a prospecting report from the late-nineteenth century written by a surveyor prospecting possible mining operations in the mountains of northern Chile. Two of these cannibal Encerrados were found trapped and starving in a cave by the author himself. He described the creatures as gaunt, malformed hunchbacks, with skin as white as milk and mouths overflowing with great curving teeth. Large numbers of these creatures were said to inhabit the infamous Caves of Salamanca and also those shunned caverns which are called Quicavi, between the towns of Chiloe and Ancud in central Chile. Further investigations revealed a bizarre system of ancient legends which elaborated the sinister origins and purpose of these unfortunate beings.

These legends told that the Encerrados were human children who had been abducted from their homes by wandering witches who prowled the mountains. These stolen children were then taken up to the stony peaks where they were blinded, mutilated, and locked away for many years deep within the mountain, in dank, subterranean pits. Here their eyes and ears were sewn shut, so that their other senses would develop to an unnatural sharpness. They were also fed a mixture of human and goat meat, and made to participate in gruesome demonic rituals; over time, they metamorphosed into hunch-backed cannibal homunculi. As was the case with the cannibals, the Encerrados were usually mentioned in association with a huge, water-dwelling monster known variously as the Invunche, or as the smaller, but much more deadly, Trelquehuecuve (which some shamans believed were only a disembodied extension of a much larger Invunche probably hiding nearby). Both are described as a flat, extended skin, spread upon the surface of the water like the hide of an enormous animal, with eyes and great flexible claw-like appendages all around its perimeter. Luring its victims down to the water's edge, the Trelquehuecuve was said to leap out and grab unwary humans, dragging them down into a whirlpool, where it wrapped itself around their bodies and digested them. Other legends describe how the Invunche does not even need to leave its lair to hunt; from afar, it is able to cast a glamour of curiosity over its intended victims, causing them to swim down to their doom in the tunnels beneath the lake.

I could not help but think that all of this bore a more than passing resemblance to the central themes and creatures of the Tiwanaku Creation Myth; a great liquid monstrosity nesting in a vast underwater cave beneath a mighty lake or river, with quasi-human minions upon the land, frightful humunculoid beings who worshipped this shape-shifting creature as a god, and made frequent sacrifices to it. It was not just the similarity of these mythic narratives that unnerved me, but the eerie number of parallels between the dreaded Encerrados and my own increasingly bizarre plight.

*　*　*　*

AFTER THESE STRANGELY EVOCATIVE INQUIRIES INTO OBSCURE myths, I decided to read several contemporary newspapers and journals, to catch up on current events and to pull my head out of the ancient past and into the present century. News of my bombing was all over the papers, and, within the subtext of these dramatic and sensational accounts, I could easily discern the implicit rationale for a police state. This did not come as a surprise to me; I knew that any retaliatory violence on the part of the workers would always be used as the justification for more police violence. The hammer of repression was coming down one way or another, but the bombings removed all subtlety from this process. The crackdown, of course, had been well underway for years and included the deportation of huge numbers of people whom they labeled "undesirable aliens."

Elsewhere in these same papers, I encountered two other stories which seemed oddly connected to my investigations. The first of these recent articles, I found in the *British Daily Mail*, where I learned of the famous English explorer Percy Fawcett, who was currently on expedition in the Amazon, in pursuit of a legendary lost city. This lost city had come to him in a dream he said, compelling him to make a lifelong career (one might say obsession) to find it and reveal it to the world. Many times he had traversed the obscure corners of the Amazon, claiming to have met large numbers of savage Indios who confirmed his notion of a lost city, buried somewhere in the unexplored backwaters of the Brazilian and Peruvian interior. Certain cannibal shamans even claimed to have visited the ruins themselves, saying they were all that remained of a once mighty civilization which had been abandoned in ancient times and subsequently been reclaimed by the all-consuming jungle. Exactly when and where this lost civilization was supposed to have flourished Fawcett was never able to determine, though he continued to collect tantalizing legends of a megalithic plaza with structures, free-standing archways, corridors with niched walls, and god knows what else. It could be reached, the Indios said, by an intrepid group of explorers, should they be able to secure a willing guide. But, as with the expedition to Machu Picchu, this business of finding a reliable guide had proved an utter impossibility. Notoriously jealous of Bingham's discovery of Machu Picchu, Fawcett (along with his son, Jack, and a colleague by the name of Raleigh Rimell) had set out to hike the unexplored upper Xingu River, an obscure backwater of the Amazon, in an area inhabited by several much-feared cannibal tribes, and sending back harrowing but optimistic reports to the press back home.

Diving into the archives of the *New York World,* the *Los Angeles Times,* and several others, I read these reports with great interest, struck by a certain parallelism between Fawcett's plight and my own. These accounts so moved me that, several times, I paused in my reading and contemplated making a journey to South America myself, both to visit Machu Picchu and to begin my own search for the ruins that Fawcett's hypothesis suggested. I suppose some part of me wondered if I wouldn't have better luck finding these lost ruins than some of my less-informed and less-intuitive predecessors. But these same articles also sometimes made ominous references to other white men (surprisingly numerous) who, possessed by mad dreams of a lost city and the gold it contained, had marched into these same jungles only to emerge, months or years later, empty handed, starving, riddled with parasites, and half-insane. If they emerged at all. A distressingly high number of these intrepid souls (Carvajal's four thousand men, Lope de Aguirre, Francisco de Orellana) were never seen alive again. Curiously, it was a frequently added footnote that these lost parties, in their intense privation, had sometimes resorted to cannibalism before finally succumbing to death by pestilence, parasites, or starvation. Though the particulars of this cannibalism were never stated, I felt I could hazard a few informed guesses with regards to which organs had been eaten and the effect they had had upon the men.

Unfortunately, Fawcett was decidedly short on money, as were his more enthusiastic supporters. At one point, he had even considered starting a mining business as a way to raise funds for his expeditions but, after doing some research on the mining industry, and the Rockefeller stranglehold, he concluded that the entire industry had been hijacked by "a nest of crooks," and he abandoned the idea.

The second set of articles I read were on the developing situation in Russia which, by the autumn of 1919, also seemed imbued with a kind of prophetic significance. The revolutionary situation, which had at first held so much promise, was rapidly degenerating into a Bolshevik power grab. Lenin, spouting ideas and rhetoric of a decidedly anti-statist type, had ridden a wave of popular support, until at long last he had maneuvered himself into a position where he was able to implement his true agenda. Despite hundreds of speeches and essays pontificating fairly convincingly about the dangers of large-scale, top-down government, he had turned around and implemented a modified version of the very system he had helped destroy. Once the political apparatus had come within his reach, he reversed his program of independent workers' unions into one of rationalization and State ownership of production. He and his minions simply replaced the despots which the revolution had ousted. The Bolshevik regime implemented the "statization" of all industry, refusing to recognize any union not directly affiliated and managed by the central government and immediately crushing, one by one, all who resisted this process. At this time, Lenin had sent his most loyal lapdog, Leon Trotsky, to exterminate whatever pockets of resistance he encountered in the countryside. There had been many triumphant moments here, including the brilliantly successful raids of the Mahknovists, but the overall picture in Russia remained grim.

Meanwhile, in the letters sections of countless scientific journals, debate continued to rage regarding the ruins at Machu Picchu. What had been the true purpose of this unusual complex of buildings? Some claimed it was a proper city, while others said it was a royal palace or retreat. Still others argued that it was an observatory, built for viewing the heavens and the surrounding landscape. To support this view they explained how the Incas believed that the creator god Viracocha had sculpted the mountains into particular shapes which communicated messages and even prophecies to those priests keen enough to discern them. Some claimed that the religious overtones in the architecture suggested that it had been some sort of monastery built in honor of Inti, the Sun God. The large number of young skeletons with deformed craniums, recently found in a subterranean vault, led to the wildest speculations.

With my inferior knowledge on these topics I was unable to determine which of these theories seemed most probable, yet I read them all with great interest, recalling also the things Howard had said about the Inca being astronomers, and inferring what I could from the various texts. Nevertheless, certain questions continued to haunt me. If, as some have suggested, Machu Picchu was a royal estate then why should so much religious activity be occurring in a place where hunting, debauching, and other leisure activities should have been the primary pastimes? The predominantly religious overtones of the ruins suggested some sort of astral cult, yet the specifics of this worship seemed destined to remain a mystery.

I found several picture books (filled with photographs of the Machu Picchu ruins taken from numerous angles) which had a rather shocking and curious effect on me. Staring at these photographs, uninterrupted, for long stretches, I found that I possessed the ability almost to enter into them, in a disembodied way, and to inhabit and explore the scenes they depicted. It was during the course of these bizarre "explorations" that I began to notice certain other curiosities which seemed vaguely suggestive of hideous things. I saw that there were little waterways chiseled into the masonry all over Machu Picchu, a series of communicating troughs and pools which enabled some unknown fluid to spread itself throughout the complex. As I stared into these photographs, strange shapes began to flicker before my eyes. I saw flashes of scenes which corresponded to the stone palace in the photos, though in my visions it swarmed with tiny human figures, leaping and moving about as if in wild celebration. In some places there were the large gazing pools which the photographs had shown as empty, but which now appeared full to the rim with a heaving, black, jelly-like substance. The Inca cultists who ventured near enough to these black pools seemed to receive curious mental enhancements for doing so, creeping forward in dread anticipation and then suddenly stumbling backwards, as if astonished or amazed by some hallucination or new addition to their ability to perceive. These visions, like the dreams of the previous winter, were so vivid and unforgettable that I did not doubt, for one minute, their authenticity.

Lastly, with regard to the many murders which I had committed, I searched and found only bland obituaries and unconnected notifications. In the case of the very wealthy victims, such as senators and governors, the deaths were invariably assigned to natural causes, while my less prestigious victims were usually considered to be missing persons. I found no references to mass mobilizations of police or warnings of a killer on the loose, nor anything of the kind — just understated acknowledgments that investigations into those few disappearances would be on-going, with the usual vague assurances of eventual success.

I would have stayed in the Harvard Library and read more but, as the afternoon had progressed, a peculiar feeling had come over me and I could no longer dispel the notion that certain people were staring at me. I left, vowing to resume these studies elsewhere at the soonest possible opportunity.

*   *   *   *

IT WAS JUST ABOUT SUNSET WHEN I EXITED THE HARVARD LIBRARY. Returning to my quiet room, I made myself a meal of bread, fruit, and a cup of Russian tea, which I heated over a candle. After this small meal, I lay upon the bed and, still dazed from all I had read, soon dropped off to sleep. I had been asleep for what seemed only a short time when I was suddenly awakened by the sound of shouting in the street below my window. By the time I made it over to the casement the commotion had passed, but I stood there transfixed for a moment, still half asleep, and gazing out at the view of the city.

Before me was a sea of crooked, lamp-lit rooftops and chimneypots, a million golden windows floating in a black void, trembling with internal shadows and rolling away toward the harbor, beneath a lowering sky of purple and black clouds. Across the river I could see the twinkling lights of Beacon Hill and, farther east, the spires of downtown Boston, dramatically lit against the starry darkness that seemed to pour up out of the sea like smoke.

I stood contemplating the lights of Boston and my thoughts drifted once again back to the conversation I'd had with Howard's mother, wherein she had warned me that my offspring would eventually leave me to find the nearest portal. Recalling how the Black Thing (as soon as it was capable of coordinated ambulation) had cut an unswervingly straight path toward the city of Boston, I wondered if it was not, therefore, logical to infer that the "nearest portal" might lay somewhere within that city, or possibly beneath it. With this in mind, I decided to walk down to the Cambridge Bridge (awkwardly named, but no less picturesque) to make a tentative exploration of downtown Boston.

I set out from my room with a half-formed plan to enter a crowded bar or café, to see if I could catch the latest gossip on the street and to listen for any rumors of brainless, mutilated corpses turning up in parks, alleys, or sewer drains. As I walked along the cobbled stonework of the bridge, occasionally gazing down into the swirling darkness of the river, I wondered what sort of strange phenomena might indicate the presence of a hidden portal. Was there, for example, some alley or park, some street or abandoned building, where a disproportionately large number of people had gone missing? Might such a location perhaps even have a local reputation as being haunted?

Before I had even formed these many divergent thoughts into some kind of cogent plan, I suddenly stopped, frozen to the spot by an overwhelming presentiment of extreme danger emanating from the maze of streets directly ahead of me. All other thoughts wiped from my mind, I knew by some irrepressible intuition, that before me, somewhere in the city of Boston, some great incomprehensible Horror was afoot, lurking stealthily through the byways of the great port city and holding its inhabitants under a spell of abject terror.

The chill winds that came rushing up Cambridge Street were perfumed with the unmistakable scent of raw human fear and herd panic. From various points on the horizon, there came to me the sounds of numerous overlapping police sirens, accompanied by a subtle but steady rumbling sound, as if some fantastically huge engine were idling nearby, unseen but deeply felt, and causing the very air to throb grotesquely. Beyond the oddly deserted neighborhood of Beacon Hill, the city of Boston itself seemed to shudder, as if in terror of some pervasive impending holocaust, the unspoken horror of its uncomprehending citizens accumulating and combining to form a dense, cloud-like miasma which, at times, was so strong that it nearly made me gag. The sidewalks along Cambridge Street and Embankment Road were practically deserted and, if not for the occasional pedestrian and automobile, I might have thought that martial law had been declared. Arriving, a moment later, on the Boston side, I turned right down Embankment Road, where, following the river, I made my way south. Peering down the side streets as I went, I began to glimpse groups of roaming soldiers, walking in twos and threes bearing rifles and fixed bayonets, stopping everyone they encountered and asking them their names and addresses.

I walked by an open window, where I paused to listen as two voices, raised in anger and fear, repeatedly made cryptic references to "the terrible situation," "that awful violence," and bickering over some unnamed and sinister "They." Recalling the things Bartolo had told me about the vicious attacks against the unarmed May Day marchers by persons unknown, I wondered what fresh horrors had been visited upon the weary populace of this strangely cursed city.

Turning south onto Storrow Drive, I pulled my hat down low over my eyes and, using my enhanced senses to track and evade the patrols, stepped into a tree-lined park which followed the shore of the river. Utilizing the trees as cover, I found an unlit footpath, whereby I was able to enter downtown Boston unobserved and unmolested. I turned left onto Berkeley Street where I cautiously made my way toward the crowded center of town. Reassured somewhat by the increasing number of seemingly unconcerned people strolling along the sidewalks, I turned onto yet another crowded thoroughfare and began searching for a pub or café where I might strike up a conversation with a talkative local.

On that starry autumn evening, in the fear-choked atmosphere of that soldier-infested city, I was walking south along St. James Street, when who should I see loping towards me up the pavement but my old friend Howard from Providence! He was scowling as he threaded a meandering course through the polyglot crowd, several times looking askance at a group of Polynesian fishermen who were loitering outside an intensely odorous fish market across the street. Upon seeing me, his face lit up, and, shaking his large head in disbelief, he came lurching toward me with an enormous smile.

"Well look who it is!" he cried, as he gripped my outstretched hand in both of his. "E.T.A. Hoffman. I have been hoping against hope that I would run into you these past few weeks! How strange that we should cross paths here in Boston. It is good to see you!"

"Yes, it is good to see you too," I said with a grin. "And, please, call me Robert. How did you enjoy those Nietzsche books I gave you?"

"Fascinating!" he shot back, nodding his head. "Quite fascinating! Mind you, I don't swallow him whole. His system of ethics, for example, is a joke."

"Well," I replied with a chuckle, "Show me a system of ethics that isn't a joke and I'll show you a..." but he cut me off with a wave of his hand.

"No time for philosophizing, Robert. We can disagree about Nietzsche later. Come. Walk with me! Lord Dunsany is speaking in twenty minutes at the Copley Plaza Ballroom and we have an extra ticket! Please say you'll come? I'm here with some friends and fellow writers. We arrived early and obtained front row seats! During the address we will be sitting directly opposite the speaker, not ten feet from him! The man is a genius and besides, we can talk afterwards, when the others have gone — I have so very much to tell you!"

He put a peculiar emphasis on this last part, so that a thrill of nameless apprehension shot through me.

"I wish I could, Howard," I said. "Honestly I do. But I am caught up in a very strange and sinister adventure of my own, and one I simply must see through to the end!"

A look of keen, almost wolfish, interest animated his features, as if, at long last, he hoped we might dispense with the formalities and get down to brass tacks.

"Oh no," I said in response to this look. "To tell you anything about it now would be to risk endangering us both. But someday, my friend, when I finally understand it all myself, I promise I shall visit you in Providence and tell you everything. Tonight, however, we haven't the time for such things. But please," I indicated the street before us, "I can walk with you as far as Copley Plaza! I've only just arrived in Boston and I was hoping to find someone who could tell me what the hell has happened here. I've never seen so many soldiers in my life! It's like the Devil himself has come to Boston."

"Can it be that you haven't heard?" Howard said, astonished.

"Heard what?" I replied.

"My goodness, man!" Howard chuckled loudly. "Have you been living under a rock?"

My reader will understand the shudder that passed through me when, upon consideration, I realized that, in fact, yes, I had, for a time, been living under a rock! Howard and I had not been reunited three minutes and, already, he was up to his old tricks again, displaying that eerie unconscious knowledge of me and my doings.

"Maybe I have!" I said defensively.

"Never mind, Robert," he said impatiently, "it's just a figure of speech. I apologize if I have offended you. It's just that... it's all over the papers! The Bolsheviks are trying to take over Boston! It started with the policemen's strike last month." Looking off into space, he said, almost to himself, "Who would have dreamed that the Reds had infiltrated the police force so completely? They attempted to initiate their pathetic *coup d'etat* by going on strike last month. I believe they were hoping for a repeat of the General Strike that happened in Seattle, only, this time, with no police to restore order!"

"Really?" I said. "That's fascinating. What makes you think that the police strike was a Bolshevik conspiracy?"

"Well, they certainly waited until the worst possible moment to abandon their posts," he continued, "what with the immigrant hordes pouring into the city like vermin, infecting the young and the gullible with their poisonous anarchistic philosophies!"

"Now wait a minute. What were these striking policemen demanding?" I asked.

"Oh, I don't know. I don't see that it matters. In times of civil unrest such as these, a police strike is unforgivable. President Wilson has called it 'a crime against civilization' and, for once, I'm inclined to agree with him!"

"Is that what's got everybody up in arms?" I asked.

"I should say so!" Howard replied with severity, "Can you imagine this city without policemen? Thank god the State Guard arrived when they did."

"Why? What happened during the police strike?" I asked.

"The city was paralyzed, that's what happened! Hooligans were running rampant! 'When the cat's away, the rats will play.' There was thieving and purse-snatching and heaven knows what else!"

"Sounds like a typical night in South Boston to me," I said.

"No, no, this was worse. There was some sort of disturbance in Scollay Square which triggered a riot! Nine people were killed!"

"My god! That's terrible!" I said, suddenly feeling nervous. "What killed them?"

"It is difficult to say." Howard mused, "Details are very murky. It was a riot after all!"

"How many of the nine people were killed by rioters?" I asked.

"None!" Howard proudly asserted, "They never gave them the chance."

"Who?" I asked. "The State Guard?" Howard shrugged with a smile. "So it was the soldiers, not the rioters, who killed nine people?" I asked.

"Details are murky," was his annoyed reply. "Nobody knows for sure who or what killed those rioters."

This statement seemed intentionally cryptic to me, conjuring up very unpleasant mental images of my offspring squaring off with an angry mob on the streets of Boston. Then, admittedly anxious to absolve my Black Thing of the nine deaths and without quite knowing what I was saying, I asked, "What sort of shape were the bodies in?"

This pseudo-casual inquiry stopped Howard in his tracks and, raising his eyebrows in a smirk, he stared knowingly into my eyes, as if he had caught me in a lie.

"Well now, that's a strange question," he said. "Why on earth would you care about that?"

"Sorry," I blurted. "I don't mean to be morbid. I just…"

"You just what?"

"I just wondered if they had been… dismembered or mutilated in any way. A friend of mine said that soldiers and vigilante mobs were running around with clubs, crippling people. I have a horror of lynch mobs and I don't like soldiers or cops."

"Why don't you like soldiers and cops?" He seemed genuinely astonished. "They may just be the only thing standing between us and total anarchy!"

"Well now, there's a thought," I replied with a queasy grin.

Wincing and tapping his impressive chin, he thought for a moment.

"You can't mean that, Robert! You can't tell me you don't feel safer with those soldiers around."

"On the contrary, my friend. I trust them less than the street thugs."

"Dear me!" Howard gasped. "You're not an anarchist are you?" He could scarcely bring himself to say the awful word aloud.

"I lack the proper labels adequate to describe what I am, Howard. But people who think as I do are often the ones found dead or missing during these so-called riots."

"Very well," he said with a shrug. "To answer your question about the bodies in Scollay Square, apart from bullet holes which someone rightfully inflicted upon them, I believe the corpses were essentially intact."

Breathing a sigh of relief, I quickly steered the conversation to other matters and we resumed our walk.

"What happened with the strike?" I asked. "I mean afterwards."

"The police department has refused to re-hire the mutinous policemen and is currently hiring on a whole new force and implementing all the things the strikers had demanded. Frankly, I don't see what else they could have done. America must purge her institutions of these Bolshevik influences or suffer the fate of the Russian aristocracy!"

Noting, once again, how diametrically opposed our perspectives were, I decided not to argue. Howard's politics were, after all, largely irrelevant to me, though I did wonder how this difference in outlook might play itself out in future interactions. More to the point, would a man of Howard's convictions feel compelled to report someone like me to the authorities? I had numerous reasons to believe that the answer would be a resounding "yes!" And yet, it was more complicated than that. For there was something underneath Howard's reactionary perspective which seemed to transcend all earthly politics. Despite the calmly rational words that came out of his mouth, Howard's eyes seemed to gaze unflinchingly into the rotting, shrieking soul of civilization itself. He was too keenly alive to the stunted and degraded condition of domesticated humanity not to recoil, in a general way, from the horror show that is the human zoo of modern society. The horror of the centuries seemed somehow reflected in those bulging and sincere eyes; I had the impression of Howard as being the sort of man who, having ventured too far into some arcane inner abyss, had glimpsed something that had changed him forever, a mind made cosmic by some unforgettable brush with infinity, an experience which had permanently attuned it to the subtler frequencies of its animal existence.

On the other hand, Howard's clearly stated admiration for the soldiers and the policemen put me on my guard, and I silently made a pact within myself to speak in a guarded way about my philosophy as well as all other delicate matters. Nevertheless, I also understood that, should Howard have some latent, half-realized ability to see into my thoughts (as I suspected he did), all attempts at verbal concealment would be utterly useless.

I was just about to ask about his mother when I saw that we were standing before the glass doors of a massive, pillar-flanked entranceway, leading into the foyer of a truly impressive luxury hotel.

Turning to me, Howard pulled a ticket out of his breast pocket and offering it to me, said, "Well, Robert, here we are — Copley Plaza Ballroom. This is my final offer. I do hope you will accept it."

Suddenly, there was a lump in my throat. The thought of sitting in the front row of a well-lit lecture hall and being introduced, one by one, to Howard's smiling friends utterly terrified me. But I also knew that I could ill afford to miss the opportunity to hear whatever it was that Howard was so eager to tell me. Deciding (rather suddenly) that I had no desire to part ways with Howard, I reconsidered my options for the evening. If nothing else, I reasoned, sitting through the lecture would give me the chance to rest my weary legs before resuming the search for my offspring and the hidden portal. Perhaps after his friends left, I might even be able to persuade Howard to accompany me on my explorations.

"Alright," I said, "I'll accept your invitation under one condition. I will sit off by myself, in case I have to get up for any reason. I don't do well with large crowds. They make me nervous."

"Very well," Howard said. "Do you want to meet my friends afterward? They are some wonderfully talented people. I'm sure you would love them!"

"Thank you, but no. I'm afraid I'm a little out of sorts just now and I don't feel much like socializing. Could I just meet up with you later, perhaps, after they have gone?" Smiling, as if in sympathetic understanding, Howard nodded his enormous head.

"Alright then," he said. "My friends and I were going to part ways shortly afterward anyway. I'll meet you here by this pillar after I've said my goodbyes to them." I nodded.

Accepting his proffered ticket, I followed a grinning Howard into the ballroom where I immediately set out to find myself a seat near the back. The event was very well attended; empty chairs were hard to come by, but, taking my seat near the aisle in the rearmost row, I kept my eyes upon the floor directly in front of me, carefully avoiding the gaze of the other attendees.

As it turned out, Dunsany arrived late, taking the stage nearly half an hour behind schedule. Edward Plunkett, 18th Baron of Dunsany, is a rather peculiar looking man; standing a little over six feet tall, he is quite slender, with fair and pleasing features, though somewhat boyish and a touch awkward. His voice is calm and cultivated, with an Irish-British accent that has a certain charm. Addressing the crowd with good humor, he first touched upon his ideals and methods of storytelling and writing. Seating himself at his reading table, he commenced to narrate a short play of his own entitled "The Queen's Enemies" which was clearly based upon the anecdote of Queen Nitocris in the second book of Herodotus. After this, Dunsany read selections from several other works of his but, I confess I heard very little of the second half of this lecture.

As the evening had wore on, I had begun to get the curious mental impression (faint at first but with increasing intensity) that somewhere beneath the streets immediately outside the lecture hall, there was some sort of subtle seismic activity going on — a series of faint migrating convulsions that seemed to be concentrating themselves in the immediate neighborhood around Copley Plaza. I was just considering the implications of this when the room suddenly exploded with the roar of deafening applause and, as Dunsany bowed before a standing ovation, I began to scan the walls and ceiling for cracks. Looking up, I saw that several of the chandeliers were swaying. I began to pick my way through the crowd, moving towards the exit as quickly as possible.

Looking back over my shoulder, I saw that Dunsany, who had come down to the front row to meet his fans, was now swarmed by well-wishers and autograph-seekers. Among these swarming fans I glimpsed Howard standing with two women, a younger and an elder, the younger of whom seemed determined to get an autograph. Stepping out into the cool night air, I took up my position near the pillar, casting long searching glances along the pavement and tracking as best I could, the queer rumblings from below. Twice they seemed to pass within twenty or thirty feet of me though, try as I might, I could not expand my senses enough to pentrate the grey stone road.

It was nearly half an hour before the three finally emerged and, after saying goodnight and seeing the two women off into a hansom cab, Howard at last turned and walked back to where I stood waiting.

"Did you get an autograph, Howard?" I asked.

"Heavens no!" he declared with undisguised contempt. "It was my young friend who wanted one. Personally I detest fawning upon the great!"

"Shall we attempt to lose this crowd?" I asked indicating the bustling street before us.

"Yes, let's," he replied, sneering at the dwindling crowd, "so that we may speak freely, without fear of eavesdroppers."

XI

AFTER SEVERAL MINUTES OF WALKING ALONG THE CROWDED thoroughfare, Howard and I entered the noticeably less populated streets which I had passed through earlier. As we walked and the crowd thinned to a steady trickle, Howard's contemptuous expression gave way to one of diabolical eagerness. Taking me by the arm, my odd friend led me along the darkened avenues, intuitively avoiding the roaming soldiers as he threaded a course through the labyrinthine streets. For several minutes we trod the darkened sidewalk without speaking, while I threw long ponderous glances into the shadowy byways, looking, listening, and feeling for any abnormalities or distortions which might betray the presence of a portal. After this period of silent walking, during which Howard seemed to be deciding how best to express his thoughts, he finally spoke.

"I am experiencing certain... augmentations, Robert," he said in a low voice, "certain... enhancements! And devilishly strange enhancements, I can tell you... but marvelous too! Absolutely fantastic!"

I looked at him sideways.

"I'm afraid I don't know what you mean," I lied calmly.

"It's absolutely uncanny," he said in a hushed voice, pointing down at the sidewalk. "You'll think I'm mad but, look there: if I focus all my attention on it, I can actually hear that centipede crawling along the pavement ahead of us! And, what is more, if I shut my eyes very tightly, I can almost glimpse this street, these mountainous buildings, from it's tiny perspective... as if I was somehow seeing it all through it's eyes!"

"What centipede?" I asked, feigning ignorance of the tiny creature whose presence I had been aware of all along.

"That one," he said, opening his eyes and pointing his finger, whereupon I stooped and looked down upon the tiny being that was moving along the rim of a great cavernous crack in the sidewalk.

"Aha," I said, somewhat theatrically. "There's the little fellow."

"Actually, she is female," he corrected. "The females give off an unmistakably sweet odor."

154

"Well," I said disconcertedly, "I suppose I will have to take your word on that score." This was entirely true; despite sniffing the air several times, even with my enhanced sense of smell, I remained unable to determine the gender of the tiny being before me.

"I'm telling you, Robert," he continued, "all of my faculties have been awakened! Not merely awakened but, somehow heightened to something like four or five times their usual sensitivity! Why, just by smelling the air, I can tell you what most of these people had for lunch today. That man there had potato soup and beer and that fellow there had pastrami, bread, and cheese. I can tell you which of these women are fertile and which are menstruating. That woman over there resting on the bench is... oh... about ten days pregnant and that poor chap over by the hansom cab has got tuberculosis. You see that well-dressed man over there carrying those bags of groceries?"

Again I looked where he was pointing and saw, not only the broad shouldered man with a bag in each arm, but a faint, vaporous, monochrome shadow, or halo, that seemed to shimmer all around him, trailing behind him like a thin smoke and giving off, as I now detected, a subtle yet insidious metallic odor. I had never seen anything like it before and, startled out of my caution, I committed my second blunder of the evening.

"What is that... thing attached to him?" I asked.

"Aha! So you can see it!" he gloated. "Just as I suspected. Excellent, excellent." Squinting at the broad shouldered man, he said, "As for our monochrome friend here, I believe it is the typhoid virus, or else something damnably like the typhoid virus. Interesting how the man himself seems to display no symptoms whatsoever."

Then, as we watched this figure cross the plaza and enter a restaurant, he raised his head to the sky and inadvertently sneezed into one of the bags of groceries.

"Dear god! Did you see that?" I asked, suppressing a shudder. But Howard, rolling his eyes, only shrugged and continued to pull me up the street by my arm.

"I can see other things too, Robert," he continued. "Uncanny things that no normal human eye should be able to see!"

"You mean like that man's disease?" I asked.

A faraway look came into his eyes and he looked into the air above our heads and inhaled deeply. I watched as his gaze began to drift, this way and that through the empty air, like a man standing before an enormous aquarium full of sharks. His face looked tight, as if making a great effort to keep his emotions in check. Smiling, he turned back to me and, pointing to the northern horizon. He said, "No, I mean things like those birds roosting there upon that old clock tower. They are rock doves and there are seven of them."

I could see the clock tower of the Custom House, located nearly halfway across town, but quite visible, standing out clear and sharp against the night sky. It had to be almost a mile away, though it was close enough for my enhanced vision to confirm the truth of his statement.

Howard seemed on the verge of saying something but I held up a finger to stop him and, still puzzling over the eerie way he had peered into the sky, I decided to put him on the spot. "What where you looking at just now Howard? Before the birds on the clock tower."

A grim determination came over his features. His jaw set and his brow furrowed strangely. He fell silent and, avoiding my eyes, he subtly increased the length of his stride so that I had to adjust my pace to keep up with him.

"One thing is for certain," he said with strange intensity. "I don't need to bother with a telescope anymore. The heavens, as such, have been revealed to me!"

This would have been a statement of exaltation if not for the curious strain behind his words. Howard seemed to be struggling with the twin emotions of awestruck reverence and cold, breathless terror.

"What have you seen Howard?" I asked. He only chuckled ominously and looking at me from the corner of his eye, was quick with a clever retort.

"I can now see the surface of the Moon well enough to confirm that the so-called 'canals,' as certain astronomers insist upon calling them, are nothing more than the rays of debris emanating from various craters. The same may be said for the supposed canals on Mars, which I'll point out to you in a few hours, when it rises above the horizon."

"You can see the surface of Mars?" I asked, stunned and profoundly jealous.

"Vividly," he said confidentially, "I also used to require a high-powered telescope to view 47 Teucani... that most distant of stars."

"And now?" I asked. Howard only smiled and shook his head slowly.

"What is more," he whispered, "I would swear that, on several occasions now, I have glimpsed, very faintly, another planet-sized mass, out beyond Neptune... a ninth world, dead, frozen."

"A ninth world," I said, mystified. "Of course!"

"Actually," he corrected himself, "It is two planet-sized objects, revolving so closely around each other that they move as one."

As intriguing as this notion of a ninth world was, I was keenly aware that these answers were not so much lies as evasions, anecdotes designed to distract, a screen of words behind which he hid the true answer to my question.

"But Howard," I asked, "is that really what you were looking at just a moment ago... when all the color drained out of your face and you practically stopped breathing?"

There was another long silence. Howard's once-cheerful face became blanched and expressionless.

"My friend," he said wistfully. "You may ask me about anything... but not that." His voice sounded unfamiliar — strangely small and distorted by fear. "The things I've seen passing through the night sky these past few months..." A visible shudder went through him and he shook his head.

"What have you seen passing through the night sky?"

"Heaven forbid that you should have such things described to you, Robert," he said, turning away from me.

"I'm not afraid," I insisted. "Please, tell me."

After a thoughtful pause he looked over at me and said, "Come. I want to show you something."

We arrived on the crest of a low ridge, practically panting from the exertion of our quickened pace. Having walked steadily uphill for the last half hour or so, we were now looking out over several hundred rooftops, with a better view of the sky than we'd yet had. We stood for a minute, catching our breath, loosening our scarves and taking in the incredible view. Howard pointed to something floating just above the northern horizon.

"Look there. Do you see that misty patch?"

"Yes," I replied, "it's a sort of milky spot. What is it?"

"In the language of astronomy, the members of that resolvable class are called 'clusters.' Those other less distinct aggregations retain the name of 'nebulae,' or the singular 'nebula.' That one is called Pegasus. Clusters of its kind may be found in every degree of aggregation."

"What, exactly, is a nebula?" I asked, a question which seemed to please Howard immensely.

"They are enormous masses of glowing gas, under high pressure, and extremely hot. Their principal point of interest is that they are nothing less than solar systems in the making! To understand this one must first grasp the nebular hypothesis of creation, as given by Laplace."

I looked at him blankly, and said, "I have never heard of it."

"It runs, more or less, as follows. Before the existence of the stars and solar systems, nothing save nebulae occupied space. These rotating, cast-off rings later hardened into planets, which continue to revolve and rotate, forming the present systems."

"So the nebulae we are seeing here tonight, are the remains of this early condition?" I asked.

"Theoretically, yes. For example, the nebula in Canes Venatici, which is now below the horizon, is a mass of light with a sun condensing in the center, while those in Andromeda, Aquarius, and Pegasus reveal rings that will someday become planets." Turning to the eastern horizon, he continued. "Over here we have Taurus and its two attractive clusters, the Hyades with its red, Aldebaran sun, and — somewhere behind these trees — the Pleiades."

"Where is the Pleiades?" I asked, eager to catch a glimpse.

Taking a step forward, Howard began to search along the horizon, craning his neck and squinting awkwardly into the distance. Then, having found it, he beckoned to me, pointing off into the starry vastness just above the treeline beyond a row of houses. Stepping up alongside him, I continued to peer out in the direction he indicated, trying with difficulty to focus my eyes upon the Pleiades and, all the while, feeling that Howard was staring intently at my profile.

"Most nebulae," he continued softly, "are so large that our solar system is an atom in comparison. But, truth be told, they will contract quite a bit as they cool."

"Oh, that's reassuring!" I said sarcastically.

"No!" Howard laughed, "It really isn't! Precious little in astronomy is what you would call reassuring!" This statement set us both laughing.

"Wait. Is that the Pleiades there?" I asked, pointing.

"Yes," he said, "the most obviously visible of all the greater nebulae... and, I don't need to remind you, a constellation of great significance to the Inca."

"It's so beautiful," I said.

Closing his eyes, Howard intoned,
"Many a night I saw the Pleiades,
Rising through the mellow shade,
Glitter like a swarm of fireflies
Tangled in a silver braid."

"Who is that?" I asked.

"Tennyson. Remarkable poet; one of the greats." Here he seemed to drift off into his thoughts, smiling strangely to himself.

"What are you smiling at?" I asked.

"Oh, nothing," he said, almost embarrassed "It's just that... ever since these strange enhancements, I have been developing a theory that some of our classical poets must have also had enhanced senses. It's the truly sensitive souls who seem most receptive to it."

I recalled the similar thoughts I'd had upon reading Henry Wadsworth Longfellow's verse about the talking trees, but I kept this to myself, determined to keep with my vow of minimal disclosure.

"Howard?" I asked, after a time, "May I ask a foolish question?"

"No such thing, Robert," he replied. "Ask away."

I hesitated here, uncertain whether or not to broach the subject so directly.

"What do the Inca legends say about the Pleiades? What exactly was its significance, for example, to the temple builders at Machu Picchu?"

"I have asked myself that very same question these past few months," he replied, "and the true answer may never be known. We may only conjecture. Lately, I have been wondering if, perhaps, the Inca cultists emphasized the Pleiades with their architecture because they believed that that is whence the Viracocha came... and to where it returned."

"Do you think such a thing is possible?" I ventured, "Do you think that the Pleiades could be..." I hesitated, "inhabited?"

Howard's face became a mask of forced ambivalence, almost accusatory in its utter immutability; I got the impression that by asking this question, I had somehow triggered the wheels of some larger hypothesis taking shape in his mind.

"Perhaps you should take a look for yourself, Robert," Howard prompted, "and tell me what you see."

"Alright," I said, feeling suddenly apprehensive.

I narrowed my eyes and began to concentrate on bringing it into focus.

As I stood squinting into the eastern sky, an awful vertigo suddenly swept through me. I was instantly aware of a hot prickling moving in waves across my face and neck, as though I had thrust my head over the grating of a furnace or looked down into a smoldering chimney. But these merely physical sensations were soon pushed from my awareness, rapidly eclipsed by the bloodcurdling awareness of a malevolent, cosmic scrutiny bearing down upon me. Out there, within that relatively nondescript configuration of glowing stars, amid the eerie silver vapor in which the greater bodies hovered, I could feel the presence of a some huge living, thinking Scrutinizer — an entity so inconceivably ancient that the sheer density of its projected awareness pressed in upon me like an annihilating Judgment, forcing the very air from my lungs. For several seconds I had the hair-raising sensation that I was being intensely inspected and examined with no possible way to escape, as exposed and helpless as a bacteria on a microscope slide. The effect was dizzying. Stumbling backward, I turned away from the eastern sky and, holding my head tightly between my hands, I staggered away, eager to place something substantial (like a building) between myself and that sinister constellation.

"I don't want to look at the stars anymore, Howard." I said, stalking off down the street, "Let's keep walking."

159

"Yes, I know precisely what you mean," he said, straining to catch up with me. "Stargazing is not something I can do casually anymore either. Ever since the enhancements it's an entirely different experience. Not only can I see the heavenly bodies with a frightening clarity, but lately, I have become convinced that, on some of them, I am sensing the presence of intelligent life!"

"Is that so?" I asked with obvious sarcasm.

"I know what I am saying, Robert," he said, "and you would do well to listen. There are Things out there watching us, studying us. I have felt them — sensed them — ever since early childhood. Now, thanks to these enhanced senses, I can look up into the night sky and actually see them! And, to make matters worse, some of them... seem able, not only to detect my intrusive gaze, but to somehow trace it back to its source and to return, through the intervening voids of space, a corresponding scrutiny of their own!"

"That is definitely the impression I got staring into the Pleiades!" I confirmed.

"I would have warned you," he said, "but some things must be felt to be believed." Another momentary silence fell between us."Oddly enough, if you avoid looking at Them..." He added, somewhat wistfully, "They will not bother you."

"They?" I asked "I saw only one."

"One?" He promptly burst out laughing.

"How many can you see?" I asked.

"Great Scott!" he sneered. "There must be thousands of them!"

*　*　*　*

A SHORT TIME LATER, WHEN I FELT CALM AGAIN, I RESUMED MY gentle interrogation of Howard, fascinated to learn the extent of his powers. Clearly his sense of smell far surpassed my own. Additionally, the thousands of beings he clearly saw swimming through the night sky were invisible to me and, curious about these apparent discrepancies, I spoke up.

"If you don't mind my asking, Howard, what else can you see? Can you, for example, see in the dark?"

"No," he said, almost disappointed. "I can see across great distances, but only if there is light."

"Interesting," I said. "Can you see through solid objects? Can you, for example, see through walls?"

"No," he repeated, looking at me strangely. "I can sometimes see when people are ill, and I can see those Things in the sky — but that is all. Why do you ask, Robert?"

"If I may," I continued, "when did you first notice these enhancements?"

He smiled knowingly. "It's funny you should ask me that! Some months ago I asked myself the same question and, oddly enough, I'm certain it all began the day after I met you. The morning you left, I had intended to run some errands downtown but by noon I felt oddly fatigued and feverish. I stayed near the bathroom all day because I kept having the feeling that, at any moment, I was going to be violently ill. But it never happened. Imbibing nothing more than the occasional glass of water, I remained bedridden for three days."

"Go on..." I mumbled, a lump rising in my throat.

"Naturally, I thought I had a virus and that, frankly, I had probably caught it from you. On the morning of the fourth day, I awoke to a dreadful nausea and after emptying the contents of my stomach into the toilet, I went back to bed and slept for several more hours, after which I awoke feeling one hundred percent better. Not only was the sickness gone, but I felt better than I had in years, like a man half my age! Ever since that day, I have been assailed with the most astounding dreams. Some incredible new ability seems to manifest every month or so!"

"Interesting," was all I could manage, my heart pounding painfully in my chest. I could not shake the image of Howard flushing his newborn offspring down the toilet. After a short pause, I put the question to him bluntly, "Howard, I need to ask you something else. Did you do anything to bring on these enhancements? Have you, for example, indulged any... unusual cravings lately?"

A startled curiosity came over Howard's features. At first, he grinned, narrowing his eyes at me until they were mere slivers of shiny darkness. Then, quite suddenly, his look melted into something more like a mischievous smirk.

"Well, have you?" I repeated. "Perhaps you have... umm... eaten something unusual?"

Howard turned to look at me, staring directly into my eyes with a grin I can only describe as ghoulish. His head jerked to one side, and shutting his eyes tightly, he stopped walking and stood perfectly still upon the pavement.

"Shh!" he hissed, suddenly opening his eyes and looking at me, "Someone is coming!"

He guided me down Beacon Hill and the poorer neighborhoods that comprise South Boston. Ahead of us, I saw several soldiers, still a block and a half away, but moving down the sidewalk directly toward us. In a few more seconds we would be visible to them.

"Come!" he said. "Follow me."

"Do you know where you are going?" I asked, but he was already off, stepping, with startling agility, into the mouth of a dingy alleyway.

I followed immediately on his heels for several minutes; we passed through a string of dark courtyards which, after another journey through a reeking grime-encrusted passageway, dumped us on Mulvey Street, in the heart of the South End. Seeing that these streets were momentarily free of soldiers, we resumed our walk, moving soundlessly through tenements, festering alleyways and pushcarts heaped with odd-smelling trash, threading past such pools of raw sewage that I actually encountered several species of odor which even my discerning nose was unable to classify. Furthermore, Howard's footsteps were like those of a cat. Each step was so carefully placed that he made absolutely no sound as he padded along on the edges of his feet, a thing which unnerved me strangely, betraying, it seemed to me, that my unusual host was apparently well-practiced in the art of creeping.

So we went, moving silently through the night, making our way down countless byways, through enchanted courtyards, past darkened houses, moonlit tree parks, and gardens withered by the autumn frosts. As we trudged along the winding pavement, I continued to glance about, half-listening for any queer vibrations which might betray the presence of a hidden portal. I recall thinking that, perhaps, the various monstrosities I had been sensing throughout the evening were, in themselves, evidence of a nearby portal; wouldn't the area surrounding such a doorway between worlds be likely to contain large numbers of newly arrived (or else soon departing) invisible monsters?

As we made our way through that squalid maze of shadows, I once again became aware of those curiously subtle rumblings which I'd first noticed back at the Copley Plaza Ballroom. As before, I noted that these encroaching tremors seemed to be congregating at some indeterminate point beneath the crust of the street, meandering in ever-shrinking circles. I intuited that, whatever these subterranean horrors might be, they were searching along the underside of the pavement, like orcas hunting beneath the surface of a frozen sea, searching blindly about for some crack or fissure through which they might press themselves into sudden and advantageous proximity to their prey. These thoughts so succeeded in unnerving me that I was soon walking several inches closer to Howard, fearful that, at any moment, some huge appendage might burst forth from the pavement, to drag me down to whatever gory fate awaited me in the darkness below. Catching up with my companion, I fell in step alongside him.

"Would you mind telling me," I gasped, "why a mild-mannered gentleman such as yourself is so eager to avoid a group of soldiers? Didn't you just get through singing their praises?"

Clearly exasperated, Howard sighed thoughtfully.

"Tho this be madness… there's method in't!" he said with a smile.

"I'm all ears." I replied, a statement that seemed to set him thinking.

Keenly aware that the curious rumblings behind us were beginning to get stronger, I quickened my pace and took the lead. Hereafter, I began to subtly direct us back towards the Cambridge Bridge where, I reasoned, we would be relatively safe, at least from subterranean burrowers. After a minute had passed, I once again prompted my companion with a question.

"Are you going to explain to me the 'method' in your madness, or are you just going to let me wonder?"

"First of all, Robert," he began, "regarding my extra-legal activities, I, like you, am not at liberty to discuss such matters candidly. So you needn't ask me impertinent questions which I could not possibly answer without compromising my own safety, and yours."

"Fair enough." I relented.

"Nor do I consider the police and the soldiery to be my enemies per se." He continued, "Soldiers and policemen are a necessary evil in a civil society, so you'd best get over your squeamishness about them. The way things are headed around here, there's bound to be more and more of them in the months and years to come, which it is long overdue."

At this precise moment we were again passing along one of those avenues which, twenty years ago must have been a bastion of middle-class tidiness and bourgeois order, but which had long since been given over to filth, poverty, and neglect. From this admittedly grim scenery, my companion seemed to be drawing a peculiar inspiration.

"Take this neighborhood for example." Howard said in disgust. "Look at these ancient houses. They were charming once, no doubt. Look at them now… they have been taken over by filthy foreigners and terrorists. This once charming New England street has become a hive of licentiousness, drunkenness, degradation, and anarchy!"

"Howard." I interrupted, "I think you are confusing poverty with depravity. It is the landlords who have let this neighborhood fall into decay. Not the renters."

My eccentric friend was not to be discouraged. His eyes burned with a fierce intensity. "If these walls could talk, tell me who would have the stomach to listen? I find it a pitiful irony that these fine, beautiful houses of brick and wood, with their carved mantles and graceful stairs, with their carefully laid stone steps and wrought iron railings, are now the trash-strewn abodes of subhuman troglodytes!"

I looked at him, startled.

"Oh yes Robert, I'm afraid the soldiers are a necessary evil." He continued, "The unwashed masses must remain subject to the will of a dominant aristocracy so long as the present structure of the brain endures. This street is a microcosm of civilization itself. These ancient houses tell the whole sordid story! What we have here before us are the crumbling facades of a once-proud English civilization, slowly being overrun by swarthy foreigners, degenerate perverts, and inbred, subhuman apes! Why, this ghetto is even worse off than the alienized suburbs of my native Providence where Hebrew, Italian, and French-Canadian squalor are spreading like a pestilence."

"The only inbred degenerates I am seeing are the members of the ruling elite who practically own cities like Boston. It is they who have made an obsession of keeping their precious bloodlines 'pure.' My god man! Some of the European aristocrats are so inbred that haemophilia wipes out half of their offspring! Believing themselves to be almost a race unto themselves, the landed gentries have been marrying and mating with their siblings and cousins for thousands of years, to keep the wealth of nations within the family. The Inca, the Egyptians, and any European Royalty you could name, all engaged in systematic incest. This practice has sharply increased the prevalence of madness among the Royal families."

I admit I was ranting, but Howard listened, with patience and thinly disguised irritation, to my sermon. As he walked, his posture and stride became quite severe, his nostrils flaring impatiently, as he seemed to be considering my words very carefully.

"I'll tell you something else, Howard," I continued, "some of these royal inbreeds get to looking mighty strange after a time... mighty strange. Inheritable genetic traits are one thing but, good god! I once saw a series of portraits depicting the scions of a wealthy Austrian dynasty. It practically looked like a Darwinian chart, arranged in reverse!"

"I believe you've made your point, Robert," he ceded, annoyed. "Nevertheless, a man of your intelligence must admit that the minds of the peon classes are woefully underdeveloped; they are little more than brute beasts. That is why the anarchic impulse is strong among them... because they hate what is superior to them, they are prone to mob up and go on the warpath against their natural superiors. They nearly took Boston by storm just one week ago tonight! Their brains may be stunted but they are no less dangerous for that!" Then almost to himself, he muttered, "Pitiful... such a waste..."

This puzzled me.

"What do you mean?" I asked "What is a waste?"

"All those underdeveloped brains," he sighed, "wasted on the lower classes. The human mind is the most precious resource we have to work with in the further evolution of our species. If only we could find a way to activate and unleash its hidden properties, I believe we could avail ourselves of untold powers. We could finally realize our destiny as a race!"

He said this just as we were passing by a group of young hooligans sitting on a stoop, who, having caught Howard's condescending look, eyed us strangely as we passed.

"That is," Howard continued in a low whisper, "if we are not bludgeoned to death in the street by these roaming gangs of throwbacks bent upon starting an insurrection! An uncultivated mind soon degenerates into bloodthirsty barbarism. The human brain is an untapped resource and if the dull-witted masses are too stupid to develop their minds to their fullest capacity, then I say, those raw materials should be put to better use elsewhere!"

This candid statement shocked me, not only because of what it plainly stated, but because of what it implied beyond that. What had begun as an incoherent rationale for a police state had metamorphosed into an implicit, and dangerously suggestive, confession.

"I can't imagine what you mean, Howard," I said.

"Look," he said in a low, conspiratorial whisper. "There are nerve bundles in the brain which, if properly stimulated, can open up whole new modes of language, knowledge, sensation, consciousness, being. We have these powers, but they are mostly inaccessible to us, locked away inside our minds like an unopened letter."

I looked at him blank-faced.

"Oh, don't look so stunned, Robert. Anthropologists tell us that primitive men have been engaging in various forms of brain experimentation for hundreds, if not thousands, of years. Most commonly it takes the form of skull-binding, stimulating inactive brain tissue through pressure by deliberately altering the shape of the skull during infancy. But there are other, less-common, methods as well."

My baffled look spurned him on.

"Evidence unearthed by archaeologists in Peru indicate that Nazca and Inca surgeons were performing large-scale, systematic trepanning operations upon carefully selected members of the peasant and Indio population, as far back as 1200 AD!"

"I recall having read about such things," I replied casually. "Pretty strange stuff. What do you think they were up to, opening people's skulls like that?"

"It is difficult to say," he replied with a sigh. "Presumably, they were manipulating, stimulating, or possibly even removing brain tissue — either for health reasons, or for mere effect. Perhaps it was the brain blood they were after. In *The Golden Bough*, Frazer speaks of the Inca fetish for collecting brain blood. They smeared it on their bodies and added it to a sacred bread, which they ate in large quantities, as a protection against predatory spirits. Who can say? Perhaps they removed certain parts of the brain and ate them. Many modern cannibal tribes claim that consuming brain tissue affords a certain mind-expanding effect."

"Mind-expanding effect?" I echoed.

"They claim it is a powerful intoxicant, and mildly hallucinogenic," he said. "It gives them visions. It enables them to see themselves, and their world, through the eyes of their god. The Nazca and certain portions of the Inca royalty appear to have believed this. Their entombed dead show evidence of successful brain surgery — actual trepanning operations being performed in Stone Age Peru!" Howard gazed out at the moonlit street, overjoyed at the very thought of it. "Think of the wonders they must have discovered, the powers they must have unleashed. Sadly for us, neither of these civilizations utilized a written language to describe what they were doing. But we are left with an impressively detailed and thriving oral tradition, as well as a vast quantity of sculptures, paintings, and woven images, many of which depict demonic portraits and enigmatic scenes of ordinary human beings interacting with supernatural entities and mythical beast-men."

"Let me get this straight," I said. "You think the Nazca were surgically creating god-like Beings by manipulating, removing, and possibly even eating certain nerve clusters in the brain?!" I was purposely trying to make his theory sound as ludicrous as possible. It wasn't hard.

"Aside from the possibility of cannibalism, it's not that different from the operations performed on vicious dogs and schizophrenic patients in Sweden in the 1870s. The removal of parts of the temporal lobes was said to have a definite calming affect, though admittedly, several of the patients did not survive the operation. But these patients were already hopelessly deranged at the outset, so the results are unreliable, to say the least."

"I am disturbed at your apparent lack of ethics when it comes to the poorer classes," I said bluntly.

"Like their ancient counterparts, modern western surgeons are going to require access to reasonably healthy human subjects if they are ever going to fully comprehend what those nerve bundles are and how they work. Many of these slum-dwellers are walking around in a state of dementia anyway! The surgeons would be doing them a favor! They might even figure out how to heal them!"

My disapproval for this line of thinking must have shown upon my face, but Howard pressed on, unaffected by my perpetually raised brow.

"There is a Welshman," he continued, "by the name of Arthur Machen, a failed medical student, an ex-Freemason, and a writer. I believe he may have observed one of these human experiments, performed upon a street urchin, a peasant girl by the name of Helen Vaughn. Machen describes the entire procedure, and its shocking outcome, in a narrative which, I believe, he was permitted to publish only because he insisted, till his dying day, that it was fiction."

"Of course elites experiment on their subjects, Howard!" I replied. "History shows that they torture with impunity, subject them to untold torments of the mind and body, all under the pretense of judicial and medical procedure. That's nothing new under the sun. What I find disturbing is the fact that you appear to approve of such things!"

"Robert, you must rid yourself of this sentimental delusion of equality." Howard said, "It is only causing you unnecessary suffering. The great masses of humanity are too stupid to run their own society. They don't have the brains for it. They grumble about it, but there is no other way."

"I once believed as you do, Howard," I said, "but I have seen too much."

"More and more," Howard said with a grimace, "they appear as a vast herd of dumb beasts on the verge of stampeding! Should they ever catch us off guard again, our quaint English civilization is done for."

"And in the event of such an uprising of the lowly horde," I asked, "you intend to participate in its suppression?"

Here he turned to me in deadly earnest. "Don't be deceived by my appearance, Robert," he whispered severely. "I am naturally Nordic — a chalk-white, Tuetonic killer of the Scandinavian and North German forest... a predatory rover of the blood of Hengist and Horsa! I am descended from the conquerors of Celts and mongrels — a son of the thunders and the arctic winds, and brother to the frosts and auroras — a drinker of foemen's blood from new-picked skulls!"

Tempted as I was to burst out laughing at this absurd self-assessment, I balked; despite his obvious hyperbole, there was something in this utterance which rang out like a confession.

"What do you know about drinking blood from new-picked skulls?" I asked.

Howard sensed his error immediately and, growing somewhat pale, he continued on in a quieter tone.

"I hold with Nietzsche that an intellectual aristocracy is the only possible way for..."

Howard never got a chance to finish his thought. At that precise moment the tremors which had been trailing us for the last three hours suddenly and mysteriously coalesced beneath our feet. Several immense shudders swept down the length of the quiet street, and I watched in numb dread as the surrounding cobblestones began to shudder and crack, become dislodged and, in some cases, even to leap several inches into the air, as if struck violently from below. There was a deep bending sound and the entire street was rocked by a colossal explosion, like a cannon blast, which emanated from somewhere beneath the paving stones directly behind us. When a house next to us began to collapse, falling noticeably toward us, we looked at each other, wide-eyed, and began sprinting away.

Every house we ran past immediately fell. Had I not seen it for myself, I would not have believed it. I could see, as I fled for my very life down that bursting sidewalk, that there was a horrific and undeniable synchronicity between our running and the falling of those houses. I have thought back on this episode many times, trying to understand how it might have happened. All I can think is that, having finally zeroed in on their meandering prey, the unseen burrowers had, in that final lunge, disrupted the foundations of those doomed houses, as they chased us up the street. On the two occasions when I dared to glance backward, I was appalled to see the sidewalk directly behind us, disappearing beneath a steady wave of falling bricks and timber.

Then, just as abruptly as it had begun, the quake was over. The roaring wave of rubble that had pursued us up the street suddenly ceased. All was still. Out of breath, I stopped running and leaned against the nearest wall, wheezing and gasping.

We had reached the top of the street and, looking back, I saw an immense chasm of broken concrete, shattered timber, and ruptured sewer mains. A great tunnel-like hollow beneath the street had collapsed, pulling one house after another down into the empty darkness below. Turning toward Howard, I found him steadying himself against a wall and staring intensely up into the empty air directly above the great pit. To my amazement, his expression was one of profound rapture; he was grinning and shaking his head in wordless awe. Inhaling deeply, he seemed to be studying the smoke that was rising out of the pit, which prompted me to sniff the air. I became aware of a smell which reminded me, oddly enough, of fresh blooming roses. Howard and I both stood there, transfixed, for several minutes, staring down from the rim of the crater, sniffing, while people spilled out from the nearby taverns and boarding houses. A crowd formed around us, ogling the damage, positing wild theories, and peering into the curious rift.

Too stunned to speak, and ruminating over the oddly abrupt exodus of the hungry burrowers, I chanced to see a wooden sign suspended by two thin chains from an iron armature bolted to the wall, just over the doorway of a Russian bakery. Howard and I were leaning against the wall of this building, this odd sign hanging directly over our heads, when the tremors suddenly ceased. Taking a step in order to examine it, I gazed up at the painted image. What I saw could best be described as a curious primitive drawing of a bearded man in holy robes, holding a book and making a cryptic sign with his right hand. Staring up at this crudely drawn figure, I was struck with the curiously forceful notion that it had been precisely this image which had stopped the monstrosities. Hadn't Howard and I been standing directly beneath the sign at the very moment that the attack had mysteriously ceased?

As the minutes passed, I was increasingly convinced of the correctness of this theory, and deeply impressed with the idea that I needed to somehow find a way to take this image with me. Pulling a fountain pen from my breast pocket, I quickly recreated the crude outlines of the figure upon the palm of my hand, as darkly and boldly as I could.

Without looking at me or noticing what I was doing, Howard finally began to speak.

"I wonder what it was that caused those houses to collapse?" he said in a faraway voice.

"I don't know," I said, "but any minute, this street will be crawling with soldiers and policemen."

This seemed to jar Howard out of his daze and, nodding to me, he followed as I pushed past the crowd and led us onto the empty pre-dawn streets that lay beyond.

"Perhaps the anarchists were building another one their infernal bombs," he postulated, "and it went off prematurely, killing its makers! Ahh, now that would be poetic justice!"

I did not contradict this theory, tempted though I was to debate its presumptions. Howard's ignorance seemed to function as a sort of shield; I decided to keep silent about what I had seen (and felt) beneath the pavement, humoring him and nodding blandly at his comments.

During our walk to the Boston Train Station, we returned to the subject of industrial civilization and I listened distractedly but with great pleasure as Howard, undeterred, once again, expounded his reactionary philosophy.

"The chief indictment against the capitalist ideal, at least here in America, is the profound, subtle, and pervasive hostility of capitalism, and of the whole essence of mercantilism, to all that is finest and most creative in the human spirit. Business and capital are the enemies of human worth in that they exalt and reward the shrewdly acquisitive rather than the intrinsically superior and creative."

"I certainly agree with that," I said. "It's just that I believe the things you are saying about America are also true of civilization in general. The power-hungry tend to dominate and to do all they can to maintain that domination."

"Yes," he said ponderously. "Ever since these enhancements, I must confess I have developed very serious doubts about the whole civilizing process. It seems deliberately designed to keep us meek and submissive."

"But surely," I added, "like the police and the soldiers, the civilizing process is one of the few things standing between us and 'total anarchy.'"

He smirked at me. "Perhaps, Robert, perhaps. You see, I am not so attached to my opinions that I am unwilling to reconsider them in light of new information. Nevertheless," he continued, indicating the industrial scenery of the approaching train yard, "nothing good can be said of this cancerous machine-culture itself. It is not a true civilization, and has nothing in it to satisfy a mature and fully developed mind. It is a treadmill squirrel-trap culture, drugged and frenzied with the hasheesh of industrial servitude and material luxury. Its denizens do not truly live, or know how to live. It is attuned to the mentality and imagination of a moron, and crushes relentlessly with disapproval, ridicule, and economic annihilation, any sign of actually independent thought or feeling which chances to rise above its sodden level."

"You have heard about the lynchings then?" I asked.

"What lynchings?"

"The lynching of anarchists, radicals, libertine philosophers and countless others who dare to advocate a world without these artificial hierarchies and restraints. These persons are routinely attacked and killed in the streets by patriotic mobs and soldiers for daring to advocate for a world without authority."

"The lynching of anarchists is something entirely different from the phenomenon to which I was referring," he corrected.

"Is it?" I asked, to which Howard responded with a shrug.

We arrived at the impressive entrance to the Boston Station and, stepping through its massive portals, we entered the cavernous central chamber, which was just beginning to fill up with morning commuters.

"I'm going to get away, Robert," Howard said triumphantly, turning to face me. "I have had an inspiration just now and I believe I've hit upon the perfect profession for myself! I shall become an investigator of bizarre phenomena; a student of crypto-zoology! I have already described how ideally suited I am for such a career. These enhanced senses enable me to perceive all sorts of new things! I shall document the phenomena I observe in the form of stories. If I could sell these stories to the better-paying science magazines, I could travel the world, expand my researches!"

"An excellent idea!" I said. "Oh... but what about your family, Howard? Who will look after your mother?"

"Oh, Robert," he said, a sharp pain coming into his eyes. "I have not told you yet."

"What is it?" I asked. "Is it your mother?"

Looking down at the floor and wincing, he said, "Aunt Annie and I were forced to commit mother to Butler Hospital."

"Oh no." I said, "What happened?"

Howard stared into the distance and shook his head sadly.

"Some months after your departure, mother's illness worsened noticeably. Distracted as I had been by my own enhanced senses, I could suddenly think of nothing but getting her the help she needed."

"What do you mean her illness worsened?" I asked.

"She began to complain of a... presence," he said, ruefully, "...a presence lurking around our house, peering in the windows at night, tracking our movements." He shook his head preposterously, as if to laugh, but the laugh never came. "Her senses began to develop at an absolutely frightening rate. Last February, the neighbors began to find her lurking about in the shrubbery, in a curious state of elation and insisting that some of the bushes and shrubs were not actually bushes, but some kind of imitation; 'imposters' she called them. I know it sounds ludicrous!" He was blushing. "When she started wandering the neighborhood, inspecting other people's front gardens, looking for these imposter plants, Aunt Annie and I decided it would be best if she went someplace where she would stop frightening herself and others. Last March she became a resident patient at Butler Hospital for the Insane." There were tears forming in his eyes but he turned away.

"I'm so sorry Howard," I said putting my hand upon his shoulder. "That must have been an exceedingly difficult decision to make."

"Yes," he said, "exceedingly difficult indeed."

We stood for a moment, then Howard suddenly looked up and, hearing a southbound train approaching the station, he wiped his eyes and said, "Well Robert, I had better purchase my ticket now. I intend to sleep the whole way home."

Realizing with great sadness that we were about to part ways, I practically blurted that I would visit him again in Providence as soon as I was able.

"Yes," he agreed. "Do visit me. I would enjoy that immensely. Every time we get together, strange and wonderfully bizarre things seem to happen! Tonight it just happened to be an earthquake!" He chuckled, shaking his head in disbelief.

"Unbelievable," I said, somewhat disingenuously.

"Well," he continued, "New England certainly has its share of anomalous seismic activity. Just ask the residents of Moodus, Connecticut, or Dunwich for that matter! Perhaps I'll write a story about it!"

"Go ahead and write your story," I said. "Just don't mention me by name, alright?"

Laughing, he replied, "Don't worry. I'll leave us both anonymous. Just a cryptic reference to two non-descript men observing an enigma. One a traveler, and the other a poet."

"If you must," I laughed.

"A writer must follow his inspirations!" he chuckled.

"Speaking of inspirations," I said, "I have a present for you. Do you have a piece of paper?"

He nodded and, removing a small black notebook from his coat, he tore out a page and handed it to me. I quickly copied the simple figure from my palm onto the piece of paper.

"Fold this into your breast pocket and keep it with you always," I said.

"What is it?" he asked, looking skeptical.

"Never mind. Just keep it with you at all times — for good luck and as a token of our friendship."

"Very well," he said, raising his eyebrow, as if doubtful of my sanity.

Looking at my friend, I had the sudden sense that this was the last time I would ever see him again and, reluctant to say goodbye, I permitted myself to gush.

Shaking his hand vigorously, I said, "Howard, you've been a marvelous friend. You can't imagine what our discussions have meant to me. You've helped me so much, with your incredible knowledge of folklore and astronomy and everything else. I shall sorely miss our conversations! I won't pretend to understand the odd ways in which our lives seem linked, but I am so very grateful to have met you."

"Well said, Robert," he replied. "I, likewise, feel the same about you. Only I, unlike yourself, am not so sure that we have seen the last of each other."

I paused.

"Did I say that I thought this was the last we would see of each other?" I asked, somewhat startled.

"No," he chuckled "you didn't say it, but you thought it!" With this cryptic statement, the train whistle rang through the air, followed by the conductor announcing the final boarding. Bringing our vigorous handshake to a close and turning to the train, Howard quickly made his way up the platform, through the turnstile and onto the waiting train. As I walked away, shaking my head, I could not suppress a laugh for, even in his casual farewell to me, Howard had once again demonstrated the almost supernatural rapport that existed between us.

I headed back to my room in Cambridge, where I packed my things and squared my bill. Setting out on foot, I headed west toward the beckoning hills. Having spent so much time in the city, I now longed for the comparative quiet of the wilderness. I loaded up on essentials, and tramped off into the forests of eastern Massachusetts once again, moving in nonsensical patterns designed to confound any would-be pursuers bold enough to try and track me.

*　*　*　*

REGARDING THE CURIOUS FIGURE I HAD DRAWN UPON THE PALM OF my hand, later research revealed it to be the portrait of an obscure 11th century Russian clergyman, by the name of Grigoriy, a character out of the old peasant folklore whose image had been taken from an ancient woodcut. It came as no great surprise to learn that the image of this little-known Saint Grigoriy was often used as a sign of protection; during his lifetime, he was known primarily as a killer of Vampyres, specializing in Incubi, Succubi, and other Pestilential Entities.

*　*　*　*

HIGHLIGHTS FROM THIS PERIOD OF DELIRIOUS WANDERING INCLUDE camping out in Sarah Bishop's cave near Ridgefield, sightseeing in the swamps of New Jersey, and the cold winter night I crept into the mansion of the multi-millionaire industrialist Henry Clay Frick, "the world's most hated man," according to the *New York Times*, where, finishing what Alexander Berkman had started back in 1892, I strangled him with his own pillowcase as he lay sleeping. This was an act of pure animal hatred, primarily to avenge the striking miners he had infamously massacred in 1892 near Homestead, Pennsylvania.

My reader must understand that this was a very different sort of killing than I had ever done before. It was done neither for necessary sustenance, nor under compulsion from any outside force or entity. This murder was, morally speaking, purely mine, a manifestation of my own heart, my own desire, my own will.

XII

SEVERAL MONTHS AFTER KILLING FRICK, I BEGAN TO HAVE experiences which could only be described as psychic. I can do no better than to relate an actual example, which occurred on a warm April evening in 1920. I was sleeping in a wooded valley just east of the town of South Braintree, Massachusetts (a name which struck me as sounding somewhat prophetic, if not vaguely instructional). On this particular night I first adopted the habit of sleeping in trees. The infrequent nightmares about lynch mobs had intensified throughout the spring of 1920 until, on the evening of April 15, I woke up sweating and breathless from a vivid dream in which I was being kicked to death by an angry crowd who had surrounded me as I lay sleeping in a wooded glen. Leaping immediately to my feet, my heart pounding in my chest, I scanned the surrounding area in all directions until, satisfied that I was truly alone, I began to pace nervously back and forth in the moonlight. This dream was so convincing, so horrifically realistic, that my body actually ached in the places where my dream attackers had struck me. Half asleep, I crawled up into the branches of a nearby fir tree. I dimly recall thinking that I would be safer off the ground, but I did not analyze it at the time.

About fifteen feet up, the trunk of this mighty fir tree diverged into two smaller trunks. About ten feet above that, one of the trunks ended abruptly, broken off (presumably in a high wind), while the other continued on, meandering skyward and blotting out half the stars with its massive branches. The summit of this broken trunk formed a sort of bowl-shaped nest of boughs, which seemed an ideal sort of bed; spreading my heavy coat over this web of overlapping limbs, I lay myself upon it. After nearly an hour of arranging and rearranging myself, I fell into a deep, dreamless sleep, from which I was awakened some hours later by a curious rustling sound coming from several points in the forest directly below my tree.

Fear swept through me. I flicked open my eyes and, turning my head very slowly to one side, I saw that the ground directly beneath my tree was full of creeping human figures. They were armed with rifles and electric torches. Moving along in a line formation, making a clean sweep of the entire area and poking about in the underbrush, they were clearly searching for

174

someone. These men did not speak to one another except in low whispers, primarily utilizing hand gestures to communicate, a thing which made me think that they were plain clothed police officers or soldiers rather than angry citizens. The extreme caution these men displayed with their movements told me two things. First, that they had a great fear of their quarry, and second, that they believed it to be very near at hand. This observation put me in a heightened state of alarm and, waiting until my noises would be covered by the sound of the wind, I managed to ease myself over to the other unbroken trunk. Taking hold of its lowest branches, I crawled, slowly and silently, bit by bit, into the uppermost limbs of the surviving trunk. I curled myself into a ball and there I waited, for nearly an hour, until the last of them disappeared over the ridge and descended into the neighboring ravine. It was then, and only then, that I permitted myself to draw a full breath.

I was initially quite relieved, but also troubled by the implications. What bothered me more than anything was the fact that I had slept through the mob's approach, a thing I would have thought impossible, given my enhanced senses. Recalling the curious nightmare (which had placed in my head the thought to sleep in the trees), I was thankful to whatever intuition had alerted me to the approach of a decidedly violent and pitiful death. I remain convinced that this premonition actually saved my life and after this first night, sleeping in trees became a preference which soon developed into a habit. Similarly, I began to consciously cultivate the habit of obeying my more unorthodox and random impulses, seeing how they generally led me to interesting insights and often signaled the onset of some strange new power or ability.

Crawling back to my original resting place on the crown of the broken trunk, I passed the remainder of the night in restful sleep. The next morning, after assessing that the entire valley was devoid of human life, I descended, making my way onto an old abandoned highway. I had been tramping west for about a half an hour, and was just cresting a small hill, when I saw, on the road about fifty yards ahead of me, several strange green rectangular objects, each about six inches long, and buzzing strangely at either end, like the ill-timed wings of a hummingbird. As I came closer I was shocked to see that these objects were, in fact, thick bundles of money! Picking one up, I discovered that each bundle was comprised of one hundred crisp twenty-dollar bills, bound in the middle with a paper ribbon and flapping in the breeze. Several more of these bundles lay in the ditch along the roadside and two more lay in the grass nearby. Before gathering these up, I made a close inspection of the area, using my enhanced senses to see if I could detect any persons hiding nearby. Finding none, I quickly gathered up every last one of these bundles and pocketed them. I returned to the cover of the forest, hiking parallel to the road for several hours.

Ten days later I learned that the nocturnal manhunt and the mysterious bundles of money were both part of the aftermath of a robbery that had occurred several hours prior to my arrival in South Braintree. The payroll of the Slater & Morell Shoe Company, almost $16,000 in workers' wages, had been robbed, during which two guards had been shot and killed. According to the newspaper accounts, two Italian anarchists had been taken into custody in connection with the South Braintree armed robbery. These two fellows, soon to be inseparably known to the world as Sacco and Vanzetti, were widely believed to be innocent of the robbery; many locals believed that they were taking the fall for the Morelli Gang, a well-known group of armed bandits active in that region. I was shocked and saddened beyond all words when I saw the photographs of those two Italian anarchists in the papers and immediately recognized them as Bartolo, the steely-eyed bookseller and his friend Freddie, the teetotaler who never swore. The initial police search for the culprits had turned up nothing, though I later learned that Galleani had been arrested at this time and was being deported. This seemed to me an ominous portent indeed.

I had no way of knowing if Bartolo and Freddie had robbed the payroll but, knowing what I did of them, it was certainly possible. On the other hand, both men were extremely principled on the subject of who did, and did not, constitute a worthy target. On this point they had far stricter standards than I, targeting only members of the extremely wealthy power elite and no others. It is for this reason mainly that I doubted their guilt. We three had spoken of a great many delicate matters, but never once did they mention armed robbery. Almost everything else, lord knows, but not armed robbery. Nevertheless, even if they had been involved in robbing the payroll, I was pleased to know that, by removing the bundles, I had deprived investigators of a significant piece of evidence.

From this point forward I never had to worry about money. One bundle was more than enough to cover my minimal expenses, the primary being travel, food, and the purchase of disguises. The rest of the money I passed off, here and there, to beggars, street urchins, travelers, anarchist propagandists, and anyone else I deemed worthy.

* * * *

FOR SEVERAL WEEKS, I WANDERED AS IF IN A DREAM CONTINUALLY moving west and avoiding populated areas whenever possible. It wasn't just humanity that I wished to avoid now, but also the Hidden Monstrosities as well (though even in the pristine forests on the eastern slopes of Mt. Greylock, I searched in vain for a gully or ravine that was not inhabited by at least one or two). Additionally, I had no luck detecting the presence of my offspring. Wherever it may have gone (if it still existed at all) the Black Thing was too far outside the range of my abilities to sense it. Leaving South Braintree far, far behind, I once again took to the green hills, determined to keep searching.

In this misanthropic condition, I camped out for several months until the cold, wet weather eventually drove me indoors. Autumn passed in a blur as I flitted from place to place, barely taking the time to notice which city I was in. I continued to move, alternating between urban and suburban landscapes and the wild wooded valleys, passing the winter in various rented rooms throughout the greater New England area. Soon enough I lost all track of where I was going. North, south, east or west... it didn't matter anymore.

*   *   *   *

SOMETIME IN DECEMBER OF 1920, I EMERGED FROM THE WOODS NEAR Ridgefield, Connecticut, and entered the city limits. I went directly to the train station where, with some of the money I'd found on the roadside, I purchased a first class, one-way ticket to Peekskill, New York. Having exhausted every other possibility, I'd finally decided to just go to the squatter camp near Leffert's Corners and to wait for the Black Thing to return.

Alone in my private cabin, I slept for the entire ten hour journey, after which I was awakened by the scream of the whistle and the ticket-taker knocking courteously at my door, informing me that we would be pulling into the Peekskill station momentarily. Five minutes later I was stumbling into the sunlight with the rest of the human cargo, bleary-eyed, half-exhausted, and absolutely famished.

The Peekskill train station, a hive of travel-weary humanity, was at once doleful and deliriously ecstatic. Everywhere, I saw the cheerful decorations which told me that the holiday season was approaching; I stood for several minutes on the windswept platform, like a watchful statue, listening to people shouting and laughing, greeting and embracing each other with great affection; I drew a strange and unexpected comfort from these displays. But I was soon jostled out of this watcher's trance by the soft collision of a passerby, after which I quickly made my way to the end of the platform and out to the road. Purchasing two large sandwiches and a bottle of root beer from a street vendor, I then wandered down to the riverfront park which bordered the station on one side. Seating myself upon a quiet bench that faced the water, I attacked my lunch with disturbing zeal.

Now and then, as I looked around, I could not help but be awestruck by the breathtaking scenery before me. To the north, across the frigid black waters of the Hudson River, loomed Bear Mountain, Storm King Mountain, and several other snowy peaks which, huge as they were, I knew were mere foothills when compared with the mighty Catskills looming behind them.

To the south lay Croton-on-the-Hudson and Ossining. Beyond that, I knew, was Tarrytown, and Kykuit, where I stood a decent chance of again intercepting John D. Rockefeller and company. Perhaps, if luck was with me, John D. might even be entertaining a guest or two (say, J.P. Morgan, Andrew Carnegie, or John Astor), so that I momentarily fantasized how I might be granted an opportunity to kill two, or even three robber barons at the same time.

Certainly enough time had passed (and my appearance changed enough) that I could safely go to Tarrytown and have a look around. By this time, I had come to feel as though I needn't worry overly much about being recognized. Upon consideration of the facts, it was entirely possible that the authorities still had no clue as to who, what, or where I was. Only one of my many victims had survived my attacks and, having only glimpsed me momentarily in the darkness, Old Man Rockefeller was not likely to give an accurate description of me to anyone. Perhaps unrecognized, I would even be able to walk right up to his front gate and sneak past his gatekeeper. Maybe, after all this time, I would finally get a chance to finish what I had foolishly left undone, and strangle the heartless miser. The old man had stayed busy these past four years and tales of his ongoing misdeeds were still being told. It was commonly understood by most, for example, that the brutal stranglehold of the coal barons was, by the winter of 1920, merely being rearranged and decentralized into smaller puppet corporations, creating the legal loopholes of blamelessness large enough for Rockefeller and his cronies to slip through.

There was another, less pleasant, consideration; despite my initial aspirations, the death of John D. Archbold had only been a minor episode in the history of the Colorado Fuel and Iron company — and that it had been largely, if not entirely, ineffectual.

In killing Archbold, I had avenged the brutal murder of Joe Hill. This was my one true reward. This understanding did not cause me to renounce assassination altogether, but rather to think of it as one of many possible options. As far as keeping myself amused, as pure revenge, or as a source of (admittedly questionable) brain meat, murdering tycoons was acceptable. But from the perspective of affecting a meaningful change in the world, it was almost worthless. Without the larger context of a full-scale insurrection to back it up, it was reduced to mere symbolism. Almost. Because it was of vital importance to remember that the seemingly untouchable plutocrats who maintain this brutal class structure are, after all, just men who have names and addresses and heartbeats. Who can pretend to know what affects a deed such as this will have? As a child, when I first learned about the assassination of President McKinley by Leon Czolgosz, I recall that I felt inspired, as if my eyes had been opened to a whole new world of possibilities. Was it really so strange to assume that others might be similarly inspired by my deeds, just as I had been by Czolgosz? Furthermore, John D. Archbold had not exactly been a well-known public figure, so the impact of his death, never even publicly acknowledged as a murder, had naturally been limited. Killing John D. Rockefeller himself, on the other hand — now that would be like slaying one of the very gods of Capitalism itself!

Despite these stimulating ruminations, a bloody return to Kykuit was not to be (at least not in the way I initially imagined), but I was about to become the recipient of a joy and satisfaction far greater than that of any politically symbolic assassination. While gazing out at the majestic Hudson River Valley, I suddenly detected the presence (and relative nearness!) of my long-lost offspring! It hit me first as an odor, then as a barely audible pulse, coming from somewhere beyond the mountains on the opposite shore. I was so overjoyed by this revelation I could barely contain myself; it was all I could do to return to the train station and calmly inquire about ferry rides across the river. I decided that, after a quick visit to the Peekskill public library (to scan the local headlines for news of any grisly murders in this or neighboring counties), I would catch the next northbound train to Red Hook.

I made my way to the public library on Nelson Avenue. Entering this imposing and impressive edifice, I had just seated myself at a table in the periodical section on the fourth floor when I became aware that I was, several times over, the subject of a hostile scrutiny. After thumbing distractedly through one or two newspapers, I stood up, and prepared to make my exit.

A chill passed through me when, from the corner of my eye, I saw that three of the watchers were also standing up and were now swiftly making their way toward me, heads lowered, with their hands in their coat pockets. Looking to my left, I saw the rear stairwell was marked as an exit; I moved to it with as much speed as library etiquette might tolerate.

Once inside the stairwell, I abandoned all pretense and ran for my life, taking the steps four or five at a time. Halfway down, I slowed just long enough to hear the sounds of rapid footfalls explode above me, as the other men entered the stairwell and took up the chase. I paused for a moment at the wide metal door, to compose myself, before calmly and cheerfully slipping out onto the bustling sidewalk. In the cold, crowded dusk, I distinctly heard, in the stairwell above me, over the rumble of pounding feet, one voice shout

out to the others, "We can't lose him this time!" to which one of the others replied, "We'll get him! We'll get him!"

Walking directly into the most crowded part of the thoroughfare, I began zig-zagging through a sea of beggars, Christmas carolers, shrieking brats having Christmas tantrums, and the legion or more of holiday shoppers, who flitted obliviously in and out of the various shops and restaurants. On the crowded winter streets of Peekskill, I had no trouble at all losing these fellows. I ran faster than I would have thought humanly possible, having no need to slow down at blind corners, dark alleys, or other areas with limited light. Perceiving my fellow pedestrians with supernatural clarity in the darkening streets, it was easy to avoid colliding with them. I was able to achieve speeds which, for a normal man, would have been reckless.

Cutting through a series of crowded plazas and alleyways, I easily left my pursuers far behind me. Yet, I was greatly troubled by the knowledge that I had very nearly been run to ground. One or more of my enemies (I did not yet know which) had finally found me; the feeling that I was safe in my anonymity was quickly replaced by the revelation that I was being hunted by a potentially limitless number of skilled assassins — cold-hearted, ruthless men trained in the art of the manhunt and extremely well paid for their efforts. Most frightening of all, however, was the certainty that, no matter how many of these fellows I managed to kill, they would never stop sending more.

This experience was also indicative of a few indisputable realities. First, my enemies must have somehow obtained a photograph of me, for they knew me well enough to pick me out of a crowd (despite my altered appearance). Second, and more disturbing still, they knew that I was fond of libraries, and had set their trap accordingly. The significance of these two facts was not lost on me and, deciding to forego so obvious a mode of transport as the train, I deemed it prudent to sneak out of town after sundown, and walk the northbound tracks to Red Hook. Half an hour later, I was picking my way through the hilly forests on the northern edge of town where, meeting up with the tracks, I followed the northern line up through Bear Mountain pass. Hiking alongside the river for several hours, I passed through the sleeping village of Cold Spring, moving through the woods whenever possible, avoiding public thoroughfares.

Sometime before midnight, I came upon a railroad bridge which I utilized, under cover of darkness, to get over to the Rockland County side of the Hudson. Once there, I picked up that long stretch of old dirt road, known as the Appalachian Trail, which would eventually take me into the very heart of the Catskill Mountains.

If I had thought for one moment that the Black Thing might be waiting for me on the opposite shore, as eager to see me as I was to see it, I was soon to be relieved of this delusion. As I was to learn over the next eight weeks, my singular progeny, once again, only lingered on the very edges of perceptibility and would venture no nearer, nor permit me to close the gap. It was almost as if it wished to spend some time observing me from afar, before deciding whether or not to approach me.

Yet, just to sense the nearness of the Black Thing was receiving confirmation that my offspring had not only survived, but returned to New England, filled me with unprecedented joy and good cheer. Uncertain of where else to go (and unwilling to stay in one place), I continued to move in a westerly direction, making my slow and steady way to Leffert's Corners.

*   *   *   *

IN LATE FEBRUARY OF 1921, WHILE TRAVERSING THE WILDS OF Ulster county, fifty miles southeast of Leffert's Corners, the Black Thing finally ceased its evasions and placed itself directly in my path. Again I saw it on the western horizon; this time it did not retreat from my advance, but permitted me to approach it on a deserted mountain road.

I was overjoyed to see my offspring. I was like a father who, believing his child to have been killed, suddenly stumbles upon him, alive and well, sitting beside a country road. Waving my arms in the air, I laughed aloud as I ran to it, while it shivered and rocked in anticipation, staring intently at me as I approached.

I could tell immediately that the Black Thing was different. When I looked into its many red eyes (each now roughly the size of a tea saucer!) I saw that it was changed, in some indefinable way, and now regarded me with a kind of sentimental curiosity. Its gaze was thoughtfully reflective now, even critical, in a way that it simply had not been before. It was as if some intense experience (or experiences) had made it more cautious, more analytical, more methodical. Seeing it alive and healthy, I finally permitted myself to acknowledge (and to laugh off) the countless awful deaths I feared had befallen it — sucked into a portal, eaten by Tree Things, captured and enslaved by the military, and countless other horrors...

I was too happy even to bother trying to form a hypothesis about where it had been. I was so thankful for this reunion that I stood there, laughing aloud, shaking my head in disbelief, exchanging meaningful glances with my kin.

This reunion, however heartwarming, was also immediately unnerving in certain respects as well. As I scrutinized the Black Thing, I saw that it had not simply grown, but had more than quadrupled in size, becoming vaguely spheroid, roughly the size of a small haystack, and looking very much like some massive, shiny black sea-sponge. It was now approximately six feet wide and seven feet tall, and vaguely barrel-like in its corpulence. I was uncomfortably reassured that it had not starved in my absence. Additionally, it now moved with a wild, almost spastic quickness, possessing an unprecedented, almost terrifying alertness.

I also noticed, after this strange greeting, that the Black Thing seemed devilishly eager to lead me in a northwest direction (in the very direction I had been walking), rushing ahead impatiently and then speeding back to my side, as though it were nervous. I had no other desire than to follow it, wherever it might lead me, so we continued toward the western horizon, moving through hill and meadow, toward the slowly rising enormity of the Catskill Mountains.

The Black Thing and I traveled well together in the country. It was nearing the end of winter and, still having that same low-level fever which made me immune to the effects of the cold, I was able to walk surprisingly long distances, along the windy hilltops of Ulster and Sullivan counties. What a sight I must have been, casually tramping through the greenery, with my peculiar companion rippling along beside me and looking for all the world like a gigantic black walrus, only with no tusks to speak of, and sporting twenty thoughtfully inquisitive eyes, rather than the traditional two.

I noticed still more strange and baffling changes which had come over the hidden monstrosities inhabiting the landscape. Not only did they suddenly, inexplicably, cease to speak in my presence; they also departed and retreated (one might even say fled) at the very approach of my Black Thing. giving it such a wide berth that I got the impression that they were all, somehow, deathly afraid of it. On two separate occasions, as we made our way through Sullivan County, whole sections of the thick mountain forest, quite literally parted for us like the fabled Red Sea, recoiling backward over hills and retreating down into the gullies, refusing to return to their original positions until we had passed several hundred yards. A feeling of awestruck terror swept through me at these times. I had felt considerable trepidation about how the hidden monstrosities might respond to my offspring, but in all my worried guessing, it had never occurred to me that the Tree Things and Boulder Things might actually be afraid my Black Thing — so very afraid, in fact, that they would avoid all direct contact and withdraw in what appeared to be cringing submission. I was not prepared to contemplate what such a response might mean. Seeing this mass retreat forced me to reconsider my assumptions regarding the presumed vulnerability of my progeny; it seemed clear that I had an inadequate understanding of its true capabilities and status amongst its own kind.

There was one more shocking revelation afforded by this reunion. Now that I was thrust into the position of locating and approving victims for my offspring to eat, I was able to observe the Black Thing hunting and killing on an almost weekly basis. Carefully leading it to the places where I knew suitable victims were most likely to be found (such as parks, public gardens, wealthy private estates), we waited patiently for the right sort of victim to come along, at which time I would whisper the cue phrase "Viva l'anarchia" and point directly at the intended victim.

I was, initially, somewhat horrified to see that the Black Thing did not simply engulf and absorb its victims whole, but rather had developed its own hideous and varied techniques of hunting and eating. Most often it became something like the crawling Tree Things, while at other times it moved on five or six elephantine legs, running its prey to ground. On one occasion, after I had whispered "Viva l'anarchia" and then, pointed to a policeman walking in a deserted park, I watched as it flew into one of the intervening trees and waited, dropping down from the branches, like some horribly carnivorous tarpaulin, and engulfing the thrashing form of the unsuspecting copper.

Regardless of the shape it took, the method of brain consumption was always the same; I had vivid illustrations of the kinds of deaths the unlucky squatters of Leffert's Corners must have met with. Catching its prey unaware, or on the run, it would pin the struggling body to the ground, spit a thin stream of some acidic enzyme into their face, burrow through the fresh wound into the skull, and force its way up to the brainpan. I was, at last, made to understand the partially exploded quality of the bodies. What remained was a severely battered corpse with a hole where the face should have been; I recalled the phrase "The Face-Eating Cult of Leng" and now understood what its author had perhaps hoped to convey.

*   *   *   *

AFTER AN ESPECIALLY DIFFICULT DAY OF HIKING THROUGH THE HILLS west of the city of Monticello, we stopped to rest upon a stony eminence and I pitched camp for the night. I had just lay down when I noticed the Black Thing rise up, very suddenly, to a height of perhaps ten feet, its many eyes peering with a curious intensity in the inevitable northwesterly direction. Standing up, I went and stood beside it, staring and listening with all my ability in the same direction.

The Catskill Mountains gleamed in the moonlight. Looking upon that spectral view of steaming hillocks and glimmering trees, I was overcome by the sense that I had been led to this beautiful, wild place to fulfill a terrible destiny, a fate which was now inescapable because, I knew, when the time came, I would embrace its horror willingly. Our destination, I felt with dreadful certainty, lay somewhere among those mighty silver peaks hovering ominously above the landscape.

The Black Thing maintained its watchful attitude for the remainder of the evening. For many subsequent nights, come bedtime, it would again rise up, gazing with rapt attention at those ghostly mountains on the western horizon. It usually maintained this vigil for many hours, and I concluded that it must have detected some Thing out there in the night that had put a terrible fear into it and made it especially vigilant.

XIII

THREE DAYS LATER, WE HAD MADE IT AS FAR AS THE TOWN OF NEW Paltz, in the foothills of the Catskills. The Black Thing (visible only as a rippling shadow upon the road) was leading the way, with me lagging about thirty yards behind. The northern horizon was dominated by Mohonk Mountain, while about six miles to the northwest lay the town of Leffert's Corners. I was walking along the Showengunk Ridge (with New Paltz still visible in the valley below me) when the peaceful stillness was suddenly rent by the ominous crack of a rifle.

Dropping instantly into a low crouch, I saw and heard (and felt) a bullet whiz past, just above my head, missing me by perhaps eight inches, striking a tree some twenty feet away. Running in a crouch toward the tree line, I heard two more shots (and in such close succession that I knew there must be at least three shooters) before diving headlong into the shadowy cover of the forest. My pursuers were near enough to me that I clearly heard one of the men swear in frustration at seeing me unhurt. Running with all the speed my tired legs could muster, I continued to move evasively; by the time I reached the crest of the next hill, I had already widened the gap between us. Using the hill itself as cover, over the slope I had just ascended and saw, to my horror, that the forest below was swarming with fifty or more charging gunmen, some wearing the uniform of the New York State Troopers, others in what looked like huntsman's camouflage.

I turned and fled, keeping the hill between my pursuers and me, running straight into a stand of trees which bordered a series of wide, sloping meadows. Glancing back, I was relieved to see the Black Thing flying along behind me, a milky grey shadow pouring swiftly over the unbent grass. Moving north to the top of the first meadow, we entered a deep, tree-filled ravine which we followed for nearly a mile. Eventually, this ravine opened out onto a lonely marsh, beside which lay a strangely shaped and unnaturally uniform, lowland flat. Stumbling out of the tree line, I entered this expanse of overgrown field, apparently abandoned but strangely criss-crossed with row upon row of odd, furrow-like mounds that looked as if they could be part of some large agricultural project of the New York Public Works Department.

I paused to catch my breath and consider my best possible options for escape. Standing beside the Black Thing, I was again struck by the odd uniformity of the mounds in this small valley as I picked my way carefully through them. Yet another rifle report echoed across the foothills, and again, I heard the whine of a bullet as it sped past me, thudding into a nearby mound. I raced along the edge of this field for several hundred yards, knowing, every step of the way, that if the shooter could see me well enough to take the shot, then he could most likely also see the curious elliptical shadow racing along beside me. What must he have thought? Utilizing the mounds as cover, I continued to run until, at last, I reached another tree-lined canyon.

This was a decision I would immediately regret. This ravine turned out to be a perfect cul-de-sac, enclosed on three sides by nearly vertical walls of mostly exposed hillside. With a mounting panic, I fled madly up the side of this convexity and, with impenetrable thorny brambles to my right and dangerously steep rocky clearings on my left, I made a desperate search for a hiding place. Moving into the upper steeps of the enclosed chasm that now encircled me like an amphitheater, I presently heard the voices of the men, now strangely amplified, as they entered the ravine and argued with each other about which way I had gone.

I saw that there were no decent trees for me to hide in, since all were either too small, too sparse, or else silhouetted against the sky in such a way that rendered them useless as hiding places. Passing by several outcroppings of large boulders, I deemed one an adequate place to rest. I collapsed in the grass behind it, gasping for air, my heart pounding painfully in my chest. I suddenly noticed that the Black Thing was no longer beside me, I raised my head and scrutinized the immediate vicinity.

About thirty feet below me on the hillside and standing in a cluster of apparently dead maple trees, the now substantial Black Thing had risen to a height of about seven feet and was quivering strangely in the sunlight, with thick, band-like undulations flowing down its sides; it almost resembled a miniature volcano overflowing with black lava which expanded its base into something resembling a huge black starfish. I had seen many shape-shiftings throughout my overland journey with the Black Thing, but this was unprecedented. It seemed to contract inward, and then, suddenly, telescoping out of itself, it poured into the air like an inverted cataract, growing to a monstrous height and putting out jagged, foot long barbs, so that it resembled a tree which had been burned in some long ago fire. There it stood, utterly motionless, like a monstrous black icicle, as the men swarmed past its base, paying it no heed in the furious search for their quarry.

The men were no less than thirty feet from me. I had just drawn myself flat against the backside of one of the larger boulders, holding my .38 special across my chest, when, to my horror and astonishment, the stone rolled away from me. I nearly lost my balance, and, turning, I watched dumbfounded as this enormous boulder (and several of its companions) rose up and went hurtling down the hillside, straight into the line of advancing troopers. Suddenly deprived of my cover, I threw myself upon the ground and watched, bewildered as the great rocks plunged, bounced, and somersaulted wildly down the side of the ravine. The troopers, seeing this avalanche descending upon them, turned and ran screaming in all directions, some tripping and stumbling down the slope, others colliding violently with one another, in their frantic attempts to avoid being crushed. The Boulder Things, for their part, did not seem to want to kill these men so much as to terrify and drive them off, inflicting painful (but not fatal) injuries upon them and knocking them down the slope. In a moment, it was all over and the ravine fell quiet once again.

I hadn't the inclination (or the time) to help those poor battered men, though I certainly felt sorry for them. These Boulder Things which had come to our aid, had not revealed themselves by feasting upon the broken bodies of the troopers; rather they kept up the ruse by making these collisions appear random and coincidental, conforming their movements to the trajectories of an ordinary avalanche, then remaining utterly motionless at the bottom of the slope. After picking themselves up, the stunned and baffled troopers beat a hasty, horror-stricken retreat, back the way they had come. Gathering myself up, I summoned the Black Thing to my side and we exited the ravine through the top, moving in the opposite direction of the withdrawing coppers.

As we continued to hike northeast along the Showengunk Ridge, leaving that gruesome scene far behind us, I could not help but be reminded of the man whom the history books called Sapa Inca Patchacuti, the Earth-Shaker, who had the ability to raise up the very rocks against his enemies; I understood all at once that, somehow, like myself, he too must have proven himself such an ally to the Boulder Things that they had, at certain times, come to his aid, just as they had come to mine.

*　*　*　*

TWO HOURS LATER, AS THE SUN WAS BEGINNING TO SET, WE ARRIVED on a bluff on the outskirts of Leffert's Corners, whose lights we saw in the valley below. We saw that it was nearly encircled by a high, meandering ridge and, utilizing this, we bypassed the town altogether, moving into the hills beyond.

At one point, I looked back and saw a large grey and white cloud descending from the heavens. A light rain was falling in silvery curtains upon the landscape we had just traversed, and heavy winds were pushing the grey and white mass directly toward us. The air seemed oddly pressurized and the smell of rain was growing stronger by the minute. Not only was a storm of considerable intensity rapidly descending upon us, but it would most likely arrive within the hour; to my relief, I saw no sign of the battered hunting party which had nearly overtaken us in the ravine.

Yet, as I gazed at those strange clouds, I was aware of the fact that there was something about them which seemed not quite right. They were a little too white and a little too cylindrical. They hung in the sky like a haze, as if on the verge of evaporating but never doing so, behaving more like the rising smoke of a brushfire than any cloud I had ever seen. Adding to the oddness, the surrounding sky in all directions was entirely cloudless (for the day had been unusually hot and dry), a fact which gave these storm clouds an eerie, anomalous aspect. I am no expert in meteorology, but this approaching cloud mass struck me, in all these little particulars, as somehow artificial. Furthermore, there was a curious darkness near the center of each cloud, a sort of huddled shadow, which I found especially repellent. I say all this to you dear reader, and yet I do not doubt that, at that very same moment, many thousands of other people, looking upon these very same clouds, would have seen nothing more than the advent of an utterly ordinary (perhaps even longed-for) summer storm. But I did not wish to be caught out in the open when those weird clouds broke overhead; quickening our pace, we retreated under the canopy of some nearby trees.

Before continuing along a tree-lined ridge, I took one last look down into the valley below, where the mighty Hudson River wound blackly through the foothills, and a great silvery mist spread its pall over the distant towns. In the distance I even heard a peal of thunder and glimpsed the occasional flashes of heat lightning. Recalling how thunder and lightning had effected the Black Thing back at the farmhouse, I grew anxious, wondering how my offspring might fair in a storm without the comfort of a subterranean basement to hide in. Nevertheless, we continued.

We were about a mile north of Leffert's Corners now. Seeing and smelling the chimney smoke from the squatter's camp, I stopped to catch my breath and to consider what to do with the Black Thing. As we had been hiking along, I had seen many rocky outcroppings half buried in the hillside, several of which appeared to have cave-like hollows between or beneath them, not unlike the one I'd found on Mount Greylock. Searching about in the steeper parts of the forest, I located a small crevice between two massive rocks, a jagged crawlspace about twelve feet deep, where I indicated to the Black Thing that I wished for it to enter the low cave, which it did. Kneeling down beside the myriad eyes that blinked at me, I explained, with a combination of words and gestures, that I needed to leave for a few hours, but that it was to remain inside the cave until my return and that it must not, under any circumstances, attempt to follow me.

It seemed to comprehend these commands well enough; I departed fairly confident that I had been understood. Following the smell of the cooking fires, I descended into a perilously steep ravine, in the side of which someone had carved a procession of ingeniously sturdy and helpful steps. Making my way down this long, winding staircase, I soon had an excellent overview of the entire camp.

There were between fifty and sixty small dwellings, eight-foot long shacks with shuttered windows and swinging doors. Along the northern edge of the camp was a stream which flowed out from a narrow canyon where, in the tall grass by the water's edge, some people were quickly pulling bedclothes off a clothesline to protect them from the coming rain. Nearby, a pack of feral-looking children were scrambling about in the underbrush, shouting and running this way and that.

Here and there, on the pathways that ran between these humble structures, I saw men and women of various ages standing in groups and talking, or else busy at various tasks, most of which seemed to pertain to the cultivation of a massive garden in the center of the camp. In one corner of the garden, countless woven hand baskets, which had been laid out to dry in the sun, were being hastily gathered and placed in a wooden shed. The air grew rich with the smell of soup and baked bread. I was almost lost in a reverie of nostalgia for home-cooked food.

The first to notice me was a troop of mongrel dogs, whose incessant barking soon alerted the entire camp to my approach.

I was only in this squatter camp for three hours, but I was pleasantly surprised by the easy-going interactions I had from the kind people who came out to greet me. Passing myself off as a hobo, I'd come with the plan of doing some labor in exchange for a hot meal (gathering whatever information I could about the disappearances) and then returning, as soon as possible, to my waiting offspring. Upon learning that I was a drifter, I was immediately invited to stay the night, an offer which I politely declined, proposing instead an arrangement whereby I would do an hour's worth of dishes in exchange for a meal. These proceedings were soon interrupted by the arrival of the peculiar rain clouds which broke directly overhead, unleashing a deluge of surprising intensity. Removing my backpack, I was invited into the dining area, a heavy canvas tent directly adjoining an impressive, and wonderfully odorous, roofed kitchen. Seating ourselves at one of the already crowded tables, we made the rounds of introductions in a relaxed and jovial manner, while outside, the downpour became so intense that we sometimes had to shout to be heard above it.

The majority of the older folks seated about the dining area spoke pidgin English and Dutch, while several of the more outspoken young people were American-born, having the unmistakable New England drawl and a vocabulary which indicated that they had, at one time or another, been the recipients of a formal education. There were several small families variously of (judging from their accents) Russian, Spanish, and Italian descent as well as two or three families of mixed race, namely, Dutch and Iroquois hybrids. Some of the elderly Dutch-Iroquois, I noticed, were held in extremely high esteem by the youngsters, seeming to enjoy being in the position of wise elders. I could not help but notice that a disproportionately high number of these elders had mismatched eyes, or, if not exactly mismatched, then with irises which, not unlike my own, were marked with curious areas of discoloration. When they spoke, these half-breed Dutch-Iroquois extolled a decidedly decadent anarchic philosophy, their various comments and jokes revealing a mocking contempt for English civilization in general. Some of these squatters were self-described anarchists, refugees from the colonies in Barre, Vermont and Lynn, Massachusetts which had recently been broken up by police. Directly to my right, I heard a group of rowdy young Spaniards speaking Esperanto and elsewhere in the room, I heard laughing and swearing in Italian. Some of these folks, as I later learned, were actually Galleanists, while others were travelers from the New York anarchist colonies in Croton and Lake Mohegan. Several were simply men and boys who had been hiding out from conscription — draft-dodgers who, now that the war was over, had concluded that communal living suited them.

At some point, numerous huge bowls of delicious vegetable soup were placed upon the various tables, along with tin trays stacked high with loaves of fresh, oven-baked bread, all of which were summarily devoured by the assembled crowd. Two other newcomers and I were given our food first, as a sign of welcome, after which the others joined the feast.

I listened closely to the many fascinating discussions going on around me, contributing sadly little but absorbing much in the way of history and philosophy. They argued over Darwin's theory of evolution and also Kropotkin's rejoinder, *Mutual Aid*. On these topics they were remarkably well-read and well-spoken, discussing these things with a critical frankness which thrilled me. Despite there being much philosophical disagreement and discord among the squatters, debates were tempered with a general sense of irreverence toward authority, rationalism, and religious morality which made it a pleasure to listen to. Each person I heard speak seemed a unique individual, wonderfully free-thinking, and self-directed; these were men and women who took their desires seriously. And though I sat quietly, I made no secret of the fact that I was also following the numerous discussions and arguments which were being shouted from one end of the tent to the other.

As I listened to these highly entertaining, overlapping discussions, I became aware that something was oppressing these squatter folk. There were several times when, after the casual mention of certain names, lively discussions would falter into an awkward silence, which the elders immediately sought to fill with cheerful talk on fresh topics. Several times I peered through the tent flaps and spotted small groups of men and women, nervously walking along the perimeter of the camp, behaving almost like a patrol, speaking in hushed tones to each other and searching along the ground near the adjacent forest. There was an unmistakable tension in the air; I had the impression that I had arrived on the heels of some tragedy, and I began to wonder if there had been another disappearance. It wasn't until an hour or so later that I would learn that, in fact, there had been another disappearance (followed by the discovery of yet another grotesquely mutilated corpse) and this just two days before my arrival. I was relieved to notice, instantly, that this recent fatality had occurred at a time when I knew that my Black Thing had been with me.

After the meal ended, I got up and immediately walked over to the outdoor kitchen (a curious, gazebo-like structure with a raised floor) where, rolling up my sleeves, I went to work on the small mountain of dirty pots, plates, and cutting boards which had been assembled near two sawed-off wash barrels, one full of soapy water, the other clean. I was not alone in my labors; I was surrounded by ten or twelve other industrious persons, all of whom were applying themselves to the task at hand with gusto.

From among this eclectic mix of folks, there eventually emerged an extremely attractive, dark-haired woman with a curious accent, who took up her position across the barrels from me, winking at me as she rolled up her sleeves. I instantly recognized her as being one of the other new arrivals, though I had not yet learned her name. She was a short, pretty woman, lean and strong, with a thick pink scar extending from her jugular vein around to where her collarbones met. Looking at this scar, I couldn't help but think that she had been stabbed directly in the throat with a large knife, and somehow, miraculously, managed to survive. She introduced herself as Carmilla, eyeing me up and down and extending her soapy hand to me, grinning as I took her small wiry hand in mine.

In less than a minute, Carmilla had been pressed and cajoled by the others to tell stories of her travels and of her native land, to which she acquiesced soon enough. She had come to New York, she said, on a ship from

Barcelona, and was soon regaling us all with vivid descriptions of the social unrest going on there.

She began by explaining how there were massive demonstrations happening all over. Growing legions of unemployed people wandered the streets of all the major cities, begging, stealing and, not infrequently, collapsing from starvation and exposure. She explained how women from the poorer neighborhoods, desperate to feed their hungry families, had begun organizing raids on grocery stores, bakeries, and lorries, attacking delivery carts and carrying off clothes, foodstuffs, and coal. She described, with obvious affection, how these large crowds of shrieking women would surge, en masse, screaming and howling, into bakeries, restaurants, and produce markets and clean them out. Initially, these raids were successfully carried out without casualties, but, increasingly, these desperate looters found themselves fired upon by the Sometent or the Guardia Civil. Once, Carmilla described how she herself, half-crazed with hunger, had participated in one such a raid upon an upscale bakery, storming the doors with about thirty other women, desperate even for a loaf of stale bread, only to be clubbed on the head by a policeman on horseback, nearly trampled, and left for dead in the street. Struggling to her feet she had miraculously managed to escape the neighborhood before the second wave of police arrived and began arresting the wounded.

Carmilla expressed a passionate hatred for the Spanish authorities and went on to describe how even Spain's neutrality during the War had been a lie. In truth, she said, Spain's capitalist class had used the war as an excuse to fill their coffers by exploiting the disruption of international commerce. Manufacturing goods and raw materials for both the Austrians and the Americans, making it so that everyone was actually working for the war, whether they knew it or not, making shoes, clothes, soap, canned goods, armaments, or machine parts for one side or the other — or, more often than not both!

As we finished up the last of the dishes, the questions directed at Carmilla began to ebb; retreating into a thoughtful silence, she only seemed to half-listen, as the discussion broke up into numerous smaller debates. Outside the noisy tent, the rain had stopped. Beyond the murmuring voices of the squatters, an eerie silence reigned. After drying her hands with a towel, she gave me an inviting look and stepped out into the darkness behind the kitchen, making her way to one of the large wooden benches which flanked the entrance to the garden. Drying my hands on the same towel, I followed her out into the cool night air.

"Your accent is unusual," I said, stepping up behind her. "Where are you from originally?"

"I was born in England," she said, "but my father raised me in Styria, near the Austrian border. But I have lived in a hundred different places since then. Most recently, as you heard, I have been staying in Barcelona."

"What brings you this far up the Hudson?" I asked.

"I am told that my great-grandmother was full-blooded Iroquois," she said, thoughtfully. "I have always wanted to visit this place and to see if I could find any of my great-grandmothers people."

I recalled things I had read back at Harvard, the writings of Charlevoix and Jean-Baptiste du Tertre. They had written vivid descriptions of the cannibal rites allegedly perpetrated by the Iroquois tribes against prisoners of war.

"Many white men think and say terrible things about the Iroquois people," she continued, staring out into the darkness, "but everyone knows that the white man's descriptions of Native tradition and belief cannot be trusted."

This statement startled me; Carmilla had responded to something which I had merely thought but had not actually said aloud. Nervous that she, like Howard, was capable of reading my thoughts, I scrambled to keep the conversation moving forward.

"Yes," I said, "That is true."

"Ahh... True, is it?" she chuckled. "What is true, Robert? Are you an Arbiter of Truth?"

"I meant no offense," I said, feeling flushed.

"None taken." She sighed, adding, almost as an afterthought, "I like you."

We exchanged a playful look.

"Have you had any luck finding your great-grandmother's people?" I asked.

"No," she replied, "not yet. But I have only just arrived. Tomorrow I will try to speak with the elders here. Some of them are Iroquois."

"I believe so," I replied.

Suddenly, in the distance, we heard the rolling crash of the approaching thunderstorm. I must have jumped involuntarily, because when I looked over at her, she was staring at me.

"Are you afraid of thunder and lightning?"

"No," I lied. "Although, to be honest, some of the thunder clouds I've seen since my arrival here seem a bit... unusual."

"Hmm." She smiled, looking at me out of the corner of her eye and nodding.

"Have you noticed this as well?" I asked. She took a full minute to answer me.

"Iroquois legends tell of a time when the Cloud Beings, the Thunder and Rain Beings, would descend from the sky to instruct humankind, to teach them new ways to survive and overcome difficulty. The Iroquois were on friendly terms with these Beings and countless legends had been passed down which describe these encounters. Even after the arrival of the white man's civilization, stories of this kind are fairly common. According to a medicine man I met on Mohonk Mountain, the Thunder, Rain, and Cloud Beings continue to assist, and even communicate with, those humans who manage to resist the poison of civilization."

"Really?" I asked, stunned at her frankness.

"Yes, really," she purred. "And those who embrace and defend civilization are treated as prey."

It was at this time that I began to notice a very peculiar sensation coming over me, something like a shiver that passed through my body in waves. I began to feel oddly disoriented, a kind of drunken sentimentality creeping into my thoughts, a sentimentality which, even in the (apparent) privacy of my own mind, embarrassed me. I became uncomfortably aware that I had been staring at her lips as she spoke; as her wide brown eyes moved slowly over my face and body with a hungry, shameless, curiosity. Additionally, there was something about her odor that was distracting, commanding more and more of my attention; I noticed that I was inhaling, slowly and deeply, as if to draw as much of her scent as possible into my lungs. Initially, this odor was rather faint; attempts had clearly been made to wash it off and cover it with scented oils. But there was no mistaking it: It was the subtle reek of fresh corpses, mingled with the lesser scent of upturned earth, exuding primarily from her hands and face. This nostalgic perfume of exhumed cadavers, with its sinister and myriad associations, was delectable to me.

"You are on the run from the authorities, no?" she said. It wasn't a question.

"Does it show?" I asked.

She nodded, giving me a long slow sideways look. "I too am hiding."

"And how do you know that you can trust me with such delicate information?" I asked.

"I can tell you are one of us," she smirked. "Looking into your eyes… I can see right through you, Robert," a statement which equally thrilled and unnerved me.

By now, the smell of this irresistibly ghoulish woman was overwhelming, at once, deliciously sweet and strangely narcotic. In addition to the curious tingling spreading throughout my body, her scent awakened bizarre mental images, drawing up from the recesses of primitive memory a long-dormant hunger, a strange and unfamiliar craving which, for me, was as alien as it was subtly loathsome. Such bizarre urges and gruesome impulses had, long ago, become a common occurrence in my life. I would even say that, on the subject of perverse cravings, I was practically unshockable. But the longings now surfacing in my mind were something apart even from the wildest orgies of brain-eating which my offspring and I had enacted; this strange hunger was for something about which I knew almost nothing. It was a longing for… sex.

Though common enough in most people, this sex hunger was, for me, a mysterious and dimly remembered thing. For the last seven years, erotic emotions had been unknown to me; even as a grown man of twenty-five, I was profoundly inexperienced with human intimacy of any kind, and a virtual stranger to physical affection. With the one exception of my abandoned fiancée in Plymouth, I had never been intimate with anyone (and even then, only twice). My reader will, therefore, understand my utter surprise at the nearly forgotten feelings of sexual attraction which now flooded through my body. I was suddenly transformed into a blushing novice, trying to carry on a normal conversation while increasingly preoccupied with the overwhelming impulse to take her in a passionate embrace and to taste her animal body. There was a curious lull in the conversation, during which we seemed to be appraising each other. Discerning these amorous feelings upon my face, she blushed, laughing softly.

"I am surprised at how much I am attracted to you," she said. "I haven't wanted to be with a man in a very long time."

"It is the same with me," I said. "From the moment I saw you, I couldn't take my eyes off you."

"Hmm…" she intoned, staring into my eyes. "You're sweet."

Peering about, as if to assess our privacy, she frowned to see that we were not quite alone. Following her gaze, I saw that several people were now hovering near the tent flaps of the kitchen, tentatively emerging from the well-lit dining tent, and moving drunkenly toward the spot where she and I were sitting.

"Now is not a good time but… I would like to see you later tonight. Perhaps we could meet… there," she pointed, "at that bench near the edge of the forest. I have something which I would very much like to show you." She flashed a toothy grin.

"When?" I asked, surprised, but not looking away.

"Midnight," she said. "Don't be late."

My mind went to work, frantically planning how I could modify my plans to keep this appointment. If I explained my reasons to my offspring, could I compel it to remain alone in the cave for several more hours? My heart was pounding at the thought of this midnight meeting.

I was still haunted by certain other pressing questions. Was Carmilla a ghoul? Was she a vampyre? Was she, like me, something like an Encerrado, a creature stuck halfway between humanity and some nameless man-eating deity? She was, most certainly, an eater of the dead. I could smell it on her. I could taste it in her breath, on her skin, her hair. More to the point, was she friend or foe? Was I attractive to her as a companion with similar inclinations... or was I prey?

I was startled out of my contemplative trance by the splashing of several large raindrops upon my head. A dull roar rose out of the surrounding darkness as the deluge, suddenly and unceremoniously, resumed. Covering my head and laughing, I shouted "I'll be there!" to which she nodded. Following her lead, I ran back to the dining tent, covering my head with my arms. Once inside the warm glow of the tent, we joined the others who were now forming a line to receive a warm mug of either coffee, tea, whiskey, or wine, which the kitchen workers had prepared. Returning to my seat, with Carmilla following behind me, I sat down at the tables, which now formed a semi-circle around a low fire burning in a large earthen oven near the edge of the tent.

Being the only other newcomer beside Carmilla, it was now, apparently, my turn to be prodded and cajoled by the others, to share my story. I related a heavily edited version of my actual autobiography, answering numerous questions, and ending with an explanation of how I was on a journey to meet a friend in Ithaca, New York, and so would be departing within the hour.

This news of my imminent departure sent a wave of unease through my many hosts, and I found myself in the most uncomfortable scenario imaginable; sitting and listening while the friends and families of the deceased squatters, in their efforts to dissuade me from entering the woods alone, told me the stories of the numerous tragic disappearances and of the subsequent discoveries of some of the brainless corpses.

These stories were invariably told in the manner of cautionary tales. Having inadvertently raised the topic, I was a captive listener, my hosts becoming quite vehement in their insistence that I remain until morning.

It was a fine and grotesque bit of theatre that I performed that night. The task before me was no less than this: to feign total ignorance and a kind of shocked, innocent disbelief, while hearing detailed descriptions of a macabre predation, by a brain-eating, shape-shifting Black Horror (whose methods, appearance and proclivities were only too familiar to me).

While I learned several valuable things from listening to these heart-breaking stories, certain stubborn questions remained. Some of the things I heard incriminated my offspring, while others absolved it.

While the three most recent killings had occurred at times when I could definitely account for my offspring's presence, a larger number of squatter deaths and mutilations had occurred in the weeks and months prior to our reunion; I could not rule out the possibility that my Black Thing could be implicated, at least partially, in some of the earlier killings. On the other hand, it seemed unnervingly clear that there was some other brain-eating entity (or entities) who were also utilizing these wooded ravines as a hunting ground. In a sense, this was precisely the information I had hoped to gain, and yet, as told by the loved ones of the deceased, it was a particularly brutal thing to hear. I was doubly sickened to think that, in some cases, my offspring might have been involved; throughout these suggestive tales, there were certain other comments which further supported the idea that my offspring was the culprit.

"It is always worse when it storms," one old woman said, "for the lightning throws the Forest Devil into a rage."

Hearing observations such as this, I shuddered. Carmilla, who was sitting directly beside me, seemed to register this with a keen interest.

As these poor, besieged people unburdened themselves of the nightmare they had been living, I was heartbroken to hear them referring to my offspring as the Thunder Devil, the Tree Devil or simply the Demon. Some of them had even glimpsed it and gave trembling, incoherent descriptions of it, a topic which eventually led to a heated debate about the Thing's shape. One man insisted that it was a great black snake while another described it as an enormous bat or vulture. Yet another claimed it was a gigantic human, while another called it a walking tree. This debate continued for several minutes, during which, disturbed by these descriptions, I listened in vain for some indication as to whether or not these attacks had been the work of one shape-shifting creature, or possibly the work of many different creatures. Certainly the descriptions of gigantic humans and crawling trees gave me pause.

"Are the brains always missing?" I asked.

"Always," said one of the elders firmly, "though not all the missing have been accounted for."

"Well..." one young lady corrected, "the last two bodies were so mutilated that their organs were indiscernible." This statement set several heads nodding.

"How long has this been going on?" I asked.

Several of them exchanged severe looks. An elderly man spoke up, slowly, but with dreadful, heartfelt conviction.

"Beginning of the last century. Since the Indians avoided this valley entirely, the region was first settled by the Dutch, sometime around 1818. They soon abandoned it. Some say it was them early settlers who accidentally awakened the horror that had been living here, others say that them Dutch were bad folks, devil-worshippers who had brought the demon with them."

I turned to see Camilla's reaction to all this, and was surprised to see her standing up, gathering up several empty mugs from the tables, and moving to the kitchen. I had an impulse to follow her, but, embroiled as I was in the discussion, I thought better of it.

After hearing several more of these stories, I expressed my deepest sympathy for their losses and acknowledged the strangeness of their dilemma. Thanking them for their hospitality, I told them that, though I was deeply moved by their concern for my well-being, my meeting on the following day in Ithaca was of such importance to me that I would rather risk my life than miss it.

"I'll tell you, mister," said an earnest young man of about seventeen, who had recently lost his father to the Demon. "You really ought to wait until morning. We've already lost three people, and it's only July."

"Why don't you just leave?" I asked, directing my question not just to him, but to all of them.

A strange silence fell over the assembly. Only the sound of the steady rain filled the void. Some people seemed to stare off into space, while others mumbled to themselves. Some just stared at me sadly, as if I were a doomed man. Throughout the duration of this curious silence, I was increasingly aware of the fact that two of my hosts were staring intensely at me, and with that blanched and decidedly fearful expression which I knew only too well. These two particular individuals, having lately entered the dining tent, had instantly developed a nameless apprehensions about me, and I felt the sudden urge to make myself scarce, as soon as possible, before such feelings against me had a chance to blossom and grow.

A minute later, large numbers of people began to excuse themselves, carrying their dishes into the kitchen and wandering off to their respective shacks. Carmilla was nowhere to be seen. I pulled on my backpack, and said goodbye to several of the people with whom I had spoken earlier, receiving only doubtful looks and shrugs in reply. Stepping out into the rainy night, I made my way back to the earthen steps that led up and out of the canyon.

*   *   *   *

AS I ASCENDED THE MEANDERING STAIRCASE THROUGH THE TREES, occasionally glancing back hoping for another glimpse of Carmilla, I wondered if it had been a mistake to enter the squatter camp. Certainly I had received valuable information, but I began to entertain fears that, by spending time with these fine, free-spirited people, I had run the risk of causing them even more trouble from the authorities than they were already enduring. Nevertheless, my meeting with Carmilla seemed oddly serendipitous and I very much looked forward to learning more about her at our midnight rendezvous.

Nearing the top of the canyon wall, I emerged from the canopy of thrashing boughs and saw that the sky above was now a dismal black cauldron of clouds, hovering above the landscape. The rain was coming down in huge, marble-sized droplets which fell noisily upon my hat. The wind, which had been practically non-existent down at the encampment, was now a fury, flinging the rain sideways (and even upwards) as it crashed violently against the massive trees, bending them low. I soon spotted the outcropping where I had left the Black Thing three hours earlier and, sprinting in that direction, I soon came to the mouth of the crawlspace. Crouching on one knee, I whistled sharply, and instantly the Black Thing appeared, looking nervously relieved to see me. Lowering myself, feet first, into the crawlspace, I lay down alongside my offspring, removing my boots and backpack, and stretching out on the dry ground.

Resting my head on my arms, I listened to the advance and retreat of the rain, savoring the warm, reassuring presence of my progeny beside me in the darkness. As I lay grinning, idiotically, in that hole, my mind flitted from one subject to another, flickering with a rapidity that was almost dizzying. Always my thoughts returned to one single image, a recurring vision which rose up before me in the darkness, blotting out all other thoughts. It was a dazzling vision and it made my foolish grin grow wider still; it was a vision of the lovely Carmilla, beckoning to me, reaching toward me, as if in a dream.

XIV

I MUST HAVE SLEPT FOR ABOUT AN HOUR WHEN THE SOUND OF thunder woke me. Turning over, I saw that the Black Thing was cowering against the rear wall of the crawlspace, as far from the mouth of the cave as it could possibly get. Looking outside, I saw that the storm was, once again, gaining momentum. Gesturing for my offspring to follow me, I dragged myself into the open air and stood up, peering cautiously into the surrounding sky as I dug my pocket watch out of my backpack. The rain was falling in sheets across the hillside and the lowering storm clouds overhead had turned a bizarre purplish black.

At first, they had seemed to be floating past at a normal speed, but careful scrutiny revealed that the clouds themselves were, in fact, stationary. All across their undersides, however, there flowed striated undulations, a vast network of ripples which, when viewed from below, created a nearly perfect illusion of motion. The wind was warm and constant. The air, once again, seemed oddly pressurized. I felt nauseous and frightened; as I pulled the pocket watch out of the pack, I noticed that my hands were trembling. It was 11:11 p.m.

Noting that the Black Thing was already in a state of fright, wide-eyed and quivering, I decided that it would probably be best to confront my offspring's astraphobia directly and at once, to nip it in the bud before it flowered into an actual panic. If I could demonstrate that the thunder was harmless, I felt confident that the Black Thing would overcome its fear. If I showed no fear of it, surely my imitative offspring would seek to emulate me. Placing my hat upon my head, I began the short hike up to the northern rim of the ravine with the Black Thing trailing at my heels, flat as a puddle upon the ground. As I trudged along the tree-lined meadows, I noted the nearby Tree Things retreating silently, surreptitiously, into the shadows, quailing, as before, at the approach of my offspring.

Walking through the rainy darkness, I became unnerved. Most of the taller trees, which stood along the crests of these many intersecting ridges, appeared scorched, burnt, or otherwise mutilated, as if by lightning. Recalling the articles I'd read back at Harvard about the unusually dramatic storms common to this region, I took a renewed interest in studying the landscape. Ahead of me, at the high point of the ridge, I saw a huge maple tree, nearly sixty feet tall and, by far, the most scarred and disfigured tree I'd seen yet.

There was something else which troubled me. While a fair number of these damaged trees were authentic oaks and maples, I soon discovered that the vast majority were actually Tree Things, present in unusually high numbers, and apparently holding their ground in what appeared to be a concerted and ongoing assault from above. These injured Tree Things were, in many cases, quite misshapen, blackened and bent, with great swollen protuberances and bizarre, inexplicable growths, as well as split, or missing, boughs and limbs. This curiously prevalent damage was so consistent that I wondered if, perhaps, the lightning strokes, rather than being the random actions of random cloud collisions, were perhaps something more systematic and intentional... perhaps even a method by which the Overlords expressed their disapproval? Could the intense mutilations evident upon these Tree Things actually be the result of some disciplinary action on the part of the Overlords against certain unruly members of this standing army? I recalled, at this time, what Legion the Giant had said about how the Dark Ones would not tolerate a nuisance to their agenda, and wondered if this could be the true explanation. Was it because the attacks against the squatters had been so clumsy and ill-concealed that the local Hidden Ones were being punished by their invisible overseers? Was there some sort of conflict going on between the Tree Things and the Cloud Things?

Finally arriving at the foot of the giant maple, I squatted down to examine the roots, which were unusually gnarled and articulated. I pulled my hat down low over my eyes and made a sweeping survey of the area. In the ravine directly to my left was the ill-fated squatter camp I had visited. In the next ravine over to my right, I also detected a sizable amount of human activity. I walked over to the edge to get a better view of what was going on below.

In this neighboring ravine there was another squatter camp comprised of thirty to forty tiny hovels, suitable for sleep and little else. Some of these were crude, shed-like structures while others were dug-outs, built into the hillside itself. It was similar to the camp I had visited, though noticeably smaller and more exposed.

As I casually watched the activities of this second encampment, I noticed several things that struck me as peculiar. First, my enhanced vision revealed that these squatters were predominantly, if not entirely, men and boys, not a single female, elder, or child under ten, among them. Second, for a bunch of gypsy squatters, they had surprisingly little gear, except for the shiny new rifles each man openly brandished. Springfields and Winchesters, these guns were government issue, the best available. In addition to these oddities, a surprisingly large number of these men were visibly drunk, staggering around the camp, flaunting their handsome new rifles and calling out strange salutations to one another. The longer I looked and listened, the more I became convinced that these were not ordinary squatters, but some sort of civilian militia, carelessly disguised as hobos and tramps. I received further confirmation from the bits of conversation I overheard, filled with ominous references to "later tonight," "God-damned anarchist foreigners," and "They ain't gonna know what hit 'em!"

More distressing still was the fact that the hovels themselves seemed genuine enough; I wondered, with a shudder, what might have happened to their original inhabitants. These tiny dwellings had clearly been ransacked, looted of any usable items and, in some cases, kicked to pieces. Various coats, blankets, and hats had been commandeered and put on for the purposes of camouflage, the rest trampled underfoot. From the care and attention they put into these costumes, it was clear that these men were plotting a deception. Whatever atrocity it was that they were about to commit, they hoped it would be blamed upon the squatters whom they had displaced.

Twice in ten minutes, I saw men run up to the intervening ridge, peer over, and then sprint back down, giving a full report to an official looking man sitting near the fire under a canvas rain fly. After observing this conspicuously sober man for several minutes, I noticed how the others seemed to defer to him; if this was a hired militia, then this man must be the one sent to guide and command them. As I watched, he stood up, calling the men over to him. Observing this commotion, I immediately understood that they were making last-minute preparations for an organized attack against the neighboring hamlet. I thought of how unprepared the squatters would be and knew that I must run to warn them.

The men in the camp began making preparations to depart. The official man called the others over to the dwindling campfire, and as the storm clouds rumbled discontentedly overhead, I listened as he instructed the men to make ready for departure, to make sure their guns were in good working order, and that each man had a pocketful of shells.

Hearing this cold, calculated recitation of the supply list for a massacre against unarmed, unsuspecting people, I was sickened to my core. Beside me in the wet grass, like a recumbent walrus, lay the Black Thing, whose many eyes gazed thoughtfully back and forth between me and that awful gathering in the gully below. Seeing this small army on the move, I flew into a panic. There was no time to warn the others. I knew I must act now or witness the slaughter of an entire village, whose inhabitants were asleep in their beds.

Glancing down at the Black Thing, my mind raced until at last, with a sharp whistle to get its full attention, the Black Thing and I exchanged a long meaningful look. With a trembling hand, I made a sweeping motion toward the armed procession making their drunken way up the side of the canyon, and then spoke aloud the phrase, "Viva l'anarchia."

Seconds after I had issued this command a dreadful and bizarre coincidence occurred; just as the Black Thing had started off the towards the men, a cataclysmic thunderclap exploded overhead and a gigantic bolt of lightning tore down from the sky, striking the gigantic maple tree not ten feet from where I stood! Stunned, I dropped to the ground, paralyzed with fright. But as frightened as I was by this near miss, the affect it had upon the Black Thing was absolutely appalling.

Until this time, I suppose I had clung to the idea that the Black Thing was a young, inexperienced animal which, despite its capacity for violence, was still, after all, just a vulnerable underling. I had even felt a sort of fear on its behalf, protective, as one would feel towards any living creature which appeared lost or disoriented. All that changed that night in the ravine.

The rainy, uneven moonlight pouring down into the grassy canyon lit it up almost like the dawn. By the time one of the men glimpsed the rippling black triangle that was gliding toward them, it was too late. The Black Thing, hideously invigorated by the lightning, was among them, upon them and, yes, *inside* them. This pitifully drunken procession of roughly seventy-five men never even made it fully out of the encampment. The thundering movements of the Black Thing as it tore through the men were a sight unlike anything words could ever hope to convey. The screams of the men (coupled with the crunch of splintering bone) echoed gruesomely off the canyon walls, and the violent rending of those many bodies created such an unholy din that (as I later learned), the squatters in the neighboring hamlets, having heard it, simply fled in a panic to Leffert's Corners, where they babbled incoherently of the nightmare massacre they had overheard.

In the ten or twelve minutes it took to perpetrate this slaughter, the Black Thing doubled, then tripled, then quadruped in size. What it had done, in essence, was to feed, as swiftly as possible, on every single human brain it could find, falling on groups of ten to fifteen men at a time, de-braining, flaying and macerating them before flinging itself at another cluster of whimpering men and dispatching them in a like manner. Those men who sought refuge inside the hovels quickly learned the futility of such measures. Others, utterly overcome with fright, ran straight into the Black Thing. Something like twenty-five of these men were simply liquefied, reduced to a shiny paste of pulverized flesh and bone. What remained at the end of this melée was less a pile of bodies and more a small lake of gore.

It must have been the sheer quantity of all this fresh human seepage that attracted those secondary scavengers — Beings, most definitely, of the extra-terrestrial sort, and utterly unlike any creatures I had seen so far. I soon learned how they too cherished a particular fondness for the meat of humankind. Alerted, I presume, by the stench of the gore, these horrible Others came burrowing up from underneath the red lake, not unlike a school of sharks in a feeding frenzy. They were great snake-like things, as thick around as a telegraph pole, and squirming out of the ground, bursting through the gore-soaked grass and reducing the turf to a ragged red upheaval. These writhing horrors emerged only reluctantly from within the collapsing lake of gore. I could form no complete picture of them, only catching partial glimpses of their meandering, unearthly anatomies. What might have been their faces were vaguely cylindrical, with clusters of shiny black eyes above awful snapping triptych mouths, straight from a maniac's dream. The sight of these Worm Things slopping about in the viscera gave me such horrors that I became nauseous with fright, reeling away from the edge and falling to my hands and knees.

My thoughts were interrupted by the fiendishly convincing sensation that the entire hillside to which I clung was somehow rocking, to and fro, as if in an earthquake. I became suddenly afraid that I was going to lose my balance and tumble headlong down the slippery, nearly vertical, incline. Such an event would have surely meant my death. Even if, by some miracle, I should have been lucky enough to miss the intervening rocks and trees, then I was sure to tumble directly into that heaving red pool of death which lay at the foot of this cliff-like slope. With my fingers in my ears and my eyes shut tight, I flung myself against the trunk of a nearby tree, where (after confirming its authenticity) I remained for several minutes, trying desperately, though ineffectively, to block out the echoes of the feast occurring in the chasm below.

The gruesome crunching and tearing sounds seemed to go on, and on, and on; I thought I might go irreversibly insane, huddled against that tree. An unknown span of minutes passed in this way until, at last, the awful din began to subside, by degrees, and eventually there was silence. Only then, in the dreadful quiet that followed, did my wits slowly return to me. Listening, I heard nothing save the rustle of the wind in the trees and the occasional rumble of the receding thunder. The storm had passed us and moved on, an eerie calm settling over the glistening hills.

*　*　*　*

IT TOOK ME SOME MINUTES TO BUILD UP THE COURAGE TO PEER INTO the gully. The seventy-five men were all corpses now (and some not even that). The Worm Things had withdrawn, to whatever foul netherworld they had emerged from; I was alone with the Black Thing which, having returned to my side, sat shimmering in the moonlight about twenty feet away on my right. It was gigantic now, the size of a small circus tent, with a shocking, almost spastic agility, and I could not help but regard it with trembling fear. Sensing this, the Black Thing (ever attentive to the subtleties of my moods) kept its distance from me while I took the time to collect myself.

Making my way down into the ravine, I had the presence of mind to avail myself of the best looking rifle I could find (a bolt action Springfield Star-Gauge), as well as fifty or so shells which I gathered up from the gore-soaked grass.

Then I ran. With the Black Thing pouring along at my heels, I ran straight into the thunder-haunted wilderness, over hill and glen, marsh and thicket. I could not say with any accuracy how far, or for how long, I ran. It felt like an eternity of running, one foot in front of the other, into a blurry vortex of wet green hills and dripping trees. I would not have guessed I was capable of such exertion, exhausted as I was; the scene of carnage I had just observed had so disturbed me that it had almost granted me the power of flight. I ran for several hours, continually hemmed in by towns and villages, covering far less ground than I had hoped. Well aware that I was in no shape to be seen in public, I refused to enter populated areas, convinced that I would be locked up on sight. Roughly twelve hours later, when I realized I had come, full-circle, back to Leffert's Corners, I could no longer deny the fact that I was dangerously exhausted and delirious. Climbing high up into another fir, I made myself a crude bivouac by wedging my backpack among the boughs and draping myself over it.

There I lay for about an hour, resting, while the Black Thing, disguised once again as a huge burnt tree, stood nearby and kept watch. At last I fell asleep, waking sometime just before dawn. Hiking north for about an hour, we stopped again to rest in an orchard. After eating my fill of apples, I watched as the Black Thing made a nervous examination of the immediate vicinity.

After being nearly struck by lightning, my offspring was never quite the same. If it had seemed volatile before, it now became downright skittish. It sometimes moved with a quickness and a ferocity that was simply appalling. Though I never once felt personally threatened, its new-found vigor made it so that, on the occasions of its feeding, a thing which I had previously found quite fascinating, I now found it necessary to look away, repulsed by the gruesomeness of its unnecessarily vicious technique. Three days later, when we ambushed a deputy sheriff near Morgan Hill, I was compelled to plug my ears with my fingers during the feeding, for the Black Thing, perhaps on account of its newfound enormity, was now oddly noisy when it fed, filling the air with an intolerable wheezing, gurgling, hissing sound, which I found utterly revolting.

After the near miss with the lightning, the Black Thing seemed to desire movement for its own sake, rarely sitting still for long, and often pacing back and forth, or in curious lilting loops, circling me like a sentry whenever I sat down to rest. As we made our way through the steep mountain passes, I frequently had to struggle to keep up with the Black Thing, since it now moved with an unprecedented speed and fluidity, at times, not seeming to care, or even notice, whether or not I was keeping up.

*   *   *   *

ON THE FOLLOWING EVENING, WE ARRIVED AT A WIDE DARK marshland, slowly being inundated with a thick silver miasma, opaque, luminous, and, at times, curiously still. I was quite disoriented at this time, uncertain whether it was dawn or dusk, and hopelessly turned around. Looking out at this strange scene, however, I intuitively knew where it was my offspring had purposely, surreptitiously, led me. A feeling of cold dread gripped me when I recognized that it must be the Great Swamp, the Grot Vly. Before me was a vast track of fetid and unusable marshland, neglected, avoided, and (according to early Dutch settlers) home to the curious Indian demon. Above us in the sky, like a hideous godhead, loomed Overlook Mountain, the shunned peak which also figured so large in the local folklore and which the Seneca and Iroquois adamantly avoided after dark.

Arriving at the edge of this huge marsh, I stopped, exchanging a long, curious look with the Black Thing. Frowning, I shook my head emphatically, to show that I did not wish to enter the swamp, stamping my foot several times upon the ground for emphasis. My offspring looked up at me inquisitively, as if puzzled, perhaps even mildly amused, but after I repeated these gestures in earnest, it rose up to a height of about six feet, eyed me meaningfully, and then, turning away from me, vanished into the engulfing mist. Retiring to a nearby grassy hill, I sat down on the ground beside a log and loaded a cartridge into the rifle. Setting the weapon across my lap, I leaned against the log, pulled out my copy of *The Ego and his Own* and began to read.

I had only been reading for about ten minutes when, from out of the foggy swamp directly ahead of me, I began to hear sounds which instantly made reading and relaxation an absolute impossibility.

It was here, upon a low grassy hillside overlooking the Grot Vly, that I spent what was easily the most terrifying four hours of my life, listening to numerous overlapping choruses of bizarre chirping, splashing, and bleating sounds— a multi-layered cacophony of hideous alien chatter accompanied, intermittently, by huge, slopping footsteps, and thunderous, undulating vibrations. If my reader were to imagine numerous dueling foghorns, rising and falling in timbre and pitch, they might have some sense of it. Occasionally, these noises coincided with strange multi-colored lights, flaring up and receding within the mounting vapors. There were strange flapping and swishing sounds, coming from the uppermost treetops, followed by curious creaking noises, as if the larger oaks and maples within the Grot Vly were, now and again, being pressed low, almost to the breaking point, then suddenly released. This odd sequence of sounds, repeated many times, implied nothing so much as the stealthy advent of numerous gigantic bodies, gliding quietly down out of the night sky, landing upon the trees, and then dismounting with a splash into the waters of the swamp. The roiling veil of vapors prevented me from seeing what was transpiring beyond it, and yet the constant, rhythmic splashing of tiny (and not so tiny) wavelets against the shore betrayed an almost ceaseless rearranging of huge unseen bodies, as well as a slight but noticeable displacement of the swamp water itself, which rose perceptibly.

It was here that I learned the limits of my ability to comprehend and translate all of these unearthly languages. Despite my earlier breakthrough, I now found that, while some of these utterances were intelligible, others, while clearly an actual language, remained wholly indecipherable. The implication seemed clear: some of the beings I was overhearing were unlike any that I had encountered before and, perhaps, something wholly apart from the (now familiar) Hidden Ones. From the little phrases that I *could* actually understand I received the most abominable revelation of all, that which laid waste to whatever shred of sanity I had been clinging to. To my everlasting despair, I learned precisely how the clearing of the earth is too come about.

The attacks would come in three successive waves. First would be the worldwide emergence of the Hidden Ones (whom they called the Feeders), those beings whom I have already described: the now familiar Tree and Boulder Things, as well as the various and innumerable man-eating ponds, clouds, mounds, bogs, and mists of the forest. On that fateful day, these creatures, freed of their obligation to remain hidden, would be permitted to feed at will upon whatever human beings they would be lucky enough to discover. The second wave would be the arrival of three enormous interstellar creatures who would come to set the world on fire. These gigantic, fiery beings were repeatedly referred to as the Flaming Three. The Hidden Ones, in their talk of such matters, deliberately avoided all descriptive references to the

Flaming Three, evoking them in name only and without any explanatory language, as if to carefully avoid calling their image to mind. The third and final phase would be the Wavemakers, whom they also called the Myriad Ones. There would be seven of these similarly non-descript Myriad Ones who would drop from the sky, throwing up huge, mountain-sized waves, which would extinguish the massive firestorms which the Flaming Three had left in their wake. These monster waves would flood the earth from pole to pole, washing away, not only the last traces of human civilization, but whatever remained of terrestrial life.

When the sun finally began to rise, this hideous chatter began to die down. Once again, I heard a great disturbance among the trees, followed by the sounds of the beating of numerous gigantic wings high above me. These sounds eventually faded away. Not long after this, as the vapor began to dissipate, the Black Thing emerged from the marsh and joined me on the hillside. Inexplicably, it had returned to the size of a haystack, a fact for which I was most grateful. Twenty minutes later we had left the Grot Vly behind. By the light of the rising sun, we started off again, heading due east. At my insistence, I took the lead, chastising the Black Thing every time it tried to go ahead of me, until, weary of my outbursts, it finally resigned itself to follow at my heels.

* * * *

I FORCED MYSELF TO CONTINUE EAST UNTIL THE OUTLINE OF Overlook Mountain was a dim shadow on the horizon. I was desperate for rest and quiet and, finding a warm dry hillside which overlooked the entire valley, I resolved to sleep away the day in the tall grass.

Having just settled into a comfortable position on the ground, a strange noise made me sit up and look around. Gazing into the darkened valley that stretched away to the south, I saw a large troop of armed men, still about a quarter of a mile away, but slowly making their way up the valley toward me. Many of these men, like the earlier posse, were also dressed in the uniforms of the New York State Troopers, and I was further distressed to see that they were beating the bushes as they came and carefully looking up into the branches of every tree they passed under. The sight made me sick to my stomach. In my panic and desperation to escape, I had woefully overestimated my powers of endurance, and had run myself well beyond the point of exhaustion. My legs buckled and I dropped involuntarily down on one knee.

Even at that distance, I could hear the barking of dogs. Near the front of this sizable posse, I saw two men, each of whom was leading a half-dozen, huge, black Alsatians on a lead-leash. I was quite dazed and found that my sense of time had become oddly unreliable. I rubbed my tired eyes for a few seconds and when I looked again, this vast hunting party was only a few hundred yards from me. I fell to staring at them and, the next thing I knew, they were at the dilapidated fence which ran along the base of the hill, pulling open the barbed wire for each other and guiding the Alsatians through the gap. The wind must have blown my scent straight down to them; the dogs exploded in a fit of savage barking. The men unleashed the dogs, and all twelve of those snarling, snapping canines came bounding up the hill, not fifty yards from me!

I looked around for a tree to hide in. Before I could even steady myself, I saw the Black Thing pouring down the hillside to intercept the ascending dogs. Spreading itself perfectly flat upon the ground and hidden by the curve of the hill, the Black Thing waited until the first of the charging dogs were within just a few yards before launching itself upward, a sight which so frightened the dogs that, almost without exception, they turned tail and fled back down the hillside to their masters. I say *almost without exception* because several seconds later, from a thickets about fifteen feet away on my right, there burst forth one final dog, whose particular route up the hillside had spared it the sight of my offspring's menacing display. Momentarily separated from the pack and unnoticed in the charge, she now came barreling toward me, snarling savagely, her white fangs bared.

On shaky legs, I attempted to retreat from my attacker but, in my weakened state, I was no match for this magnificent animal. Before my offspring could repeat its terrifying performance, this Alsatian had smashed into me, catching my outstretched hand in its mighty jaws and sinking its fangs deep into the tender flesh between my thumb and fingers. From the corner of my eye, I saw the Black Thing fly up, and the now terrified dog instantly released her hold upon my hand and fled, yelping, toward the armed procession. Turning my back on the Black Thing and the posse, I managed to retreat with haste, along the sloping ridge, desperately looking here and there for a place to hide, with blood pouring from my mangled hand.

At last, about a hundred feet down that same ridge, beneath an oddly shaped furrow, I found a curious hole, rather like a badger's sett, only considerably larger; detecting no life within, I quickly crawled inside. I followed this passage some ten feet, following its curve sharply to the left. Here I squatted, struggling to catch my breath, occasionally peering back at the entrance from behind the safety of the corner. Looking at the wall directly across from me, I spied The Black Thing (or a portion of it) embedded, or rather implanted, grotesquely, in the side of the tunnel, and visible only as a dark stain full of blinking, migrating, eyes.

Outside, the barking of the dogs grew louder until at last I knew that the hunting party was gathering just outside the hole. I heard several stern voices commanding the Alsatians to enter the tunnel, a thing which the poor beasts simply refused to do, even when, a moment later, the men began to beat and whip them with the lead-leash. I heard the dogs whining and howling miserably, in terrible agony, a thing which eventually led to some harsh words between the troopers and the dog handlers.

Undoubtedly frustrated by a long, tiring, and, ultimately fruitless chase through the hills, the enraged troopers did a rash but understandable thing. They suddenly unloaded their weapons into the hole; to escape the noise and the chance ricochet, I was forced to retreat ever further into the recesses of that awful burrow. I hadn't gone but fifty feet, around several more corners, when I came upon a curious oval-shaped chamber, just off the main tunnel. Entering, I collapsed upon the convex floor, breathless, terrified, and lightheaded from blood loss. The bite wounds on my hand, now caked with tunnel dirt, were still bleeding profusely and the painful throbbing was quickly becoming so intense that I could think of almost nothing else. Pulling off my backpack and dumping it out on the floor, I clumsily wrapped my injured hand in an old shirt, after which I promptly drank an entire canteen of water. I then collapsed against the side of the cave.

*   *   *   *

I NOTICED THAT WE WERE ENTIRELY ALONE. NOT ONLY WERE THERE no large animals hiding inside the surrounding tunnels, but there were no grubs within the walls, no worms within the soil, no ants or pill-bugs traversing the earthen floors. I say that we were entirely alone, and this was demonstrably true; yet a heavy musk-like scent permeated the burrow, an odor simultaneously revolting and oddly appealing. With my enhanced sense of smell, I could take this odor apart, isolating and identifying its separate components — a list which, oddly enough, seemed to include rotting fabric, decaying flesh, dust, moldy leather, and rust. As informative as this was, I remained fearful that the inhabitant of this subterranean nest (whatever it might be) would return at any moment, to find me helplessly crippled by exhaustion, and tastefully doused in my own fresh blood. After several days passed without incident, however, I convinced myself that the lair was indeed abandoned.

I remained laid up in this antechamber for several days and nights, feverish, enfeebled, and with a dwindling water supply. I had recently stocked up on apples which, along with a loaf of stale bread, sustained me throughout this period of physical agony. Beneath the dirt-caked shirt I'd used for a dressing, my hand soon became badly infected and, lacking the mobility to find a stream or spring, I was prevented from giving it a proper cleaning. I remained in this pitiful condition for an unknown span of days, guarded over by the Black Thing, who watched patiently as I writhed and moaned through my convalescence.

Helpless as a baby, I could feel, and hear, and sometimes even taste in my mouth, billions of poisonous microbes pouring from the epicenter of the infected area and spreading throughout my body. Some phases of this slow recovery were worse than others, as my body fought back tirelessly against the tiny invaders. My hand, within the span of a few days, soon became badly discolored and swollen with pus, throbbing painfully anytime I failed to keep it elevated. The worst symptoms, by far, were the hallucinations in which I was vividly privy to the progress of my microscopic attackers; even when I closed my eyes, I saw horribly enlarged scenes of my own necrosis. It was as though I were floating over vast, mountainous landscapes of pink meaty tundra, inundated with swarming crab-like Things, who feasted and tunneled into the ragged topography of my collapsing flesh. Just as it had been in those other prophetic and apocalyptic dreams, it was as if I were watching it all happen from some strangely elevated position, suspended high in the air.

Occasionally I heard human voices, whining dogs, even gunshots, coming from the area just outside the hole. As before, there seemed to be a universal refusal to enter the burrow itself, and I remained there, unmolested by man or beast.

*   *   *   *

WHEN, AT LAST, MY FEVER BEGAN TO SUBSIDE, AND I RECOVERED A modicum of my strength, I dragged myself to the mouth of the tunnel to savor the sunshine and fresh air, and to gaze upon the surrounding countryside. From the safety of this hidey-hole I was also able to monitor, in a limited way, the furious activity going on in the valley below. Several times over the first few days, the countryside was crossed and re-crossed by wave upon wave of sheriffs' posses, vigilante mobs, search parties, reporters, and platoons of State Troopers. I deemed it prudent to remain hidden until I was fully recovered.

Another thing I learned from my vantage point just inside the mouth of the cave was that, despite my initial impressions to the contrary, the surrounding forest was, like the interior of the tunnel itself, strangely, inexplicably devoid of animal life. Careful listening revealed that the chittering, chirping, and whistling noises I had occasionally heard echoing across the landscape were, in fact, fake — nothing more than the imperfect mimicry of the Hidden Ones (who, once again, accounted for a distressingly large percentage of the surrounding wilderness). Twice I thought I saw high-flying ravens, but, upon closer inspection, I recognized that these too were imposters, shape-shifting Hidden Ones.

I was forced to wonder what manner of thing could it be that had driven away the rest of the wildlife? Certainly not the Hidden Ones, for I had observed countless Tree and Boulder Things co-existing alongside the native fauna without incident; the Hidden Ones preyed exclusively upon humankind, so wildlife had no fear of them. The same held true for myself and the Black Thing. With increasing trepidation, I was forced to ponder the inevitable question: what might this thing be, this unprecedented monstrosity, whose nesting place I had inadvertently inherited?

I also gave considerable thought to the notion of punitive lightning and Overlord supervision. What the Goliath had said seemed the only plausible explanation. The attacks occurring near Leffert's Corners were obviously being carried out by an inexperienced underling, untrained in the art of subterfuge, whose overt violence posed a threat to the secrecy of all. These hypothetical Overlord beings could not very well stand by and allow such wanton indiscretion to compromise their positions or betray their presence. A rogue creature such as my offspring, inadequately experienced in the art of concealment, presented a very real danger. Perhaps the uncanny lightning strikes I had seen were part of this larger system of intimidation and control. It would certainly explain why my offspring would have such a great terror of them.

Despite these aborted insights and wild speculations, I always returned to the central question of what might cause such a tight concentration of frenzied attacks in one specific area. Was there a reason why so many of the Hidden Ones had come to this particular mountain region? What was drawing them to this remote and desolate mountainside? I wondered... could there be a nearby portal?

* * * *

DURING THESE SHORT STRETCHES OF BASKING IN THE sunlight, I became aware that there was, in fact, one life-form which was not only present, but surprisingly plentiful. Here and there, drifting over the green hills, I saw great clouds of swarming flies, some of which passed directly over me, in an almost exploratory way, alighting upon me fearlessly. These flies were of the shiny blue and green variety, sometimes called flesh flies. Later research would reveal them to be Calliphorus erythrocephala, and Phormia regina of the genus Sarcophaga, the kind sometimes seen on dung and decaying organic matter. These particular specimens looked plump and well-fed. I couldn't help but wonder if perhaps there wasn't some large corpse, or corpse pile, rotting somewhere nearby, giving rise to these wandering over-stuffed swarms. Furthermore, could this curious phenomenon be related somehow to the absence of wildlife?

Moreover, I experimented with a way of cleaning my infected hand that, thankfully, did not involve leaving the safety of the burrow. Recalling something I'd once read in a medical book, I adopted the habit of allowing these remarkably fearless flies to land upon my wounded hand, permitting them to feed upon the pus and to lay their eggs directly inside the torn folds of the wound itself. Shortly thereafter I was pleased to feel these eggs hatch and the maggots to commence their feasting. Once inside the wound, these burrowing larvae ate only the necrotic cells. All that remained when their feasting was through was the pink, still-living tissue, licked meticulously clean by several hundred tiny tongues and now free of infection. This method also proved quite painless (compared to re-opening, rinsing with water and stitching). The only slight discomfort I experienced was the ceaseless squirming and wiggling of the maggots themselves, a tickling, pulsating sensation, unscratchable because it was beneath the skin. In time, even this ceased to irritate me and, eventually, I even grew to enjoy it. Four days after applying the maggot cure, I rinsed the wound in a nearby stream, where I let the tiny nibbling minnows clean it yet again.

With the infection gone, my fatigue and fever quickly faded and my strength returned.

XV

ONE NIGHT, WHILE RETURNING FROM A MIDNIGHT RAID ON A NEARBY orchard, I happened to glance up at the windswept peak directly above my cave and glimpsed, through the trees, an illuminated window, nearly obscured by the branches of an enormous tree. Moving closer, I saw that this window was part of a much larger structure whose breadth was almost perfectly hidden by trees, bushes, and a low hillock. Surprised that I had not noticed it sooner, I continued along the hillside through a light rain, staring fixedly at this spot until, at last, I discerned the outline of an enormous mansion situated near the summit of the mountain and well over a hundred yards above my hiding place. Inside the house were three human figures whose warm silhouettes I clearly saw (despite the intervening wall) huddled together in one of the upper bedrooms.

Curious to get a closer look at this structure (and its occupants), but unwilling to travel overland through an increasing downpour, I wondered if there might not be a subterranean route. Returning to the burrow, I quickly confirmed that the main passage beyond the chamber I had expropriated ran in an apparently upward, straight line toward the summit of the mountain, and at an almost identical angle to the outer slope. Within minutes of entering this unexplored passage, I encountered many intersections; I concluded that, true to my intuition, the entire hillside must be riddled with similar tunnels. While most of these side tunnels ran horizontally, I found several that sloped noticeably upward in the direction of the peak. Was it a stretch to think that one of these many passageways might communicate directly with the mansion? With a sharp whistle I summoned the Black Thing to my side, pointing into the central tunnel and motioning that I wished for it to go first.

I could not always see my offspring in the dark. From the time that it was very small, it had possessed the ability to hide from me, despite my enhanced senses; during the first few days of its life, it was only its bumbling clumsiness that had enabled me to locate it in the dark cellar. Rather than mere happenstance, this had been a conscious choice on the part of the Black Thing. In fact, it could radically manipulate its temperature, density, and color.

214

As we entered the darkened tunnel, the Black Thing increased its temperature. Not only did it warm the chilly subterranean air around us, but it became distinctly visible to me in the dark, pouring over the contours of the tunnel floor like a dimly luminous carpet, nearly thirty feet long. This luminosity, in these surroundings, laid bare the internal composition of my offspring, and I received a brief but startling education in its alien anatomy. I saw the things which must have been its organs, veins, and muscles, pumping and writhing curiously beneath the stretched and glowing outer membrane, keeping time with its bizarre form of locomotion.

With thunderheads crashing outside, we began to make our way through the interior of the mountain. This low passageway soon merged into another, larger, tunnel which was several times bigger than the others I had seen. I found I could stand completely upright in it, a fact which simultaneously relieved and unnerved me; relieved that I didn't need to crawl or walk in a painful crouch, yet anxious that whatever had made this tunnel must be roughly the size of a full-grown bull elephant; it was for this reason that I made the Black Thing go first. I followed as close behind it as I could without actually stepping on it. Roughly ten minutes later, I spied a place where this steep tunnel abruptly ended and ascended vertically, like a chimney, toward the surface. Regrettably, my enthusiastic offspring also saw this opening and, before I even had a chance to object, it had hastened to the spot with a startling speed, and promptly vanishing.

Running to catch up, I approached the opening with mounting apprehension. Cautiously sticking my head through the hole, I peered into the vast sub-cellar of a huge rectangular building, confirming my intuition; the tunnel had brought me directly underneath the mansion. All around me in this cellar grew a wild profusion of brambles which, in the moist shelter of the many-windowed basement, had grown to a shocking and unprecedented size. The intermittent moonlight poured through the window on my left. In the southeast corner of the decaying framework above, through the intervening floors and walls, I discerned the warm outlines of the three human figures I'd seen earlier, laying side by side upon what appeared to be an enormous bed. From their slow heart rate and respiration, it was plain that the three men were fast asleep.

But I was not the only one making a careful study of these figures. Moving along the southern wall of the cellar, like a huge black snake, and seemingly oblivious to my presence, I saw my offspring, its many unblinking eyes trained upward and fixed upon the three silhouettes. Feeling distinctly uncomfortable with this stalking behavior, I immediately made a low short whistle, followed by an emphatic gesture that I wished for my offspring to come to me at once. I was, however, unrepentantly ignored, and I watched, dumbfounded, as the Black Thing raced defiantly across the remaining floor, spilling, ink-like, up the wall and then, to my utmost displeasure, vanishing into a large crack in the plaster.

Panic-stricken, I crawled the rest of the way out of the hole and, steadying myself against a large brick chimney, looked around for an opening in the brambles. Finding one, I quickly began to work my way through it, moving as quietly as possible, taking solace in the fact that the three figures, still clearly visible above me, remained horizontal, asleep and apparently undisturbed. I was, however, unable to locate the Black Thing. A minute later I had reached the base of the rickety wooden stairs which led up to a door on the ground floor. As carefully as possible, I managed to climb the stairs, open the door, and step through it, without making any discernible noise. I entered an enormous paneled foyer which, in its day, must have been truly magnificent. Now, however, its oaken balustrades were rotted through, collapsing in places and caked with a black fungus which gave off a sharp, peppery odor. In the center of this vaulted chamber rose a massive curving staircase which led to the upper floor. From the many fresh footprints I saw on the dusty flooring, it was evident that this mansion had recently been entered, explored, and possibly even ransacked, by a fairly large group of people. Doors and cupboards stood open, shelving had been ripped down, and all the drawers had been pulled out, their contents dumped upon the floor. Mounting the moldy staircase I drew comfort from the sound of snoring.

I was only halfway up the stairs when I heard another sound that stopped me in my tracks. Between the aforementioned snores there was a soft, rhythmic sound, a gurgling, slurping noise, almost lost in the roar of the wind and the rain which assailed the outer walls, but growing steadily louder and coming from the same spot as the snoring. Peering in the direction of the occupied bedroom, I now saw that, beyond the thin partition that stood between us, two of the three silhouettes upon the bed had grown inexplicably dim and strange of shape, jiggling curiously from side to side, and writhing silently upon the bed. Creeping up the remaining stairs, I moved down the hallway to the door, and hesitated. Hearing the awful slurping sounds within, my nerves nearly failed me. Visions of the horrendous slaughter I'd seen in the squatter camp flashed through my mind. I clenched my teeth and drew a deep breath in a vain attempt to steady myself. I could detect the overwhelming stench of fresh human meat, warm, salty, and overpoweringly sweet to my nose. Grasping the doorknob with a trembling, reluctant hand, I slowly and silently pushed the door open about three inches and peeked inside.

From the sheer size of this chamber, I gathered that it must be one of the main bedrooms. It was about twenty square feet, with an enormous window overlooking the valley to the south — the same window, in fact, which I had seen from below. These details were soon eclipsed by the fact that the room was coated in fresh blood from end to end; had I not later learned the true cause of this carnage, I might well have thought that a bull, or some other large animal, had been slaughtered and butchered there. This blood had not been splashed thickly upon the walls, but rather sprayed, as if a bloody fog had passed through the room and left its shimmering red dew upon every surface. Pushing the door open a few inches more, I glimpsed the fireplace and the antique bed, upon which I saw a vision of such unearthly grotesqueness that I froze, paralyzed with dread at the sheer, incomprehensible wrongness of it.

There in the darkness, laying upon the bed, was the Black Thing, its body, oddly bifurcated into two separate blobs, one running down either side of the mattress and connected only by a thin arm-like appendage which was draped over the middle man, miraculously still asleep in the center of the bed! Of the three recumbent figures, only this middle man was visible. The other two had been completely engulfed within the liquid mass of the divided Black Thing. These two separate blobs (each containing the still-struggling form of its disintegrating victim) began heaving gently from side to side, with curious ripples running down their length. Through the action of some unknown type of peristalsis, it was attempting to digest them. As I watched, the blob on the left side of the bed began to pour itself, through the intervening appendage, into the body of the blob on the right side of the bed, which, naturally, began to grow exponentially, spilling onto the floor and rising into the air beside the bed, filling the emptiness of the room like some bizarre, twenty-eyed tree.

Half-roused by these curious movements, the sleeper in the middle, whose back had been to me, began to stir. With a low groan, he rolled himself over, lifting his sleepy head and turning his face to me for the first time. Seeing his features, I gasped in disbelief, recognizing, at once, that it was Howard from Providence!

It was as if an abyss suddenly opened up beneath me. My mind reeled as a thousand questions went ripping through me. How could it be that, of all people, Howard was here? What could possibly have brought him to so desolate a place as this derelict mansion in the Catskills? More to the point, what exactly was happening on that bed? My rambunctious offspring, taking note of my presence, seemed to pause in the air, like a child caught stealing a cookie. Having interrupted its scrutiny of Howard, the Black Thing now directed its full attention at me, glaring at me, it seemed, with something like annoyance and exasperation.

As far as I could surmise, the Black Thing was seconds away from ingesting my friend Howard. I suddenly knew that, once again, I must act, or else stand by passively and witness the brutal maceration of my one and only friend! What could I do? How might I hope to stop it? When I had tried to call it back to me down in the cellar, it had willfully ignored me. Had I lost all control over my progeny, or might I still retain some power of influence? These questions did not come one after another, as I have written them, but all at once, like a painful explosion inside my head. I screamed, as loudly and as strangely as possible. I screamed in an attempt to gain and hold my offspring's attention, to frighten or distract it long enough to give Howard a chance to escape. I screamed to wake Howard up and to alert him to the danger that was poised above him. I screamed in anguish and fear for the well-being of my dear friend, now threatened by a polymorphous fiend of my own creation, and I screamed because the idea of my offspring killing someone whom I cared about horrified me like nothing else I could imagine. I screamed for all these reasons, and countless more. Startled by the horrible intensity of my own voice, I clapped my hand over my mouth and fell silent. Alas, it was too late. The effect of this aborted screaming, now echoing off the walls and down the hall, was profound and two-fold.

Flicking his eyes open and jerking his head off the pillow, Howard suddenly sat up, blinking, squinting, and fumbling for his glasses in the pitch darkness. Instantaneously, the Black Thing recoiled its tendril, withdrawing all its limbs into one consolidated mass, and moving abruptly to the window. Just then a colossal bolt of that oddly (suspiciously) well-timed lightning flashed across the sky, lighting up the room for several seconds, which caused my astraphobic progeny to leap, spasmodically, into the air. It cast a ghastly shadow upon the chimney, before dropping soundlessly onto the wood floor and vanishing through the boards, pulling its grotesquely pliable, human-shaped cargo along with it.

The next thing I knew, Howard was on his feet and running, wildly, madly, straight toward the very door that concealed me. In a panic, I stepped into the room across the hall, flattening myself against the wall, just as Howard burst into the corridor and flew out of the house. Stepping quickly to one of the front bedroom windows, I watched as he fled back down the mountain, shrieking and howling incoherently as he went. Two minutes later, I heard the distant roar of an automobile engine, followed by the sound of tires spraying gravel as Howard sped off. I watched from the window as his tiny headlights appeared in the valley far below, careening along the meandering road in the direction of Leffert's Corners, before finally disappearing over a hill.

Returning to the cellar, I searched about unsuccessfully for the Black Thing. Finding nothing but a great smear of blood leading into the tunnel near the chimney, I lowered myself into the opening in pursuit. Scrambling through the steep darkness, I returned to the oval-shaped chamber where I found the Black Thing, huddled pathetically against the back wall and staring at me with round, apologetic eyes.

* * * *

THAT NIGHT I LAY AWAKE FOR MANY HOURS, MY THOUGHTS RACING from one unanswerable question to the next. I wondered what might have possessed Howard to come to this remote region and then, recalling his stated plan to become an investigator of strange phenomenon, I theorized that, having read of the squatter massacre in one of the Providence papers and, intrigued by the diabolical legendry connected with it, his curiosity must have been profoundly aroused. For a man of Howard's temperament, I knew that a mysterious tragedy of this kind would have been an irresistable enticement, in his present state of mind.

I pondered the implications of my offspring's disobedience. Could I reasonably expect to retain control over a monster who had grown so big and powerful? A few times before retiring for bed, I issued a few minor commands to the Black Thing, to see if it would obey me. It did, almost too eagerly; I concluded that there must be some other explanation for what had gone on in the mansion. The unprecedented manner of feeding was also something of a puzzle. Why had it eaten the men whole, dissolving them entirely? Why had it eaten Howard's companions while carefully avoiding Howard himself? Perhaps it detected, as I had, that there was something about Howard that seemed almost beyond human. Had my offspring spared Howard because he carried some other Being inside him? Was Howard (to use the Goliath's phrase) pregnant? Had I not seen his pupils flare in that curious way? I recalled his descriptions of being ill immediately after my visit and, for the first time, I permitted myself to wonder: had I infected Howard with a Black Thing? Had a tiny fragment of the piece living inside me, implanted itself inside my friend? More ghastly still, had I inadvertently infected Howard's mother, Susie, and, thereby, somehow contributed to her subsequent collapse?

* * * *

AFTER RECOVERING FROM THE SHOCK OF THIS EPISODEE, I IMMEDIATELY began to make a systematic investigation of the entire tunnel system. Initially the Black Thing was eager to take the lead and, since I remained nervous about who or what we might encounter, I assumed the role of follower despite my reservations. Once again emitting the warm glow, it launched itself into the tunnel, slowing to a reasonable pace only after I had sternly admonished it.

The Black Thing led me first down a long southbound passageway. This relatively straight tunnel sloped downward for nearly a mile, and soon widened into something the size of a narrow hallway. Twenty minutes after entering this passageway, I grew alarmed when the air became thick with the unmistakable stench of decay. This odor was so strong that, after considering the distance and direction we had gone, I began to wonder if we had not perhaps drawn near to the squatter's camp where the massacre had happened. Shortly afterward, we came to a place where this descending tunnel reached its lowest accessible point: a wide tapered chamber, perhaps fifty feet long and roughly twenty feet high near the center. The stench soon became intolerable. After negotiating several huge boulders which lay in the middle of this room, I suddenly came upon the source of the unfortunate odor.

The downward sloping tunnel before us was flooded — quite literally clogged from floor to ceiling, with human gore. From the angle of the ceiling it was clear that, though the passageway continued on for some distance, the remaining portion of the tunnel was filled-in, submerged in this sea of rotting blood, meat, entrails, and various other (discernibly human) fragments.

The Black Thing was in the lead, with me following close behind it, and this was true — that is, until it became clear that my offspring intended to plunge directly into this pool of moldering viscera, to swim through it, in fact, and to explore whatever lay beyond. Stopping short, however, I stamped my foot upon the stone floor and folded my arms across my chest. Having already entered the rotting pool, the Black Thing stopped, pointing its many eyes at me, as if in confusion.

"I do have my limits, you know!" I said. "There are some things that I will not do, even for you!"

The Black Thing blinked uncomprehendingly.

"Come on," I said. "We are going back!" And then I turned, as resolutely as possible, and started back.

Suddenly, from behind me, I heard an astounding thing… a perfect echo of my own voice, right down to the intonation, saying, "Come on. We are going back!"

Spinning around, I shouted, "You can talk!"

"You can talk!" it answered, its voice emanating from a curious little blowhole which had appeared in the center of its broad back.

"Can you understand me?" I asked, dumbfounded.

"Can you understand me?" It repeated.

"I am your father," I said softly, smiling, tapping my fingertips against my chest, "I created you! I brought you into this world! You came from inside me. Do you remember?"

"I am your father." It repeated, "I created you! I brought you into this world! You came from inside me. Do you remember?"

Several more questions along these lines revealed that my offspring, while capable of doing a miraculous, pitch-perfect impersonation of me, was merely a mimic, showing no sign of actually comprehending any of the words which it had spoken. It quickly grew bored of our little game of call-and-response and, returning to the edge of that awful red mire, once again beckoned me to follow it.

"I am not swimming through that!" I said, pointing, "Now… come!"

I began walking back to the tunnel. I had only gone about five steps when my offspring went racing past me, taking the lead once again, back the way we had come.

Before leaving this half-flooded chamber, I paused and turned back. I scrutinized the stony walls for any sign of an adjoining passageway, finding nothing but densely-packed rock, clay, and soil. Peering up at the ceiling directly over my head, I made a conscious effort to expand my awareness to include the landscape above me, hoping that I might recognize something familiar. After several seconds, I began to see, as if in a dream, the ghostly topography of the hilly countryside above us. There, in the ravine directly overhead, just as I had suspected, I saw the rough outlines of about twenty crude structures, strewn with debris and empty of inhabitants. The chamber I was standing in lay directly beneath the squatter camp where the militia had been slaughtered.

I ran to catch up with the Black Thing, which was thoughtfully waiting for me in the passage ahead.

*   *   *   *

SHORTLY AFTER OUR DEPARTURE FROM THE GORE-CHOKED sinkhole, we resumed our explorations of this shockingly vast labyrinth of tunnels which seemed to underlie the entire region. At one point, we found a mile-long passage that brought us out upon a hill which overlooked the Grot Vly. A few days after that, we found a passage that led to a cemetery within Leffert's Corners and, a few days on, we emerged from a long uphill tunnel and found ourselves on a neighboring peak which overlooked the mansion on the hill where the Black Thing had eaten Howard's friends.

Aside from these local attractions we also sometimes traveled vast distances through these surprisingly extensive tunnels. We spent several

221

weeks exploring several of the longer passageways, seized, at times, by a feverish and inexplicable curiosity to see where certain tunnels led. Most of the time, however, the longer tunnels never came to the surface at all, but rather opened out onto huge, irregularly shaped chambers. Some of these were quite spectacular — great cathedral-like catacombs, gymnasium-sized hollows full of curious odors, shadows, and tremulous echoes. Other tunnels, however, seemed to go on forever, so that we eventually gave up and turned around. One we followed due south for about four hours, finally emerging in a wooded glen, beside a cemetery near the town of Crawford. Another huge westbound tunnel, which we followed for about eight hours, led us to a massive sewer drain located in a park inside the city limits of Wallkill, New York. This proved most fortuitous, since I was able to enter this city, stock up on food and other essentials, and return to the tunnel in less than an hour. This quick jaunt into civilization, which was pleasantly uneventful, enabled me to remain underground for several weeks more.

There were certain other things which I noticed during these investigations which troubled and intrigued me. By its eagerness to return to the half-flooded chamber beneath the sinkhole, it seemed evident that the Black Thing longed to return to the scene of the massacre, frequently lingering near the mouth of that passage and looking at me expectantly. Several times, after we had returned from these longer journeys, my progeny tried to slink away from me in that direction. To be truthful, the scene of horror which I had witnessed at the squatter camp was still a source of tremendous unease to me, an unwelcome memory which I was able to banish only with the greatest mental exertion. The too-vivid recollection of my offspring carnivorously whipping through that crowd of men like some horrendously enlivened, man-eating circus tent, was so upsetting to me that it was often accompanied by chest pains and nausea.

* * * *

MID-OCTOBER, ONE OVERCAST AFTERNOON, AS I LAY IN THE OVAL-shaped chamber reading *The Ego and his Own*, I noted the prolonged absence of the Black Thing and, after a brief search, I found it huddled, predictably, near the mouth of the passage which led to the gore-flooded chamber. I called it away in the usual manner, but it did not budge, staring at me wide-eyed and nodding emphatically in the direction of the tunnel. I shook my head sternly and frowned, a thing which prompted it to hiss and bristle in frustration.

"That tunnel is impassable!" I shouted, annoyed, "It is a dead end!"

This pushed my offspring well past the point of exasperation and after glowering at me for several seconds, it suddenly sped off down the tunnel, looking back aggressively as it went, blithely ignoring my shouts of protest. Enraged at this insubordination (and frightened of it, too) I took off running after it, determined to corner it somehow and explain to it, once and for all, that it ignored me at its own peril. Twenty minutes later, having failed to overtake it, I entered that familiar gore-clogged chamber. Clambering over the boulders once more, I now saw that the tunnel which had previously been flooded with human gore had somehow drained, revealing a blood-slicked passageway now accessible for exploration. Cautiously, I made my way down into the malodorous pit.

Ahead of me in the darkness, I saw a dim and diffuse light, streaming down from some unknown aperture in the ceiling. Bathed in these curiously uneven beams, and positioned directly beneath the aperture, I saw the Black Thing, rising and swaying like a gigantic cobra, peering tentatively into the opening above. Following the direction of its gaze, I expanded my awareness to include the landscape above. Within seconds, I saw the outline of the ravine, and of the cluster of ransacked hovels which stood at its base. These hovels were abandoned, as before — that is, except for one, wherein I perceived the warm silhouettes of two human figures, one sitting, one standing, inside a cabin not fifty feet from the hole.

The Black Thing made no attempts to evade me as I came and stood beside it, so fixated it also was upon the two human silhouettes in the cabin. I gazed up, as if into a narrow, earthen chimney, and glimpsed the mighty storm clouds passing overhead; these great brooding cloudbanks occasionally parted to reveal the darkening sky beyond. The intermittent roar of the downpour, as well as the huge drops of rainwater that occasionally hit my upturned face, indicated that the storm was well underway. A sudden blinding flash of lightning, and the rumble of thunder that followed, caused my offspring to recoil violently and to retreat from the opening; its fear of the lightning had been the only thing which had prevented it from emerging into the rain-swept ravine.

My gaze returned, again and again, to the two figures in the cabin. There was something familiar about one of them, the tall, lank frame, the overly-large head, the curiously monochrome quality of its silhouette. It was Howard. I could sense it, feel it in my bones, and I was seized with a desire to see him and to speak with him. Thrilled (and troubled) by the presence of my eccentric friend in this dangerous place, a part of me wished to march up to that cabin, pound upon the door, and implore Howard and his friend to leave this place immediately. Perhaps, I fancied, I would even go with them! But as much as I missed Howard (and longed to speak with him), I also understood that, with his questionable loyalties, and his stated antipathy for anarchists, I could not, under the present circumstances, risk compromising either of us by allowing him to see me. Being the subject of an extensive manhunt, I thought it best for all involved if Howard and his friend remained entirely ignorant of my presence. Perhaps, I reasoned, if I could get close enough, I could eavesdrop on the two men and learn their reasons for visiting this devil-haunted mountain.

Pulling myself onto the rocky wall, I managed to enter into this vertical, chimney-like aperture and, utilizing the ample foot and hand holds I found here and there, I climbed up, until at last, I poked my head and arms out of the hole and surveyed the wild scenery around me.

Through the many shifting gaps in the clouds, the afternoon sun cast her errant beams, which meandered across the landscape in a manner distressingly reminiscent of slow-moving searchlights. Despite the fact that it was still early afternoon, the sky was a patchwork of accumulating gloom. Looking out across the ransacked squatter camp, I could not help but be reminded of the mind-bending violence I had witnessed there. I saw it all over again in my mind, in a series of flickering flashbacks which made my mouth go dry and set my heart racing. All around me the slick, grassy canyon walls stretched up to the sky, eerily lit by the muted sunlight glowing through the rain, the grass blades dancing this way and that beneath the lashing wind. I noted this wind inflicting a disturbing amount of violence upon certain trees along the upper ridge, blasting them with unrelenting ferocity, tearing off leaves, even whole branches, and flinging them into the gully below. Unable to shake the impression that I was witnessing a conscious, deliberate struggle between two warring tribes of sentient beings, I lingered for some minutes, utterly mesmerized by the frightening spectacle. Inside the cabin, one of the glowing figures must have lit a match; there was a flash of heat which caught my eye, and I was pulled instantly from my trance.

Looking down the hole, I whistled for the Black Thing and, after a few seconds, its many upturned eyes appeared beneath me.

"I want you to stay!" I said, kindly but insistently. "Stay right here and I will return shortly, as before."

My offspring, clearly unhappy with this idea, widened its eyes in dismay. Turning (with palpable reluctance) it disappeared, withdrawing into the recesses of the pit.

Crawling out of the hole and feeling the wind hit my face, I was immediately aware of my vulnerability. Should either Howard or his friend have suddenly decided to peer out the window, they most certainly would have seen me. I was standing at the bottom of a mostly treeless ravine beneath a ceiling of low-flying clouds which had already proven themselves capable of producing both thunder and lightning. The idea that I might be struck by one of these random (or not so random) bolts caused me to look around for possible protection. The light rain suddenly grew into a downpour of considerable strength; seeing no better shelter, I took off toward the cabin occupied by Howard and his friend.

Crouching low, I trotted along the edge of the intervening hill (carefully approaching the cabin from the side without windows) and arrived undetected in the narrow shelter provided by the eaves. While the walls of this cabin were made of logs and hard-packed earth, the roof was comprised of a straw thatching parts of which, if I could find a way onto the wall, would be easy enough to pull aside for the purposes of spying. Recalling Howard's remarkably enhanced sense of hearing, I made special efforts to make absolutely no noise whatsoever, hoping that the thundering downpour had covered the sound of my approach. I reassured myself that Howard, despite his enhanced senses, had not developed the ability to see through walls. Nevertheless, I knew that if I made any irregular noises, even one misstep, I would betray my presence to those keen ears, so I moved with an exaggerated stealth.

Slowly and silently, I followed the wall around to the rear of the cabin where, utilizing a sheltered woodpile, I carefully hoisted myself onto the portion of earthen wall which formed the backside of the structure. The sound of the wind upon the thatch was a constant rustling roar which seemed likely to drown out any noises I might have made. Knowing that this straw would not support me, I was careful to keep my weight upon the top of the wall, drawing my legs up silently, one at a time, and squatting upon the topmost edge, utilizing a crude, tin chimney to steady and maintain my balance.

I could now hear that the two men inside the cabin were thoroughly engrossed in conversation, which seemed to confirm that my presence had not been detected. Relieved, I slowly and carefully stood up and surveyed the immediate area. I had a full panoramic view of the entire ravine and, confirming that no others were present, I once again crouched down and, with minute care, pulled aside the thatching, to see if I could catch any part of their conversation.

Beneath me in the dim lamplight, I saw Howard and the other fellow (a lean, balding, pale, middle-aged man) sitting upon rickety boxes, passing a pipe back and forth and talking. Howard was responding to a question which his companion had asked him about his dreams.

"Well, what did these dreams entail?" the man had asked.

"They were awful!" Howard replied with a shudder. "You might say they were… apocalyptic in nature."

"You're dreaming about the end of the world?" The man chuckled.

"I wish I could laugh about it, Arthur, I really do. But the fact of the matter is…" Here he sighed, looking gravely at his incredulous listener. "I am beginning to suspect that, in these dreams, I am actually receiving messages — cryptic warnings sent by Beings from beyond our solar system." The other man frowned sharply, but Howard continued. "These Beings have detailed information about a series of cataclysmic events which will occur on this planet sometime in the next hundred years — events so earth-shattering, so catastrophic, that they shall mean the end of the world as we know it!"

"Sounds rather biblical to me," Arthur said. "You know I don't go for that kind of stuff."

"The Christians don't have a monopoly on the end of the world, you know," Howard said severely. "Besides, the Christians have got it all wrong anyhow. There will be no Angels of Mercy, no Rapture, no Eternal Reward. There will be no Last Judgment to sift the good from the bad. The earth will be cleared of all life! None will be spared! The surface of the earth shall be razed and resurfaced. These Beings have such detailed information about why, and when, and how it will happen that I find it increasingly difficult to..." Howard trailed off here, too upset to continue.

"What did they tell you, Howard?" his friend asked. "What did the Beings say will happen?"

Howard looked up at his companion and nodded, as if to acknowledge that it was a fair question. His face, however, was ashen as he seemed to be deciding how best to answer his friend's query. After taking a long slow pull upon the pipe, Howard sat up straight, folded his arms across his chest, and exhaled thoughtfully. Then, speaking in a pensive monotone, he described a familiar scenario.

"The clearing of the earth will happen in three distinct waves, Arthur," he began. "Without question, the first wave shall be the worst. The beings in my dream spoke of a vast horde of monsters whom they called the Feeders, and made statements which told me that they, themselves, belonged to this first group. The Feeders are already here among us, hidden from sight but poised to strike. When the Feeders come..." Here he paused again, lay a trembling finger upon his lips and winced. "When the Feeders come, they shall hunt man to extinction. Next, after the Feeders, will be a trio of gigantic beings they call the Flaming Three, who will scorch the earth, burning up the carnage left behind by the Feeders, and reducing the world to ash and rubble. The departure of the Flaming Three shall herald the arrival of the Myriad Ones, allegedly the most horrible of all. Luckily, humanity won't live long enough to see them. These beings shall bring about a terrible global flood, which will wash away any surviving remnants of terrestrial existence. Make no mistake... with this chronological onslaught, they aspire to one outcome only... the brutal suppression of all earthly life."

Hearing these descriptions, I was naturally quite stunned. I had barely begun to consider the implications of Howard's uncanny dreams when I heard a sound behind me — a curious chirping noise. Turning my head, I saw the Black Thing, raising itself out of the hole, apparently in a desperate frenzy to get my attention. Reluctant to exit the hole, however, it lurched and bobbed in the rain, peering fearfully into the cloud mass overhead and cringing pathetically. Waving my arms in the air, I got its attention and then made a gesture with my hands indicating that I wished for it to return at once to the safety of the tunnel. But to my horror, I saw that the Black Thing was now making tentative moves toward emerging more completely from the hole, intending, so far as I could guess, to come join me on the roof.

Suddenly, from the hulking grey storm clouds above us, a massive bolt of lightning shot down, splitting magnificently in two, one of which struck a large tree on the ridge.

The other, effecting a breathtaking arc down into the ravine, aimed itself directly at my emerging offspring, blasting into it so violently that, amid the smoke and sparks, I saw it split open, ragged pieces flying into the air. So great was this impact that the Black Thing was thrown several yards up the side of the ravine, where it immediately collapsed onto its side, revealing a massive ragged wound, charred, burning, and oozing a thick, translucent syrup. When the smoke cleared, seconds later, I saw that the deadly bolt had hacked into my offspring with such force that it had succeeded in amputating a significant chunk, which now lay steaming in the grass about ten feet away from the point of impact. Immediately, my injured offspring beat a hasty retreat down the ravine, vanishing instantaneously into the hole.

Once the Black Thing disappeared, my attention was drawn back to the piece of my offspring which the lightning had severed, now bubbling and shuddering in the wet grass. Suddenly, this severed piece (which was roughly the size and shape of a grand piano) erupted into the most hideous spasms imaginable, flipping and flinging itself into the air in writhing somersaults of agony, its two gigantic eyes bulging as it flopped about, bucking this way and that, until at last it fell still upon the ground. This appalling display of raw animal suffering gripped my heart and, enraged, I began to look around for the quickest way to dismount from the roof. My plan was to follow my offspring into the relative safety of the tunnel, where, out of range of the deadly lightning, I could assess its injuries.

I had just begun to step off the roof when the severed piece of the Black Thing, whose huge staring eyes had been searching the landscape for any sign of movement, suddenly found me. An icy terror washed over me as I watched it rise up. Setting its sights upon me, it began gliding stealthily toward me, drifting along the grassy slope and glaring hungrily as it came. I began to

227

gesture (somewhat frantically) at this approaching mass, indicating that I wished for it to stop, turn around, and go back down into the pit and rejoin the Black Thing. I was ignored. In those wide staring eyes there was no recognition, no trace of the sympathetic familiarity that existed between my offspring and me. This detached fragment, now clearly an organism in its own right, was an entirely different beast. Instead of the rapport I had hoped for, I saw the cold, determined look of a hungry, desperate animal, speeding headlong toward the first edible thing it could find. With an awful eagerness, this creature was quickly closing the gap between us, steadily gaining momentum as it came. I froze, certain that my death was at hand.

Seeing no possibility of escape, I resigned myself to die hideously, within the folds of the approaching segment. From past experience, I knew (only too well) the manner in which I would be consumed. Bracing myself for a face full of acid, I tried to console myself that, if nothing else, it would at least be a quick death.

Fate, however, intervened. Without knowing what he was doing, the man whom Howard had called Arthur suddenly, and inadvertently, saved my life, unfortunately by sacrificing his own. In the cabin, directly below me, the awful crash of this final blob-splitting bolt had caused Arthur to rise from his seat, and walk over to the window where, by the light of his pocket torch, he fumbled about for the latch.

Just as the shapeless fiend was drawing near to the shack, Arthur removed the shutters and thrust his head out into the rainy darkness, as if to ascertain the damage which the massive lightning stroke had caused. Turning his head quickly to one side, he glimpsed me in his peripheral vision, craning his neck to see me better. It was for this reason that he did not see the approaching mass. Crouching low against the thatching, I heard him whisper, breathless with terror, "Howard! There's someone on the roof!" Hearing this, I peeked down one last time, to ascertain the progress of the rapidly ascending monstrosity.

The portion of my offspring, scared half to death by this human head suddenly thrust into the air directly above it, dropped flat upon the ground, crouching there just long enough for Arthur to catch sight of me. No sooner had he mumbled to Howard when the ravenous fragment launched itself at his head.

The fragment moved with a dreadful savagery, a fury all the more brutal because it was fueled, I could sense, by a desperate, uncomprehending terror. It leapt, like a striking snake, straight into the poor man's face, plunging itself into the nostrils and eye sockets and boiling over the upper face, like an expanding pool of black jelly. I watched just long enough to recognize that, like the Black Thing itself, this lesser fragment was also an enthusiastic brain-eater who gained access through the eye-sockets, forcing its way through the brainpan with a barely audible crunch. Seconds later, having melted its way through the upper face, it was greedily, silently, feasting upon the brain of its rigid victim.

With my heart in my throat, I turned around and jumped from the top of the wall, clearing the woodpile and landing in the wet grass behind the house. Careful to keep the cabin between that awful carnivorous fragment and myself, I ran down the hillside toward the hole. At one point, I looked back and saw the cabin door ajar and Howard standing in the threshold looking out. I ducked below the curve of the hill and ran the rest of the way in a low crouch. Had my friend looked into the ravine just then he might have seen me — but, as another backwards glance revealed, his eyes were fixated upon the curious clouds overhead, which seemed to be breaking up and dissipating with a startling and unnatural rapidity.

When I reached the hole, half a minute later, I dropped into it to my armpits, looking back one last time to see if the thing was pursuing me. It was not. I am fairly certain I saw it enter the forest beyond the ridge. Looking back at the cabin, I saw that, though the door still stood open, Howard had gone back inside.

Howard's scream came ringing out of that cabin like a shriek from the Abyss. It was the kind of scream which the human larynx can only achieve under the most mind-boggling of circumstances. I knew that Howard was gazing upon the faceless corpse of his friend. That my offspring and I had caused this remarkable man such horror, that we had macerated, almost before his very eyes, not one, not two, but three of his friends, was a pain I would have to live with for the rest of my days. His heart-rending scream was the last sound I heard as I slipped back down into the stinking, blood-soaked pit.

XVI

IN THE GORE-SLICKED HOLLOW, THE WOUNDED BLACK THING was nowhere to be seen. There was, however, a trail of the translucent slime, which I promptly followed up into the sloping tunnel which led back to the oval-shaped chamber. As I trudged along this passageway, alone with my thoughts, I noticed I was in a queer sort of delirium. I was bathed in sweat and there was a low roaring in my ears which no amount of head-slapping could dispel. My thoughts, oddly jumbled, revolved around two concerns. I needed to find my offspring, and, in the meantime, I needed to understand what had just happened.

I was beginning to feel as though invisible forces were conspiring to make a mocking ruin of my every effort to accomplish certain goals. My initial intention of putting an end to my offspring's rampage had failed miserably, resulting, ironically enough, in a massacre of unprecedented proportions — the largest loss of human life yet. My efforts to spare Howard and his companions from an encounter with my overzealous progeny had also been a dismal failure, resulting in the deaths of three harmless men. Howard, though present for all of these deaths, had been inexplicably spared, a fact which also continued to perplex me. The more I thought about it, the more it seemed as if Howard and my offspring had almost been drawn to one another. It was an eerie symmetry; presumably, Howard had come to the Catskills to track down my offspring, while it had, in turn, immediately begun stalking him. Worse still was the fact that the Black Thing seemed determined to kill and eat every one of Howard's companions. I could only imagine that he must have felt horrifically singled out.

A ghoulish thought occurred to me and I began to wonder if perhaps I had not misunderstood my offspring's repeated attempts to take me down to the site of the massacre. Had the Black Thing been trying to lead me to Howard the whole time, slaughtering those others as a crude way of emphasizing or indicating Howard himself. Had I just been too dense to understand?

There were other reasons why I was beginning to feel cursed. My apparently fortuitous meeting with Carmilla had been tragically canceled by a

230

devastation of my own making. I had made the worst possible impression upon the inhabitants of the squatter hamlet, leaving them to conclude that I was either mad, stupid, or evil — and possibly all three! I had left the camp under a cloud of generalized suspicion, not to mention the two gentlemen I had seen gawking at me. When I had first come to the squatter camp I had very much hoped to put an end to the nightmare that they had been living through, to give the besieged squatters some reassurance that there would be no more deaths — for, once I regained control of my offspring, I intended to lead it far, far away from those kind people. This too had been a failure.

Somewhere, the Black Thing was badly hurt, possibly even dying, and, if I didn't find it waiting for me in the oval-shaped chamber, I had no idea where else to look. Almost everything I had set out to do had gone terribly wrong.

As I reached the main junction of the tunnels, however, my nostrils were suddenly assailed with the curiously layered odor which had permeated the oval-shaped chamber upon my arrival. As I passed through several familiar intersections, where six or seven other reeking tunnels joined up with mine, I continued moving as quickly as possible. Crouching low, I entered the smaller passageway which led to the oval-shaped chamber. I noticed numerous fresh tracks on the floor of the tunnel before me. These prints were essentially human, only smaller so that, for a moment I had a ludicrous vision of a pack of feral, cave-dwelling children.

I hadn't gone more than five paces when I intuited that I was not alone in this tunnel. I had just begun crawling on my hands and knees when something diminutive and grey, roughly the size of a small dog, shot past me in the darkness, missing my arm by mere inches.

This pale shape which flitted past me in the darkness was soon followed by several others, speeding past me at regular intervals. To my keen eyes they appeared as little more than morphous shadows but, after the fifth or sixth one passed me, I began to grow concerned. After several yards of crawling, I was nearly overcome by raw panic. Increasing my speed, I fairly flew up the remaining passageway. Though no more shapes passed me by, the odor of corpses and rotting textiles became noticeably stronger. In the passage behind me, and still a way off, I heard a curious rasping sound, as of many little mouths breathing heavily and chittering softly to one another — a sound which, while still quite far away, powered my limbs with a primal dexterity.

Arriving at the oval-shaped chamber, I quickly shoved my assorted books and clothing into my backpack and, leaving only the rifle behind, exited the burrow through the same bullet-ridden passageway which had been my original point of entry. Emerging onto the deserted hillside, I scrambled down the slope, looking back only once to make sure that the things hadn't pursued me out into the late afternoon sun. They hadn't, and I was so overjoyed by this revelation that I almost fell on the ground and wept with relief. My elation, however, was tempered considerably when I looked back and saw that the hole I had so recently quitted now appeared to be teeming with curious trembling shapes — a cluster of pale, whitish shadows with shiny eyes that seemed to watch me as I fled down the rain-soaked incline. I was convinced that, whatever they may have been, the burrow's original tenants had finally returned to reclaim their abandoned lair. Had they come five minutes earlier, I am certain they would have overtaken me. Some visceral awareness assured me that I would not have survived this encounter.

Wishing to be as far away from the hole as possible by sundown, I headed toward the nearest town with a train station, which turned out to be Crawford, about three miles away. Before leaving this wooded area, I sat down upon a high eminence and, collecting my thoughts, began focusing my attention in an attempt to locate my offspring upon, or within, the landscape. When this failed, I concentrated on trying to call the Black Thing to me. After about ten minutes, having neither seen nor heard any sign of it, I gave up and set off for Crawford. Nervously uncertain about where the ravenous fragment had got to, I remained keenly aware of the peril it posed. Should it have the opportunity to intercept me before I reached the town, I felt certain it would not hesitate to make a meal out of me. With this in mind, I kept up a steady pace and stuck to the open meadows, glancing backward often, and scrutinizing the scenery as I went.

*　*　*　*

TWO HOURS LATER I WAS WALKING DOWN A CROWDED SIDEWLAK IN Crawford. At the train station, I purchased a one-way ticket to Albany. I cleaned my face, hands, and neck in the washroom sink, then put on the cleanest outfit I had. Seating myself in a nearly deserted rear car, I put my hat over my face and pretended to sleep. My mind raced with more questions, enigmas, and theories which, while utterly ludicrous, were also damnably, hideously, plausible.

It now seemed irrefutable that there was some sort of conflict going on between the various monstrosities I had observed. All those battered and blasted Tree Things along the high ridges, assailed by the supernatural wind and lightning, resembled the wounded rear guard of a brutal military campaign. Additionally, I felt certain that the lightning bolt which had struck my offspring had been intentional — a punishment for insubordination which, I was painfully aware, was most likely an indirect result of my inadequate parenting.

After contemplating the Worm Things I'd seen in the lake of gore, coupled with the vast network of underground tunnels, I had to conclude that the surrounding mountain range was fairly well infested with this species of tunneling horrors. Add to this menagerie my offspring and also its enlivened fragment, now roaming the area in a voracious frenzy. Were there others as well, recalcitrant monstrosities who, having grown weary of their Overlords (the prevailing Cloud Things), now sought refuge in tunnels deep below the surface where they could escape punishment? Could it be that the vast tunnel system beneath the hills functioned as a sort of refuge for the rogue monstrosities inclined to desertion, a huge subterranean hive of intergalactic, polymorphous turncoats and mutineers?

The varying sizes and shapes of the tunnels implied that numerous distinctive creatures had participated in the construction of this hive. Did they all inhabit it together? What was their relation to one another? During, and immediately following, the massacre, the Worm Things' refusal to emerge more than two or three feet out of the bloody sinkhole seemed to convey a profound fear of the Cloud Things lurking above. Conversely, these same Worm Things had seemed utterly unconcerned about my nearby offspring, a thing which stood in sharp contrast to the cowering Tree Things upon the ridge who had fled before us.

What of the multi-form monstrosity that had come to reclaim its burrow — that half-glimpsed, many-headed Thing whose tracks vaguely resembled children's hands and feet? My offspring and I had slept in its nest for several weeks undisturbed. Where had it been? Had the mere presence of the Black Thing caused it to relinquish its burrow? Is that why we were never attacked? Was there some other factor which prevented it from killing me in the tunnel when it had the chance? Had it spared me out of ambivalence, or because it had felt some affinity for me? I did not recall seeing it on the night of the massacre. Why not? Surely such an epic melée, so close to its burrow, could not have escaped its notice. Had it been away? If so, where had it gone? Finally, and most importantly, what manner of creature (or creatures) was it? Despite my near encounter, I still could not say with certainty whether or not it had been one multi-form creature or many.

*   *   *   *

ARRIVING ON THE BUSY STREETS OF ALBANY, I ATE A SIZABLE DINNER AT a crowded restaurant, after which I rented a room at a nearby inn and slept until sunrise. In the morning, I showered, dressed, and paid my bill, all before 9 am. Originally a Dutch trading post, Albany is a city built on a hill that slopes down to the edge of the vast, mirror-like Hudson, with remarkable vistas of the wide river valley which it overlooks. Making a brief circuit of the city, I loaded up on various essentials, including a new suit, which I donned immediately.

I found Albany to be an unusually handsome and picturesque city, particularly its architecture; its numerous cathedrals, towers, and government buildings (including City Hall) all revealed the strong Gothic influence imported by early Dutch settlers and kept alive by men like Henry Hobson Richardson. Inquiring about the ferry, I was directed to Steamboat Square. I boarded a southbound ferry, a four-hundred foot long "floating palace of steel and glass" (according to the banner), owned by the Hudson River Day Line, capable of transporting six thousand souls 130 miles in just under nine hours. Its final destination was the Desbrosses Street Pier in Manhattan.

The steamship was a quadruple-decker sidewheeler which, chugging along at a solid 30 mph, dwarfed every other ship on the river. For the first few hours of this journey I slept in a private cabin but, awakened by the sound of drunken revelers in the hall outside my door, I rose and wandered out to the rear deck for some fresh air.

Here I met the captain, a friendly, chatty Dutchman by the name of Van Woert, who informed me, with much pride, that the *Washington Irving* was the largest passenger-carrying steamship in the world. When I prompted him, he told me the lengthy history of this remarkable vessel.

As I listened to the drone of his voice, I chanced to peer down into the wake of the boat, letting my gaze explore the curious ripples and bubbling eddies which the huge sidewheel left on the surface of the water. My eye caught a glimpse of something through the foam. The sunlight sparkling on the surface of the churned water, in addition to the vast patches of dissipating foam, made it difficult (at times, impossible) to see what was going on even just a few inches below the surface. Nevertheless, several times in the span of a minute, there were sizable gaps — clear patches where the roiling water suddenly and briefly became as translucent as glass through which I caught startling glimpses of what appeared to be an enormous black shape, vaguely triangular and perhaps forty feet across, meandering along in the wake of the boat. More disconcerting still was the fact that, upon closer inspection, I thought I glimpsed, in among the islands of foam, the unblinking gaze of numerous upturned eyes, almost perfectly camouflaged within the dissipating bubbles. Looking at Captain Van Woert, I saw that, having come to the end of his most recent anecdote, he had lapsed into a thoughtful reverie.

"Do you see that?" I asked, pointing a finger down at the glimmering foam, "What is that?"

"What?" he said, carefully searching the waters.

"There!" I repeated, "There is a huge dark shape under the water, like a big triangle, following us…" I waited until I saw it again then pointed. "There! Right there!" I said but, after another moment of scrutinizing the water, he shook his head and wrinkled his brow at me. "Probably just the shadow of the ship," he said with a bewildered grin, "or else a reflection of one of these huge mountains."

We were now passing through the Hudson Highlands, just south of Newburgh, gliding along beneath the towering bulk of Storm King Mountain, which rose up so dramatically that it blotted out the entire western sky. At this moment a young man in a white uniform approached us and told the captain that his presence was requested upon the bridge. With a firm handshake, Captain Van Woert bowed slightly before following the young man across the deck and vanishing into an oblong portal.

*   *   *   *

I DECIDED TO WALK THE DECKS, EVENTUALLY WANDERING INTO the dining lounge where I sat down at a table and refreshed myself with assorted delicacies from the buffet. A half hour later, I had returned to my cabin; I was hoping for another hour of sleep before arriving in New York City.

I had only just nodded off when I was promptly awakened by a nightmare so intense that I lay panting for some minutes. This unusually vivid nightmare had been most disconcerting because it involved the violent collision and subsequent sinking of the very steamship upon which I was a passenger! In it, I was lying down in a cabin identical to the one I currently occupied, when I felt the ship lurch violently to one side, as if struck. I was flung from my bunk, smashing into the opposite wall. A deafening shriek of tearing metal and bending steel resounded through the entire structure as the ship slowly came to a shuddering halt. Opening the door, I encountered a great crush of bodies as the passengers stampeded, shouting and scrambling through the passageways and across the foggy decks, sweeping me along. Once outside I saw, to my horror, that the ferry was hemmed in on all sides by a vast wall of utterly opaque fog. Past the railings nearest to me, there hung a dense, immutable curtain of vapor, swirling yet oddly stationary, and whose eerie immobility instantly recalled to mind the miasma I'd seen at the Grot Vly and the swamp in Somers. The ship listed heavily to the port side and, as the water came creeping up across the angled deck, there was a mad scramble in the opposite direction.

The dream ended there. I sat for some minutes, breathlessly trying to collect myself and wondering what it meant. Soon I rose and, making my way along the deserted passageway, I went to the rear deck to confirm that we were not, in fact, engulfed in fog. The weather outside was as bright and clear as one could possibly hope for. Still, I remained watchful. Looking over the rail, I once again spied the sinister black triangle weaving and meandering patiently through our wake, and, worried that my dream had been some sort of clairvoyant warning, I resolved to do two things. First, to find, and warn, the captain about the coming disaster, and second, to disembark at the next available landing.

In the twenty minutes it took us to get to the dock at West Point, I searched in vain for the captain. He was most likely in the engine room, or some other restricted area. I asked three different members of the crew if they could help me locate him but, as we were just now arriving at the pier, I was told politely that "the captain is too busy to visit with passengers at this time." I considered writing him a note and asking a member of the crew to deliver it to him, but, upon consideration, wondered what, precisely, I would write in such a note. Should I tell him the story of my shipwreck dream? Should I warn him to avoid sailing in heavy fog? What could I write that would not sound like the scribblings of a lunatic? How could he possibly take anything I had to say seriously? Besides, even if I had foreseen the tragic fate of the *Washington Irving*, I still did not know *when* it was going to occur; how could I issue an effective warning? Unable to come up with anything remotely plausible, I abandoned the idea.

I could not help but note the irony of my situation. What practical good is a clairvoyant ability if nobody will listen to you or take your warnings seriously? To move among doomed people, and to see this doom approaching, inexorably, day after day, and yet to remain utterly unable to alert them for lack of credibility, was to feel a sense of estrangement which mere words cannot convey.

Arriving at the West Point dock I disembarked and, after climbing several, interconnected staircases leading to the huge stone observatory, I gazed upon the wide river and the doomed ship below, already letting out from the dock and continueing south. I felt a dull and hopeless grief as I watched the ship dwindling in the distance. Seeing no fogbanks anywhere along the southerly route, I hoped I had been wrong. Perhaps, I mused, by getting off the boat, I had spared it from the destruction I had foreseen.

I made my way across the West Point campus, moving amongst the sightseers and the visiting guests who ambled along its many footpaths. Moving across the various lawns and sport fields, I saw squadrons of young cadets, bright-faced boys with forced stern expressions, eyes locked on their superior officers, obediently awaiting instruction.

It depressed me considerably to see all those young men in formation, marching in time to their Drill Sergeant's hypnotic, submission-inducing intonations. They were so young, mere boys really. I pitied them, even as I loathed the murderous automatons I knew they must one day become. Uncle Sam had grim plans for these boys and they were too young and too inexperienced to understand what was being done to them. They seemed to take it for granted that it must be good for them, but the indoctrination these boys were receiving was designed to break them down, mind, body and spirit, so they could be made to commit murder, even serial mass murder, at the snap of a finger. They were being taught to obey without question, to submit their will and their intelligence, to their superior officers, to accept their place in the military hierarchy. These boys were like the many animals I'd seen in the various menageries I'd encountered; I had an overwhelming urge to set them free, to show them that they were being used and to explain that what was being done to them was part of a larger system that was enslaving humanity. I wanted to tell them that by submitting to such a program, they would permanently stunt their minds, confuse their instincts, and implicate themselves in atrocities that would leave them deeply, permanently, scarred. Unlike the animals however, the liberation of these boys was a thing not so easily accomplished. How could I hope to describe such things to them without sounding like a madman?

Leaving the West Point Academy behind, I headed south along a wide two-lane country road, which soon brought me to the town of Highland Falls. In an ongoing effort to confound any would-be pursuers, I walked several miles, through frog-infested marshes and steep headland forests, until I came to the village of Fort Montgomery. Arriving just before sunset in this tiny mining hamlet, I purchased supplies at the local market and then prepared to resume my journey southward.

At the edge of town, I came to a park, located at the foot of a grassy hill which sloped upward into the forest that is at the northernmost border of Bear Mountain State Park. Here, near the crest of this hill, I sat down upon the grass, admiring the twilight scenery, and making a small meal out of the food in my pack. While I was doing this, four policemen entered the park. After making a brief exploration of the area, one of the coppers finally saw me, pointing me out to the others and gesturing curiously. Seconds later, they all looked directly at me, regarding me for some minutes. One of them waved and whistled to me but, pretending that I had not noticed them, I finished my meal, stood up, pulled on my pack and headed straight up the slope and into the forest beyond. Still about a hundred and fifty yards away, they would have had to run very fast indeed to catch up with me.

Near the top of the hill I encountered a wide dirt road. I followed it along the ridge, walking at a leisurely pace, even pausing to admire the breathtaking views of the river, eighty feet below, which was occasionally visible through the intervening trees. Veering off the road (but keeping it in sight), I entered the trees which overhung this shadowy lane, marching at a steady pace toward the dark, conical bulk of Bear Mountain.

It was now evening. Hearing the noise of the nearby cities, and the subtle rumble of the river itself, I picked my way between the ash and maple trees, casting sideways glances at the river. I must have been walking for about twenty minutes when I caught sight of several electric torches bobbing up and down in the darkness behind me. My pursuers were still far behind me, but moving quickly enough that I knew they would be upon me in no time. Suddenly, in the trees to my right, I saw several more torches appear. These were only about a hundred yards off; I was being surrounded and run to ground. Was it the police? Had they called for reinforcements and taken up the chase? Was it State Troopers from Leffert's Corners? Rockefeller's death squad? Patriotic vigilantes? Or a deadly combination of all four? I took off running, moving low along the backside of a small hill, to see if I could spy a narrow chasm that might serve as a hiding place or an escape route. Closer inspection revealed that the hillside below me quickly steepened into an actual cliff face, which, I surmised, was so sheer that no sane attempt could be made to descend it.

Panicking, I ran along the rim of this curving cliff. The shimmering river was now about a hundred feet below me. From the base of these palisades, the distance to the shore looked to be about thirty feet, a distance I knew I could never cover even with a running start. Every second, bobbing electric torches were spreading throughout the forest until, at last, I was hemmed in on three sides. I heard the crack of an automatic and the now-familiar whiz of a bullet as it sailed over my left shoulder.

I came out in a small clearing which afforded a view of the ravine into which I had run. Far below, along the floor of this canyon, I could see the glimmering surface of a deep, wide creek, swollen from the recent storms, winding its way out of the gorge and joining up directly with the Hudson River itself, just a few hundred yards downstream. Spanning this gorge, a short distance from me, I was relieved to see an iron bridge, an ancient viaduct or trestle, about ninety feet above the creek and, from the look of it, long since fallen into disuse. I headed toward it, arriving there just a moment later. Shaking in the moonlight, I considered my options gravely. I knew I could cross the span of this bridge in about five minutes, running at top speed. Prompted by the sound of footsteps in the forest behind me, I ran in low sweeping zig-zags, onto the surface of the bridge.

I was only about a quarter of the way across the trestle when, directly ahead of me on the far side, I saw four more electric torches appear out of the blackness, as well as a bright flash. Another bullet came whistling toward me out of the night, missing me by about six feet. I had finally run out of ground. Pausing to confirm that both sides of the bridge were, in fact, blocked by my enemies, I continued to run along this trestle, wondering if there was some way I could climb underneath it. There wasn't. I was now about midway across, positioned directly above the middle of the creek which, I realized, was my only chance of escape. From this angle, even my enhanced vision was of no use in determining the depth of the water. Peering tentatively over the edge, I searched about for any indications of submerged rocks, trees or floating debris. I found none. Uncertain whether it was six feet deep or sixteen, I did not allow myself time to think. Stepping up to the edge, I inhaled sharply and dove, headfirst, into the empty air.

As soon as my feet left the bridge, time froze. The world around me vanished and, with only the noisy flapping of my clothing as a reference point, I was aware of nothing but the sound and speed of falling. Shrugging off my backpack (with the hopes that it might possibly serve as a decoy, and draw fire away from me), I stretched my arms out and dropped headfirst into the roaring blackness. All my concentration went towards keeping my body rigid. I had deliberately chosen to go headfirst, knowing that if I was going to hit bottom, I would prefer to die instantly upon the stony creek bed rather than to risk floundering there, crippled in the shallows, gurgling and bleeding, as my pursuers gathered along the edge of the trestle and used me for target practice. Tucking my head between my outstretched arms, I emptied my lungs and then filled them to their fullest.

Upon feeling the smooth, cold shock of my body entering the dark water, and the jarring change in velocity, my first thought was to become horizontal as soon as possible, and to head immediately back toward the surface. This I would have done, had it not been for the hail of bullets which, seconds later, began to rain down from above. Terrified, I swam deeper and deeper down, submerging to a depth of about twelve feet, at which point the bullets became harmless, glancing off me like tossed marbles. The water at this depth was noticeably colder, and I shuddered as I continued to propel myself away from the bridge, toward the Hudson as quickly as possible.

Startled by the swiftness of my progress, I was preparing to return to the surface for air when I noticed that, though I'd easily been underwater for over a minute, I felt no need whatsoever to draw a breath. I was able to continue swimming with no discomfort.

I knew something strange was occurring when, three minutes later, I still felt no need to surface! Incredulous, I continued to swim until at last I entered the stronger and deeper currents of the Hudson River.

How can I express the shock of this revelation? Had I transmuted yet again? Had my lungs expanded so monstrously that I could remain under water for long periods? Did I require less oxygen now, or were my lungs, after some unnoticed metamorphosis, simply making better use of the air I had inhaled? It had never occurred to me that I might have developed still more curious abilities which had not yet come to light, though I am unsure why I felt so certain that my transformation was complete.

Peering up through the shimmering water, I could see the flickering stars and the wavering, egg-like moon. Here and there, along the eastern shore, I glimpsed the undersides of ships, large and small, pulled alongside docks and piers, or else anchored offshore. Not surprisingly, the best scenery was below me. I was swimming through a half-lit dreamworld of granite canyons, giant, mossy, witch-haired boulders, and sunken skeletal trees, drifting over, and through, the canyonesque landscape of the river bottom, whose lower depths remained curiously shrouded in a murky darkness. Seeing this strange opacity flowing along the river-bottom sent a shiver through me and I recalled the black triangle I'd seen trailing behind the *Washington Irving*. I spent several moments peering nervously in all directions, searching for any odd movements or inexplicable shapes speeding toward me. There was nothing but the occasional meandering bass or herring in the surrounding waters. Below me, the rocks swarmed with various species of crab and crawling things, all of which, I could tell, were of the wholesome, earthly type. The only oddity was that curiously darkened trench that ran along the bottom of the river. As far as I could tell, it contained nothing but several hundred tons of black, algae-like slime.

Incredibly, the breath I had drawn, nearly twenty minutes earlier, was still sustaining me. Dumbfounded, I continued to drift and to swim at my leisure and found that I lacked neither air nor strength. Furthermore, a strange fever burned in my limbs. I was not at all bothered by the cold river water.

When I did finally surface for breath nearly thirty minutes later, my attention was drawn to the eastern shore where I glimpsed the glowing spires of Peekskill. Recalling the deadly trap that had been laid for me at the Peekskill Library, I couldn't help but regard these lights with a certain dread. It was, however, tempered by the fact that I now had access to a place of concealment and a mode of transport which, while not exactly comfortable, kept me entirely out of the reach of my numerous human enemies.

Over the next few hours, I learned that one deep breath of air could sustain me for forty-five minutes, slightly less if I swam continuously. It took some time for the sense of stunned awe to wear off long enough to notice certain other changes.

For example, I'd been swimming underwater for about forty minutes when my eyes began to burn and sting just as they had with Galleani, Howard and the Goliath named Legion. I stopped swimming altogether, allowing myself to drift while I rubbed both eyes vigorously with my knuckles. Unlike before, however, this tickling did not subside after a minute, but grew into something much worse: a painful burning beginning in the inner corners of my eyes and spreading along the edges of my eyelids. It was as if I had soap in my eyes. This discomfort could only be relieved by direct and constant pressure.

In the midst of this vigorous eye-rubbing, the initial relief gave way to a curious and even more painful ripping sensation along the bottom edges of each of my eyelids. Feeling with my fingertips, I discovered that my upper eyelids had, somehow, split into inner and outer membranes, which could move independently! These new secondary (inner) eyelids were transparent, like the membrane on a frog or fish eye, a protective lens which perfectly covered my already protruding eyeballs. This nictitating membrane, as I later discovered, is common to many birds, reptiles, amphibians, and some mammals, but unheard-of in humans. Initially, looking through these nictitating membranes was like peering at the world through a dirty window. For about an hour or so, I saw strange halos everywhere, curious and inexplicable patches of blinding light which seemed to approach me and then speed away, or else to follow me at a distance. By the time I reached Croton-on-the-Hudson, my underwater vision was as clear as if I were wearing motorcycle goggles, and, looking about, I saw that the curious light patches (whatever they had been) had now vanished.

*　　*　　*　　*

ONCE MY VISION HAD BEEN RESTORED, I STARTED TO experiment with different ways of propelling myself through the shadowy depths. Never having been much of a swimmer, I tried several different techniques before I finally settled on the most optimal. With my arms pressed tightly against my sides, and moving my legs in tandem, I soon found that I could achieve shocking speeds. I instinctively kicked loose of my clothing (a thing which increased my speed considerably), while the aforementioned fever continued to insulate me against the effects of the often frigid water. So greatly did I underestimate my own speed that when, after another hour or so of this mostly submerged swimming, I once again broke the surface, I was amazed to see the Manhattan skyline. I had swum a full fifty miles in less than three hours.

I became aware of the sheer might of the currents that carried me, though I saw no place where a naked man might come ashore unnoticed. Floating past Battery Park, cautiously avoiding passing ships, I listened in awe to the low thunder-like rumblings of this daunting metropolis.

With my nearly telescopic vision, gazing up at the grotesquely articulated and luminous agglomeration of buildings was like looking at a gigantic cemetery built by demons from another world. Mesmerized by the outlines of the huge shimmering towers standing tall and stark against the purple darkness, I could not help but imagine them as living things, monolithic, million-eyed beings, intelligently scrutinizing the ant-like humanity who swarmed in and around them.

Then I heard it — faint at first, but growing louder with each passing second, steadily becoming more and more distinct. It was a low and incongruent murmur coming from somewhere beyond the generalized rumble of the city, a low chorus of volleying noises, which my sensitive ears focused on with a loathsome familiarity. At first it seemed to come from everywhere, but slowly, as I made further efforts to trace it, my attention was drawn back up to the uppermost portions of those glistening towers. A half a minute of concentrated listening and staring erased all doubt. Upon the outer walls of these colossal structures, I saw things that looked like heat mirages — places were the masonry seemed to ripple, subtly, as if seen through a mist. My thoughts became confused and my chest began to heave. There was no question about it; several of the taller towers were clearly infested with Boulder Things, which were faintly singing to each other across the vast, canyonesque cityscape. Their mimicking voices, disguised accordingly as foghorns, roaring engines, and various other common urban sounds, blended in perfectly with the general noise. As I floated past this nightmarish scene, staring up in wonder and terror, I could almost make out the content of their cold, merciless exchanges, as these ancient horrors gazed pitilessly down upon the hordes below.

Dazed by the sudden awareness of the city dwellers' profound vulnerability, my mind reeled at the implications. Had the granite masonry that comprised these buildings been unwittingly chiseled out of sentient stone? Had these towers, in fact, been built out of Boulder Things, by people unknowingly in the thrall of an alien inspiration? Had the builders and designers been under the subtle guidance of the Boulder Things themselves? Worst of all, what would happen on that fateful day when the Hidden Ones burst forth? What spectacular carnage would ensue when those embedded monstrosities emerged from their sky-bound hiding places to feast on

242

humankind? A dizziness came over me. I could no longer tell where the checkerboard lights of the Manhattan skyline ended and the starry vault of the sky began. It was as if the two were grotesquely merged, spilling strangely into one another, surrounding me and pressing me down, threatening to crush me under the black waves.

I continued to drift away from Manhattan Island and out into New York Harbor, past the Statue of Liberty, Governor's Island and the twinkling lights of Red Hook. Still bewildered, not only by my strange, dimly horrifying new abilities, but also by the nightmare I'd seen in downtown Manhattan. I lost all track of time and space; I discovered, almost too late, that the current was pulling me south and dragging me out to sea. The tide was also going out and, contending with the several million tons of water pouring out of the mouth of the Hudson, I was nearing exhaustion as I struggled to remain in New York harbor.

Recognizing the potential danger of my situation, I turned myself over in the water and, floating on my back, kicked my legs vigorously while allowing the rest of my body to go limp. In this manner, I traversed several hundred yards of water where, at long last, I felt the current finally loosen its grip upon me. By this time, I had been dragged so far out to sea that the lights of the mighty metropolis now appeared as little more than a string of luminous shapes hovering along the western horizon.

Taking a few deep breaths, I once again filled my lungs and went deep, to see if I could escape the rip current by circumventing it. Swimming along with my arms pressed against my sides, I found a place where a back-current veered toward the Jersey coast. I had just entered this southwestern current when a curious set of movements directly beneath me caught my eye.

Far below me, the murky darkness near the bottom had finally dissipated enough to reveal that which it had previously hidden, namely, a surprisingly deep trench, several hundred yards wide, and many thousands long, which had been gouged along the floor of the coastal shelf, presumably, by the action of the river. This massive trench ran, like an ever-deepening canyon, straight out to sea — a huge, shadowy rift that cut through the sea-bottom itself as it sloped away toward the vast ocean deeps.

As I drifted along about twenty feet below the surface, my eyes adjusted to the murky depths far below and I beheld a sight that chilled me to my core, obscuring all thought of heading ashore.

All down the length of this massive trench, I saw Hidden Ones — Boulder Things, Tree Things, and numerous others crawling by the thousands, by the tens of thousands; the entire floor of this sloping canyon teemed with an unending procession of marching, swimming horrors. This awful parade was multi-directional, half of these monsters moving west, emerging from out of the vast deeps of the Atlantic itself and moving up into the spewing mouth of the Hudson River, the other half running in the opposite direction, leaving the river behind them and heading out to some fiend-infested abyss that lay hidden beneath the turbulent sea.

The majority of these Hidden Ones were only too familiar. There were the aforementioned Boulder Things and the mantis-like Tree Things, as well as numerous other, now familiar, shapes which swam, crawled, slithered, or else dragged themselves along. Several other types were entirely new to me. There were great scrambling alligator-like things, some twenty and thirty feet in length, with gruesomely splayed heads, where innumerable orange eyes peered out between great cartilaginous thorns of grey, elephantine flesh. There were swimming things which resembled huge multi-colored anemones, cyclopean spheroids and winged red cylinders with multiple heads. At one point I saw several of the great black triangles gliding along, identical to the one I'd glimpsed in the wake of the steamship.

These were not the worst. There was a third and final category which were, quite simply, beyond all sane conjecture. In the upper and lower portions of this downward sloping canyon, swimming alongside and above this ghastly underwater procession, I occasionally saw the sleek pale bodies of human beings! I stared, doubting my own eyes, as several hundred naked men, women, and children, in a manner reminiscent of a vast pod of dolphins, poured through the canyon. I noted with especial horror how they held their arms flat against their sides, and moved their legs tandem, precisely as I had done, not four hours earlier. These apparently aquatic human beings flitted and darted (with remarkable facility) among the other marching monstrosities. Like the procession itself, these human swimmers were both descending into, and emerging out of, that greater expanse of watery blackness just beyond the coastal shelf.

I must have floated above this strange procession for about ten minutes, stunned into paralysis, before a feeling of exposure gripped me, causing me to swim back up to the surface in a panic. It wasn't until my head broke the surface that I knew that I had been on the verge of drowning. My limbs were going numb and I was finding it exceedingly difficult to keep my head above the water. My thoughts became incoherent, and I began to slip in and out of full consciousness. Enthralled with my new submarine abilities, I had woefully overestimated them — and now, I felt certain, I was going to pay with my life for this miscalculation.

What happened over the next two and a half hours is not entirely clear. I recall that, on several occasions, I was certain that I had submerged for the last time, only to feel myself curiously bolstered to the surface by some odd upwelling of seawater. At some point, I saw the lights of a ship steadily drawing near and, knowing that this was absolutely my last hope for survival, I forced myself to swim, feebly, towards it. I knew that if I could somehow get ahold of this ship, I would be able to rest long enough to recover my strength and eventually climb into it. Slipping under the water, I was overjoyed to see that this decrepit old steamer was dragging behind it about forty feet of loose line, a thin but sturdy hemp rope, not unlike the ones I helped make in Plymouth. Grabbing ahold as it passed and, twining it around my arm, I let the ship drag me, while I dedicated my last remaining strength to keeping my face out of the water.

After a few minutes, I recovered my strength (and my curiosity) well enough to look back, one last time, at that monstrous underwater procession still pouring through the trench behind me. What would have happened if I had lost consciousness and sunk down into that demon-haunted canyon? Would those other aquatic humans have saved me? Would they have whisked me off to some alien necropolis hidden in the depths of the ocean floor? And who were these strange people who seemed to share my peculiar mutations? Could I learn more about them?

I continued to look back at the dwindling, two-way parade of horrors, observing one final, chilling detail which had previously escaped my notice. Of these two complementary processions, the ocean-bound monstrosities pouring out of the mouth of the Hudson were noticeably, considerably, larger than the incoming horrors. I could not avoid the inference that the latter, fattened from covert feedings, were returning to the abyss and making way for the smaller, leaner, hungrier monsters who sought to trade places with them.

XVII

I DID NOT ENJOY THE SENSATION OF BEING DRAGGED BACK TO THE fiend-infested skyscrapers of Manhattan, but I was not in a position to choose. As the ship turned north, entering the increasingly polluted waters of the East River, I avoided looking at the towers above me, searching instead along the opposite bank for a place where I might safely come ashore. I have a dim recollection of passing beneath the great iron silhouette of the Williamsburg Bridge, starkly skeletal and dinosaur-like against the orange grey sky, but I was hallucinating badly at this time and unable to trust my still-swollen eyes.

Just as I felt my arms go completely numb, I saw something looming out of the pre-dawn haze. A small island, with six or seven official looking buildings on it, their pale bulk outlined against the increasingly cloudy sky. More importantly, this island had a wide beach, surrounded by low shrubs, hidden from the rest of the island by a steep embankment which ran its length. I unwound my feeble arm and let go of the rope, allowing myself to swirl away through the ship's wake.

Glancing up at the receding steamer that had saved my life, I read the word painted across the stern and was both startled and amused to realize that I recognized it. It was the decrepit steamship *Yorrike* which I had seen nearly three years earlier on the Charles River, on that fateful day of the awful Molasses Flood in Boston. Certain that I had encountered the name somewhere before, I tried my best to recall where. Then it came to me. It was from *Hamlet*, the graveyard scene. The skull which the gravedigger unearths, the skull of the King's Jester whom Hamlet mocks and pities, is the skull of a man whose name was Yorick (perhaps an old English or Scandanavian spelling). Wondering at the eerie significance of this familiar exhumation scenario, I shivered, unable to shake the feeling that it was yet another taunt from the Overlords themselves.

Rolling over in the currents, I lacked the strength to propel myself to the beach and, fearful that I was yet again in danger of drowning, I tried, however feebly, to kick my legs in the general direction of the shore.

Just then, I became aware of several large glowing objects meandering, very swiftly, through the water directly beneath me. As before, I felt myself

246

eerily, inexplicably, bouyed. This upsurge, riddled with these curious luminous masses, began to propel me across the rushing currents towards the island beach. At one point during this strange transport, I allowed my head to slip beneath the low waves and saw that the shallows before me were swarming with strange darting white lights. So weakened was I by then that I feel certain that, had these curious lights not whisked me to the shore, I could not have made the journey. Deposited there, half dead upon the sandy shoal, I managed to drag myself clear of the waterline. Unable to rise, or even move, I lay exhausted, listening to the chirping of the morning birds and the low rumble of the surrounding metropolis, weeping tears of joy for the solid ground beneath me.

From out of that cluster of silent, mist-enshrouded buildings that covered the island, I heard a distant shriek, high and sharp and definitely female, coming from somewhere beyond the buildings, tainting my initial relief with a decidedly ominous undertone. Despite wondering what this eerie wailing might indicate, my eyes simply closed and, face down in the sand, I lost consciousness for an unknown period of time.

* * * *

UPON WAKING, I SENSED THE PRESENCE OF SOMEONE STANDING nearby. Looking up, I noticed a woman in a dingy grey lab coat, standing some twenty feet away, smirking. Her arms folded resolutely across her chest, she looked to be in her early fifties, with great reams of brownish red hair pinned up in a bun. Although she clearly saw me struggling to get up, she made no move to help.

In a lilting Irish brogue, she said, "If you're waiting for the welcoming committee there young fella, you can forget it. I'm under government quarantine and the Law says I'm not allowed to touch you... even if I wanted to." She raised her eyebrows when she said this last bit, staring approvingly at me. I knew I was stark naked, with only a dim recollection of having kicked free of my clothing at some point during the swim.

"Well, you're a lovely specimen, ain't you?" she smiled. "Are you some sort of selkie then?"

"A what?" I asked.

"Or else a kelpie?" she laughed.

"You don't happen to have a towel handy do you?" I asked, but she shook her head and shrugged, grinning all the while.

"Where am I?" I asked, rising to my knees and looking all around. The sun had still not risen, though the sky was pale along the eastern horizon.

"You're on North Brother Island... brother." She looked at me expectantly, waiting to see if I recognized the name.

"Never heard of it." I said, brushing the sand from my face and chest. "Care to enlighten me?"

"Don't read the papers much do you?" she asked.

"Not if I can avoid it," I said.

"This island is a quarantine facility for Riverside Hospital. An isolation unit for people with highly contagious diseases," she said. "Most of the people living here have tuberculosis."

"Is that a fact?"

"I'm afraid so," she said cheerfully.

"Do *you* have tuberculosis?" I asked, but she shook her head.

"No, not exactly."

Casting all modesty aside, I struggled to my feet and began to make my way, slowly and haltingly, up the beach toward the lawn. Several times my legs nearly failed me; I was still dangerously exhausted. The muscles in my legs went limp, and after going about five paces, I fell back down upon my knees.

"My name is Mary," she said, making her way down the slope to meet me. "Mary Mallon." Again she scrutinized my face, to see if I would recognize the name.

"That sounds vaguely familiar," I said. "Are you famous for something?"

I sat back down upon the sand and watched this woman coming down the little hill toward me. I saw something which had initially escaped my notice — a thing which promptly answered my many questions. Not unlike the man Howard and I had seen in Boston, she had a kind of subtle shadow, a silvery grey halo, which clung to her like a mist as she moved. My gaze was drawn irresistibly to her chest where I saw, stirring within her upper torso, the dim outline of a luminous organism, a strange spider-like "passenger" whose warm silhouette I could clearly discern, as it pulled itself through her chest cavity, moving among her organs, like an octopus cautiously rearranging itself in an underwater cave.

"I am Robert," I said, extending my hand. She looked at my hand, and shook her head.

"I don't have tuberculosis, Robert, but I should warn you. I'm here because the Health Department believes I am infected with something."

"Infected with what?" I asked.

"Well, they were calling it typhoid fever..." she shrugged, "But now... I reckon they don't know what to call it."

"Well we can still shake hands, can't we?" I asked but she recoiled and folded her arms across her chest, clearly annoyed by my ignorance.

"You can't catch typhoid fever from a handshake," I added.

After a minute of eyeing me suspiciously, her face warmed into a reluctant smile.

"So," she said at last, "you've got brains as well as looks, eh? That's a rare combination in a man."

"Not as rare as you might think," I replied.

"Oh, trust me, boy!" she laughed. "Rarer than the unicorn! Take it from one who's been searching."

Once again, I attempted to rise to my feet but I reconsidered and sat back down on the sand.

"What brings you to our lovely island facility, Robert?" she asked. She was regarding me now with intense interest, her eyes moving up and down the length of my body again. I began to suspect that she could see my passenger.

"Well," I said, "I was on a ship and, to make a long story short, I ended up in the water. I'm rather surprised I didn't drown. I was in no condition to swim but..." I glanced over at the shoreline as the memory came back to me. "There were these things in the water. I was carried here by... something. There were strange lights, hundreds of them, all along the shoreline."

"Ah, so you saw Them," she replied with a smile.

"Who?" I asked.

"The Things in the water. The Shining Ones."

"What are they?"

"Nobody knows," she sighed. "Just a legend really. But, on occasion, they have been known to save people from drowning."

"Who saves people from drowning?" I asked, unnerved.

"Who can say? Kelpies? Selkies?" She squinted at the lapping shoreline. "Ghosts?"

"What ghosts?" I asked. This seemed to catch her off guard and she looked away from me suddenly, peering thoughtfully into the distance.

"Well, sonny," she said finally, thrusting her hands deep into her pockets, "Let's just say you're not the first body to wash up on this beach."

"What do you mean?" I asked. She raised her eyebrows in surprise.

"Surely you've heard of the *General Slocum*?" she chided.

"No," I admitted.

"Good Lord, son! It was only one of the worst shipwrecks in the history of America," she countered, "second only to the *Titanic* in death toll, with over a thousand people drowned! But, you know, since it was mostly a bunch of poor immigrant women who died, it is less known." Then, turning fully to me she asked, "Is any of this ringing a bell, sailorman?"

"No," I replied "I think I would remember that."

"The *General Slocum* was a rather odd ship with a very peculiar history. Some said it was haunted, or cursed. It was involved in a surprisingly high number of accidents and mishaps. Five collisions in eight years is certainly an indication that something is going on. Once, in 1901, it was hijacked by several hundred drunken anarchists, though this mutiny ultimately failed." I shrugged and shook my head, momentarily amused at the idea of several hundred drunken anarchists taking over a steamship.

"What happened then?" I asked, "Did it finally sink?"

"One day, in 1904, the *General Slocum*, loaded down with over a thousand passengers, mostly woman and children from a Lutheran Church in Germantown, caught fire on Long Island Sound. The crew quickly assessed that there was nowhere to dock without running the risk of setting the wooden wharfs ablaze, so the pilot did the only thing he could do — he just kept going till at last he ran her aground, here on this island."

"That's awful," I said. "Weren't there any lifeboats, or life preservers on board?"

"The lifeboats had been freshly painted to look like new but when the passengers tried to make use of them, they found that nearly all of them had been painted firmly in place. The ship was also equipped with fire hoses but these had never been replaced and immediately fell to pieces when they turned them on."

"There must have been hell to pay for the company!"

"Actually," she said, "the president, treasurer, secretary, and commodore of the Knickerbocker Company which owned the *General Slocum*, despite being indicted, were somehow able to pin all responsibility for the disaster on the lowly captain. In the courtroom he took the fall for the entire Company and despite all the criminal neglect on the part of the owners and the inspectors, none but the captain was held liable."

"What happened to him?" I asked.

"He served three and a half years in Sing Sing, and then Taft pardoned him. It's really a lovely judicial system you've got here in America. Just lovely…"

"Yes, it really only works on the poor," I said. "It operates on the principal of fall-guys, patsies, and scapegoats. The wealthy businessman is quite above the law. If you have enough money, you can get away with anything."

"How many passengers died?" I asked.

"Over a thousand. The ones who didn't burn or drown were inevitably drawn into the paddle wheel and bludgeoned to death. Many jumped in with life preservers on, only to have them disintegrate immediately. In some cases babies and small children were outfitted with life vests and thrown overboard, only to sink like stones. It was later discovered that many of the life vests had actually been loaded with lead pellets to meet regulation weight. Incredibly, the Law did not bother to pursue the manufacturer of the life vests!"

"How many survived?"

"About three hundred and twenty survived out of one thousand five hundred," she said. "I read about a wee lad, who survived by hanging onto his stuffed bear. He floated several hundred yards downriver and was eventually discovered by rescuers. Oddly enough, it was the captain and most of the crew that survived. It was one of the worst shipwrecks in US history and most of the bodies washed up right here, along this very shoreline." She looked off towards the lapping water again. "Sometimes, in the hours before dawn, I stand here on this embankment and look out across the water. Every once in a while, when they are feeling playful, they permit me to see them."

For nearly a minute, we both stood there, silently staring out at the shimmering waves.

Thinking about all those drowned people, I began to ponder once more on those things I'd seen in the water, the strange underwater lights that had swum beneath me and pushed me to shore. On the subject of ghosts, I was undecided. If anything, I was inclined to believe that most (if not all) so-called ghost sightings had, in all likelihood, been sightings of Hidden Ones, accidentally noticed on the move by observant humans who misconstrued what they had seen. On the other hand, the glowing things beneath the water were unlike any Hidden Ones I'd seen. I must have had a curious look on my face because she smiled at me.

"Do you think those things in the water are..." I hesitated to use the word. "Ghosts?"

"I have seen many strange things along this shoreline these past twelve years," she said wistfully. "Ah... but you probably wouldn't believe me if I told you."

"You would be surprised what I'll believe." I laughed.

From somewhere behind my increasingly interesting hostess, a door slammed and Mary fell silent, casting several long glances over her shoulder before turning back to me.

"Perhaps I'll tell you about it some other time," she said. "Right now we have got to get you out of sight — the staff will be arriving very soon."

"I need help getting up," I said. "I don't think I can walk unassisted."

"But I already told you I am infected," she said flatly. "Aren't you afraid of contracting typhoid fever?"

"Do I look like I'm afraid of contracting typhoid fever?" I asked reaching my arms up to her.

"Suit yourself," she said with a smile, gripping me firmly by the armpits and hauling me, effortlessly, onto my feet.

Once upright, my vision became confused. The darkened lawn and buildings became a vast smear of grey, green, and black. The scenery began to sway from side to side. Even Mary, standing directly beside me, was little more than a shapeless blob.

Hearing another door close nearby, I whispered, "Are we still alone?"

"For the time being, yes, but the sun is rising. Do you need medical attention?"

"No!" I said emphatically. "No doctors! I just need sleep... and food."

"Good," she said. "We'll feed you and put you to bed in my cottage."

Pulling my arm across her shoulder this powerfully built woman dragged me up the lawn to her cottage.

Upon entering this cabin-like structure, I became aware of many strange smells. I was greeted by a large friendly dog, who immediately took to sniffing me and licking my dangling hand. Crossing the floor, I heard Mary gently shoo the dog as she lay me out on a narrow cot and then went immediately to work preparing some warm vegetable soup. I was completely blind now and I suspected that my newly exposed eye membranes had become irritated, possibly even infected, from the filth of the East River.

Considering the last twelve hours, I was dimly amazed to still be alive. I had narrowly escaped getting shot by diving off a railroad trestle. Then I was nearly swept out to sea and devoured by god only knows what, only to wash up on an island that's under government quarantine. And now, to top it off, I had gone blind!

"Your eyes are going to be fine..." she said, "...though God must hate you something fierce to have delivered you here, sailorman."

"I'm not a sailor." I corrected her, to which she replied, "I should say not — you couldn't even manage to stay on your ship!"

This set us both laughing.

"But I'll grant you the point," she continued. "I reckon the proper term for you now is castaway."

I dimly recall being spoon-fed warm soup and hunks of toasted bread, though I was teetering on the brink of exhaustion. She set me down again and covered me with blankets, putting a warm wet teabag over each eye to bring down the swelling. With the warm soft bulk of the dog pressed up against me, I slept for next 72 hours, sprawled out on a pile of thick blankets carefully arranged underneath Mary's cot.

* * * *

In the crawlspace beneath the cot, I was permitted to convalesce for a period of days, reflecting on all that had transpired. One morning I found that my nictitating membranes, no longer swollen, had retracted. My vision returned to normal and I was able to assess the structure which housed me. This cottage was about twenty feet square, consisting of a large living room with an adjoining kitchen, and a washroom in the rear. A large oak table stood in the center of the room, flanked by several old-fashioned chairs with cane seats and backs. A few old colored prints decorated the walls; boxes, bags, and clothing covered most of the floor. The cot which concealed me was situated against the south wall.

The dog was my constant companion, a friendly Dalmatian, whose name was Daisy. I lived in a pitiful state of intermittent semi-consciousness for nearly a week, waking up only when Mary brought me meals, which I devoured with enthusiasm and gratitude. Several times I awoke at odd hours to find her gone, though she always left a plate of food for me and a note explaining where I could find such necessities as I might need or desire. Her hospitality was stunning and, feeling myself wholly undeserving of this reception, I vowed to find some way to repay her in kind.

Under Mary's care, I was spoiled with some of the best home cooking I'd ever had, as well as being the grateful recipient of her intuitive healing abilities, which included frequent warm salt baths to relieve my tired and strained muscles. Having been a nanny, Mary Mallon was also a gifted storyteller, full of weird, Irish legends and fables which she dispensed with minimal prompting.

Over the course of two stormy afternoons, as we sat sipping peppermint tea in her cottage, she told me all the Irish, English, and Scottish legends she knew that pertained to man-eating ogres, trolls or giants. During these discussions I learned of the Beast of Lettir Dilan, a misshapen humanoid said to be the offspring of a mortal mother who had been attacked and impregnated by a lake-dwelling monstrosity. Mary also told me of the dreaded Fomorians, a pre-human race of monster-men described in the *Lebor Gabala* ("Book of Invasions"), an ancient Irish codex from the 12th century. Similarly, I heard the legends of the Kelpie, the Ciudach, the Gaborchind, and the English Hobyah, all monstrous troll-like creatures, all hunters of men. Mary also told me the legends of Sawney Bean, Cutty Dyer, Christie-Cleek, and the Jarman of Colne Brook, in Berkshire England, famous cannibal killers who, I theorized, may also have been Encerrados. Every one of these legends contained those familiar details — the recurring themes of predation by strange cannibal beings with curious deformities.

It might have been a fine existence but living in such intimate proximity to Mary, I soon learned the grim truth of her life upon North Brother Island.

She had been quarantined on this island for over a decade, during which time the government doctors had continued to run her through a battery of tests, excessive even for a supposed sufferer of typhoid fever. These tests included the biweekly collection of stool and urine, as well as frequent blood tests and daily physical examinations. Every morning at 8 a.m. there was a soft knock upon the door and Mary would rise, dress, and walk, under escort, to one of the large grey buildings where they collected her secretions, took her temperature, measured her pulse and otherwise documented her various bodily functions.

This puzzled me. Surely they had long since confirmed that she was infected with typhoid — so why all these ongoing invasive tests? Occasionally, she said, the doctors encouraged her to try one of the medicinal drugs they were testing, though none of these experimental cures ever altered or improved her condition. As Mary told me later, she would often amuse herself during these exams by fabricating curious and inexplicable symptoms, distorting and exaggerating her answers, or otherwise misleading the various doctors and nurses attempting to study her.

As the days passed, I came to understand that Mary was remarkably adept at concealing my presence from the hospital staff. She repositioned the blankets upon her cot in such a way that I was curtained off from any curious eyes which might have peered in at me from the windows. Mary also helped matters by keeping her cottage in a state of constant, intentional disarray, with the piles of clothes, boxes of books, and personal effects heaped upon the floor around the cot. This mess had the twin benefits of discouraging intruders and also providing me objects to hide behind. In the space beneath the cot, I played games with Daisy to pass the time, napping frequently, and stretching and massaging my still-aching limbs.

One of the first things Mary did was to bring me a hospital staff uniform (which she had stolen from a supply closet), admitting, with a grin, that she had felt some reluctance on this score. In her thoughtfulness, she even brought me a stack of books and magazine, on a wide array of topics, which, once the exhaustion passed, I perused with interest. Among the warm blankets with Daisy, I spent several hours a day reading through this literature. Some of these magazines even contained articles about Mary herself; these represented a vast assortment of perspectives on her experiences with the Health Department. From these various articles I was able to piece together a general idea of my hostess' rather unusual history.

Mary Mallon was born in 1869 in Cork County in southern Ireland. Nearly nothing is known of her life prior to immigrating to the United States in the late 1880s. Like myself, Mary was entirely without any living relatives. It was the first of several eerie parallels. She was alone in the world, with no one to trumpet her cause but the occasional sympathetic commentator or journalist. Two or three of the authors I read even crassly intimated that she might have inadvertently killed off her own family with typhoid, though they provided no evidence to support this insinuation. What is known is that she arrived in New York City sometime around 1900. An unusually gifted cook, she immediately found work cooking for numerous wealthy families throughout the greater New York area.

In the summer of 1900, she was hired by a family in Mamaroneck, New York. Not long after her arrival, however, a young man visiting the house contracted typhoid fever. Mary departed shortly afterwards. During the winter of 1901-02, Mary worked for a family in New York City. A month later, the laundress became ill with typhoid fever. Mary continued on with this family for nearly a year before departing. Throughout 1902, she had worked in Dark Harbor, Maine, for the family of J. Coleman Drayton, a prominent New York lawyer and son-in-law to Mrs. William Astor. Seven out of nine family members soon fell ill and Mary, at the request of her employer, remained on for over a year to help nurse the sick. Two years later, there was an outbreak of typhoid fever in Sands Point, New York, at a home where Mary was employed. In 1906, she was hired by Charles Henry Warren, the wealthy banker and president of the Lincoln Bank, summering in Oyster Bay, Long Island. Shortly thereafter, six members of the household contracted typhoid. Three weeks after the epidemic began, Mary quit. At no time during these occurrences did anyone link these outbreaks with the healthy and able-bodied cook.

The concept of the healthy diseased carrier was still a controversial new theory, and much doubted, even by many established scientists. Displaying no symptoms whatsoever, Mary would have had no reason to think that she was involved in these outbreaks, though it must have occurred to her that something strange was going on. If she had noticed anything at all, it might have seemed that typhoid fever was stalking her which, of course, she would have known was impossible. I mention these things because the matter of her intentions... the question of her conscious ambivalence, or malevolence, would later become of central importance.

During the winter of 1907, Mary was hired by the Walter Bowen family on Park Avenue. Two months later, the chambermaid fell ill with typhoid, followed by the youngest Bowen daughter, Annie, who later died. Called upon by her employers to nurse the dying child, with whom she had formed a deep attachment, Mary remained for several months. It was here that she was first confronted by an investigator named George Soper and informed that she was a spreader of disease. Upon learning this, her reaction appears to have been one of panic and disbelief, lashing out violently at her bizarre accuser.

Later, much would be made of this irrational response and what it might mean about her character.

Shortly thereafter, Mary Mallon was incarcerated on North Brother Island for a period of three years, during which time extensive tests were conducted to determine how it was that she could be a spreader of disease while remaining perfectly healthy. In 1910, she was finally permitted to go free on the condition that she promise never to work in food preparation again. She agreed to this and, signing an affidavit to that effect, she was released from custody. For a time she worked as a laundress but in 1915, unable to earn a decent living outside her chosen profession, and perhaps skeptical of her healthy carrier status, she changed her name to Mary Brown and was hired at Sloane Maternity Hospital in New York City as a cook. An outbreak of typhoid soon followed and she was recaptured, amid much fanfare, and returned to North Brother Island. During this outbreak at Sloane Maternity, twenty five hospital employees fell ill. Two of these infected people later died.

It must have been bad enough being identified as a "walking contagion," but the most damning insinuation of all was that Mary Mallon had intentionally infected others with typhoid. In 1909, after being told that she was a healthy carrier of typhoid, she had taken a job where she prepared meals for many hundreds of people. In total, Mary had been linked to forty seven cases of typhoid and three deaths, most of these after she had been informed of her infected status. Worst of all, she had gone to work at a maternity hospital. While reading these various accounts, I admit that I began to feel a bit strangely about Mary myself. Had she knowingly spread typhoid to the men, women, and children who ate her food?

Certain authors dwelt morbidly on the fact that Mary, like me, had no living relatives to speak of, and many seemed to feel that this lack of familial connection was further evidence of something suspicious in her character. The overall impression one took away from the more insidious articles was that these minor outbreaks were probably just the tip of the iceberg and that Mary Mallon had likely caused many more outbreaks, back in Ireland and elsewhere. Mary Mallon, as depicted in these articles, was a threatening figure, a foreign-born criminal hiding out in America from an obscure and sinister past, and spreading her disease to the inhabitants of New York and beyond. Another mark against her was the fact that she had neither married nor bore children, a circumstance which was similarly used to imply that she was abnormal. Add to this the fact that she was a poor Irish immigrant, and her transformation into a living symbol of contagion, corruption, and decline was complete.

As damning as all this was, there were things about this story which simply did not make sense. It reminded me too much of my friend Howard's remarks about immigrants in general. Howard (and countless others) had compared incoming immigrants to a disease, gnawing away at the otherwise wholesome foundations of American society. In the shadowy figure of "Typhoid Mary," these racist analogies had found a suspiciously cogent literalization.

Most, if not all, of the descriptions of Mary's supposedly sinister behavior came from George Soper, the investigator initially hired to track her. It was clearly to Mr. Soper's advantage to dramatize, as much as possible, the pursuit and capture of his death-dealing quarry. The more monstrous she was thought to be, the more heroic he appeared. The temptation to exaggerate must have been great. In his descriptions of Mary herself, he was barely able to conceal his contempt. He called her "peculiar," "fearful," "obstinate," and "distinctly masculine." He said she was "careless," "disordered," "hysterical," and "impossible to deal with rationally," a fact which my observations of Mary did not bear out. These descriptions, echoed and embellished by reporters who were also inclined to exaggerate for the same reasons, formed the basis of the public view that Mary was a menace.

*　　*　　*　　*

LATER THAT SAME AFTERNOON I READ TWO MORE DOCUMENTS WHICH further altered and illuminated my perspective on the case against Mary Mallon. The first of these items was a medical report containing the documentation of all known typhoid outbreaks in the United States over the last twenty years. This report gave the names of numerous other "healthy carriers" registered with the New York Health Department, who, like Mary had been linked to outbreaks which included the deaths of several people.

One was a restaurant owner from New York City. This man, whose name was Tony Labella, was registered as a confirmed "healthy carrier of the typhoid virus" and was positively linked to multiple typhoid epidemics; in all, one hundred and twenty-two confirmed cases of typhoid fever, five of which had been fatal. Labella was detained for two weeks and then realeased. He apparently continued to run and operate a restaurant in defiance of the Health Department, a fact which had eventually resulted in another outbreak. There were more examples like this, numerous unnamed "healthy carriers" who had broken their promises to avoid food handling. I read about a man by the name of Alphonse Cotils, a confirmed "healthy carrier" living in New Jersey, whose chart revealed that he too had been positively linked to multiple typhoid outbreaks, some of which had occurred after being informed of his "healthy carrier" status. The Health Department had agreed to let him go if he promised not to cook for people again. Yet Cotils, like Labella, had returned to work in food preparation, even after being told that it could result in the deaths of innocent people. He, too, had been permitted to go free, despite his fatal violations.

Further down this same page I read about the case of Fredrick Moersch, a confectioner from Brooklyn who was identified in 1915 as the cause of a typhoid epidemic which infected fifty-nine people. Moersch, like the others, had also willfully disobeyed the Health Department and resumed food preparation. And again, like the other men, Moersch had been released, at which time he too resumed working as a baker. More outbreaks followed. In fact, according to these reports, there were hundreds of examples of people who had either escaped, out of the view of authorities, or else defied them outright and continued to work in food preparation. Once caught, some of these people were temporarily detained, though all were freed shortly thereafter. Having Mary Mallon isolated on North Brother Island for her first offense, and then permanently incarcerating her for her second offense, while numerous other repeat offenders remained free was a discrepancy which Health officials never bothered to explain.

The second thing I read which changed my perspective was an old issue of *The Starry Cross*, an anti-vivisection magazine, where I found a fairly sympathetic article about Mary's case. "There is one common characteristic of 'dangerous' carriers," the author stated. "It never varies. They are always plain people in humble circumstances. Those with more money and influence who could fight back are, somehow, never pronounced 'dangerous.'" The typhoid chart I'd read earlier seemed to bear this out, confirming that it was only the most impoverished and vulnerable members of society whom the authorities were penalizing. In the case of Mary Mallon they had not even bothered with a pretense of legality.

I wondered why the papers had gone to such lengths to demonize and vilify Mary Mallon specifically. Did she simply have the horrendously bad luck of being the first "healthy carrier" to be successfully tracked and caught? Why single her out, when men, who had been responsible for far worse outbreaks than she, were neither detained nor vilified? Why the permanent incarceration and public disgrace? Why all these tests, examinations, and the harvesting of her bodily fluids for years on end? What were these doctors doing to Mary Mallon that they felt they needed to monitor her so closely?

Additionally, why were these articles so quick to suggest that Mary had spread typhoid fever intentionally, and was therefore dangerously aggressive? They said she kicked like a mule when the agents came for her. According to one article, she had bloodied more than one nose and had to be hauled bodily into the wagon by the squeamish coppers. Perhaps, learning of men like Frank Labella, Fredrick Moersch, and Alphonse Cotils, Mary had reason to doubt the validity of the charges against her. Several independent laboratories had tested her stool and found nothing. Perhaps she had reached the plausible conclusion that there was some other unstated reason for her incarceration. Maybe it even gave her a reason to doubt the validity of her diagnosis. Reading the typhoid report again a second time, I found myself doubting it as well. There was certainly no reason to think that her ignorance of her healthy carrier status was not authentic prior to 1909. Many leading scientists did not even believe there was such a thing as a healthy carrier.

* * * *

I MENTIONED THIS TO MARY WHEN SHE RETURNED FOR DINNER THAT evening. As she prepared soup for us both on a double burner stove, I told her of the articles I had read about her case.

"The way you've been treated by the Health Department is bizarre, to say the least," I said. "They really rolled out the red carpet for you, didn't they?"

"Tell me all about it, sailorman," she laughed. "Thank god I wasn't in Chicago in 1892!"

"What happened in Chicago in 1892?"

"A typhoid epidemic that wiped out ten percent of the city's population! They probably would have blamed that on me too. Ha! If they only knew the truth!" She paused, as if she were in deep contemplation. "They were trying to blame an epidemic in Ithaca, New York on me as well," she said, "but gave up when they saw I had never even been to Ithaca!"

I shook my head in disgust.

"Neither I, nor anyone I knew, had ever heard of such a thing as a 'healthy carrier!'" she went on. "The papers said I changed jobs because I knew I was spreading typhoid. Such lies! Those three who died from their contact with me, Annie, Allison, and Victoria, were kind decent people! I bore them no malice! On the contrary, I cared about them a great deal! Little Annie Warren was like a daughter to me! If I had had any idea that I was..." She clenched her fists and looked away. "And now Soper has got everyone believing that I spread the virus on purpose? What the public must think of me! If I lived for a thousand years, I could not hope to live down such monstrous, heartless lies."

She scowled hatefully.

"I'd like to go a round or two with Soper! Just the two of us. Then he'd find out about us Irish girls — how different we are from the fawning flowers he's used to!"

Concerned that my questions had provoked her rage, I attempted to redirect the conversation in a less vengeful direction.

"Your continued incarceration on this island makes no sense, Mary, and there's a fair bit of public outrage about it, you know."

"There is certainly some," she sneered, "but the way the Health Department has suppressed the details of my ongoing detention shows how much control they have over the papers. They mean to make some sort of example out of me. Bacteriology, my arse! They want absolute control over certain members of the population, and they'll use any crisis, real or imagined, as a pretense to get it!"

"What I don't understand," I added, "among other things, is... why the ongoing tests? They should have learned all they could years ago."

"I thought the same thing," she said, finishing up the soup and pouring it into two bowls to cool, "But now I'm beginning to wonder if..." She fell silent, turning her back to me.

"Wonder if what?" I asked tentatively.

She turned and, putting her wooden spoon down on the table, folded her arms across her chest and narrowed her eyes at me.

"I'm beginning to wonder if, perhaps, they haven't seen something... felt something... inside my body, which they have never encountered before... something they cannot fathom... something they need to study."

She had put on a brave face but there was fear in her voice now and her eyes were wide with a kind of muted terror.

"They are keeping you imprisoned here to study you..." I said. "And they have made you out to be a fiend in the newspapers to justify it."

"You are very observant, Robert," she said in a low voice.

"But what about those others I read about? Cotils, Labella, Moersch... documented cases of other healthy carriers who also violated their agreements with the Health Department, people who harmed far more than you have, yet have not been denied their freedom. "

"Nothing can clear me in the eyes of the Health Department, Robert, because they want to make a showing of me! To put me on display as some monster whom they have captured. They will forfeit my freedom so they can take credit for protecting the rich!"

As I heard these words, I immediately began to plot a way to get Mary Mallon off North Brother Island.

"There's two kinds of justice in America," I said. "One for the rich and another for the rest of us."

"I've been flung into prison without even a pretense of a fair trial. Known murderers at least get that much!" She looked away in disgust, though it soon faded into a curious smirk.

"Do you want to hear the greatest irony of all, Robert?" she asked.

I nodded.

"I don't think I ever even had typhoid fever."

This puzzled me; I frowned at her in confusion.

"Oh, make no mistake," she clarified. "There is something living inside me alright! But, unlike these doctors, I don't pretend to know what it is. I have, however, managed to learn a few things about it."

"Like what?" I prompted, sitting up and giving her my full attention. She leaned towards me conspiratorially.

"Well," she went on in a low voice, "it behaves rather like a disease, and is sometimes sickening... or even fatal, to others in my proximity. Whatever it is... it is reproducing itself at an alarming rate, using my body as a nest or an incubator for its young. And it permits me to live symptom-free because I am its host... and a very convenient vehicle for getting close to its desired prey."

"Its desired prey?" I asked.

"Yes, it feeds on living tissue. Secreting itself inside my body has provided it with ample opportunities to get up close with its preferred quarry."

I shrugged.

"Human beings, Robert," she said. Her voice was small and distant now. "Like little Annie Warren, Allison the laundress, and Victoria the chambermaid. My... or rather, our victims seem to experience an acute swelling of the brain and gall bladder, followed by perforation and deterioration of the intestines. Not long after that, death by septicemia... or else peritonitis. In the papers, the doctors called it typhoid fever, but they were wrong." She looked away as she said this, though not before I saw that her eyes were brimming with tears.

A feeling of empathy passed between us and I looked away uncomfortably. My skin began to crawl and I shuddered. Collecting myself, I continued to ply her with questions.

"Do you have any sense at all of what this thing inside you might be?" I asked. She shook her head.

"Whatever it is, it has found a way to disguise itself as the typhoid virus. Even after eight years of careful scrutiny, the doctors here were convinced that I had typhoid fever. Hence my charming nickname..." I shook my head and she continued. "Oh, but there are still a great many things under the banner of heaven which the ruthless scalpel of Science cannot discover, a great many things which cannot be viewed through a microscope or telescope."

Picking up the sufficiently cooled soup bowls, she stepped carefully through the cluttered room. Placing my bowl on a nearby chair she seated herself on the bed above me.

"There are other forms which life takes... whole cycles of existence, a vast multitude of Beings, unseen and unfathomable, which have not permitted themselves to be discovered by the blundering representatives of humankind."

A long, thoughtful silence followed this statement, during which I ate several large spoonfuls of soup.

"You mean like those Shining Things that carried me to the beach?" I asked.

"Precisely," she said. "And a thousand more besides. They are all around us, Robert, yet hidden from view."

"You think it is one of these beings who has taken up residence inside your body?" I asked.

"These things are mimics, Robert. They can impersonate ordinary forms so perfectly that they are able to avoid detection. This thing inside of me has perfectly synchronized its bodily functions with my own. For example, its pulse, for lack of a better word, is hidden beneath my own pulse. Every now and again, our pulses fall out of step, though it is always quick to correct this. On very rare occasions, they slip up and permit themselves to be seen or heard or felt... but, since those who observe them are never believed, their existence has remained a secret."

"Of course," I mumbled, thinking of the many Hidden Ones I'd observed, and of their uncanny mimicry. If they could disguise themselves as trees, rocks, clouds, and shadows, then why not diseases as well? When considered alongside my prior knowledge, it made perfect sense. If they could colonize the human body without killing it, and cloak their presence behind a veil of familiar (but misleading) symptoms, then they could spy on us from inside our own bodies, a thing which would make their subjugation and surveillance of us all the more absolute.

"You're saying that your body has been colonized by some kind of undiscovered organism. Are the doctors here close to figuring out what it is yet?"

"I think they have known for some time now that this thing inside me isn't typhoid fever. Now they are just determined to figure out what it is. At the cost of my freedom! I have been a peepshow for everybody. Even the bloody interns had to come see me and ask about the facts already known to the whole wide world! For a while there the doctors tried to convince me I had to have my gall bladder out. I told them to go piss themselves because there was nothing wrong with my gall bladder! As soon as I put up a fuss, they dropped it. Later Doctor Wilson admitted to me that removing my gall bladder wouldn't have helped anyway!"

I shook my head in disgust.

"You should stop giving them your bodily fluids, Mary," I said.

"I tried!" she hissed. "Back in January of 1919, I told them I was done giving them samples. A large male intern returned two days later and threatened me! He started dropping comments about how awful it would be if something should happen to me, implying that, in the event of an accident, I might not get the care I required." Her hands were shaking and her face twisted into an angry scowl.

"So now they are keeping you on permanent quarantine from all but a few masked and gloved hospital staff?" I asked.

"No," Mary smirked, "My situation is even stranger than that! While I have been separated out from the other typhoid patients, I am permitted, even encouraged, to mingle with the tuberculosis patients. Similarly, I spend several hours a day with various members of the staff. I even volunteer in the labs sometimes, working alongside the white coats, covertly learning what I can about the research they are doing on me."

"Incredible!" I said.

"That's not all, Robert. They even permit me to bake and sell bread and muffins to the employees and visitors to the island. They all *rave* about me bread!"

"Wait a minute. You are permitted to mingle with the other patients at this facility? And to sell them food which you have prepared?"

"Yes. And how on God's green earth is that allowed? Why aren't they worried that I'll spread typhoid to these already sick people? Can you explain that?"

I remained silent.

"No, you can't, can you? You know what else you can't explain? The tuberculosis clinic has a nursery. They sometimes ask me to tend to the sick children there — even the wee babes!"

I recalled reading about this in articles from both *New York World* and *New York American*, but I had dismissed them both as exaggerations at the time. I was stunned to learn otherwise.

"So then, sailorman, I'd like to hear you explain what's going on here."

I shrugged, genuinely baffled.

Some time after this we fell silent. From where I was, I could just see Mary's profile in the moonlight. At one point I noticed that she seemed to be staring intently, fearfully, at something in the darkness and, following the direction of her gaze, I saw and heard the source of her interest. In the yard outside the cottage, there was a large tree, whose windblown branches, every so often, scraped gently against the window casement. Using my enhanced senses, I made as careful a scrutiny of this tree as my position would allow. Studying its outline intently for several minutes, I saw nothing to indicate that it was anything but an ordinary tree. Vaguely reassured, I soon fell into a deep sleep.

Mary, however, apparently kept up her vigil for most of the night. Several times before dawn I awoke to find her still staring at the window, her face oddly lit by the dissipating moonlight, an expression of mounting terror contorting her features.

XVIII

THE FOLLOWING MORNING, AT ABOUT 8 A.M., THE SOFT KNOCK CAME came again and Mary dutifully rose and departed for her daily examination. She did not return for several hours, spending the rest of her morning baking muffins, biscuits, and loaves of bread. Spending all morning with Daisy, I had ample time to contemplate calmly the various insights of the prior night's conversation, distressing though most of them were. I attempted to make sense of the numerous parallels that existed between my curious hostess and me.

We both were, or had been, carriers of an unknown and unidentifiable organism, a dangerous quasi-parasitic being so unusual, so unprecedented, and so elusive, that it had baffled the very best doctors that the US Health Department could summon. Like me, Mary Mallon was also the end of her family line — a runaway who had, at a young age, packed a few bare essentials into a carrying case and, saying goodbye to everyone and everything she had ever known, had struck out alone, to make her way in the world. Like my own, Mary's parasite nested inside of her in the manner of a virus, utilizing her as a medium for its gruesome predation of humanity but leaving Mary herself unharmed. As a result we had, both of us, carved unusually solitary paths through the world, each leaving a damning wake of human damage behind us.

In sharp contrast to myself, however, Mary was not an active participant in this predation and did not share in the spoils of these attacks. Whereas I had been enlisted, mind, body and soul, she appears to have remained a more passively unconscious intermediary, reflexively unaware and uninvolved. Finally, and perhaps most importantly, Mary Mallon, like myself, was a member of the lower class who had dared to bring harm, wittingly or unwittingly, to members of the ruling class, earning us both the unmitigated and energetic hostility of the authorities.

Mary returned to the cottage later than usual that night. It was nearly 10 p.m. when she came in, depositing yet another bag of books, folders, magazines, and newspapers on the cluttered table before collapsing onto her

265

cot with a sigh. After exchanging a few pleasantries, she got up and offered to cook me some more soup, an offer which I politely declined.

"Can I ask you a very complicated question?" I asked after a few minutes.

"Of course," she said, looking at me wide-eyed.

"I already told you last night what I think is going on around here. What I really wanted to know was, what exactly do *you* think is going on at this facility?"

Mary sighed and, putting a kettle on to boil, she came over and sat on the cot above me, looking straight into my eyes, her hands folded tightly in her lap.

"The people confined to this Island are being exposed to multiple contagious diseases, simultaneously," she said, "but only some of us are contracting them."

"They are experimenting on you," I prompted.

She nodded. "As I see it, there are only two possible explanations. The most likely explanation is that they have quarantined us, under the unassailable pretense of the public health, because, secretly, we all display certain… inexplicable traits or talents."

"What do you mean?" I asked.

She smirked at me. "Not the brightest star in the sky are you, pretty eyes?"

"What are you talking about?" I muttered, feeling suddenly nervous.

"There's a lass they keep locked up in building C who can hear people's thoughts. I've tested her several times myself and she's never been wrong. An elderly woman on the first floor of the same building can heal dementia patients just by talking to them and touching their faces. Most of the people on the third floor have extraordinarily good vision, and on the fourth floor are the people with… let's just be generous and call it preposterously acute hearing," she laughed. "Some of them are probably listening in on us right now!" She looked out the window, toward a large four-story building about two hundred yards away, and let her gaze run along the row of darkened windows that faced us.

I scoffed unconvincingly, "That's impossible."

"Is it?" she asked confidentially. "Several of them insist that they can hear the trees whispering and humming back and forth to each other at night. And there's a young girl on the fourth floor, just ten years old, who swears she can actually hear the earth turning! The poor little dear. At night she has to stopper her ears with cotton because she claims she can hear certain stars, as she says, 'roaring back and forth to each other!' Fancy that!"

These examples, seemingly chosen at random, intrigued me intensely, though I was careful to keep a disinterested expression upon my face. "I certainly don't envy anyone who has that particular power," she went on in a low whisper. "All the ones with the exceptional hearing are a bit mad. It's not good to hear everything all at once, like that."

"And what about you, Mary?" I asked. "Do you have any peculiar abilities?"

She hesitated, eyeing me thoughtfully, looking slightly surprised.

"Do you really have to ask, Robert?" she smirked. She looked at me suspiciously now, accusing me with her eye. I grew nervous and scrambled to keep the conversation moving forward.

"Well, I understand, of course, that you are apparently immune to a disease which kills thousands every year. I'd definitely call that a peculiar ability. But I meant... beside that."

"I'll tell you a little story," she said softly, "and then you will understand."

Leaning back on my elbows, I nodded.

"When Soper and the rest of those bastards first brought me here, back in 1907, I was so angry that I got into all sorts of mischief." She shot me a look which told me that this was, in fact, a gross understatement. She continued, almost boastfully. "I used to sneak out, late at night, strip off me clothes and go wading into the river. I didn't know how to swim back then, but I had a secret plan to teach myself as quickly as possible and to, one day, swim for my freedom. Swimming in the river was, of course, strictly forbidden but I was very careful, and they never once caught me. I was a younger, fiercer woman back in those days... and angry; very, very angry. Night swimming was the only thing that kept me sane, you see, for it allowed me some small degree of... privacy." She paused here and her eyes welled up with tears, though she quickly wiped them away with her thumbs. "That's when I first glimpsed those Shining Ones who you saw gathered along the beach. I would stay there for hours, immersed in the water, trying to observe them, catching fleeting glimpses and trying to guess what on earth they might be. One night, I was out there... you know... trying to get a closer look. I'd been swimming up and down the beach for nearly an hour when I suddenly felt a sharp pain in my eyelids! I rubbed them and rubbed them, but the pain only got worse." Noting the look of fearful interest upon my face she smiled approvingly before continuing. "And would you care to hazard a guess as to what happened next, Robert?"

A long silence fell. I struggled with the impulse to tell her everything. She was toying with me, and I was still uncertain whether or not I could trust her. I decided to play.

"Hmm… Don't tell me. Did your eyelids spontaneously split in two and you suddenly found that you had thin, translucent membranes over your eyes that enabled you to see perfectly underwater?"

"Well now," she laughed, "Would you mind telling me how on earth you could possibly have known that?"

"Lucky guess?" I shrugged. Then, before she was through laughing, I asked, "What did you do then?"

Grinning triumphantly, she got up and went into the kitchen, emerging a few seconds later with two steaming cups of peppermint tea, one of which she placed on the floor beside me. Sitting down, she resumed her tale.

"I got out of the water as quickly as possible and groped my way back to my cottage where I placed peppermint teabags" — she glanced at my cup — "over my eyes to bring down the swelling. Later one of my eyes swelled up and became quite infected, which I attributed to the large amounts of raw sewage in the river water. It took a few months to heal but soon enough it was right as rain."

"Sorry to hear that," I said. "The mint leaves reduce the inflammation rather quickly I'd say."

"Yes, they really do." She winked at me. "Glad I could help a fellow sufferer."

"Thank you," I said.

We fell silent for a few moments, savoring the quiet and the pleasure of each other's company. After several sips of tea, Mary told me a story about how, earlier that day, one of the young nurses had approached her in a friendly way, inviting her to sit and talk out on the patio. They had only been talking for a few minutes when the nurse had begun to ply her with questions, and Mary abruptly excused herself and returned to her baking.

"I don't tell these bastards nothing about my life!" she said. "Nothing true anyway. They ask and ask and ask and I tell them lies. It's true that I am subjected to their tests… but they don't know what I hide. They may have my body but they will never have me. They think they've got me all figured out, and I let them believe it."

"So mysterious," I said. "What are you hiding, Mary Mallon?"

She studied me for half a minute.

"Wouldn't you like to know?" she asked.

"Yes. I would." I replied.

She seemed to consider this for a moment before answering. "Fine. Tonight, after the island has shut down for the night, I will show you."

"Show me what?" I asked.

"You will see."

"Where is it?"

"Outside. I'll take you there in a few hours."

Looking up, it was now apparent that my hostess was exhausted, and, feeling a bit guilty that I had kept her up talking, I brought the conversation to a close. I knew she could not rest unless I went to bed; feigning exhaustion, I told her I was going to try and get some sleep. Quickly stripping down to her undergarments, she stepped over me and, crawling beneath the sheets of her bed, I saw Mary, once again, fix her gaze upon the window casement across the room where the soft swishing of the leaves against the glass formed a kind of uneven, drunken melody. I studied the movements of these branches from my vantage point upon the floor but, as before, I saw nothing to justify Mary's alarm. It wasn't long before I heard her soft, gentle snoring.

*   *   *   *

STILL FEELING RATHER STIMULATED BY OUR DISCUSSION, I DECIDED to begin making my way through the fresh stack of books, newspapers, magazines, and folders which Mary had so thoughtfully brought for me. Quietly pulling them over to me, I lay in the dark perusing several recent newspapers, to catch myself up on recent events.

It was now the autumn of 1921. In several different papers I learned of the nightmare unfolding in and around Russia in the wake of the Bolshevik takeover. One article described how an estimated four million people had starved to death as a direct result of the government's requisitioning of grain supplies, a death toll which the author pointed out, was higher than both WWI and the Civil War combined. In the famine-induced delirium that was sweeping the region, there were even reports of cannibalism in the rural districts of Ukraine and elsewhere, but these were little more than rumors.

But there was hope in Russia and there had been numerous instances of rebellion and mutiny, not just against the grain requisition but against the Bolshevik state in general. The worker's reclamation of the island naval base of Kronstadt was an inspiration that fed my heart, and descriptions of the ongoing raids of Nestor Makhno continued to amaze and impress me. In one magazine, I learned of the "Pitchfork Uprising" of 1920 wherein 50,000 starving Russian peasants had risen up against the soldiers sent to collect their grain. This uprising had lasted nearly forty days and it ended in the brutal massacre of three thousand peasants, offering the world a candid glimpse of life under the new regime. It was becoming clear that the Bolsheviki, now residing in the palaces and embassies of the Czar, were not so different from the aristocrats they had dethroned, especially when viewed through the eyes of the starving peasantry. They had far more in common than they had differences, especially when it came to sacrificing the lower classes to the national economy.

Further down this fresh stack of literature, I found a very old copy of the *Saturday Review* from 1901 which contained several items that attracted my interest. In it I found, among other things, a scathing article on the philosophy of anarchism. The author of this diatribe could barely conceal his horror of anarchists. The notion that anyone could want to live in a world without authority seemed to fill him with uncontainable dread. Among the typical, predictable demonizations and clichéd mischaracterizations, I was startled to come upon an extremely curious quote, the phrasing of which I found especially haunting and troubling. "Anarchism," the author stated, "has no program but murder, and any teaching that organized government might, could, or ought to be abolished should be treated as part of the murderous conspiracy... It has become a disease which is transmitted from one mad anarchist to another as hydrophobia is transmitted from one mad dog to another; and the mad dog and the mad anarchist have about the same capacity of reasoning as to the source from which they get their virus, or the objects they propose to themselves by biting."

Not entirely unrelated, in an old issue of *Arena* magazine from 1902, I found an article by R. Heber Newton which contained a similarly curious analogy, this time specifically denouncing Leon Czolgosz, the anarchist who had assassinated President McKinley in 1901. Once again, it was the particular metaphor the author had chosen. Referring to Czolgosz, the author stated, "Despite the fact that the assassin of our President was born on our soil, he was to all intents and purposes alien; he was of alien birth and alien stock; his whole mind was alien."

My initial response to these articles was to laugh at the absurd, almost mawkish overstatement. The authors engaged in the most ludicrous hyperbole, in addition to contradicting themselves. How, for example, could Czolgoz be American, but not be American? How could he (or I, or anyone for that matter) be one of "us" yet "alien?" This pathetic attempt to disown Czolgoz, to wash America's hands of him, was idiotic, cowardly, and mentally lazy on its face.

On the other hand, as I read and reread these curious passages, another more troubling question began to oppress me. What if there was some truth in these apparently absurd *ad hominem* exaggerations? What if these authors, patriotic sycophants though they plainly were, had glimpsed, almost unconsciously, some larger truth about us? It was certainly not the first time that I had heard anti-anarchist rhetoric which described anarchists as a race apart, almost a separate species, from ordinary human stock. It was just that, for the first time, I permitted myself to wonder if perhaps there wasn't some grain of truth in it.

The next set of papers I found, bound up in a folder bursting along its seam, appeared to be a set of legal documents, written by a lawyer, and containing a brief outline of a possible legal defense for Mary Mallon. These documents were at least ten years old, a fact that made me think that it was a legal defense that had been assembled and then promptly abandoned by someone who must have seen that it was a hopeless case. It was in the course of going through this folder that I learned several things, including the little-known fact that, since her incarceration, Mary had sent samples of her urine and stool to the laboratories of George Ferguson, a reputable bacteriologist in Manhattan whose lab results had repeatedly come back negative, a fact which had been duly ignored by the committee assembled to assess Mary's eligibility for release.

In this same folder I found an examination report confirming that, in 1907, Mary had suffered an "unknown injury" to her eyes, specifically to her left eye. I knew this to have been the spontaneous growth of her nictitating membranes, and the subsequent infection but from this document it was clear that, at the time, neither Mary nor the medical staff had any idea what was occurring.

Attached to this report was a copy of a letter which Mary had written to her lawyer in 1909. In this letter, Mary lamented the fact that there had never been any attempt by the medical authorities to rehabilitate her, pointing out how this had been a top priority with almost every other carrier they had found. Later in this same letter, she told the story of her injured eye, though she necessarily concealed the true nature of her malady. Mary understood perfectly well that the Health Department meant to keep her a prisoner for the rest of her life, and that her jailers were not interested in her health and well-being. She described her traumatic arrival on the island and the fact that it had so upset her that she had fallen ill. As for her curious eye injury, she believed it was due to the strain of the callous and thoughtless manner of her arrest and abduction, during which she was held (inexplicably) incommunicado. When her left eye became paralyzed, she became concerned and mentioned it to the doctors; the doctors had done nothing about it and refused to see her. She did not even get a cover for her eye and had to hold her hand over it while going about her day. At night she had had to tie a bandage on it. This had gone on for over six months.

During this time, Mary learned that there was an eye specialist who visited the island three or four times a week; he was never asked to visit Mary. Why not? In December of 1907, a new physician, Dr Wilson, took charge. Mary met with him and told him all about her eye. He promised Mary he would send her medication immediately. He never sent it. For the duration of her painful eye infection, Mary had remained unable to convince the doctors to look at it. "My eye got better thanks to God Almighty," she wrote, "and despite the medical staff!"

*   *   *   *

IN THE SILENT HOURS JUST BEFORE DAWN, MARY WOKE ME GENTLY and invited me to come down to the water's edge with her.

"Do you still want to see what it is that I hide from the medical staff?" she asked.

"Yes," I replied, "I do." I quickly got dressed and followed her silently out the door.

It was the first time I'd been outside since my arrival. The cool breeze on my face felt good, despite the eerie menace that hung in the air. Scanning the island with my heightened senses, I could see that there was not a soul about. The only warm silhouettes I detected were motionless, horizontal, and located within the confines of the locked residential buildings. To the east, across the river, the shoreline was completely shrouded in a thick grey fog that was pouring off the river. Above this mounting wall of vapor, several hundred feet high, I occasionally caught a glimpse of the desolate skyscrapers, appearing and disappearing intermittently within the sea of low-lying clouds. To the south, I saw the silhouette of the Williamsburg Bridge spanning the misty gulf below.

Arriving at the narrow beach, not far from where I had come ashore, Mary and I sat down upon the cool grass, beside a clump of tall reeds. I could hear the water lapping gently upon the sandy shoal.

"I know what they are after when they take my blood, stool, and urine every few days," she said matter-of-factly. "They can tell by the state of my hormones that I am a new mother and have been, almost continuously, since my arrival here."

"A new mother?" I asked.

"Yes Robert. I am a new mother, though I have managed to keep it a secret from the whitecoats."

"Oh, they can tell something is going on inside me alright but... they really have no idea what it could be. They still have not seen the biggest, most revealing, piece of the puzzle."

"And what is that?" I asked nervously.

Grinning like a fiend, she reached over and pulled aside the reeds not two feet away, beckoning me to lean across her and peer into the rippling pool beyond. It took a few seconds for my eyes to adjust, but when they did, I gasped in surprise and almost fell across her lap. There before me, in a tiny lagoon not more than six feet across, and perfectly shrouded on three sides by a wall of cattails and rushes, was a most incredible sight. Splashing gently about in the shallow water were several hundred tiny White Things, identical to my own offspring in its earliest infancy. Several of these White Things had reddish centers, a thing which told me that, while still primarily embryonic, some of Mary's tiny offspring had eaten enough flesh to begin the colorization process. Turning to Mary, I smiled.

"Incredible!" I said.

"Yes, they are wonderful aren't they?"

"How do you keep them from swimming away?"

"It is the most remarkable thing, Robert," she said, "but would you believe the Shining Ones actually tend to them!"

"You mean... the ghosts from the *General Slocum*?"

"I've sat here upon this very beach and watched them herd minnows by the thousands into these shallows for my little ones to eat. Once, several weeks ago, I saw one of the little White Things try to escape. The Shining Ones immediately surrounded it and redirected it right back to this pool, like a mother duck collecting an errant duckling."

"Amazing," I said, instantly lamenting the fact that I had had no such assistance throughout my own offspring's infancy back in Sudbury.

"Every night," she went on, "as you can see, the Shining Ones form a protective ring around them."

It was true. The shoreline immediately surrounding this hidden lagoon was dense with a legion or more of low-lying Shining Ones, huddled in close and forming a significant barrier between Mary's litter of White Things and the stronger currents of the open river.

"How have you managed to keep this a secret?" I asked.

"Oh, it's easier than you might think. You see how easy it is for me to keep you a secret."

I wondered if Mary's offspring ever forced her to go out and get sustenance for them. Being trapped on an island, I reflected, would pose some considerable difficulties for a foraging parent.

"What do you feed them?" I asked, scrutinizing her face for any trace of alarm at this question.

"I smuggle food out here... No one suspects a thing. The doctors here all think I like the view of the river but really this hillock provides me with a perfect overview of my water babies."

"Interesting." I said but, unwilling to let her steer the subject away from feeding, I continued. "What exactly do they eat?"

"Oddly enough, pig intestines!" she said.

I sneered.

"Oh come now, Robert!" she laughed. "You eat sausage don't you? It's not so different from that."

"I do not eat pig intestines." I corrected her. "I am practically vegetarian. And where the hell do you get pig intestines out here?"

"Hell is a pretty good guess. You're closer than you think. There is an old Irish fellow who works as a porter here on the island. His name is Tom Cane and I think he's a bit sweet on me — does me favors. Once a week he brings me pig intestines from a butcher shop in Hell's Kitchen."

This struck me as odd, as my many experiences with these curious offspring had indicated that they craved human meat only.

"Your offspring really eat animal flesh?" I asked.

"It's not ideal of course," she sighed, "but what am I supposed to do?"

The implications startled me and prompted me to ask the obvious question.

"What kind of meat would be ideal, Mary?"

Another long silence passed between us before Mary said, somewhat annoyed, "For a man who doesn't reveal anything about himself you sure ask a lot of questions."

I stared at her, unable to think of a decent response.

"Also, it occurs to me," she added wistfully, "you're taking this all rather well. Most people would have run away by now! Are you sure you have no prior experience with this sort of thing?"

This statement embarrassed me because I knew that she was right. My reticence no longer made sense. The request behind her mockery was obvious enough and, tired of keeping my nightmarish experiences to myself, I decided to tell her the truth.

"I only ask about the meat because..." I narrowed my eyes at her.

"Yes, Robert?"

"I only ask about the meat because, as you have probably figured out by now..." I rolled my eyes at the cloudy sky. "I too have... um... produced a similar being."

She grinned victoriously.

"But," I continued, "I should tell you that I only ever had one offspring... and it was many years ago."

"So we are not so different after all... you and I?" She appeared overjoyed at the very thought but I felt moved to stop her.

"Wait," I said, holding up my hand. "There is another key difference between us."

"And what might that be?" she asked in a low voice.

I nearly faltered, but forced myself to say the words "My offspring would eat nothing but..." I looked at her, almost ashamed, wondering if she would judge me. "It would only eat brains."

"What sort of brains, Robert, if you don't mind me asking?" she purred.

"Pig brains," I lied. I looked into her eyes now, in an attempt to ascertain whether or not she believed me, but she turned aside. There followed a lull so intolerable to me that I soon interrupted it with a practical question.

"How did you know that you should feed your offspring intestines, of all things?"

"Believe it or not," she said, "I actually saw it in a dream!"

"You dreamt of feeding intestines to those things out there?"

"Yes!" she said. "Those dreams were so vivid. So shockingly clear. I recall thinking that it was almost as if I was being given instructions..." She looked at me, utterly perplexed, blinking several times before continuing. "I know it sounds daft but... later I did some research on the unfortunate people who died from their contact with me, Victoria, Allison, and little Annie Warren. I read their autopsy reports, and the attending doctor's descriptions of their symptoms."

"That was brave of you," I said. "What did they say?"

"I learned that, first and foremost, whatever had killed those three women had perforated their intestines, dissolved them... just like the typhoid virus would have done. This led me to guess — correctly as it turns out — that my little water babies might desire something similar to nourish themselves."

"A logical deduction," I said, distinctly queasy at the candid nature of our talk.

"Right around this same time, I recall that I myself began craving raw meat in general, and uncooked sausages in particular. And there were other bizarre urges too. I also had another series of ghastly nightmares, which seemed somehow connected to the raw meat cravings."

"How so?" I asked.

She paused, clearly disturbed by the recollection.

"Every night, for a period of about three weeks following each birth, my sleep was invaded by terrible visions of carnage. In these dreams I observed myself, in various settings, doing... terrible things."

She was staring off into space now, half-stunned. Then her gaze fell to her feet.

"What sort of terrible things?" I asked.

She swallowed hard and steadied herself, but her face was ashen.

"I dreamt I was attacking people," she whispered, a glazed look of astonishment pulling her features into a frown. "It was like I was some sort of crazed werewolf. I appeared to be blissfully intoxicated, chasing my victims down, knocking them to the ground, tearing them open with my bare hands and eating their entrails!"

I swallowed audibly.

"It took a tremendous amount of willpower," she went on, "but eventually I mastered these terrible urges and, shortly thereafter, the nightmares went away."

"Wait a moment," I asked, "you mean you resisted the urge?"

"Certainly! What would you have me do?"

"But your offspring needed intestines, and it was your duty to provide them."

She squinted at me, pursing her lips oddly.

"Obviously I couldn't find any surplus human intestines on North Brother Island. I had a thought that maybe pig or cow intestines would do the trick. I placed my order with Tom Cane and he went by the butcher shop in Hell's Kitchen and gathered what he could."

I was stunned, but remained calm. Mary, in her innocence, had nearly been drawn into the same life I had, but had avoided it by successfully resisting the initial promptings towards cannibalism. I could not help but to compare my plight to hers and to imagine how differently my life might have been if I, and my offspring, had been content with pig brains. Clearly, being a carrier was more complicated and varied than I had initially assumed; hearing this shattered any notion I may have had that I understood the motives of the various Hidden Ones. More than anything, it implied that I had seen only a small piece of what must have been an infinitely complicated scenario. Clearly, not all these reproductive parasites were the same. They affected their hosts differently and required different forms of sustenance. Mary's offspring, all one hundred of them, had apparently learned to make do with the occasional bucket of pig intestines. How many other variations existed?

I thought of all the famous cannibal lunatics of history, the vampires and werewolves of Euro-American legend. Was Gilles De Rais, the infamous cannibal and butcher of Machecoul, France, merely the human host and parent of a bloodthirsty brood? Had famous cannibals like Vlad the Impaler and Elizabeth Bathory merely been gathering sustenance for a litter of offspring which they had managed to keep hidden from authorities… and the world at large?

I was pulled from these macabre musings by the sound of Mary's voice.

"I am still uncertain how this contagion spreads," she continued, "but, once inside the body of its chosen victims, my parasite immediately goes to work dissolving the small intestines. Why it feeds exclusively on the intestines, I have been unable to figure out, though I have a few theories.

Perhaps human intestines possess some vital enzyme or compound which my parasite needs to survive. Perhaps it cannot acquire this compound in any other way. In every case so far, the parasite has digested its victim's intestines. All evidence of their predation is made to perfectly resemble the classic typhoid symptoms; eroded intestines accompanied by a swelling of the liver, spleen, and brain."

We shared a pained look.

"Now you see why I have had to hide these things from the whitecoats. I tell them nothing! If they only knew the truth of it, they would waste no time. They would etherize me in a heartbeat, do an autopsy to formulate their theory... and then bottle up my parasite, my offspring, and my corpse and pack us off to an Army laboratory."

"They would be killing the goose that laid the golden egg," I said.

"Oh, they don't care about that!" she sighed. "I'm changing Robert, slowly but surely, and they damned well know it. I believe they mean to keep me here forever, studying me and harvesting my secretions to develop some horrendous new biological weapon."

Her rage, and her grief, were palpable.

"Would you like me to help you escape?" I asked bluntly.

"Oh, that's very kind of you but I leave this island all the time... in my own way."

"You do?" I asked, too loud.

"Shh," she scolded in a whisper, her finger across her lips and peering over at the buildings. "I already told you that I taught myself to swim several years ago."

"You can leave the island anytime you like?"

"I can leave the island, Robert, but I can't go ashore anywhere. My face has been in the papers too many times. Someone might recognize me, spot me in a crowd and then...." She shrugged and scowled. "Who knows? After what they've been told about me, the damned fools might just try to lynch me!"

Suddenly we heard a door slam, somewhere far off, on the other side of the island. Peering over at the taller buildings, she said, "Come on. Let's get you back inside."

Halfway across the lawn, however, I heard a sound which stopped me in my tracks. It was a long low scream, identical to the one I had heard on the morning of my arrival, and emanating from beyond that cluster of grey buildings near the center of the island.

"What the hell was that?" I asked, making no effort to conceal my horror.

"One of the patients," she said curtly, continuing to lead me up the grassy slope. This strange scream went on a few seconds more before ending abruptly on a curiously high note. Concentrating my hearing upon this scream, I realized that the voice was slightly muffled, as if the sound had come from a basement or sub-cellar, at least partly underground.

"That's the scream I heard upon my arrival here," I told her. "Do you know who it is?"

"No." she lied. "Who knows? There's a hundred patients here."

"Yes," I said, keenly aware of Mary's evasion, "but that person sounds like they're in a lot of pain."

"Well of course they are in a lot of pain, Robert! You try being abducted by your own government, plucked out of the stream of life while still in the glow of youth, and then forcibly isolated here on this god-forsaken island, thrown away like a piece of human garbage!" She was suddenly furious again, not at me, but at the awful cruelty and inhumanity of the situation.

"You try being banished like a leper under government quarantine. Reduced to the status of laboratory rat while, eight hundred yards away," she pointed towards the distant lights on the opposite shore, "the jolly happy world carries on without you! I think you'd wake up screaming too!"

As curious as I was about this unseen screamer, I made no response except to nod my head. Seconds later we were walking up the front steps and entering the warm, still air of the cottage. Daisy lifted her head as we entered but did not rise to greet us.

Once we were safely back inside, Mary and I both undressed in silence and got into our respective beds. As before, Mary joined Daisy in her silent vigil of the windblown branches, maintaining her watch for about a half hour before finally dropping off to sleep — at which time I, once again, endeavored to make my way through the pile of literature she had brought for me.

*   *   *   *

NEAR THE TOP OF THE STACK, I FOUND A CURIOUS FOLDER WHICH contained two bulging envelopes, one marked "1911-1920" the other marked "1902." In each of these envelopes there were several sets of collected articles, some neatly clipped from newspapers, others wrinkled and jagged along the edges, as if they had been hastily torn out of books and shoved into a pocket. Taken together, they formed an ominous collection; each article was a detailed account of some catastrophic event or seismic upheaval which had resulted in the deaths of many thousands of people as well as the complete destruction of whole cities, towns, provinces, and, in one case the leveling of an entire island.

The first of the enclosed articles told the story of the 1911 eruption of Mt. Taal, in the Philippines, an event which killed approximately 1,300 people and decimated an entire island. The author of this article included, within the body of his essay, a harrowing eyewitness account given by a Catholic missionary who had been present at the time of the quake. The missionary described the great plume of black smoke which darkened the sky, followed by exploding geysers of magma, flaming boulders hurtling down the mountainsides, and numerous interweaving rivers of glowing lava which oozed down into the populated regions, setting fire to everything they touched.

Another set of clippings in this same envelope referred to the fairly recent Gansu earthquake in Haiyuan County, Ningxia Province in China. On December 16, 1920, a few minutes after noon, a series of devastating earthquakes ripped through the area, leveling several cities and killing an estimated 240,000 people. Survivors of the devastation later described walking through vast stretches of shuddering countryside, some 200 miles wide, where not a single house was left standing. As I would later learn, the aftershocks from this quake continued for three years.

The next item in the envelope was a short essay, just four pages long, which told the story of the deadly eruption of Mt. Kelut, in Indonesia, on May 19, 1919. On that day, in the region of East Java, after a series of thunderous shockwaves ripped through the populated countryside, the volcano finally erupted, demolishing several cities, towns and fishing villages, killing well over five thousand people.

Folded into this essay, I found a newspaper article telling the story of the infamous Florida Keys Hurricane of 1919. This item described how a deadly sea storm had come ashore, blasting a path of carnage and destruction through the Florida Keys, crossing the Gulf of Mexico and entering southern Texas, killing nearly one thousand people along the way and causing extensive damage to the cities of Key West and Corpus Christi.

Clipped together with the essay about the eruption in Indonesia, and with the dates vigorously underlined, it seemed clear that whoever had collected these many articles had seen something significant in the fact that both the eruption in Indonesia and the Hurricane in Florida and Texas had occurred in 1919, within just four months of each other.

The contents of the second envelope were also newspaper clippings about catastrophic events and similarly grouped by year, with dates circled throughout. Significantly, all the disasters described in this second envelope had occurred in 1902.

The first was the October eruption of Mt. Santa Maria, in Guatemala, a catastrophe which claimed the lives of approximately six thousand people.

The next two articles told of the twin eruptions of both Mt. Soufriere, on the island of St. Vincent, and of Mt. Pelee in Martinique, in the Lesser Antilles. The death toll on the island of St. Vincent was 1,680, but the much larger eruption of Mt. Pelee, several hours later, had claimed the lives of nearly thirty-three thousand people, profoundly interrupting the economic development going on in these areas.

Interestingly, these last two eruptions had occurred quite near to each other, and right in the heart of that region of the western Caribbean said to be under the control of those notorious cannibals, the Caribs, from whom the words cannibal and Caribbean are derived.

As I quietly read these assorted clippings, an appalling idea began to creep into my thoughts. Rolling onto my back and staring up at the ceiling, I began to wonder... could it possibly be that this was one of the ways in which humanity's progress was being steered and guided by the Hidden Ones? Had our alien Overlords simply mastered the art of choreographing their deadly interventions to look like natural disasters such as hurricanes, volcanic eruptions, floods, and earthquakes? All of these disasters would be easy enough for the Hidden Ones to simulate. In fact, the more I thought about it, the more I saw that it was perfect camouflage. A legion of Boulder Things somersaulting down a mountainside and burying a city would be construed as an avalanche. Flooding rivers could provide the perfect cover for any number of marauding Water Things, and the stories of volcanic eruptions made me wonder if there might not also be Lava Things, flaming, liquescent shape-shifters, incinerating and devouring everything in their path. All dead and missing persons would be attributed to the disaster itself. Ordinary human spectators, without the benefit of enhanced senses, and reassured by the notion that nothing exists beyond what scientists has discovered, would have absolutely no way of comprehending what they were seeing. Best of all, though men would ascribe all sorts of meaning to such catastrophes, calling them Acts of Nature or Acts of God, eventually they would pick up the pieces and return to the drudgery of life, resuming whatever mode of civilization they had chosen to shackle themselves to, unaware of the true nature of these cataclysmic events.

Some of these articles even went so far as to outline the role these catastrophes had played in shaping human history, bringing up numerous historical examples, both ancient and modern and leaving me to wonder if their wasn't some vast, underlying intentionality to it all.

Numerous ancient cities had been wiped out, at the height of their influence, by mudslides, volcanoes, or fire, immeasurably altering the course of history. Numerous civilizations had teetered and collapsed because of dust storms, heat waves, famine, plagues, flooding, tidal waves, fires, earthquakes, and volcanic eruption. Minoan civilization was thought by several historians to have collapsed as a direct result of the eruption of Mt. Santorini and of the massive tidal waves that followed, which destroyed numerous Cretan settlements. Further inland, ashes raining down from the volcano had killed many thousands of panic-stricken refugees, suffocating entire cities and encasing whole towns in a layer of ash.

Another author pointed out that the reigning Xia Dynasty (the first dynasty to be described in the "Records of the Grand Historian," circa 1600 BC) might have also collapsed chiefly as a result of the eruption of Mt. Santorini. Others attribute the great famine in China to this same eruption. The most well-known examples of influential cities being destroyed by an Act of God are perhaps the Roman cities of Pompeii and Herculaneum, both demolished in the eruption of Mt. Vesuvius in 79 AD. As I soon discovered, there have been countless others — cities, towns, empires, and whole nations, undermined, destroyed, or redirected by various, and seemingly random, natural disasters.

The earthquake which devastated southeast Sicily in 1693, killed an estimated 20,000 people and permanently altered the course of history throughout the surrounding regions, and beyond. Beneath the two envelopes in this stack, I also found a reprinted excerpt from Charles Gardiner's book which documents the repeated destruction of the city of Dunwich, in Essex England, by several particularly violent sea storms. This small port city was destroyed for the first time in 1286, when a hurricane washed it into the sea. Later rebuilt further inland, it was washed away again in 1328 and then again in 1347. Elsewhere, I found several references to the complete annihilation of the politically and culturally influential port city of Lisbon, Portugal in 1755, and was made to wonder at the effects this annihilation had had on the growth and direction of civilization in the surrounding areas. There was the 1906 Earthquake which nearly destroyed San Francisco, California, whose deadly fires raged for weeks, reducing whole sections of the city to a sea of blackened and burned-out ruins.

Who could deny that these various catastrophes and disasters had profoundly influenced the course of human history? Undoubtedly, the vast majority of these tragedies were genuine acts of Nature, as inevitable as the flow of history itself. After all, the steadily increasing frequency (and fatality) of large-scale urban disasters went hand in hand with the rise of the new industrial city-state and mass society in general. All seismic and weather-borne disasters were many times more deadly when they occurred within the dense terrain of the overcrowded modern metropolis. In light of these catastrophes, and the general misery of urban life, it had never seemed so precarious, so fragile, as when confronted by the sheer force and magnitude of the elements.

Further questions came to me. Were these types of cataclysmic events increasing or decreasing in frequency? Were they subject to random ebb and flow or were they on the rise? Was anyone tracking and collating these statistics? If so, did they have any hope of understanding what they were seeing?

What else might this collection of catastrophes reveal? When viewed from the proper perspective, did these seemingly random disasters secretly spell out the agenda of the Hidden Ones? Did these articles represent someone's successful (or partially successful) efforts to track their interventions? Is that why they had been assembled and organized by date? Did they reveal some tell-tale pattern or commonality? Which cities had been wiped out intentionally, and why? What exactly were the criteria for these cloaked extermination campaigns? Was there some common trait or custom which these eradicated populations shared?

My mind continued to be haunted by these and other questions concerning the reasons why these locations had been slated for destruction. Had these disasters occurred in cities and countries which displayed the most extreme authoritarian tendencies? A quick review of these many articles seemed to disprove this theory, owing to the fact that these besieged locations represented a wide spectrum of political styles ranging from autocratic industrial states to primitive communitarian tribalism. The pattern seemed random, the stricken areas showing few similarities. I wondered if these disasters weren't perhaps the work of multiple competing agendas, resulting in mixed and varied outcomes. Was I overestimating (or underestimating) the precision of these interventions? Was I wrong to assume that only one criterion underlay them all? I'd heard the Hidden Ones say the human experiment was getting out of control, fast approaching its end date, and I wondered if these efforts lacked coherence because human civilization was already so far gone. Then again, as my experiences in the Catskills had indicated, I knew that these Hidden Ones were not one unified group, but rather numerous competing groups, with varying plans and strategies, which they hoped to exert and impose, however imperfectly, upon the human herd.

There was also a strong possibility that I was fooling myself. Perhaps these numerous disasters were part of an agenda so far beyond all human comprehension that I could never hope to decipher it. I was grasping at straws, groping about in the darkness. Nevertheless, something deep inside me told me that I was on the right track, a barely conscious intuition, which was every bit as wonderful as it was dreadful.

XIX

I STAYED WITH MARY ON NORTH BROTHER ISLAND FOR ABOUT SIX months, from the winter of 1921 on through to the spring of 1922. During this time, Mary and I became very close, spending several hours every day conversing on a seemingly limitless array of topics and themes. Mary Mallon possessed a brilliant mind and a brutal wit that spared no one; it was a pleasure to hear her views on whatever topics happened to arise. She had no illusions about the world or her place in it and it made her a refreshingly frank and lucid conversationalist. My hostess was also a gifted joke teller who, numerous times, had me laughing so hard that tears ran down my cheeks. This sort of extreme merriment was, for me, a strange and novel experience, though not entirely disagreeable. Sometimes she talked for hours, with me in the role of listener, as she sorted out her thoughts on everything from what was happening inside her body, to peculiar and auspicious world events, to what she should do about her carnivorous brood in the rushes. Once a week, Tom Cane stopped by with a bucket of pig intestines, cleverly concealed beneath the overcoat he wore draped over his arm. Hours later, Mary and I would slip out, under cover of darkness, and feed her offspring, a sight which never failed to cheer me and gave me fond memories of my own newborn offspring during that fateful autumn of 1918.

I was grateful to be tucked away in Mary's cottage. The outside world had become so inhospitable, so fraught with unknown dangers, that North Brother Island soon came to feel like paradise — the perfect haven, ironically enough, from the long arm of the Law. Had I been an ordinary man, with an ordinary immune system, I may well have died from eating Mary's cooking and sleeping directly beneath her. As I was not an ordinary man, I thrived in this peculiar context, surrounded by mess and disease, sleeping on the floor with a smelly old dog, in my vaguely coffin-shaped crawlspace. The piece of my offspring still living inside me continued to induce in me a constant, low grade fever, which, in addition to fortifying me against the cold, immediately killed any hostile organisms that entered my bloodstream; in the course of inhabiting my circulatory system, my passenger seemed to purify it of any and all germs and viruses. Obviously, this also included Mary Mallon's apparently contagious, sometimes fatal, passenger.

I wasn't simply immune from Mary's so-called disease. The fact of the matter was that Mary's passenger and my passenger seemed to get along quite splendidly, perhaps rather too splendidly.

One night, Mary and I were discussing the Labor Movement. I was just giving my views on unionism when we were suddenly interrupted by the eerie recognition that our bodies were, in fact, singing to each other, very, very softly, through the stillness of the room. We fell silent, astonished, and more than a little bit frightened, at the low trilling noises which we heard (and felt) emanating from deep within our own torsos. We sat staring for a full minute, utterly dumbfounded, gazing back and forth from my chest, to her chest, and back again. Mary closed her eyes tight and cocked her head, as if to listen in and overhear what our passengers were saying to each other. While I was still considering what to think of this shocking development, I was unexpectedly overwhelmed by an arresting and intoxicating odor. An odor so compelling that it immediately eclipsed all other concerns.

It was as if the sweat which dampened Mary's skin were laced with some powerful narcotic, which I knew I could never get enough of. It was abundantly clear from the look in her eye that she was as hungry for me as I was for her. My skin began to hum and to flush as every part of me awakened to her magnetic presence — the heat and glow of her skin, the multi-layered scent which she exuded — until, at last, we gave in to it, desperately and without hesitation.

I suppose we were like two starving wolves who, at long last, were permitted to eat their fill. The Black Thing inside of me awakened to the White Things inside of her and then they merged, pulling our not unwilling bodies along with them.

An hour later we were side by side on the floor, staring listlessly up at flickering shadows on the ceiling.

"You are immune to the effects of my parasite," she said finally.

"The negative effects," I replied. "In fact, since my arrival here, I feel noticeably better, like I have been given new life."

She wrinkled her nose at this statement then shook her head laughing as she turned away.

"It has been a mistake to think of these changes as the symptoms of a disease to be cured," I continued. "Even if I am dying, which I don't think I am, the effect it is having upon my mind and body has been stunning. Overall, despite the pain of transforming, I feel better, stronger, even smarter than I have ever felt before, so much so that I am tempted to think of myself as only half-alive prior to the onset of these... changes. It's as if my mind had, previously, only been half-awake."

"You talk funny sometimes, sailorman," she said, "but you're starting to grow on me."

*   *   *   *

THIS INITIAL SEXUAL ENCOUNTER WITH MARY AWAKENED IN ME A fever for sex, as if I had suddenly gone into heat. Previously I had been almost without any libido to speak of, but there was now a raging hunger inside me. This was incredible not just because of who I had been previously, but because of how eerily perfect the timing was.

One evening Mary returned from the cafeteria kitchen with a pot of steaming soup and a guilty smile on her face. Pouring the soup into two bowls, she placed them on the table before me, smirking at me all the while. She drew the curtains and, sitting down in a chair opposite, she removed her shoes.

"What are you so pleased about?" I asked.

"Oh nothing," she said. "It's just that... word of your presence has spread among some of the patients. I told several trusted friends, and said that they could tell others only on the condition that they maintained utter secrecy. Needless to say, it spread like wildfire."

"So I must go?"

"No, no," she said reassuringly. "On the contrary, the ladies here are a fine sort. Your secret is safe with them. They will keep it all hushed up, you watch."

I scowled disapprovingly at her.

"Don't worry, sailorman, your position has not been compromised. In fact they are all very pleased to have such a unique visitor. We don't get much excitement around here, you see."

"Are you certain they won't tell?" I asked skeptically.

"Absolutely," she winked. "There are a great many things which we patients are able to do behind the backs of the staff without them knowing it. These women are trusted comrades. We see things from a... common perspective."

"What's that?"

"Like me, they delight in anything which subverts the status quo around here. Most of them hate the medical staff as much as I do."

"Bless their hearts. I only wish there was some way I could express my gratitude to them."

The sly grin returned to Mary's face and she looked down her nose at me.

"What?" I asked.

"You're a bit slow aren't you?" she leered impatiently.

"Why are you smiling like that?"

"I'm smiling, you damned fool, because I came here to tell you that there might just be a way that you can express your gratitude to them, if you catch my meaning."

"I do not catch your meaning." I said, still rather mystified.

"As soon as I told the other ladies that there was a handsome, half-naked, contagion-proof man, hiding out in my cottage..." She shook her head at my naiveté, "Well, what do you think they said?"

"I have no idea." I said defensively, pulling the blanket up around my neck.

"I was practically bombarded with requests to 'borrow that young man for the night,' you fool! Two of the gals asked me to bring them here, straight away, to have proper introductions!" She laughed to herself. "When I said no, they all insisted that I describe you in graphic detail!"

"What did you tell them?" I asked, struck to the core with a thrill of embarrassment.

"Well, I told them the truth," she laughed. "I said you are exceptionally well-built and very easy on the eyes. Just the mere description of you had them groaning like a bunch of Jersey cows!"

This statement puzzled me, as I had always considered myself to be rather ugly, partly on account of my deformity and partly due to the general revulsion my looks had inspired in others. I was puzzled to hear her describe me in such flattering terms, though I laughed about it with her, despite myself.

"Yes but what did they say in response?" I asked, my vanity getting the best of me.

"Well," she continued, sighing at every third or fourth word, her cheeks suddenly quite red, "some of them... no, perhaps most of them... or possibly even... all of them... were hoping that you might be interested in coming up for a... a visit. You know... some night... very late after the staff had all gone home. Very hush-hush, you see." She began to eat her soup with a forced, almost theatrical casualness, avoiding my eyes.

"You didn't actually tell them that I would..."

I was unable to finish this sentence.

"You are certainly under no obligation, Robert," she said into her soup. "I just thought that a man of such unique... immunity and stamina... stranded on an island... with two hundred undersexed women... might enjoy such an opportunity. "

"I don't know," I lied. It took everything in my power to keep from grinning like an idiot. "Sounds risky. I can't afford to be prowling around this place at night. If I got caught I would be immediately…"

"Well, actually," she interrupted, "because we are on an island, the one and only night watchman sits in a booth down by the dock. I've roamed this island after midnight a hundred times or more with no trouble at all. It would be easy enough for you to get around, if… you were so inclined."

"Let me think about it," I said, and Mary winked knowingly. In less than a minute I was smiling and nodding my head at her.

"That actually sounds great right about now," I said. "You have awakened something inside me!"

"Are you any good at creeping around in the dark?" she asked.

I laughed heartily. "You have no idea," I said, at which she grinned perversely.

* * * *

THOUGH I HAD WASHED UP ON THE SHORES OF THIS BIZARRE ISLAND facility as little more than a virgin, I soon became a veritable jackrabbit in heat. I was awkward at first, I'll grant you, a mere boy sent to do a man's job — but, after I got over my initial sqeamishness, I came to love this new activity, delighting in the challenge of executing these covert excursions undetected, and receiving a sexual education in the process.

In the space of two months, I went from being a know-nothing novice to something approaching a character from a decadent French novel. My sudden virility, stamina, and appetite for sex, alarmed and amazed me. Not only was I able to try every bawdy act which had ever passed through my mind, but I was introduced to several hundred other exotic practices related to the art of sexual intimacy as well. In eight wecks' time, I had been utterly, splendidly, debauched, having experienced every form of perversion possible between man and woman, and savoring every minute of it. Among the many women I visited, I formed several sweet, but necessarily short-lived, friendships.

I have since read part II of Sir Richard Frances Burton's English translation of the *Kama Sutra* and, I confess, I found precious little which shocked me. There were approximately two hundred female patients in the North Brother Island facility, roughly half of whom had requested a nocturnal visit. Some of the things those women asked me to do shocked me, though Mary was always there to explain the physics of the thing and to allay any fears I had about my health. Usually she just laughed at me when I told her my various escapades. Once, when I asked her if it made her jealous, she shrugged and said coarsely, "As if I could hog you all to meself! You're too much for me, Robert. Keeping you satiated must be the work of many women, not just one. You'd exhaust me in a week!"

*   *   *   *

AS I CREPT THROUGH THE GLOOMY COMPLEX OF BUILDINGS, ON MY way to and from the women's dormitory, I occasionally glanced up at the darkened windows of the large official buildings, wondering what sorts of horrors were going on inside those sterile clinics and laboratories. These doctors had access to an almost unlimited number of human subjects, snatched off the streets of New York City. I couldn't help but wonder what sorts of experimentation they were engaging in.

There were other, more tangible, things about this island which frightened and disturbed me. On several occasions, generally toward midday (when most of the other patients were having lunch in a commons on the opposite side of the island), I again heard those curious bouts of semi-subterranean screaming coming from somewhere beyond the cluster of buildings. These cries usually began as low weeping and shouting but would increase, over a period of about four minutes, into crescendos of sporadic howling, before ending abruptly. At other times, usually very late at night, I heard a low, raspy singing emanating from this same direction — a deep, oddly rhythmic groaning which sometimes formed into weird little, short-lived melodies, some of which were so haunting that I can still recall them, even five years later. Had I had a direct line of sight on the structure which housed this unseen singer, I might have at least glimpsed a tell-tale silhouette from which to deduce the condition of this isolated prisoner. As it was, several large, inexplicably opaque buildings prevented me from making such observations.

One day, in mid-November, after hearing a particularly disturbing bout of midday shrieking, I resolved to ask Mary about it directly. The first time I had inquired after this tender topic, I had permitted her to silence me with vagaries and hyperbole. But it was my distinct impression that Mary knew quite a bit more than she had let on; I decided to try a more cautiously candid approach. That night when she returned, I put the question to her again.

"Who is it that screams in the basement on the northern side of the island?" I asked.

Her face became ashen and her eyes grew thin and secretive.

"Are you referring to those random screams we heard a few weeks back?" she asked.

"And numerous times since then, yes," I added with a nod. "It's the same voice every time. Isn't it?"

"It's a common occurrence around here," she said with a shrug. "You are in a prison after all — a human zoo. Were you expecting good cheer and merriment?" She busied herself once more in the kitchen, looking as if she were going to leave it at that.

"The first time I heard her was on the night of my arrival," I said, "the very moment I crawled ashore." Mary looked up at me vaguely alarmed, as if this fact may have had a secret significance. "Then, I heard it again, with you, the night you showed me your offspring. Now I've heard her several more times since then and I want to know: who is she?"

Mary winced but did not look away.

"She is Prisoner Number Nine," Mary said. "None of us patients have ever seen her. Those on the upper floors say they brought her here in a steel-reinforced crate about six months ago. Most of the staff seem genuinely ignorant of who, or what, she is… with maybe three or four exceptions. Twice a week, one of these doctors escorts two men of military bearing out to the little concrete bunker where they keep her. The listeners on the fourth floor have sometimes been able to eavesdrop on these little visits. That is how we learned that she is referred to as Prisoner Number Nine. The army thugs usually stay for about an hour, making a full written report of Number Nine's progress and condition, and then leave very discreetly. During these visits she usually can be heard to cry out, though never for more than a few minutes. Whoever… or whatever she might be, she is an extremely well-guarded military secret."

"Indeed," I said, staring into the distance.

There followed a long silence, during which Mary stirred the soup mechanically, absorbed in her thoughts. Finally, after nearly five minutes, she spoke up.

"You once asked me, Robert, if there was anything you could do to repay my kindness. Well, I've thought of something…" I looked at her inquisitively. "You have certainly proven that you can move about undetected on the island. Before you leave, do you think you could steal me the key to that concrete bunker?"

I raised my eyebrows in undisguised alarm.

"You want to meet Prisoner Number Nine face to face?"

"No," she replied. "I want to set her free."

"Is she… dangerous?" I asked.

"I don't know and I don't care," she said. "I want to free her." Another grave silence followed as I considered her words.

"Alright," I replied. "I will help you."

"Hallelujah!" she said. "You have no idea how long I've been trying to steal that goddamn key!"

I SOON BEGAN TO MAKE REGULAR NOCTURNAL FORAYS TO THE NORTH side of the island, with the hopes of discovering which structure housed Prisoner Number Nine. I learned the basic layout of the buildings, roadways, and footpaths. The pathology lab where Mary volunteered was adjacent to the morgue, whose enormous brick smokestack rose nearly sixty feet into the air. The coal house was located near the chapel and had its own miniature dock for the steady supply of fuel which powered all the necessary machinery on the island. Beyond this was the U-shaped nurse's residence and the maintenance building. Nearby, there was a guest cottage used to house visiting doctors, surgeons, and other specialists. There were several other buildings, though I was unable to learn what they were. On the western shore was the ferry slip, overshadowed by a large gantry crane used for unloading bulk supplies, as well as a tiny security booth which overlooked the dock and surrounding shoreline.

In the course of my nightly excursions, I took the opportunity to make numerous brief detours to the north side, where I discovered a small concrete bunker, like the one Mary had described. Getting as close to this mysterious free-standing bunker as caution would allow, I was able to make a casual inspection.

From the outside it appeared to be a tiny, twelve-by-twelve, isolation cell, half-subterranean, with windowless walls of solid concrete several feet thick. Its builders had designed it to be virtually impenetrable, excessively fortified against any who did not hold the key to the one narrow steel-reinforced door. Although I was eventually able to swipe a key from the guard, as requested, I never did take the opportunity to enter this building, nor to gaze directly upon its solitary inhabitant.

One rainy night, as the night watchman slept soundly upon his desk in the security booth by the dock, I reached in quietly through a small, unlocked, sliding-glass window and silently removed the key ring from a hook on the wall above his head. I quickly made my way over to the bunker, where I tried each key until at last I found the right one. Carefully relocking the door without opening it, I removed this key from the ring and pocketed it. As I turned to leave, I felt a curious sensation.

I cannot describe this feeling except to say that it was if someone, or something, was calling out to me, drawing me back to the bunker. Walking slowly and quietly around the perimeter of this building, I tried, in vain, to project my awareness through the walls, and to search for any trace of a warm silhouette within. When this failed, I stepped up to the wall of the bunker and placed my ear and my chest flat against it.

I was overcome with the immediate (and now familiar) feeling of arousal which I have described earlier, different only in that this feeling was oddly mingled with a barely articulated dread — a lurking undercurrent of inexplicable yet poignant revulsion. Before I could withdraw, I became aware of a presence bearing down upon me; a thinking, reasoning intelligence, very close at hand, and coming straight to me through the wall. This was followed by the overwhelming conviction that the being within was now pressing itself against the corresponding inner wall, so that our faces, though separated by a thick concrete wall, were a mere arms-length apart. I experienced something fluttering against my breastplate, followed by a sudden shock, like a blow from a fist or a stick. Certain that something had bitten into me, I tried to withdraw but was unable to push myself away. I experienced a brief, but exquisitely painful, sensation, like a hand reaching into my chest, which so startled me that I finally succeeded in wrenching myself away.

Staggering back in a panic, I looked down at my chest, fully expecting to see a small geyser of blood pouring out of a fresh wound. But there was nothing there: even my shirt was intact and unharmed. Looking back at the wall, I saw nothing but the smooth featureless expanse of grey concrete.

In less than a minute, the pain in my chest faded. I turned and fled, back in the direction of the security booth. I returned the key ring to the hook above the still sleeping guard, and sprinted noiselessly back to the cottage where Mary lay sleeping. Gently pressing the key into the palm of her outstretched hand, I watched disconcertedly as her fingers closed spider-like around it. A strange smile played across her lips and then, still fast asleep, she resumed her snoring. I lay awake for some time before my pulse finally slowed enough for me to fall sleep.

After this disconcerting experience at the bunker wall, there followed a period of intense nightly dreaming which lasted for approximately three and a half weeks. These dreams were strangely empty and uneventful, though what they lacked in actual incidence they more than made up for in pure, horrifying desolation.

In these dreams I observed strange and barren vistas, utterly void of life, though imbued with an oddly pervasive sense of lurking menace. The bizarre texture of this alien expanse, sculpted by the driving winds and unusually erratic gravitation, had conspired to shape the landscape into grotesque and improbable shapes and forms. Several of the larger mountains upon the horizon looked like huge broken cylinders and there were places where rows of ash-colored hillsides curled up and over themselves, like frozen waves on a grey sea. The skies in these dreams were similarly unfamiliar, and I shuddered when I realized that I could locate no familiar constellations anywhere. In dream after dream, I gazed upon empty haunted canyons and wind-sculpted chasms. I observed broken hillsides and mountains collapsing into vast, ash-clogged rivers which in turn vanished down ravines stranger and deeper still. There was, however, one recurring dream which differed greatly from the others. Occasionally, I dreamt that I was a shackled inmate imprisoned inside a square concrete cell, pitch black, cold, and bare.

The common feature of all these dreams was the overall emotional impression which they left me with. I often awoke in a state of utter confusion, everything around me seeming preposterous and unreal. Several times I baffled Mary with bizarre and enigmatic statements which, upon hearing them repeated back to me, I could neither comprehend nor remember saying.

*   *   *   *

AFTER THE WELCOME CESSATION OF THESE STRANGELY terrifying dreams, there followed a period of relative inactivity and restfulness. When I wasn't visiting the women's dormitory, I remained safe within the confines of Mary's cottage, eating, sleeping, dreaming strange dreams, and eagerly consuming the literature which my hostess brought in by the bagful. Daisy was a playful and thoughtful companion, always ready for a game of tug-of-war, or to wrestle, or to stay quietly alongside me for warmth. Sometimes we would just sit, calmly staring into each other's eyes for the better part of an hour. Many times I explained to her the various revelations which my extensive reading inspired, and many times I swore I glimpsed in her eyes something like interest, or curiosity, perhaps bordering on comprehension.

Throughout this same four-month period, Mary and I also got to know each other better. Sometimes we spent whole afternoons in deep conversation, talking about everything under the sun, from disease epidemics, to the class war, to the anti-philosophy of Max Stirner. Other days were passed in silence, reading, thinking, and staying out of each other's way, exchanging nothing more than an occasional smile all evening. More often than not, however, we stayed up talking for hours on end, sometimes several nights in a row. I began to feel as if I had known Mary for years.

We told each other our life stories and the history of the places we were from. She told me the story of her misspent youth, and I told her mine, each extending to the other the courtesy of omitting unnecessary and damning specifics. We told each other these things in confidence, but it would not be a violation of her trust to confirm that Mary Mallon was indeed the end of her family line, had always felt different, or set apart, from her peers and that, not unlike myself, she had never really had a true friend. "I don't need friends," she once told me. "I mostly find that I enjoy my own company best. People disappoint me in so many different ways. I generally find it best to keep my mouth shut. I get on well with the ladies here but at the end of the day... I am always glad to be alone with my Daisy." Having been deceived and misrepresented, again and again, by people like Soper, the Health Department, and the countless doctors and nurses on North Brother Island, who could blame her for feeling this way?

Mary also told me a fair bit of Irish history. With obvious pride, she told me the story of the 1916 Easter Uprising in Ireland and of the ongoing need to fight against British rule. When I asked her about it, I received a condensed education in the history of Irish colonization by the English. The story which animated her most was the Great Famine, which had occurred in her parent's lifetime. Between 1845-1849, over one million Irish peasants had starved to death as a direct result of crop exportation. During this time, the primary land-owning merchants in Ireland, working in concert with the British and Irish governments, had continued to export most of the national grain and potato crops, as well as boatloads of livestock, to England for sale. Without money to buy the corn which was growing all around them, and which they themselves had tilled, the Irish peasant classes slowly began to starve. Records indicate that when the famine was at its worst, most of the food being grown in Ireland was being exported, under armed guard, to England, so that the bosses continued to make profits despite the complete breakdown of the local economy. "Bourgeois Vampirism," Mary called it, and I did not disagree.

Mary also confided in me her private thoughts on various topics, some of which interested me intensely. One night while discussing the utter strangeness of being a healthy carrier, she said a remarkable thing.

"Had I known that I possessed this ability," she joked, "I might have put it to good use!"

"What do you mean?" I asked.

"Well, you know Robert, those people who died because of me were not bad people. They didn't deserve to die."

I shrugged.

"Had I known that my peaches á la mode were fatal," she looked at me sideways, laughing, "I might have made efforts to serve them to more deserving folks."

"Like who?" I asked with a laugh.

"Like the bloody robber barons who suppressed the Pitchfork Uprising. Next in line would be Lenin and his Bolshevik thugs who have betrayed and exploited the people's hard-won revolution. There's certainly no shortage of worthy targets here in America either."

Clearly, this was hyperbole said in jest, and yet for obvious reasons, it made me chuckle heartily to hear her advocate such things.

On another occasion my hostess confessed that she sometimes liked to fantasize that she would someday become a kind of typhoid assassin who targeted the super rich, killing "enemies of the working classes," as she put it, with her peculiar ability. Similarly, this passing joke haunted me, as I considered whether or not Mary was speaking, at least partly, from unconscious knowledge.

* * * *

ONE EVENING IN APRIL, MARY CAME IN AND, AS SHE GREETED ME, stopped suddenly and stared at me.

"Good Heavens, Robert!" she said. "You've got to get some sunlight on you boy! You're deathly pale. You been nocturnal for too long. You look like a damned ghoul!" Her accent always got thicker when she was making fun of me. I scowled at her, unamused. "Look in the mirror if you don't believe me!" she chuckled.

I went over to the mirror that hung on the wall by the sink. Stepping up, I gazed upon my own reflection, admittedly, for the first time in several years. What I saw looking back at me came as a bit of a shock.

What Mary had said was true enough. My skin had grown thin and milky white; the veins beneath were distinctly visible. There were strange creases coming down from my eyes and the outline of my skull was visible to a degree which I found alarming. My beard, previously blonde, had turned a golden coppery red.

"My god, what's happened to me?" I asked. "How can I feel so good, yet look so terrible?"

"Now you listen to me, Robert," she said intently, "and you listen good. I didn't speak up sooner because I assumed you already knew and had done it on purpose…"

"Done what?" I asked.

"You must have noticed by now that you are very, very pregnant."

Technically speaking, this was not news to me, yet I suddenly understood that I could no longer avoid facing it. Nevertheless, I was feeling argumentative.

"How do you know I'm pregnant?" I asked.

"I can tell by looking at you. A blind man could see it! If you don't get somewhere safe before your gestation is complete, you could end up in serious trouble."

This statement infuriated me, primarily because I knew she was correct. My body did feel different. There was a subtle heaviness to my extremities, which I had been effectively ignoring for about ten days.

Yet I had a strong urge to argue with her, to insist that she back up her bold declaration with some kind of proof. When I opened my mouth to speak, nothing came out.

"There's no point in trying to bury your head in the sand, Robert. You are presently incubating well over a hundred different embryos."

"How can you tell?" I asked, trying not to sound too horrified.

"Mostly, I can see it in your eyes," she replied, "but also, I can smell it on you." She inhaled through flared nostrils and raised her eyebrows suggestively at me.

"How long do I have?" I asked, somewhat hopelessly. "Can you tell by looking at me how far along I am?"

She stepped back and regarded me carefully from head to toe. "I know almost nothing about the gestation cycle of the human male," she said, "but you look pretty far along, I'd say." Leaning in very close to me, she stared straight into my left eye, a thing which caused my pupils to tingle slightly.

"Lucky for you, it looks as if you still have a month or so... so you have a little time yet. Of course it all depends on your diet..."

This was a reference to cannibalism, I think, but she had left it mercifully ambiguous. Searching myself, I found no trace of that craving for brain meat which had, at one time, been the hallmark of my existence.

I was, however, anxious at the thought of siring any more offspring. I wasn't sure I had it in me to endure such a thing more than once. The thought of going through all of it again filled me with a paralyzing dread.

"Don't look so forlorn," Mary said. "I've sired well over a hundred and I'm healthy as an ox!"

I scowled at her, but she only laughed.

"You forget lad, I have been continuously pregnant for nearly twelve years. I've learned a thing or two about how it works!"

I nodded reluctantly.

"Now that you mention it," I said, "I was wondering if you could perhaps clear something up for me."

"What?" she asked, practically beaming with pride.

"I don't know about you but, as best I can tell, my offspring has been dormant inside of me since earliest childhood. What I don't understand is how did it happen that I was impregnated? I mean, initially."

"I have pondered that myself for many years now, Robert," she mused, "though I only have a few vague theories to show for it."

"Well if you don't mind sharing, I'd love to hear them." I said. She looked at me warmly and nodded.

"Like you, my passenger came to me in the early days of childhood," she began, "though I do recall a time when it was not with me. It's a distant memory however, as I was still a very young girl. Back then, we lived in an old stone cottage which my parents had built on the edge of a wooded grassland. This was in the backwoods of County Cork, in southern Ireland, sometime around 1882. Back in those days, I was always hearing queer noises at night, like roaring lions out on the moors. In the morning, when I asked my folks about it they had no idea what I was talking about and looked at me strangely. That's when I first realized that something queer was going on. Understanding that I was the only one who could hear these noises, I quickly learned to shut up about them. One fateful morning, after a night of hearing some particularly frightful howling, I awoke to the horrendous knowledge that I was no longer alone in my own body. No longer alone in my thoughts even..." She inhaled sharply.

"Yes, but how..." I began.

"So far as I can tell," Mary said, pulling her chair closer to me, her eyes lit with a keen, conspiratorial interest, "impregnation probably occurs in one of two ways. My first theory is that these beings start out as microscopic organisms, a bacterium or germ, which floats down from the sky like a fine dust, landing on unsuspecting human hosts and entering the bloodstream through the skin, growing inside the hosts body until eventually..."

"What's your second theory?" I asked.

"Well, my second theory pertains to my own personal experience as well as some of the old Irish legends I grew up hearing — the ones about strange creatures hiding out in the secret places and preying upon unwary travelers and the like."

"You mean like the cannibal ogres you mentioned earlier? The Ciudach and the Gaborchind?"

"No," she replied gravely, "this Thing I'm thinking of was something altogether different."

I nodded in encouragement.

"There is an old Irish legend," Mary said with a wink, "of a beast known in the old country as the Donn of Cualgne. It was said to be the monstrous offspring of a woman who later claimed she had mated with a..." she eyed me thoughtfully, "...with some sort of monster from the bog. The product of this union was reported to be a misshapen fiend who, shortly after its birth, fled into the wild hills of County Ulster. There it lived in secret, for many years, till at last it grew large enough to conduct raids on human towns. Local legends described this gruesome progeny as a great horned creature that occasionally went berserk, terrorizing the countryside, eating cats, dogs, livestock, and even several people!"

"That is all very fascinating," I said, "but what does an old Irish legend have to do with my..."

"The story goes that the Dunn of Cualgne, among other things, possessed the uncanny ability to impregnate nearby cattle just by roaring at them. Any cow that was within earshot of this bellowing beast soon swelled up gigantically. Months later, if they lived that long, these cows gave birth to deformed, shapeless monstrosities which, sadly enough, members of the local sheriff's posse did not permit to survive. Things I've heard since, however, have made me think that a few of them must have managed to escape. There was another creature who made an appearance several hundred years earlier, in the counties of Cork and Munster, who possessed the same ability — impregnating its chosen hosts by roaring at them."

I shrugged, dumbfounded.

"Perhaps this is how it happens with us, Robert," she continued. "Perhaps just hearing these Things roaring in the distance is enough. On the eve of my impregnation, I heard those terrible noises coming from the moors. What if these passenger eggs, or embryos, or whatever they are, are implanted in the host through sound..."

I scratched my head and considered it. My thoughts centered on two things simultaneously. The first were the embryonic larva which the sarcophagus flies had implanted in my wounded hand back in the mountains. The second were the curious roaring noises I had heard at several different points throughout my journey.

"Nothing would surprise me at this point." I said.

Then, suddenly, Mary paused and stiffened, her head jerked at the sound of the tree tapping harmlessly against the window. Looking over at the casement, I saw nothing unusual, though I was intrigued that such an ordinary sound should elicit such a dramatic response.

"What is it?" I asked. "Why do you always stare at that tree?"

"Nothing," she said, almost ashamed, "I've been on this bloody island too long. Sometimes I'm afraid I will lose my mind if I don't get out of here."

I projected my awareness through the thin cottage walls, and, staring intently at this tree for several minutes, I remained oddly unable to confirm whether or not it was authentic or a Tree Thing. Not wanting to further alarm Mary, I changed the subject. Even if there was some Thing eavesdropping on us, I was determined not to let it ruin a perfectly good conversation.

For a time we discussed the situation in Russia, which led to a discussion about the class war in Ireland and Spain. Eventually Mary grew sleepy and rolling over, fell quiet for a time. During this silence, however, I could see that Mary was, once again, focusing the last of her dwindling awareness upon the tree branches at the window. Soon after, I heard her snoring away.

I was awake for a long time, thinking and petting Daisy, who had wandered over at some point and lain down alongside me. Every now and then, Daisy would suddenly raise her head, peering in the direction of the window, as though she too were listening intently for something. Despite my heightened sense of hearing, however, I heard nothing unusual; I was unable to discover what it was that had troubled her.

Then a hideously strange thing occurred which seemed to me so much like an omen that I interpreted it as nothing less than a flat-out warning that I must leave North Brother Island immediately, with or without my generous hostess, or else suffer some unknown but certainly terrible consequences. Like my discovery of the photographs of Machu Picchu that day in the Boston Library, seemed too conspicuous to be an accident.

Seeing a previously unnoticed book overhanging the edge of the night table, I decided to take my mind off these ponderous subjects and read something unrelated to my numerous topics of research. The book I had selected from Mary's night table was a slim volume of poetry by Robert Frost. I set the book down upon my pillow, and it fell open to a particular page, that had clearly been pressed open many times. On the right hand side of the page was a beautiful illustration of a tree. On the facing page, I read the following poem.

> She had no saying dark enough
> For the dark pine that kept
> Forever trying the window latch
> Of the room where they slept.
> The tireless but ineffectual hands
> That with every futile pass
> Made the great tree seem as a little bird
> Before the mystery of glass!
> It had never been inside the room,
> And only one of the two
> Was afraid in an oft-repeated dream
> Of what the tree might do.

This poem struck me to the core. Like the shipwreck dream I had aboard the *Henry Wadsworth Longfellow*, I was struck with an overwhelming impulse towards flight. Convinced that something awful would happen if I remained in Mary's cottage much longer, I spent my last night on North Brother Island preparing for an abrupt pre-dawn departure.

At four a.m., I gently woke Mary and informed her that I needed to go. She looked sad for a moment but then smiled wide and said, "Get somewhere safe before the month is over. You'll do just fine."

"Will I ever see you again?" I asked.

"I certainly hope so, Robert Henry Pearce."

We hugged for a long time, and then, without another word, I kissed Daisy goodbye and I left.

I made my way down to the water's edge. Once there, I stripped off all my clothes, waded out into the East River and began swimming due east. In less than an hour, I was passing, mostly underwater, through Eastchester Bay, where the East River meets Long Island Sound, along the shoreline past City Island and Hart Island. Following the coast north, I eventually came ashore in Larchmont where, entering the locker room of an upscale yacht club, I rifled through the lost and found and pieced together a passable outfit. Bracing myself for a long journey on foot, I set off with a vague plan to make my way back to the house in Sudbury, taking a short detour to Providence, Rhode Island.

XX

IT WAS NOW FEBRUARY OF 1922, AND THE FOLIAGE BLOOMING ALL around me perfumed the air with a thousand delicious springtime odors. For several hours I followed the train tracks through one industrial town after another, along deserted side streets, through vacant lots overgrown with meadow grass, past rows of prudish, immaculate houses, bustling shops, schools, churches, and parks. All the while I was thinking longingly of Mary. The loss of her and Daisy's companionship was physically painful, despite the fact that I was exceedingly glad to be off that frightful island. Keeping to the forests (which contained surprisingly few Hidden Ones) I headed north, eventually arriving in the city of Stamford. At the station I booked passage to Providence. Twenty minutes later the train lumbered slowly into the station, hissing and shrieking and reeking of oil.

Making my way among the other passengers, I chose a seat by the window, beside a rather large elderly woman (fast asleep and snoring pleasantly) whose radiant heat warmed and soothed me almost as much as the midmorning sunshine pouring through the window.

I was still feeling cautious, uncertain how long it would take my many skilled pursuers to locate me. I remained casually watchful of the strangers around me. Thankfully, this journey was entirely free of incidents and I was even able to sleep for an hour, with my head propped up, first against the window-pane and later against the huge soft shoulder of my snoring neighbor.

Upon waking nearly an hour later, I sat up and stretched, taking the opportunity to glance about at the other passengers, all of whom, strangely enough, were asleep. Seeing several newspapers on a nearby bench, I quietly looked through them with half-hearted interest, almost afraid of any further revelations on the state of the world. I did not need any more evidence that civilization was coming undone around me. Just glimpsing the headlines and article titles was enough to induce nausea.

In Massawa, Eritrea, a deadly earthquake had destroyed most of the harbor of the overcrowded port city, killing an unknown number of people.

In the mining town of Mount Mulligan, in far north Queensland, Australia, a huge underground explosion had killed seventy-five miners.

In Oppau, Germany, there had been a massive explosion at a munitions storage warehouse, killing nearly six hundred people and seriously wounding thousands more. Much of the surrounding city had been leveled in the blast.

In Texas, more than two hundred people had drowned in a flash flood which had practically washed away the town of Thrall. The unusually heavy storm had risen up in the Gulf of Mexico and several meteorologists had noted the curious manner in which the dark rain-laden clouds had seemed to travel in a straight line directly to the town of Thrall. Once there, the storm seemed to stop abruptly, holding above the town as the clouds unleashed a fatal downpour.

I had seen enough. I arranged these newspapers into a tidy stack and returned them to the bench where I had found them. There was one final headline I could not resist: "Deadly Pandemic Ravages Europe!" Taking up this one paper, I read an extensive article about the recent influenza epidemic which had spread across the civilized world between 1918 and 1920. This epidemic was thought to have been the worst outbreak of its kind, second only to the Black Plague, and claiming an estimated 80 million victims, fully five percent of the overall human population on earth.

In the course of explaining how and why the virus had spread so quickly across the globe, the author showed, through numerous examples, how it was modernity itself which had enabled this virus to travel so far and wide, chiefly through the mediums of mass public transportation, the modern metropolis, and, most of all, the soldiers' barracks. The soldiers fighting in the war at the time of this pandemic, weakened as they were by fatigue and exposure to chemical weapons, were especially susceptible. The influenza had swept through the ranks on both sides, killing many thousands of enlisted men and influencing the course of the war itself.

The author suggested that it was here, inside the European war machine, that the influenza virus had, in fact, mutated into something far worse. It would have encountered numerous other viruses — the various experimental germ cultures that the English, German, and American militaries had mixed with chlorine and mustard gas. These cultivated viruses were now sweeping through the cities, the battlefields, the barracks, and the bodies of the troops themselves. It was this collision of hazardous organisms, in the ideal breeding ground of the war camps (with their virtually endless supply of weakened bodies in which to breed and multiply) that enabled several of these many viruses to merge, giving rise to a mutation and yet another even deadlier epidemic, the so-called second wave of the influenza outbreak. The article noted that mortality among Austrian and German soldiery had been so extreme, and had come upon them so much earlier in the war, that it had played a key role in the Allied victory. The virus was then brought to the US by the soldiers returning home from Europe, killing many thousands of American civilians before suddenly, and mysteriously, disappearing.

Most scientists claim the epidemic ended there. But a stubborn minority say that the virus did not vanish, but rather mutated, once again, this time into an entirely new virus, called encephalitis lethargica, a disease which, since its first appearance in 1915, has now, once again, (at the time of this writing) reached epidemic proportions.

The implications of this article unnerved me terribly, being uncomfortably similar to certain aforementioned theories which I had been developing. It made me think of the consequences of all those biological weapons which both armies had employed along the Western Front and beyond — the flu bombs, the germ clouds, and the other lesser-known compounds. Where had these viral clouds gone? Where had the wind carried them? Did anybody know, or care? It also made me think of North Brother Island and all the ongoing disease research and experiments in cross-contamination that were occurring there. More specifically, it made me think of Mary, a prisoner of the government being exposed to multiple diseases in quarantine, having her bodily fluids harvested by military scientists, right under the noses of an unreflective, disempowered, and horror-stricken public.

Returning this final newspaper to the opposite bench, I fell to staring out the window for a time, thinking of all that I had just read and recalling one particularly poignant conversation which I'd had with Mary on the subject of germ warfare.

We were sitting out by the rushes, having just fed her offspring, and were enjoying the cool night air when Mary spoke up.

"They want to use us as weapons," she said. "Human plague bombs, walking, talking, disease dispensers — the new and improved, immune-enhanced, chemical warfare soldier. The Human Dreadnought, a biologically superior superhuman who can be controlled, manipulated... made to obey any command."

"The Automaton which Percy Shelley wrote of," I replied.

"It's like something out of their bloody bible. A bringer of plagues. The Four Horsemen of the Apocalypse. The weapon of the future will be the soldier who can move invisibly through crowds on a city street, to spread disease secretly among those designated as enemies of the state. They have already begun to manufacture diseases in the laboratory. They keep live cultures of all of them. I've seen them myself. When this sort of warfare becomes the norm, then we shall truly see a disaster of biblical proportions. They are so bloody obsessed with their apocalypse that they can't see how they themselves are bringing it about!"

Hearing this, I was startled, but not surprised. I could think of nothing to refute it. It all sounded too damned plausible.

Being on a crowded train, the irony was undeniable. If I had grabbed twenty random strangers off the streets of New York City and said to them each in turn that the United States government was, under the guise of promoting medical science, incarcerating and experimenting on its own citizens, exposing them to multiple contagions simultaneously, and then monitoring the outcome, with military applications in mind, more than half would have laughed in my face and called me a lunatic. Some might even threaten bodily injury if I did not cease such unpatriotic drivel. "Not here!" they would extol, "in this freest of all countries!" God bless the average American! He is so damned eager to sacrifice himself, so eager to please and impress his withered father figures. He is too grotesque for pity.

Other statements Mary had made — like "human plague bombs" and "immune-enhanced soldiers" — kept coming back to me at odd moments. It was strange just how many of Mary's passing comments later returned to haunt me. Things she had said almost seemed like the disconnected clues to a larger riddle, which she had casually inserted into an otherwise ordinary conversation.

In reference to the Chicago typhoid outbreak of 1892, Mary had ended her mocking description with the statement, "If they only knew the truth!" At the time, I had let this pass. Clearly, however, this rejoinder contained a definite implication that Mary believed that the Chicago typhoid epidemic was not what it had appeared to be, and that the authorities had never discovered the true cause. Naturally, this made me think of Mary's notion of imposter viruses, Hidden Ones who imitated various plagues. I recalled how, once, when I had made reference to the Black Plague, Mary had chuckled and, when I questioned her, expressed doubts about the official scientific explanations, implying that there was something the scientists had overlooked.

I arrived at the inevitable question: If the Overlords steered humanity's progress through natural disasters like earthquakes, volcanic eruptions, and floods, then wouldn't they also orchestrate mass exterminations under the mechanism of disease epidemics? Mimicking the symptoms of any disease they chose, such organisms could easily simulate any contagion without the risk of being exposed. As with the natural disasters, human observers would seek no further explanations.

*   *   *   *

303

THERE WAS ONE MORE QUESTION WHICH HAUNTED ME AT THIS TIME I had not previously considered it, though my visit to North Brother Island, as well as Mary's frank statements about Human Dreadnoughts, had brought it to the fore. Might the authorities have, in their employ, persons like Mary and myself — individuals who (as a result of some undisclosed indulgence) had induced in themselves the same sensory enhancements, and expansive consciousness, that Mary and I were experiencing? But who were patriotic, unlike us, and had endeavored to use their powers to assist the cause of the authorities? I had not encountered any pursuers who had demonstrated any such enhancements; nevertheless, I could not pretend that such things were outside the realm of possibility. Indeed, I even pressed myself to try to imagine them, to anticipate what it might be like to encounter one or more of them, with the hope of devising a plan for how I might succeed in evading (or else defeating) them.

These same fearful conjectures also brought to mind certain memorable opinions which Mary had expressed on the topic of immune-enhanced super soldiers. During one discussion, I had expressed the idea that sensory-enhanced individuals like ourselves might join the side of the cops and soldiers. "Heaven help us if the authorities ever managed to get a few of us on their side. Imagine cops endowed with our powers of sight and hearing."

"I thought of that actually," she said with a smile, "and I don't believe it is possible."

"Why not?" I asked.

"Think about it," she said. "You have encountered others like us, yes?"

"Several," I said with a nod.

"Have you ever met one who wasn't an outlaw or a rebel, in retreat from society and hiding out in the shadows?"

I thought about it… and then shook my head. "I don't believe I have."

"I have a theory, Robert. Authoritarianism, like religion, and patriotism, rather hinders, or limits, the mind's development — like a yoke limits a cow's movements, or shackles limit a man's."

"What do you mean?" I asked.

"The authoritarian mind," she continued "lives on ritualized discipline and obedience for its own sake, rewarding a rigid dogmatism, and a total subjugation of individual will. This requires an intense suppression of the intuitive mind. All military personnel, at whatever level, must prostrate themselves, mentally and physically, before this hierarchy. They must conform themselves to its parameters or suffer humiliating and grueling punishment. The whole military apparatus is preoccupied with rank, constantly reinforcing these artificial categories with uniforms and salutes, until it becomes second nature. As a result of this, the military mind is oriented toward servility, toward obeying the will of the superior, and it atrophies along the same lines. Each soldier's intuition is suppressed and replaced with the desire to please authority. That's why military men, even clever ones, are so bloody dense. They are like potted plants, stunted, obedient, broken. They remain suspended in a child-like state of submission and arrogant superiority, receiving and obeying instructions without question or complaint. Even if they advance to a higher rank, these well-heeled soldiers only know how to obey, or command — to dominate or to submit. They become emotional imbeciles; too often their minds cannot break out of this dichotomy."

"Do you think this would prevent them from developing their hidden mental powers?" I asked.

"Yes," she replied, "It seems to me that this experience requires expanding one's will, not shrinking and suppressing it. Those boys in uniform would not permit themselves to wander so far from the morality of the herd. They would not permit themselves to deviate from the parameters set down for them by their masters, and so they remain cut off from the possibility of... developments."

Her theory appealed to me for a myriad of reasons — and yet, intriguing though it was, it was only a theory. For all I knew, there was an army of super soldiers, armed to the teeth, waiting for me in the shrubbery outside the Providence train station.

*   *   *   *

HAPPILY, WHEN I STEPPED OFF THE TRAIN IN PROVIDENCE, I FOUND IT bereft of lurking policemen. I recalled with a wave of pleasant nostalgia, the night I'd spent here with Howard, and our rambling adventure through the hilly streets of this fantastic city, I was overjoyed at the idea of seeing my friend again and so decided to walk directly to his residence. I had decided to tell him the whole story of how (without ever intending to) I had shadowed him on his peculiar journey through the Catskills. I very much looked forward to hearing why he had gone there and what he had learned. Furthermore, I made up my mind to keep no secrets from him, to tell him, at long last, everything that I had seen, and learned, and done, hoping to have his honest opinion of everything. Moving through the increasingly familiar intersections, I made my way along several shady tree-lined streets whose names I recalled from my hike with Howard. At last, I came to Angell Street and, turning left, stood before Howard's three-story townhouse. It was about five o'clock in the afternoon.

305

The windows on the first and second floors were shuttered, and, despite the plentiful sunlight, the porchlight was on. Mounting the steps in a single bound, I knocked gently upon the door and then, recalling their penchant for courteous formality, I took a step backward. A moment passed, with no response. I took two more steps back and, gazing up through the walls of the house, I discerned a warm human form very slowly making its way down the stairs. This was not Howard's distinctive silhouette, but the figure of an older female, moving cautiously and with a painful slowness. Recalling what Howard had said about his mother being placed in an asylum, I guessed that this must be Howard's Aunt Annie. In a moment, the curtain beside the door fluttered and then I heard the bolt thrown aside. The door opened about six inches, revealing the face of a middle-aged, white-haired woman in a light blue housecoat.

"May I help you?" she asked in a flat monotone.

"Yes, my name is Robert Henry Pearce. I am a friend of Howard's. We met some years ago here in Providence and then again last year in Boston. He made me swear that I'd come by for a visit if I ever came back here. I was hoping he might be home."

Aunt Annie looked at me gravely and shook her head.

"I wish to god that he were here." she said ominously, glancing over her shoulder into the shadowy foyer behind her. "I'm afraid he left six days ago for New York City. He will be there for another week, then home for two days, then off to Cleveland for another two-week trip."

"Oh, I see," I said, unable to conceal my disappointment. The thought of Howard spending his days beetling about in the shadows of those demon-haunted skyscrapers, moving along the canyonesque avenues of New York, shoulder to shoulder with the teeming swarms of deranged humanity, sent a shiver straight through me. Aunt Annie, however, interrupted these musings with a sudden gasp.

"Wait! What did you say your name was?" she asked squinting, cocking her head to one side.

"Robert Henry Pearce," I said.

Suddenly her eyes flickered. "How silly of me," she said apologetically. "Of course! Howard said you might come. There is a letter which he instructed me to give to you, should you come looking for him. Excuse me for one moment and I'll get it." She disappeared into the darkened recesses of the living room.

Without her there to hold the door shut, it slowly creaked open, revealing the dismal, cave-like, interior of the house which, for the hour, was shockingly dark and cavernous. Since all the windows on the lower floor had been shut tight, the only light came from a single lamp in the far corner of the sitting room.

There was something else about this glimpse of the interior of Howard's house which unnerved me. I had the distinct impression that the place with infested with unseen things, a disturbingly large number of oddly flickering shadows peering out at me. Additionally, despite the dense, almost-suffocating quiet of the house, there was one discernible sound: a soft rustling noise, eerily familiar, and coming from several of the carefully curtained off windows. It was a familiar dragging and tapping sound, the soft squeaking strokes of windblown branches brushing against window glass. I thought of the tree outside of Mary Mallon's window, the poem by Robert Frost, and felt the hairs on my neck and arms stand up.

A moment later, Aunt Annie returned, holding in her hand a sealed envelope, which she held out to me. "For Robert Henry Pearce," was written on the outside.

"Howard returns from New York City in eight days' time," she said matter-of-factly. "I am quite certain that he will want to see you."

"Thank you," I replied. "I will try. I have a physical condition which might make this impossible, but I will certainly try."

She nodded suspiciously. With a tip of my hat, I bid her good day.

Desperately impatient to read Howard's letter, I crossed the street and, seating myself upon the curb directly opposite 598 Angell Street, I tore open the envelope and read the letter inside. It was five pages long and covered in Howard's cramped but legible handwriting.

Dear Robert,

I haven't much time so I shall be brief. If you are reading this, then all has gone according to my plan and, though I am sad to have missed you, I am grateful that you kept your promise to pay a visit.

I'm presently writing you from the innermost circle of Dante's Inferno, also known as Manhattan Island, where I am staying with a good friend who is just mad enough to actually LIKE this place! For myself, I don't know how much longer I will be able to remain here. This city has exceeded my darkest expectations with regard to the state of its inhabitants. Moreover, every night at sunset, many of the larger buildings seem to exude a curious stench, a kind of poisonous desolation which, apparently, only I can smell. New York is the New Babylon, Robert, even more terrifying than the original. In no other modern city have I seen such a vivid depiction of Darwin's evolutionary theories. Some of the faces one glimpses here and there along the wharf would barely qualify as humanity! To see such beings dressed in pants and a jacket is an affront to civilization itself. There is something detestable in it; like a frog or an ape dressed in human attire. Such a vividly pictoral depiction of humanity's evolution from simian and sub-simian origins was never so indisputably apparent. I am a BELIEVER, Mr. Darwin! I am told that, down by the river banks, there are man-made tunnels, inhabited by degenerate Irish gangs, that even the police will not enter. Each day brings fresh lunacy-inducing horrors! Someday, this pestilential island shall cave in upon itself. Mark my words, Robert. One day, Manhattan shall sink into the sea!

Enough about this place. I shall get right down to the real reason for this letter. I am leaving in half an hour to meet several friends and may not have a chance to write again for several days.

Dear friend, where shall I begin? You recall, no doubt, the last time we parted, my vow to become an investigator of bizarre and supernatural phenomena I have made good on that promise and now find myself in possession of such facts that I can scarcely bring myself to put to paper. I have gone searching for horrors untold... and I have found them! I have glimpsed unspeakable truths which have utterly demolished all prior understanding. I have only just returned from a place called Leffert's Corners in the Catskill Mountains, where I made several shocking discoveries which have altered, forever, my understanding of myself, and my place in this world. Time does not permit me to tell the whole story here. If you would like to read a more complete account, I have collected all my findings and am presently organizing them into a chronological narrative, which I expect to have published shortly, under the title "The Lurking Fear," with the understanding that it is a fictional tale of horror, in the style of Arthur Machen. I have already spoken with a friend who is an editor at Home Brew magazine. You may expect to see it there soon.

Originally, I went to the Catskills as an investigative journalist. I had heard stories of an inexplicable massacre in a squatter hamlet which I hoped to investigate and to write about. The local squatters I spoke with were extremely helpful, though what they had to say tested the bounds of credulity. In short, they claimed that this massacre of nearly seventy-five people had not been committed by any earthly being, but by an evil Spirit of the mountain which has been terrorizing the region for centuries. Some of them had even glimpsed the Thing lurking nearby, in the weeks and months leading up to the tragedy. These squatter folk informed me that this monster had made its nest in the cellar of an abandoned mansion, located on a neighboring

308

mountain. Research into the history of this curious mansion, however, revealed a macabre puzzle.

According to local historians, the original inhabitants of this mansion had been a wealthy Dutch family by the name of Martense, whose too strict adherence to a code of isolationism eventually led to their extinction. Arriving sometime in 1670, the well-known and well-liked Martense clan, headed by the eccentric Garret Martense, were known locally as kind, trustworthy people and friendly neighbors. Soon, however, they began a slow but steady withdrawal from public life. Each generation was more misanthropic than the last, eventually shunning the outside world and sequestering themselves for several generations within the confines of their remote family estate. Waited on by a staff of mongrel gypsies native to that region, the Martense family appears to have remained in undisturbed isolation for almost 300 years! Rumors of inbreeding, degeneration and murder soon spread throughout the county. Some claimed the Martenses had poisoned their stock by interbreeding with their mongrel servants. Others cited incestuous practices. Still others claimed that they had clandestine dealings with a band of rogue Iroquois secretly living on Overlook mountain. These displaced and relocated Indians had, according to local legend, secretly snuck back into their native lands and were living in remote caves, observing the white man's civilization and conducting secret raids. Nevertheless, a whole clan of parents, grandparents, uncles, aunts, cousins, and siblings, sequestered away in a palatial mansion, intermarrying, interbreeding (with each other, red Indians, and their curious staff), was hard enough for the stalwart local community to abide. But then when people began to go missing, the situation quickly became intolerable.

The missing people were mostly travelers, at first. The locals issued warnings and posted signs discouraging sight-seers and picnickers. The mansion itself was shunned. For want of any promising leads, the local authorities did nothing. Years went by. People continued to disappear. Widely believed to be the victims of the "Martense Monster," most of these people were never seen again. Every once in a while, however, some hunter or hiker would come upon a body in the woods. Always these bodies were horrifically mutilated, half-eaten, gnawed beyond recognition. Several local legends posited that the monster responsible for these killings was the unnatural offspring of incestuous union, the inevitable by-product of isolated spawning and cannibal nutrition. For the generations that came of age after 1816, much of this history had assumed the status of legend.

Sometime, shortly hereafter, neighbors noted that they no longer saw lights in the Martense mansion windows at night, and thus concluded that the last of the bizarre clan had finally expired. The house has since fallen into decay.

I went there myself. It is uninhabited... by humans. However, the odd disappearances, and the occasional mutilated corpse, have continued up into the present day. The recent massacre appears to have been the culmination of almost three hundred years of carnage.

So you see, you were right about the breeding habits of the wealthy, Robert. It happened just as you said it might. In fact, in hindsight, your comment about wealthy inbred families seems curiously, almost conspicuously, prophetic.

It is also believed by many of the older half-breed squatters that these incestuous Dutch hermits were also occultists — "devil-worshippers"— who summoned up unspeakable Things in a secret underground chamber, located beneath the foundations of the mansion itself, and connected to a vast maze of tunnels. But even this was not the crowning horror! This maze of tunnels, as I later learned from the squatter elders, was believed to conceal some kind of hidden gateway which communicated between this world of ours, and numerous parallel worlds. Some claimed that this portal had been ceremoniously opened centuries earlier, by the original patriarch of the Martense clan, for an unknown purpose. But this gateway, however it had come about, and why, had, either through neglect or design, remained open for centuries; over the years, numerous monstrosities had slipped through, feasting upon the inhabitants of the valley and giving rise to a whole cycle of legends, dating back to the 15th century. Slowly, over the course of this investigation, I became obsessed with finding out precisely where this "Martense Monster" was coming from, and where it went when it departed. Believe it or not Robert, one night, while under the spell of an admittedly ghoulish curiosity, I went and crawled into one of these tunnels. And though I saw many dreadful and baffling things that night, I was unable to locate anything so useful as a portal to another world.

Nevertheless, Robert, it is my heartfelt belief, based on my experiences in the Catskills, that these portals are REAL, that there are hidden doorways in the landscape, "ruptures in the ether" (as the late William Hodgson poignantly called them), where a man may pass out of this world and into an entirely different realm of existence. Where the denizens of those other realms may, in turn, enter unbidden

310

into our own. But these portals are not always open, nor are they easy to locate. I believe that some of these portals, like the one beneath the Martense Mansion, are guarded by sentinels... inconceivably horrifying creatures who kill and eat any who get too close. My exploration of these tunnels was cut short when I came face to face with just such a creature. It appeared only seconds before a merciful stroke of lightning collapsed the tunnel between us. Sadly, this collapse was so extensive that it obliterated any hope of discovering the hidden portal. Shortly thereafter, I left the Catskills and returned home to Providence, badly shaken but none the worse for wear.

Others were not so lucky as I. All this knowledge has come at an awful price, Robert. Three brave, open-minded, men were killed in the course of these investigations, and it is only by some incomprehensible law of improbability that I did not die along with them. I am not prepared to speculate upon the nature of the creature that devoured them, but can confirm that, in all three cases, death came quickly when it did.

Upon returning to Providence, I immediately began research into the notion of portals as they appear in English and Irish folktales, as well as the mythologies of countless primitive peoples. I was soon interrupted in my researches when I received a curiously timely letter from a friend in New York City who was, incredibly enough, making investigations into an idea not dissimilar to my own. Curiously, this friend explained how he was examining places in New York City where, like the hills west of Leffert's Corners, there seemed to be high concentrations of inexplicable, apparently supernatural, phenomena; everything from vanishings to hauntings to unsolved occult murders. Thinking once again of the portals, I interrogated my young friend through correspondence and was not disappointed with what he told me. Within a week, this same friend had made a map of Manhattan Island highlighting locations where there have been concentrated reports of unexplained deaths and disappearances. This list included everything from haunted hotels, beaches, and taverns, to hospitals where suspiciously high numbers of patients had checked in, and then promptly vanished. This adventure was too much for me to pass up. Twelve hours after receiving this letter, I was on a train bound for New York City. I arrived here just two days ago... and have been in a state of subdued horror ever since.

I will be here for one week, making systematic investigations at these aforementioned locations. After this, I will return to Providence for several days before departing again for another ten-day trip to

Cleveland, where I shall conduct similar investigations with a knowledgeable friend. After this, I shall return to Providence once more. Depending on how I am faring, I may take a trip up to the Maine Coast, where I plan to make an investigation of Boone Island, yet another place with a conspicuous history of... let's just call it unusual phenomena. From what I've read of its history, Boone Island has all the requisite features to indicate the likely presence of a portal. We shall see! Perhaps, after I return from this trip, we can meet up and compare notes. I look forward to a time when we might sit down and have it out, once and for all.

There is one final thing I must mention to you, before I end. Ever since I saw you in Boston two years ago, I have been assailed by the most macabre nightmares imaginable! Once or twice a week, I wake up shrieking from apocalyptic nightmares; grotesquely vivid visions of decimated cities, tidal waves, and burning landscapes. What they mean, who can say? But I must tell you truthfully Robert, mad as it sounds, I feel it in my bones that there are dark times ahead. I cannot shake the feeling that these dreams are a harbinger, a glimpse of humanity's possible future. It is my belief that our gently spinning Earth is on the verge of cataclysmic events. There are ancient Horrors, Robert, timeless monstrosities which are here, hidden amongst us, floating across our skies, ingeniously disguised as natural phenomena, mingling, scrutinizing, examining us... preparing for the day that they will reclaim this earth.

I have good reason to believe that Boone Island conceals one of the last open portals in the New England area. The one beneath the Martense Mansion is half-buried now and far too well-guarded for human exploration. It is my belief that, when the disaster comes, portals like these shall provide the only hope of escape. I must try to locate one so that I can observe it and see how it works. My strong sense is that the disaster is still several years away. Nevertheless, get there soon if you can, Robert, for there is a Horror coming to the world of men.

As I write this, I look out my window and see a quaintly charming street scene which Norman Rockwell would envy, and yet, I tell you, old friend, I feel like shrieking! None of these people have even noticed the change in the earth and the wind. There is something in the air which sickens me and makes me dizzy. It is not so much a smell as a vibration or a hum. The clouds that linger above the city are of a very unusual type, and the sunlight that filters through them is harsher, sharper, too bright, and too hot. It burns my skin after just a *few minutes and makes my eyes ache from the glare. Even the trees and the grass here in Central Park, and along the side streets, seem inexplicably changed... wrong in some indescribable way. I'll tell you truthfully, there are certain trees which, if one watches them, as I have, very carefully, over an extended period, one begins to see certain inexplicable movements, not natural to a tree, some merely odd, or improbable, others absolutely terrifying. This, too, seems a dreadful confirmation of my impressions of a looming conspiracy. Having noticed, perhaps, that I am becoming one of them — these hidden things no longer take the trouble to conceal their presence from me.*

I'm afraid I have still darker news. It is my sad duty to inform you that my poor, long-suffering mother died last May, during a bungled operation to remove her gall bladder. What can I say of this? I suppose I am still in shock, since I often imagine that I glimpse her in crowded places and hear her calling to me in the small hours of the night. Saddest of all, these sightings of moving trees and shrubs only serve to remind me of one of the cruelest ironies of my mother's descent into madness. I refer here to dismissing my mother when she came to me and spoke of her imposter plants. It pains me no end to consider how, after years of ignoring her assertions that some of the plants in the garden were imposters, unidentified organisms masquerading as shrubbery, I am now forced to admit that she may have been absolutely correct! For reasons I may never understand, my mother appears to have developed the ability to perceive these hidden creatures, just as I, during this same period, developed the ability to see those floating horrors which I described to you in Boston. Unfortunately, Mother's unselfconscious (and ultimately self-destructive) response was to draw attention to these imposter plants, inspecting any and all greenery, throughout the neighborhood, whose authenticity she doubted. Shortly after this discovery, she began to complain of dizziness, and of increasingly long spells of forgetfulness, wherein her mind seemed transported to another place and time altogether; upon recovering, she had to be reminded of who, where, and even what, she was. Were these long spells of forgetfulness a punishment, inflicted upon her because of her attempts to expose the hidden horrors? Just prior to the onset of her powers, mother insisted that some sort of invisible being, a "presence" she called it, had come into our home. Some unseen observer, sent to study us and to spy on our doings. I shudder to think that she may have been right all along. What's more, if I could perhaps learn something about the being (or beings) that did this to her, then I might just be able to find some way to avoid sharing a similar fate.

If I can discover, and utilize, the portal on Boone Island, I expect to have the answer to these questions and countless others. I very much hope to see you upon my return to Providence in eight days. If that is not possible, then perhaps after I return from Cleveland, ten days hence.

Sincerely,
Howard

P.S. When we do speak again, remind me to tell you about the fascinating young woman I met on the train ride back from Leffert's Corners. Her name was Carmilla, like the novel by LeFanu, and, amazingly enough, she said she knew you! She was half-Iroquois, she said, and told me several Iroquois and Seneca legends which greatly assisted in my research.

What was I to think of this incredible letter? By now, my readers will know just how many provocative statements this missive contained. Where to begin? The incredible history of the Martense clan? The encounter with Carmilla? A thousand questions, theories and brachiated hypotheses crowded into my head.

How was it that Howard had known, almost to the day, that I was coming? The uncanny arrival of his letter, here just one day before my random and unannounced visit, seemed in itself evidence of an almost clairvoyant knowledge of my whereabouts. Was he now able to see the future, and to perceive my approach upon the landscape? Clearly he had developed something not unlike the altered and expanded awareness that I was experiencing, though it had developed much more rapidly with him it seemed, and was accompanied by what I can only call curiously intense authoritarian leanings.

This led to another, much more disturbing question. Did my friend Howard represent some other kind of Encerrado? An authoritarian Encerrado? Mary Mallon's theory that the authoritarian mind was incapable of such expansion seemed to obliterate the possibility of such a being. Yet, here I was, faced with a possible contradiction, or at least one exception, to that theory. Howard, like me, possessed the symptoms of a profound inner transformation, yet he held views that were the very inverse of my own — so much so that I feared we would never be able to speak to each other with utter frankness. Up until this time, all the other Encerrados I had encountered had been men and women who had seemed distinctly libertarian, people who had, consciously, and purposely, directed themselves and their energies away from, and even against, the flow of bourgeois civilization. People like Bartolo, Galleani, Legion the Giant, Carmilla, and Mary Mallon, while distinct from each other in many ways, had a certain shared ambivalence toward the civilized mode of existence, as well as a rapport with one another which seemed to indicate some kind of shared consciousness. All had removed themselves from the squirrel-trap of authoritarian society, or else they were spit out by a civilization which could not tolerate them. Like me, they were rebels against the prevailing order. But, if a proud reactionary like Howard could develop the same heightened senses and the same altered and expanded awareness that I had, and still harbor such a profoundly authoritarian outlook, then I was forced to consider that perhaps Mary had been wrong.

There were certain other casual statements from this letter which gave me pause; mere asides which contained monstrous implications. For example, what was the significance of Howard's mother Susie dying while having her gall bladder removed? I had learned from Mary that gall bladder removal was an experimental procedure sometimes used when trying to deal with typhoid fever, which was believed by some to lodge exclusively in that organ. A tough lady like Mary had put up a fight when they tried to remove hers. From Howard's description, it sounded as if Susie had been in no condition to protest against much of anything.

Another of these shocking asides was the reference to the fact that Howard and Carmilla had met on the train. What was I to think of such an event? By what sinister machination of the cosmos had this chance encounter occurred?

Finally, what was I to think of Howard's talk of portals? Naturally, it came as a tremendous relief to me to consider that the countless squatter deaths near Leffert's Corners had, most likely, been the work of numerous portal-bound monstrosities which had been passing through those hills for decades, giving rise to a whole cycle of local mythology surrounding the haunted mansion. This would certainly explain the long ghastly history of missing persons who had turned up half-eaten within the vicinity of Overlook Mountain. It was a disconcerting theory, but I knew better than to dismiss any possibilities. Reflecting upon the many-headed Thing I'd glimpsed leaning out of the burrow, I wondered if perhaps this "Martense Monster" was not also the original inhabitant of the oval-shaped chamber which my offspring and I had taken as our own.

This idea of portals — isn't that too supported by countless prevalent myths and legends the world over? Tales of magical gateways, hidden in the landscape, sometimes in the form of a pond, or a cave, or a ring of trees, are a common theme in the folktales of the world. Could it be that such gateways to other worlds actually exist? Is it not then logical to expect that out of these portals there might occasionally emerge beings and entities so unlike anything we know on this earth that they are fathomable to us only as ghosts, monsters, or evil spirits? I had learned first hand, that sometimes even people could be portals. Why not an island off the coast of Maine?

I peered about the street, dazed. I folded up the letter, slipped it into my breast pocket, and stood up. Across the street two children were playing soldiers. Further down the sidewalk there was a woman pushing an infant in a perambulator beneath some over-arching branches. Recalling Susie's comments about "imposter plants," I made a casual inspection of the shrubbery and counted not one, not two, but *three* different Hidden Ones, masquerading, quite convincingly, as common bushes. They were standing motionless amongst the other vegetation, not three feet from the sidewalk where the woman with the pram had passed seconds before. Susie, as it turns out, had been correct! There *were* imposter plants peeking in the windows at 598 Angell Street. And not just there! Recalling Howard's stories about finding Susie inspecting her neighbor's shrubbery, as well as her own, I made a slow, reluctant, panoramic inspection of the entire neighborhood.

Gazing out across the sunny street into the gardens of neighboring houses, I saw that nearly every house along this quiet street had at least two Hidden Ones on the premises. Many were actual Tree Things, whose lofty heads towered ominously above the roofs of the houses. Others were shrubs, perfectly resembling raspberry, honeysuckle, or azalea. Most of these swayed harmlessly in the afternoon breeze, but, here and there, I saw a stray branch or two gently fumbling against the window casement, groping against the edges of the windows in an exploratory manner, as though feeling about for a point of entry. Appalled at this horrific scenery, I quickly departed Angell street.

I would have gone to visit Susie's grave, to place some flowers, and pay my respects to that kind and gentle woman, but I concluded that I had run out of time. I had turned onto Doyle Avenue and gone about a mile when I had to stop and rest, breathless from a sudden pain in my gut. There was no mistaking it. Within me like a steadily growing fever, I could already feel the craving for brain meat returning, welling up inside me like a blind rage.

I came to the northern edge of town and, entering a small, deserted woodland area, I climbed a slope that overlooked the rooftops, and collapsed in the grass. Plagued by hallucinatory visions of death and murder, I was suddenly so hungry for brains I was unable to stop the gnashing of my teeth and the rapid pounding of my heart. After about an hour of drooling into the tall grass, I fell into a deep, dreamless sleep.

XXI

I RESUMED THAT LIFESTYLE WHICH I NOW UNDERSTOOD TO BE AN unavoidable part of late-stage gestation. Once again, I became the murdering cannibal, with even more zeal than before; this time, I was not simply "eating for two," as the saying goes, but eating for two hundred. This renewed brain-eating frenzy lasted approximately nine months.

My first victim in this second wave of killings was a famous neurologist and psychiatrist, Dr. Pearce Bailey, then living in eastern Massachusetts. An avid eugenicist, Bailey had been heavily involved in the creation of the National Committee for Mental Hygiene and had been appointed head of the Division of Neurology and Psychiatry in the U.S. Army during the war years. Most importantly, he had authored the definitive work on identifying and weeding out "mental defectives" for the purposes of sterilization, not just in the Army but among the general civilian population as well. For a time, he had even worked as a surgeon at Bellevue Hospital, performing experimental brain surgeries on patients. His oft-stated goal (for which he was much celebrated and admired) was the mass sterilization of all "mental defectives" currently living in the United States. According to his widely accepted system of identification, fully one-fifth of all Americans were "mentally or physically deficient" enough to justify rejection from military services and to qualify for sterilization. Under his system of classification, many hundreds of thousands of enlisted men (mostly Negroes) were sterilized, in many cases without either their knowledge or consent. On the night that I killed him, Dr. Bailey was still serving as the Chairman for the New York State Committee for Mental Defectives, implementing his vision of a glorious and hygienic America with the full support of the United States Government, as well as the medical establishment as a whole.

Crawling into his mansion through an unlocked second story window, I killed and de-brained him in his own bathtub, retreating immediately into the forest behind his estate, where I devoured my prize in a moonlit creek bed. Collapsing, minutes later, in a nearby field, I had a singular experience which I must relate in detail. It seemed to be the culmination of what I had come to see as a steadily growing intimacy between the Hidden Ones and me.

317

After so long a period of abstinence from brain meat, the narcotic effect this had upon me was profound and far-reaching. Having lost whatever tolerance I may have developed, it hit me almost as intensely as my first brain, on that fateful day back in 1915. Again I had the well-remembered sensation of a heavy presence bearing down upon me, accompanied by feelings of extreme euphoria. Again I glimpsed odd shadows on the periphery of my vision and heard the grass swishing all around me.

Trembling, my muscles convulsing (as if rearranging themselves upon my skeleton) with waves of pleasure pulsing through me, I became aware of a curious and inexplicable tickling sensation along the edges of my body. Forcing my eyes open, I was startled to see that the grass upon which I was lying was actually moving, leaning into me from all directions, caressing me in a tender, exploratory way and combing, fingerlike, through my hair! Horrorstruck, I looked around and confirmed that the grass blades on the slope above and below me were alive with curious ripples and undulations, standing endwise and waving in the air like the raised forelegs of several thousand enraged tarantulas, advancing in waves upon me. It wasn't just the grass. Some of the surrounding vegetation, including several nearby bushes, were now violently agitated, as if whipped by a savage wind, though the night was still and calm. It occurred to me that these must be Hidden Ones who had (for whatever unknown reason) finally decided to cross that last threshold of intimacy and actually touch me. This direct physical contact was initially quite terrifying, yet I was soon moved almost to tears by the unexpected tenderness with which they examined me. I lifted my hand affectionately and attempted to return the touch of this curious grass, though it recoiled from me with a spidery quickness, withdrawing back into the ground and avoiding, at all costs, contact with my outstretched fingers.

A minute later, I lapsed into a hallucinatory stupor. I had yet another terrible vision of the ancient stone palace now known to the world as Machu Picchu. My eyes rolled painfully into the top of my head and then I must have fainted.

As in my earlier vision, I again perceived that I was standing in the midnight courtyard of that hoary stone temple, atop the domed peak which overlooks the famous megalithic Inca stronghold. Only this time, I had the advantage of knowing exactly where I was. I was clearly in the Peruvian Andes, high above the Urubamba River, roughly fifty miles northwest of Cuzco, on a peak that the Inca called Huayna Picchu. The question that haunted me most was not so much where I was, but *when*. There was no wind, despite our tremendous height, and the rank, dewy air was curiously still and quiet. Stepping over to the edge of the cliff, I made a careful inspection of this vast panorama.

Above the vast range of surrounding mountains, the black sky was riddled with pulsating stars. In the spaces between these ancient mountains, the great sea of impenetrable mist prevailed, obscuring the serpentine windings of the mighty Urubamba which lay beneath it. My eyes were drawn to the torch-lit construction on the ridge directly below me. As in my earlier visions, this magnificent complex of stone houses, temples, stairways, and porticoes was peopled with several hundred figures, all of whom seemed to be engaged in a ritual of utmost profundity, leaping, cavorting, and chanting in the central courtyard, and directing their gestures toward the starry vault above. The throbbing music which inspired these movements was a mixture of thunderous drums, various sorts of rattles and noise-makers as well as several hundred pan-pipes, whistling out the notes like a vast swarm of shrieking birds. Some of these worshipers wore yellow robes, others wore red. Many were adorned with bracelets, neck bands and tiaras of solid gold. I saw that well-remembered group of women with the curious wicker helmets, dancing near the temple steps. I could hear these songs and sounds with a startling clarity. This utterly incredible spectacle held me spellbound for some minutes; I was overcome with wonder, terror, and curiosity.

Several of the dancers began to scream out of rhythm with the others, gesturing at something beyond the walls of the stone palace. The crowd of worshipers suddenly fell silent, and all heads turned toward the southern horizon. Looking up from the red-litten palace, I too began to scan the skyline in that direction.

At first, I saw nothing but the grey mountains standing tall against the night sky. Then, in the distance, I perceived a great patch of moving blackness, inconspicuous yet discernible in the otherwise starry firmament — a gigantic flapping Thing advancing up the valley toward us. This enormous shadow seemed to expand impossibly as it drew nearer; I was soon overcome with great feelings of terror at the idea that this huge, vaguely triangular, shadow might actually be coming to the peak upon which I stood. Climbing higher and higher above the horizon, this strange patch of darkness blotted out whole constellations as it drew nearer, winging its way out of the southern sky like a gigantic black manta ray. Behind it, spread out across the distant horizon, was the great sprawling grey shadow of Lake Titicaca, from which this flapping horror had most assuredly emerged. As it vaulted ever onward, it continued to expand monstrously; it was as wide across as a medium-sized lake, noticeably thicker at the center and using its thinner, wing-like extremities to pull itself laboriously through the air.

As this Thing drew near to the palace, it began to change, thickening across the mid-section, its gigantic wings melting into an ever-widening torso, out of which their soon emerged a huge, tapered black head, festooned with several thousand bulging, blinking red eyes, each roughly the size of a wagon wheel. Most of the worshipers in the great courtyard remained in prone, silent supplication, as the colossal winds, created by the flapping of those two-hundred foot wings, swept over the entire complex. Beneath this blasting air, the people huddled in terror, many scrambling away from the advancing Titan and clinging to each other in desperation. Their garments flapped violently against their bodies and, in some cases, were ripped away completely. Wicker helmets were torn from their wearers and dashed to pieces against the temple walls and stairs, or else swept over the edge of the cliff, plunging downward into the abyss below.

It was here, also, that I understood why the strange red torches had been placed so deeply into the curious niches. Despite this blasting whirlwind, they had remained lit.

The great stone palace, indeed the entire mountain, shook thunderously as the Flapping Thing landed the central courtyard, using the tips of its massive triangular wings as feet. The few people who had remained standing throughout the creature's advent were now flung pitilessly to the ground where they huddled, petrified, with the others. Pouring itself out of the air, this shape-shifting leviathan melted into something oddly reminiscent of a hundred-foot tall raven, which stepped awkwardly across the flagstones in a manner which immediately called to mind that long ago day in Sudbury when, having observed the ravens in the upstairs bedroom, my tiny offspring had taken on an infinitely smaller version of this very same shape.

This familiar avian form was only one phase of a much more elaborate transformation. Seconds later, the Thing collapsed into several great shuddering hills of black fat which oozed, slug-like, in several different directions. In less time than it takes to write, this vast liquid horror had poured itself into that system of troughs and waterways which honeycombed the entire complex, filling the many channels and pools with a thick, lustrous oil, just as I'd envisioned back at the Boston Library. For a moment, all was still. None dared move. Then, as the minutes passed, I heard a low hum, rising up from many throats, all holding the same deep note, and with a steadily rising intensity.

The worshipers maintained this mournful note for nearly a minute. Some of the priests and priestesses tentatively rose to their feet, stepping forward, as if to receive the strange gifts of perception which proximity to the Black Thing evidently bestowed. I watched them creep forward in dread expectation and then suddenly leap backward, holding their heads in their hands, laughing, covering and uncovering their ears, or rubbing their eyes vigorously with their palms.

The vision ended there and, opening my eyes, I found myself in the grassy field under the stars, dazed and slightly nauseous. The lights of the late Pearce Bailey's mansion were still visible through the trees, though I sensed no disturbance there. Sitting up, I confirmed that the grass beneath me was, once again, of the normal earthly type. I gathered my things and departed into the wild hills, trying desperately, though unsuccessfully, to push all thoughts of my hallucinatory vision from my mind.

It seemed to be yet another confirmation of the Tihuanaco creation legend. I was left with the ominous impression that I had been made a witness to one more of the secret rituals wherein the Inca priests had summoned up (and had communion with) that deity whom they called the Lord of the Void, the ancient Horror that nested in the cavernous depths of Lake Titicaca, the "Apu Qun Tiqsi Wiraqutra," also known as Con Tiki Viracocha.

* * * *

AFTER THIS RENEWED INITIATION, I ONCE AGAIN BECAME A KILLING machine, resuming my cannibalistic predations with a frightening ease and proficiency. My views having evolved somewhat on the subject of who constituted a worthy target, I came up with a slightly modified criterion by which to select my victims. Having learned from those issues of the *Starry Cross* all about vivisection, I decided, for a time, to target as many of these heartless torturers as I could find. There were plenty within my immediate vicinity, and I rid the world of a dozen or more of these unfeeling cowards in just under three months. For those who do not know, vivisectionists are doctors who perform nerve experiments upon live animal subjects such as monkeys, dogs, and cats. They usually cite Scientific Progress or "a better understanding of the nervous system" as a rationale for these procedures, but these platitudes left me cold. I haunted the Universities where vivisection was practiced, and identified, through campus newsletters and bulletin boards in the Biology Departments, who these men were — and where I might hope to catch them unawares. Utilizing this simple method, I achieved immediate success. These vivisectionists (including several technicians who assisted with thier experiments) comprised a new record for me, by far, my highest number within a three-month period.

I admit there was an unprecedented ferocity in my harsh treatment of these particular individuals. I wished to strike terror into the hearts of vivisectionists everywhere, so I tended to leave these corpses in a gratuitously unappealing and hamstrung condition.

I resumed this hunting lifestyle with a confidence that surprised me. It came so naturally to me now that, horrible as it may sound, it all unfolded effortlessly, like the unraveling circumstances of an epic and momentous dream. As I trudged through the wild countryside, I noticed several things indicative of changes going on in and around me. I arrived at the understanding that it had been The Black Thing, not me, whom the Hidden Ones had been retreating from back in the Catskills. Not only were they not afraid of me, but these Hidden Ones actually seemed to take a vested and renewed interest in me and my very pregnant body. Three times in one month, I awoke in the small hours to find myself encircled in a ring of curious and inquisitive Hidden Ones, fascinated, apparently, by my ever-swelling body and eager to inspect every inch of me.

*　*　*　*

AFTER THIS GLUT OF VIVISECTIONISTS, I FELT IT WISE TO TAKE MYSELF on a whirlwind tour of the countryside, spreading out my crimes over a larger area and drawing on a more diverse array of victims.

On March 11, 1922, I went to Cambridge and murdered General William Amos Bancroft, businessman, soldier, and politician. Having faithfully served the interests of the local power-elite for two years in the Massachusetts House of Representatives, two years on The Board of Aldermen (of which he eventually became President), and four years as Mayor of the city of Cambridge, I felt certain that his crimes must be numerous beyond calculation. He had proven himself such a loyal lapdog to the city's ruling interests that they had even permitted him to be re-elected two more times! He had also been the first President of the Boston Elevated Railway, wherein numerous pre-existing transportation monopolies (including the West End Railway Company, which dominated streetcar routes, and the various privately owned subway and motorbus companies) were systematically bought out and merged into one huge bureaucratic conglomeration which he himself controlled, taking the decision-making power which had previously been in the hands of several thousand individuals and putting it into the hands of just one. From these positions of power and influence, Bancroft was able to facilitate and perfect the stranglehold of his own far-reaching business monopoly and to extend similar favors to his many millionaire friends. Finally, and most repellent of all, William Bancroft was a Brigadier General in the Massachusetts Militia and the United States Volunteers, wherein he oversaw the indoctrination of countless new recruits, helping to persuade many hundreds of misguided, directionless young men to sacrifice themselves to the interests of the American ruling class and to offer their bodies to the patriotic war machine. This wretched man met my criteria for being a worthy target many times over. I found the one-time Mayor of Cambridge relaxing in his sizable backyard. I garroted him, de-brained him, and left his corpse propped up in his lawn chair, as if he were asleep.

A month and a half later, while passing through Tarrytown, I revisited John D. Rockefeller's mansion, with high hopes of a gory reunion. Alas, Kykuit was as empty as a tomb; I was forced to settle for his wretched brother, William, living in Rockwood Hall, located nearby on the Pocantico Hills estate. Like his older brother John D., William Rockefeller was also an ambitious and aggressive monopolist, using his considerable family money to expand their influence as far he possibly could. Original co-founder of Standard Oil, he had quickly expanded to run a comparably vicious monopoly in the copper mines of Montana, succeeding beyond his wildest dreams, building what would eventually become the Anaconda Copper Corporation, the fourth richest corporation in the world. Setting up numerous puppet corporations, the Rockefeller brothers had played a bureaucratic shell-game to avoid accusations of monopoly, executing one brutal corporate buyout after another through these dummy corporations and taking advantage of the numerous loopholes which their millions entitled them to.

It is a curious footnote of William Rockefeller's life, and death, that on the night I killed him, he was already dying of multiple viruses which he had apparently contracted a week earlier. The newspapers had called it "double pneumonia," though I had to wonder at such a mass of strange and ominously suggestive facts. While visiting his boyhood home in Richford, New York, the 81-year-old William Rockefeller had been caught in a downpour of unexpected and unprecedented strength and frigidity. Underdressed on this particular occasion, he became instantly ill, his sickness steadily worsening throughout the week until, just seven days later, he was too sick to rise from his bed.

In the hours before sunrise on June 24th, after the attending relatives and nurses had finally fallen asleep, I let myself in through the patio door and made my way up to his bedroom. Gazing down at his sleeping body, I saw that his anatomy was completely infested with several different species of hostile organisms (some familiar, some not), all plainly visible to me. It took me three minutes to strangle him and about four to remove his brain, after which I absconded into the forest and feasted.

Curiously, though not surprisingly, the obituaries I read later, once again, neglected to mention that my victim had been strangled and de-brained, instead attributing his death to "double pneumonia." Later, one newspaper headline, which also blamed the weather, even went so far as to say that he had been killed by a "fatal rain." This curious, seemingly inaccurate, phrase immediately called to mind another provocative theory. Eerie descriptions of the oddly purposeful rain clouds which had unleashed the fatal flash flood in

Texas came abruptly to mind, as well as my own recollections of the seemingly sensitive thunder clouds I had seen waging war against the Tree Things near Leffert's Corners. Most compelling of all, however, was the anomalous lightning bolt that had savagely cleaved my offspring in two, which seemed to lend an appalling credence to the killer cloud theory. Relatedly, I found myself thinking about those vast and mysterious germ clouds, which several different governments had deployed on the battlefields of Belgium and France, and wondered if some of them hadn't perhaps been blown across the Atlantic to come ashore in America. I wondered if William Rockefeller had not, perhaps, been targeted by the Cloud Things as well. Admittedly, the fact that his death had come about through the combined efforts of the Cloud Things and me led me to wonder if there might not be some overlap between their agenda and my own, a certain similarity of purpose I had not previously considered.

I also paid a visit to Dr. Stephen Smith, yet another famous surgeon who was convalescing in the home of his sister in Montour. The 99 year-old surgeon was the author of such remarkable books as the shamelessly self-aggrandizing *The City That Was* as well as the widely read, ideologically driven, *Who Is Insane?*, in which he reiterates the bigoted notion of "mental defectives" (whom he deemed worthy of both incarceration and sterilization) and provides a rationale for ongoing surgical experimentation on the brains of incarcerated lunatics. Furthermore, as the State Lunacy Commissioner, and founder of the State Board of Health, Dr. Smith, like Dr. Bailey, had spent many years as a brain surgeon at Bellevue Hospital, performing hundreds of experimental surgeries and frequently lecturing on the subject of brain manipulation. Regarding his motives for these grotesque procedures, Dr. Smith states in his introduction that his "intent and purpose is to illustrate with as few technicalities as possible the illusive nature of insanity, its origin in the derangement of the functions of the brain cells, the extreme impressibility of these cells and our power to increase or repress their activities." In other words, Smith, and his many celebrated colleagues, were advancing the science of mind control, testing the limits of the mind's "impressibility," and looking to test and perfect these methods on their human subjects. Spearheading the formation of both the Metropolitan Board of Health and the American Public Health Association, the celebrated Dr Smith was perhaps best known for his belief, widely accepted by such men as John D. Rockefeller, that one hundred years was the correct lifespan for a human (a theory I would later have considerable reason to doubt). It gave me tremendous pleasure to kill this pathetic man.

On November 30th, I successfully infiltrated 292 Madison Avenue in New York City, the private residence of William Goodsell Rockefeller, Jr, son of the late William Rockefeller, and nephew of old John D. himself. As with the other Rockefellers, the apple had not fallen too far from the tree. William Goodsell had been a profoundly ambitious and power-hungry man. Shortly after graduating from Yale, William Goodsell had contracted the typhoid fever which very nearly killed him. Immediately after recovering his health, he was taken under the wing of his father and uncle at Standard Oil where he was "schooled in the intricacies of corporation management, using Standard Oil methods," which is to say, suppressing strikes and ruthlessly eliminating all competition through hostile buyouts. On the night I killed him, this well-connected robber baron was listed on the boards of the Brooklyn Union Gas Company (of which he was vice-president), the New York Mutual Gas Light Company, The Consolidated Copper Company, Oregon Short Line Railroad, Oregon-Washington Railroad and Navigation Company, and finally, The Consolidated Textile Company, where he served as director.

At nearly six feet tall, William Goodsell was giant of a man. His body, like his fathers, was similarly riddled with hostile organisms, several of which I could not identify. Killing and de-braining him was the work of a few short minutes though, here again, I had the feeling that I was merely performing the coup de grace on an already dying man. Like his father before him, William Goodsell was also said to have contracted "double pneumonia" from an unusually frigid rain, while attending a football game at Yale a week before his death, reviving the unsettling notion of killer clouds whose choice of targets occasionally paralleled my own.

*   *   *   *

ROAMING THROUGH THE MASSACHUSETTS WILDERNESS DURING THE winter of 1922, kept warm by the raging gestational fever that consumed me, I felt invigorated beyond words. Not only was I made aware of a further enhancement of my already heightened senses, but I had an almost disturbing amount of physical energy; I found that I could walk thirty miles, through snow and ice and wind-blasted countryside, without noticeable fatigue. Twice I was caught in a freezing rain which soaked me to the bone. Both times I was deep in the frozen wilderness and forced to continue walking, yet I never once felt cold. Once I slept in a drainage ditch, in two inches of freezing cold water, and, though wet, I awoke refreshed, happy, and warm. However cold the outside air, my body seemed to compensate perfectly against it, maintaining an unshakable warmth, even in my extremities.

Had I not been "extremely pregnant" (to use Mary's unnerving phrase) I would have traveled directly to Boone Island. Ten miles outside of Sturbridge, however, I could tell that my gestation was coming to an end; very soon I would begin the terrifying process of birthing the horrors that were growing inside of me. Luckily, I was only about thirty five miles from Sudbury. I caught a bus from Oxford and made it to the house on Arnold Lane just as the sun was setting. There were a few children playing in the snowy fields south of the house but, other than that, the neighborhood was deserted. Crawling in through the open window, I saw no evidence that it had been entered. The layer of dust and mold on the hardwood floors revealed no human footprints; large sections of the walls, floor, and ceiling, however, contained the warm silhouettes of hundreds of nesting rodents.

Before checking the bones in the attic, checked the burrow in the basement. Making my way down the creaking, cob-webbed stairs, I approached the ring of stones and peered down into the hole which I had fallen into nearly four years earlier. The rusty shovel lay precisely where I had dropped it, unmoved in the intervening years. Upon lowering myself halfway down into this opening, I noted that the walls and floor of the tunnel were now crumbling to dust and that the ceiling had, in places, collapsed as if from dryness. In one spot, further along the left-hand passageway, the tunnel was so clogged with rocks and fallen debris that it was impassable. Moreover, the tunnel itself was hung with the unbroken webs of numerous spiders, a thing which seemed to prove beyond a doubt that these tunnels were no longer in use. I was reassured and, deeming the house to be free of lurking tunnel-dwellers, I resolved to settle in for what promised to be a long and difficult nativity.

I spent the next twenty-four hours cleaning up, wiping down the floors and counters, pulling down all the cobwebs and reinforcing the many barricaded windows and doors, at the same time being careful not to make any changes which would be visible from the outside. Several of the window curtains were beginning to rot through in places, threatening to fall, so I carefully replaced these with pieces of matching bed sheet, torn into squares, which I found elsewhere in the house. When I went to check on the bones in the attic I was overjoyed to see that the army of rats, hav taken up residence in the walls of the house, had also gnawed a great many of these bones away to almost nothing, reducing them to a fine grainy dust in pursuit of the tender marrow within. This suited my purposes perfectly and endeared me even more to these remarkable (though widely hated and misunderstood) creatures. I took this as a good omen; perhaps fortune was, once again, turning favorably in my direction.

Just two days after my arrival, however, I was once again overcome with that familiar feeling of debilitating nausea. Dragging my trusty box spring and blankets downstairs, I retreated into the cellar to await the inevitable.

PATIENT READER, TIME DEMANDS THAT I DESCRIBE WHAT CAME next in a fairly truncated overview rather than to give a detailed, chronological account. My time grows short and I must hasten to the end of my tale.

Of the many incredible things that went on over the next two-and-a-half year period, it would perhaps be best for me to avoid too many specifics. It would take too long to describe in detail the many perilous circumstances, the countless eerie omens, the innumerable gruesome developments that I encountered throughout this time. On a cold night in late December, after two days of tossing and turning on my make-shift bed, I began to vomit up vast numbers of larval offspring, including countless little white blobs which quickly grew into the familiar Red Things. These various offspring tended to come in waves, or litters. A single litter usually comprised about fifty or so, arriving over a period of several weeks; I was typically "delivering" between two or three offspring per day, for a period of about thirty days. Mercifully, between these stretches of contiguous birthings, there was always a corresponding, month-long reprieve when none occurred, and I was able to rest. When I wasn't convalescing on my mattress in the cellar, I was constantly, frantically, hunting, bringing home as much food as possible, both for myself and for my hungry brood. During that time, I became a portal of sorts, my body serving as a gateway by which these countless multiform beings inside me were finally able to enter our world.

I should take a moment here to describe some of these remarkable, and disturbingly numerous, offspring, whose size, shape, and behaviors were as fantastically varied as they were terrifying, simultaneously endearing and disturbing. Among the first litter there were many which I immediately recognized as embryonic versions of the Hidden Ones themselves. There were tiny Boulder Things (mere pebbles actually) and fledgling Tree Things, living puddles, sentient slime, shambling tripods, oozing cylinders with fins, and miniaturized Worm Things, as well as a whole host of unknown creatures who looked as if they might have come straight from the ocean floor. At a rate of roughly four a day, I continued to expel one fantastic being after another, until at last my quiet little farmhouse on Arnold Lane was utterly overrun.

These newborn creatures, while intensely eerie, were also strangely playful and garrulous, chasing and wrestling each other like puppies and emitting humorous honks, squeaks, and growls, high-pitched precursors to the deafening roars and bellows I had heard in the wild hills. The Walking Sticks (as I called the fledgling Tree Things) whistled and oscillated their appendages at each other, while the tiny Boulder Things emitted a sound not unlike the yowl of a tomcat. The white and red blobs were, in every case, entirely silent.

Approximately half of these curious larva departed within a week's time, never to return, while others lingered for months and clearly required further assistance. The more complex organisms were helpless for much longer periods, while the more primitive ones usually left when they were only three or four days old. On account of the many hungry newborns who stayed behind, I continued my lethal prowling in the nearby cities and towns, collecting countless corpses and smuggling them back to my waiting brood. Happily, my old hunting grounds were just as abundant as I remembered them and I had no trouble finding accessible victims. Maintaining a strong predilection towards vivisectors, military recruiters, and judges, I was a generous provider to my litter, keeping my many little man-eating horrors well-fed and well-cared for.

In short, this nearly three-year period of incubation, gestation, and murder was a nonstop carnival of horror. During those grueling months, I saw the human body crushed, shredded, picked-over, melted, absorbed, disintegrated, liquefied, and broken down to its most basic components; soon such sights simply ceased to shock or even upset me. I received an education in the various appetites (and feeding methods) of this trans-galactic, trans-dimensional menagerie. There were the brain-eaters, the heart-eaters, the skin-eaters, the blood-drinkers, the bone-melters, and just about every other sort of revolting dietary inclination one can imagine. The blobs, as a distinct group, seemed inclined towards brains in almost every case while the Walking Sticks were acid-tongued bone-eaters. The tiny, crab-like Boulder Things monopolized the ears, noses and lips, while the proto-Worm Things (winding red millipedes several feet long) had a strong preference for the tongues, eyes, and genitals. All, however, were opportunistic feeders, taking what they could from a finite source. Moreover, there was a strangely harmonious quality to the feasting of these many divergent creatures.

Often I had a ghastly mess to clean up, for what remained after these bloody feasts were heaps of body parts which, for whatever reason, had been deemed unfit for consumption. Diseased or otherwise poisoned tissue and organs, such as the lungs of smokers or livers swollen from heavy drinking (belonging mostly to the judges, as it turned out), were strictly avoided. Naturally, as had been the case with the Black Thing, the fingers and toes of these many corpses were also universally rejected.

Initially, with regard to disposing of all this rejected meat, I received unexpected and much-appreciated assistance from the rats in the walls. Many times, I saw these intrepid rodents emerge from their hiding places, and surreptitiously gorge themselves upon the offal left behind by the feasting monstrosities. Unfortunately, as my larval offspring grew and became more mobile, they began to chase, stalk, and otherwise harass the scavenging rats until, at long last, the rodents departed from the house, unwilling to cohabitate with my increasingly rambunctious and antagonistic litter. I never once saw any of my offspring actually kill, or even hurt, a rat — a fact which seemed to confirm that it was only civilized humanity who had reason to fear them.

* * * *

AS BEFORE, WHILE OUT STALKING MY QUARRY, I ALSO FOUND TIME TO visit various libraries, bookstores, and newsstands, to stay abreast of world events, especially those that pertained to my particular situation.

Finding myself in Cambridge once again, I was able to pick up a copy of Howard's "The Lurking Fear," in the newest issue of *Home Brew* magazine. The multi-generational horror which Howard's remarkable investigation unearthed is too large to be outlined again here; I can do no better than to direct my reader to seek out this singular narrative, bearing in mind all that I have described, and to judge for yourself. Reading Howard's account, I finally learned the true nature, and origins, of the chittering, many-headed horror whose burrow the Black Thing and I had inhabited. It was also from this account that I learned of the final fate of that dreadful fragment which the lightning had cleaved so brutally from my offspring, that night in the abandoned squatter hamlet. I was given cause to reflect, once again, upon my theory that there was a conflict going on between the Tree Things and the Cloud Things, and that the inhabitants of the tunnels beneath both Tempest and Overlook Mountains were recalcitrant Hidden Ones who had retreated deep into the bowels of the earth, where the punitive bolts of the Cloud Things could not reach them. Though, in the end, Howard had seen far less than I, there was nothing in his version of events which contradicted my theory — and numerous things which confirmed it.

Reading Howard's story made me long to see my friend again. Surmising that he must be back from Cleveland by now, I even considered going to visit him in Providence, but decided against this. As much as I wanted to see him, there was simply no sane reason to further endanger Howard, Aunt Annie, or myself, by showing up unannounced at their home and throwing everything into chaos yet again. Based on some of the things Howard had said in Boston, it was clear that my first visit to 598 Angell Street had coincided, almost to the day, with the onset of both Howard's enhanced senses and Susie's "hallucinatory madness." I had good reason to suspect that I may well have infected two out of three members of their household with my strange contagion.

And what about Aunt Annie? She was living like a prisoner in her own dark and shuttered house, locking herself away from those Hidden Ones who lurked in her front and side gardens, those imposter plants which I had heard pawing ceaselessly at the ground-floor windows of that gloomy townhouse. For all I knew, after my brief exchange with Aunt Annie on the doorstep in Providence, she too had developed enhanced senses and commenced creeping about in her neighbor's shrubbery.

There was still another reason why I did not go back to the house on Angell Street. I was haunted by the inexplicable feeling that I was going to see Howard again, soon, perhaps even at Boone Island. Nevertheless, I missed my friend terribly and I must have reread "The Lurking Fear" a hundred times or more over the next three years, as it was the closest I could come to being in his presence.

Housebound, often for days on end, I read numerous books, articles, and treatises, on a diverse array of subjects, including cannibalism, literary criticisms of civilization, essays on Natural Law, and the emergence of a curious art movement gaining momentum in France. To begin with, I read numerous classical philosophical texts, many of which, surprisingly enough, discussed the problem of cannibalism at great length.

The French philosopher Michel de Montaigne, for example, was known for making unfavorable comparisons between western civilization and the numerous cannibal societies of the world, concluding that the former was just as vicious as the latter, if not more so. In his essay "On Cannibals," I found the following anecdote. The tribal chief of a savage region, after visiting Rouen, France, was asked what he thought of the great and proud city. "Very strange!" the chief famously replied. "Strange that there were amongst us, Men full and cramm'd with all manner of Conveniencies, whilst in the mean Time, their Halves were begging at their Door, lean, and half-starv'd with Hunger and Poverty. Strange that the starving Wretches did not take the others by the Throats, or set Fire to their Houses."

I read Daniel Defoe's *Robinson Crusoe*, Locke's "Essays on the Law of Nature," and Montesquieu's "Essay on Natural Law," whose convoluted ethical discussions of cannibalism intrigued and amused me no end.

In *Histoire et Description Generale de la Nouvelle France*, Francois Xavier de Charlevoix seems to excuse cannibalism only when it is done by marooned Europeans, only to avoid starvation and, ideally, with the victims' consent. He condemns, however, the cannibalism of savages in all cases. In his treatise "The Law of Nature and Nations," Samuel Pufendorf warns the reader not to condemn morally those who kill and eat their fellow man, so long as they do so only to avoid starvation. Nearly one hundred years later, Jean Barbeyrac, the French physician, professor and translator of Pufendorf, agreed, adding that we may only kill and eat someone who is less useful to society than we are. Like Charlevoix, however, both Pufendorf and Barbeyrac roundly condemned the cannibalism of pagan savages. Bound up in these arguments, inevitably, was the question of who legitimately possesses the sovereign right to kill and make use of his fellow man. In most cases, these philosophers ended up arguing that this right is reserved for kings only, revealing, in a curious way, the extent to which a king's legal right to kill and punish his subjects as he sees fit is one of the shaky foundation stones upon which all modern civil authority rests. These readings revealed the political uses of labeling people as cannibals and pagans, since doing so robbed them of any legitimate right over their lives, paving the way for the expropriation of their lands. A disturbingly large percentage of these philosophers wrestled with the question of whether or not cannibals were even human. Aristotle himself argued that cannibals were so inherently degraded that they were useful only as slaves.

On the other hand, I also encountered men like Rochefort, Raynal, Du Tertre, and Rousseau, who argued that the cannibal natives of the Caribbean, among others, had been grossly misrepresented by travelers and historians and that, in actuality, these primitive natives were, in most cases, happier, healthier, and even more beautiful than Europeans. To this end, they formed arguments against the slaughter and enslavement of Indians and even called into question the religion which provided a rationale for such practices. Often times these self-appointed defenders of the Noble Savage argued that taboos against cannibalism were in fact merely cultural, filling many pages with graphic descriptions of American and European customs which would be considered abhorrent by citizens of the so-called savage nations (such as animal husbandry, the disciplinary whipping of children, and even colonialism itself). These thinkers seemed to follow in the footsteps of Herodotus who, quoting Pindar, once proclaimed, "nomos panton basileus" (culture is king of all). Or, as the Abbé Noel-Antoine Pluche once said, Mankind's biggest problem is an "excess of Reason." Elsewhere, Abbé Pluche boldly states, "The dominion of man is universal and he does not degenerate into barbarity except when the respite of his conscience transforms him into a monster." Obviously, I had many good laughs making my way through all this strangeness, though some of it (like the idea that civilized humanity is suffering from an excess of Reason) gave me pause.

Several months later, I came upon a fascinating document called the *Surrealist Manifesto*, which, in a language perfectly mirroring my own feelings on the subject, contained nothing less than a refutation and rejection of the basic principles of rationality itself. The author of this remarkable document was the French writer André Breton, whom I immediately recognized as a kindred spirit and comrade. The criticisms put forward in the Manifesto thrilled and inspired me almost as much as the many anarchist books which Bartolo had sold me all those years before. One may easily imagine my astonishment when, in the course of reading this manifesto, I came upon the following remarkable passage. I trust my reader will indulge me if I quote at length.

"Under the pretense of civilization and progress, we have managed to banish from the mind everything that may be rightly or wrongly called superstition, or fancy; forbidden is any kind of search for truth which is not in conformance with accepted practice... But if the depths of the human mind contains within it strange forces capable of augmenting those on the surface, or of waging a victorious battle against them, then there is every reason to seize them!"

On the subject of the future, Breton was rather optimistic.

"On the basis of these discoveries a current of opinion is finally forming whereby the human explorer will be able to carry his investigation much further, no longer confining himself solely to the most summary realities. It is my belief that the collective imagination is on the point of reasserting itself."

These sentiments recalled to mind Galleani's comments about how hierarchical civilization was hampering human development, creating a society of lop-sided, under-developed automatons, increasingly cut off from their own far-reaching and limitless power. Howard had spoken of the same problem when he had mentioned the manual stimulation of nerve clusters in the brain, in both ancient and modern times, as a possible solution. I also thought of Mary's notion that the fully indoctrinated mind, mired in its own systematized rigidity, might be incapable of accessing its own hidden powers.

Recalling Howard's mother Susie, as well as the little girl on North Brother Island who could hear the stars roaring back and forth to each other, I had to wonder at a society that had labeled both of these uniquely gifted women "mad" and locked them away in hospitals. I had to wonder at the increasingly widespread suppression of anyone who described events, situations, or beings which fell outside the parameters of what was considered "sane and rational reality." There is no doubt in my mind that the asylums of the world must contain vast numbers of inmates whose only crime was that they had glimpsed, or possibly even interacted with, Hidden Ones, and had been naive enough to share these experiences with others. In this, our Golden Age of enlightened Psychology, to make such statements publicly is to invite incarceration.

Elsewhere in this Manifesto, while advocating that people permit themselves to "go insane," Breton strongly emphasized the importance of heeding ones dreams. Near the end he laments, "It is, in fact, inadmissible that this considerable portion of psychic activity has today been so grossly neglected. I have always been amazed at the way an ordinary observer lends so much more credence and importance to waking events than to those occurring in dreams... Thus the dream finds itself reduced to a mere parenthesis, as does the night. And like the night, dreams generally contribute little to furthering our understanding. This curious state of affairs seems to me to call for certain reflections... I believe in the future resolution of these two states, asleep and awake, dream and reality, which are so seemingly contradictory, into a kind of absolute reality, a surreality, if one may so speak. It is in quest of this surreality that I am going, certain not to find it but too unmindful of my death not to calculate to some slight degree the joys of its possession."

Considering the prophetic, revelatory and, at times, downright instructional nature of most of my own dreams, I was in no position to disagree with such sentiments.

Among the many rebel prophets who had signed this Manifesto, I came across one Antonin Artaud, surrealist filmmaker, poet, and playwright, in whose writings I found chilling descriptions of horrors which were only too familiar to me. In several poems he made references to a vast, sentient mass of "Black Fat" which was stalking him, calling to him, and trying to engulf and suffocate him. In dreams, he described graphic visions of entire cities and towns crushed and engulfed beneath shimmering waves of this same "Black Fat." These descriptions made me think of the huge flying Black Thing from my dream and I wondered if perhaps the Con Tiki Viracocha, or else some lesser manifestation thereof, was not also visiting Artaud in his dreams, just as it had done with the Sapa Inca Hatun Tupac, and all the other Sapa Incas as well.

At the library at Harvard, in the hall of rare and forbidden books (which I was able to sneak into after hours), I read large sections of an illegal English translation of de Sade's *Juliette*, published in France in 1907. In the pages of this abominable tome, I was horrified to discover the character of Minski, the cannibal giant, who seemed, from the description given, to be an Encerrado of the highest type. Furthermore, through the medium of this cannibal character, de Sade was able to make numerous astonishing and unnervingly familiar declarations.

Shunning all but human meat, the character Minski advocates a purely cannibal diet, extolling its many health benefits and chiding his reluctant guests (in the style of Rousseau) for their squeamishness. Regarding a proffered piece of human meat, he states, "Try some! It is absurd to turn up one's nose at anything. Aversions are based upon nothing but the lack of habit. All viands are fit nourishment for man. Nature offers them all to him

333

and it is no more or less outrageous, after all, to eat a human than to eat a chicken."

Elsewhere, Minski states, "Much philosophy is needed to understand me. Yes, I know it. I am a monster, something vomited forth by Nature to aid her in the destruction whereof she obtains the stuff she requires for creation. I am without peer in abomination, alone in my kind... All the invectives the lesser beings gratify me with, I know them by heart. Powerful enough to have need of nobody, wise enough to find sufficiency in solitude, to detest all mankind, to brave its censure, to jeer at its attitude toward me, experienced enough, intelligent enough to explode every creed, to flout every religion, to send every god to hell for the Devil's fucking, proud enough to abhor every government, to refuse every tie, to ignore every check, to consider myself above every ethical principle, I am happy... I dread no man, and I live content."

I shall probably never have occasion to be buried in an earthly grave. But in the event that I should somehow be killed before I have a chance to depart this earth, my only request would be that this last quotation be engraved upon my tombstone.

*　*　*　*

IN THE MANY NEWSPAPERS I READ WHILE IN TOWN, I FOUND numerous portentous tragedies — a preview (as it now seems to me) of what was to come. Looking back on it, there was no shortage of evidence that civilization was coming undone.

My reader may well imagine my distress upon reading of such catastrophes as the Great Kanto earthquake and fire in Japan on September 1, 1923, where the death toll had reached 140,000.

Reading through these same papers I also came across numerous references to the still-rampant cholera epidemic, then sweeping through India and North America. These two nations, whose citizens lived primarily in urban centers, were especially vulnerable on account of population density. This led me to medical journals where I read several articles documenting its fatal progress through the affected regions, wiping out millions of lives and leaving social and political chaos in its wake. I learned that this most recent outbreak was actually the sixth wave of a shockingly virulent cholera pandemic which had been ravaging its way across the globe for 100 years, from India to China to Europe and beyond. It eventually spread to Russia, Germany, the British Isles, America, Mexico, Spain, and Arabia. By 1923, the overall death toll was already in the hundred millions and it showed no sign of abating.

I learned of the many cholera riots which had erupted throughout the affected areas, where hundreds of thousands of people who had been labeled "infected" had fought back violently against a quarantine program, which they insisted was being selectively enforced. The most well-documented riots occurred in Russia, Germany, and England in the latter half of the 19th century. In Russia, the riots had been triggered by the widely held belief that the Tsarist government was exploiting the cholera epidemic and using it as a way to deliberately exterminate or infect certain undesirable portions of the peasant population. These Russian riots, the largest of which had occurred in Sevastopol and Tambov, were eventually suppressed and the impoverished rioters exterminated exactly as they had originally predicted. This was not a new phenomenon. In Liverpool, at the height of the 1832 epidemic, local people had rioted against the police quarantine and the medical authorities when it was observed that the doctors, who were using the many cholera victims for anatomical dissection, were only protecting the wealthier sections of the city's population, allowing the poor to die in droves. Eventually however, the local clergy were able to persuade the rioters to desist and to comply with the quarantine programs. A similar situation had occurred in Hamburg Germany, though bayonets, rather than religion, were used to quell that crowd's fury.

Leafing through several international newspapers I learned of the latest political developments in the Russian situation. Here I was sickened to learn of the slaughter that had happened on the island naval base of Kronstadt, where over two thousand sailors, soldiers, and citizens who had mutinied against Bolshevik state control had been gunned down by soldiers. Their demands had been simple. They wished to run their own city and for each citizen to own his home or farm. They demanded freedom of the press for everyone, including the anarchists, and to elect their own leaders through small locally run elections. For this they were exterminated. Leon Trotsky had led the charge. Those not killed outright were summarily labeled "dangerous insurgents" and executed through the Bolshevik court system.

Throughout this period, the phenomenally talented Ukrainian peasant Nestor Makhno had had stunning tactical victories against German, Austrian, and Ukrainian nationalist armies. By the beginning of 1921, Makhno and his Black Army of stateless anarchists had been crushed in a series of battles with Bolshevik forces along the Ukrainian border. Lenin at this time was quite ill, having suffered several strokes which had left him unable to speak. It seemed to me that the whole world was watching Russia with bated breath, realizing perhaps that the way things went in Russia would have implications for us all.

*   *   *   *

THE YEARS PASSED, AND IN SO BIZARRE A MANNER THAT I AM reluctant to describe more. During this period, from December of 1922 to June of 1925, my ever-replenishing brood and I continued to eke out our strange cannibal existence in the abandoned farmhouse. There were many times when I was moved to tears by the strangely beautiful Beings in my care, whose intelligence, adaptability, and eagerness to learn often astounded me. The offspring who stayed behind needed constant food and attention; to amuse myself and the little ones, I often invented absurd games to pass the time, teaching them such standards as hide-and-go-seek, fetch, and follow-the-leader. I soon learned that they loved when I told them stories or sang them songs. I would sit down in an old rocking chair, like some alien Mother Goose, and they would gather at my feet, like a flock of schoolchildren at story time, peering up at me with eyes full of wonder and curiosity, as I regaled them with fabricated tales of fantastic adventures, or else sang them the few nursery rhymes I recalled from my own youth.

Among that final litter of miniature monstrosities, there had been one tiny Tree Thing which seemed to struggle with some sort of developmental impairment. It was noticeably smaller and weaker than the others of its kind, and often had trouble keeping up with the other Walking Sticks, stumbling and falling painfully on the hardwood floors and emitting a sickly mewling. Twice I saw it walk straight into a wall and, when at last it fell down the stairs and injured itself, I began to pay it special attention. Feeding it separately from the others and observing it closely, I made a special effort to learn precisely what was ailing it. To give it the benefit of plentiful food, I fed it the corpses of two local judges, whose skeletons it single-handedly devoured over a period of six days. This extra sustenance seemed to help immensely, and afterwards I noticed immediate improvements in both its balance and coordination.

In addition to these many heartwarming moments, there were also times when I feared I might lose my mind from the sheer monotony of this life of predation and parenting. I was, at times, so physically exhausted that I would lock myself away in the upstairs bedroom for hours, desperate for silence, solitude, and undisturbed sleep. The nights were often maddeningly full of disruptions and disturbances, incidents of noisy squabbling and fussing which sometimes made getting a good night's sleep impossible. Some of these tiny monstrosities were simply nocturnal, while others, like the tiny Tree Things, would frequently yelp and bark fearfully in their sleep, as if tormented by frightening dreams. The tiny Boulder Things were incessant snorers; I sometimes had to nudge them, or else roll them over, to get them to stop.

Many times, I felt like some sort of latter day Jack the Ripper — that is, if Jack the Ripper had also had a full-time job as a zookeeper.

XXII

"And there was afterwards writ a careful and proper treatise, (which) set out that there did be ruptures of the Aether, the which did constitute secret and horrid Doorways In The Night, as those more fanciful ones did name them; And through these shatterings, which may be likened unto openings — there did come into this particular Condition of Life, those Monstrous Forces of Evil that did dominate the Night, and which many did hold surely to have been given this improper entrance through the foolish and unwise wisdom of those olden men of learning that did meddle overfar with matters that did reach, in the end, beyond their understanding.
William Hope Hodgson

IN LATE DECEMBER OF 1925, THE LAST OF THIS STRANGELY rambunctious tribe of monsters moved on, vacating the sanctuary of the barricaded farmhouse and heading east towards Boston. Interestingly, before they left, many of these departing offspring actually came and sought me out. Sometimes alone and other times in groups, they would linger near my feet and serenade me, emitting all manner of tender noises, expressing their gratitude for the nurturing and nourishing environment which I had provided. This endearing display brought tears to my eyes on several occasions. Some of these little serenaders had lush droning voices, dimly reminiscent of bagpipes, awkwardly played and badly out of tune, while others emitted curious wheezing vocalizations not unlike the mewling of a kitten or the braying of a mule. Each creature had its own unique sound, though the blobs remained eerily silent.

The impaired Tree Thing lingered for about three weeks after the others had gone, not quite able to hunt for itself yet and still perfecting its spider-like mode of ambulation. Not quite ready myself, I remained in the farmhouse, assisting the injured Tree Thing and even taking it hunting with me twice, so that it would know how and where (and upon whom) to feed. It wasn't far behind the others, and four days after our second hunting trip, I awoke to find that it too had disappeared into the surrounding forest. Shortly thereafter, I too departed from the farmhouse, heading north toward Boone Island.

Stopping off in the town of Woburn to replenish my supplies, I glimpsed a portentous newspaper headline which chilled me. It announced the disappearance of the aforementioned Percy Fawcett, the eccentric English explorer who had dreamed of an ancient stone metropolis buried in the Amazon jungle. Amid much fanfare, set off with his son and a friend to find it. There were numerous articles in numerous papers, and I read every one I could find. In telling of his disappearance, many of these articles also described some of his earlier explorations, several of which contained details that frightened me in that old familiar way. I learned how, on his 1913-14 expeditions, Fawcett, and several associates, had tramped through the jungles of northern Bolivia, where he had spoken with elders of the Siriono', Echojas, and Lengua tribes, receiving from them more confirmation of the lost city of his dreams. Upon learning that Fawcett had actually gone and spoken with elders of the Lengua tribe, I recalled what I'd read of the ghoulish Corpse-Eating Cult of Leng, feeling my skin crawl, and shuddering on his behalf.

As I now learned, tragedy had struck the most recent Fawcett Expedition and, sometime in June of 1925, deep in the jungles of northern Brazil, Percy Fawcett, his son Jack and a long-time friend by the name of Raleigh Rimell, had disappeared without a trace. After months of steady communication, in the form of weekly hand-delivered progress reports, which were dutifully reprinted in several of the major papers, thousands of readers had become fascinated by the search for Fawcett's hypothetical city. Reports of the expeditions mysterious disappearance made the front cover of most of the major newspapers and several very public rescue attempts were already in the offing. At the time of their disappearance, the Fawcett Expedition had just entered the dangerous Upper Xingu River region, an area known for its hostile cannibal natives, purposely avoided by the many surrounding tribes. Fawcett had gone and spoken with several similarly shunned groups before, alone and unarmed, and always he had returned unharmed and with more corroboration of his lost city. Certainly, he had proven many times over that he was uniquely skilled at befriending even the most dangerous cannibal tribes (the dreaded Cult of Leng, no less!), yet his disappearance did not bode well. The newspapers and journals were full of frightful speculations.

I also learned several more things about Percy Fawcett which intrigued me and reminded me, in a startling way, of myself. Despite his pretentious Victorianism and his sadly typical fondness for eugenics, for example, the man had unabashedly rejected civilization as a whole, explicitly spurning its many modern conveniences as "enfeebling," spending vast portions of his life far outside its borders.

Of foremost interest to me, however, was the way in which, over the course of his extensive travels among these cannibal tribes, Percy Fawcett had grown increasingly disenchanted, even disgusted, with Western civilization in general, making bold statements against it. Not content merely to criticize modern social conditioning, he even went so far as trying to consciously cleanse his mind of what he considered to be civilization's many crippling effects. To this end, he was a self-styled Nietzschean, a non-believer in systematized morality, a believer in transgression for the sake of enlightenment. One article quoted Fawcett to this effect. Contrasting his experiences among the Amazon tribes with the social and moral instruction he had received as a child, he had said, "I sought to uncivilize myself. I transgressed again and again the awful laws of traditional behavior and, in doing so, I learned a great deal. One might say... I found hidden parts of myself I never knew existed. There is absolutely no disgrace in 'going native.' On the contrary, in my opinion it shows a credible regard for the real things of life at the expense of the artificial. Civilization has a relatively precarious hold upon us and there is an undoubted attraction in a life of absolute freedom once it has been tasted."

More to the point, having observed (and secretly participated in?) countless cannibal rituals, Fawcett was boldly protective of the cannibal Indians he had met. After describing one ritual, in which the body of a beloved relative was "roasted over a fire... cut up and divided amongst the various families," he implored his Western readers not to condemn what they didn't understand, and to try to consider these things in a larger, less bigoted way. Like Montaigne, he was also in the habit of making unfavorable comparisons between modern society and tribal life. In his ongoing camaraderie with these primitive cannibal tribes, he stated, "My experience is that few of these savages are naturally 'bad,' unless contact with 'savages' from the outside world has made them so." Elsewhere, I found an intriguing statement he'd made in reference to public outrage over the cannibalism of the South American Indians. While careful to avoid anything that might sound like advocacy, Fawcett did not mince words. "Cannibalism," he stated, "at least provides a reasonable motive for killing a man, which is certainly more than you can say for civilized warfare." The more I read about this fellow, the more I liked him.

This was just the beginning of the eerie similarities which existed between Percy Fawcett and me. I also learned from these many articles that Colonel Fawcett was also known to be of an unusually, almost freakishly, hearty constitution. He was able to endure conditions no ordinary human being could bear. His prior colleagues and assistants who had accompanied him into the jungle were universally astonished at his almost inhuman stamina. James Murray, previously of the 1907 Shackleton Expedition to Antarctica, had famously accompanied Fawcett on a 1911 trek up the Heath River, marching from the shores of Lake Titicaca, through that lowland jungle which lies about a hundred miles due west of Machu Picchu and the Urubamba River Valley, in search of Fawcett's dream city. Murray, like so many of Fawcett's assistants, utterly unable to match Fawcett's superhuman pace, soon fell gravely ill. Three weeks into this trek the other members of the group began to succumb, one by one, to the unusually prevalent, fever-bearing parasites rampant in the surrounding jungle.

Henry Costin, who was also on this expedition, reported how over a succession of nights, he and the others were attacked in their sleep by vampire bats, who left bloody wounds upon their heads and hands. Upon waking to this awful discovery, Fawcett, despite having lost large amounts of blood through the bite-marks on his scalp, was unperturbed. Fawcett himself described how, early one morning, "we awoke to find our hammocks saturated with blood. For any part of our persons touching the mosquito-nets… or protruding beyond them were attacked by these loathsome creatures." Soon after, a fellow by the man of Manley fell ill with malaria. Costin was not far behind him, contracting an unknown jungle fever a few days later. Three days after that, James Murray noticed that his legs and arms had become infested with some kind of maggot, tunneling painfully through his flesh and causing sores that itched and burned. His body began to stink of decay and his feet swelled so monstrously that his shoes no longer fit him. Astonishingly, Fawcett remained immune through all of this and, despite repeated personal contact with his sick and infected companions, maintained an inexplicably perfect health. Numerous commentators remarked on the strangeness of this. In several different papers Fawcett was described as "fever-proof," possessing, as one writer put it, "a virtual immunity to tropical disease… There were other explorers who equaled him in dedication, courage and strength, but in his resistance to disease he was unique."

Others who had gone on expedition with Fawcett had similar tales to tell. Ernest Holt and Lewis Brown, who had traveled with Fawcett on the doomed 1920 expedition, had barely survived the experience. Like the others before them, they had returned diseased, infested, and infected, while Fawcett, despite months of immersion in the same hostile environments, remained immune. Even the various bloodsucking flies and mosquitoes seemed to avoid him, a thing which mystified all who traveled with him.

Hearing these descriptions of Fawcett's immunity to jungle conditions, I was further unnerved. Recalling how I had walked through freezing cold blizzards unaffected, engulfed in a fever which made me immune to cold, fatigue, and illness alike, I had to wonder if these anecdotes were not evidence that Percy Fawcett, like me, had a passenger which cleansed his blood of viruses and regulated his temperature, thus enabling him to endure the insufferable heat and pestilence of the jungle.

Fawcett himself attributed his constitution to his unique diet. Unwilling to elaborate on the particulars of his mysterious eating habits, he was once asked if he ate fish, to which he replied, "I never eat the flesh of beasts." Reading this, I wondered if Fawcett was not, like me, a vegetarian with the one exception of human meat.

Infinitely more horrifying, Percy Fawcett's curious air of invincibility had been apparent not just in the pestilential jungles of Amazonia, but in the trenches at Flanders where he had fought five years earlier. As a former military man, Fawcett had also raised eyebrows with the many horrors he had endured on the battlefield.

My reader will understand the uneasiness I felt upon learning that in December of 1917, while serving as a Lieutenant Colonel stationed in France, Percy Fawcett, along with many hundreds of other soldiers had been engulfed in a cloud of germ-infested mustard gas and thoroughly poisoned. Most of the soldiers did not survive this attack, but Fawcett and a few others managed to pull through. These survivors lay helpless for weeks and months on end, shrieking in agony, covered in blisters and oozing sores, blinded, gagging, and complaining to the nurses that their throats were closing and they were on the verge of suffocating. After being gassed, Fawcett was troubled for some time by the effects of the poison. His wife Nina was quoted in one article as saying that, after this incident, he was never "quite right."

There were certain statements which Percy Fawcett had made that revealed how it had been the War itself that had shattered his illusions and left him utterly disenchanted with civilization. In a letter reprinted in one of the English papers, Fawcett, writing from the trenches, had given the following description: "If you can, imagine 60 miles of front, to a depth of 1 to 30 miles, literally carpeted with dead, often in little hills. It is a measure of the price paid. Masses of men moved to the slaughter in endless waves, bridged the wires and filled the trenches with dead and dying. It was the irresistible force of an army of ants, where the pressure of the succeeding waves forced the legions in the front, willingly or unwillingly, into the shambles. No thin line could withstand this human tidal wave, or go on killing forever. It is, I think, the most terrible testimony to the relentless effect of an unbridled militarism. Civilization! Ye gods! To see what one has seen, the word is an absurdity. It has been an insane explosion of the lowest human emotions." Of the twenty million killed in the Great War, Fawcett was quoted as saying, "the whole business was suicide for Western civilization. For myself, I withdraw in disgust and I imagine many thousands must have come through those four years of mud and blood with a similar disillusionment." Like myself (and Howard, and Susie, and Mary, Bartolo, Galleani, and who knows how many more?), Percy Fawcett had somehow developed the ability to see through the Great Lie, the waking dream that is the myth of Human Progress, the myth of civilization. Something had enabled him to remove his nationalistic blinders and to see straight into the rotten heart of Modernity itself. Reading this, I was reminded of the *Surrealist Manifesto* and, reflecting on his statement that "many thousands must have (felt) a similar disillusionment," I knew that the true number must be significantly higher.

For all these reasons and more, I wondered if Percy Fawcett was an Encerrado, a mortal man who, like myself, was slowly and inexplicably taking on the attributes of an ancient Peruvian Demon.

Simultaneously eager and reluctant to reach my destination, I resumed my final journey north to Boone Island which, according to my map, was located about six miles off the coast of Maine, near Cape Neddick.

*   *   *   *

BEING MY LAST YEAR ON PLANET EARTH, I SUPPOSE I WILL ALWAYS BE sentimental about 1926. At every opportunity, I scoured the papers furiously, uncertain what I was looking for, but strangely certain that I was on the brink of an amazing discovery. All I can say is that there seemed an unusually high number of tragedies, group folly, plagues, crushed rebellions and otherwise ominous events afoot.

And yet, as always, Civilized Humanity was carrying on, marching endlessly forward with (as Fawcett said) "the irresistible force of an army of ants, where the pressure of the succeeding waves forced the legions in the front, willingly or unwillingly, into the shambles," seemingly without regard to the larger nightmare unfolding around them. Alongside articles documenting the many horrors of the war and its aftermath, the newspapers told many idiotically cheerful stories, to counterbalance the real-life nightmares with inanities designed to inspire a kind of abstract, almost child-like, optimism toward Western Civilization. One such story especially caught my interest on account of the fact that it involved two themes dear to my heart: ancient mythology and grave-robbing.

Having been, at one time, an amateur exhumer of corpses, I took a particular interest in the discovery of Tutankhamen's tomb in October of 1925. Most of my readers will already know the story of how the British archaeologist Howard Carter, during his years-long exploration of the Valley of the Kings, finally penetrated the hidden room which held the six-hundred year-old mummified corpse of the pharaoh Tutankhamen. "Tutmania" was sweeping through the English and American press, as readers clambered for a glimpse of the mummy, imbuing it with an almost religious significance. Ruminating on the descriptions of the well-preserved corpse, I could not help but wonder how an ancient brain such as Tutankhamen's might taste, and what effects, if any, might come of eating it. Sadly, as I later discovered, the Egyptians, believing the soul to dwell in the heart, ascribed no particular significance to the brain and so disposed of it along with the other viscera.

I picked up a newspaper in Medford and was astonished to learn of the sinking of the *PS Washington Irving*, the steamship I had ridden from Albany to West Point and, upon which I had had that frightful premonition of a shipwreck, five years earlier. As in my dream, the wreck had occurred while the ship had been engulfed in a heavy morning fog, near the Debrosses Street Pier, where it had collided with an oil barge. Happily, most of the passengers survived. Three persons were said to have drowned; a steward by the name of B. Woods (whose body was later found in a submerged cabin), a woman named Wylma Hoag and her three-year-old daughter, Mary. The bodies of Wylma and Mary Hoag, however, were never recovered. Curiously, several eye-witnesses, who say they saw the mother and daughter go down for the last time, swore that the bodies, visible on account of their white clothing, had not actually drowned but rather, after sinking a few yards below the surface, suddenly became rigid and swam off, fishlike, into the depths of the river. Naturally, these descriptions were dismissed as the ravings of "panic-stricken" persons.

Most grievous of all to me, however, was news of my friends Bartolo the bookseller and Freddy the teetotaler, in the ongoing, increasingly hopeless, trial. Despite a flimsy case against them, evidence of extreme judicial bigotry, countless letters of protest (by such well-respected thinkers as Albert Einstein, George Bernard Shaw, and H.G. Wells), and repeated mass demonstrations in all the major cities of Europe and beyond, I feared that my friends were going to be executed. The authorities wished to make an example of them and, apart from an actual jailbreak, there seemed precious little hope of freeing them. The uselessness of peaceful protest was never more pitifully apparent. If I had thought I stood a ghost of a chance, I might have gone and tried to break them out of the Charlestown State Prison myself. Alas, despite my numerous enhancements, I was not bulletproof. While passing through the woods north of Lynn, Massachusetts, near the barn where I had once been made a temporary member of the Galleani Gang, I sat down upon the hillside and wept for my friend Bartolo and the soft-spoken Freddy.

As for Luigi Galleani, he was gone, "deported with the rest of them," as one newspaper gloated. I could not help wondering where that incredible and seemingly indestructible man would turn up next.

What did it all signify? Was there a pattern to all this apparent mayhem — the disappearance of Fawcett, the vicious and ongoing persecution of rebels, ships colliding in the fog? The newspapers endlessly documented these tragedies, but no meaningful analysis was ever forthcoming. Was there something to be gleaned from it all? Were certain alien influences triumphing over others? Or was it just the usual, mostly random, horror that is our modern industrial age? More and more, as I looked around, it seemed that the collapse of civilization was well underway.

*   *   *   *

ON A COLD, CLEAR DAY, I ARRIVED ON THE ODDLY DESERTED STREETS of York, Maine. Determined to learn all that I could about Boone Island and to see if I could discover any peculiar legends or bizarre disappearances associated with it, I set off directly toward the harbor. Walking along Long Sands Road on that December afternoon, I recall that the sky was thick with (fairly normal looking) clouds and that the air was oddly still. Walking through the empty streets, I had the impression of a city under quarantine. Many of the windows were shuttered, despite the midday sun, and a curious pressure in the air, an almost electrical tension, seemed to grow stronger as I approached the center of town. Following the signs, and the cries of the gulls, I made my way down to the harbor. Along the wharf, I noticed a distressingly high number of patrolling coppers, who, disappearing and reappearing along the avenues, seemed to be searching the faces of all they met. Careful to avoid them, I cut through an alley behind a row of warehouses and continued on to the docks.

Arriving at the far end of the harbor, I saw a group of men smoking and speaking in low voices. They were sailors of various ranks, some lowly, others of obviously higher status, standing out on the very end of the longest pier. They were not looking out at the sea, as one might expect, but were gazing back, almost apprehensively, at the city itself. From the moment I stepped out onto the causeway, I felt them watching me with an unblinking scrutiny, studying me as I nonchalantly made my way down the road. Thinking that they might be a good source of local information, I headed toward them.

Still several hundred yards away, with my enhanced senses I could see and hear them quite clearly, their lowered voices coming across the water. A grey-bearded man was telling a story which held the others rapt. Upon hearing the very first sentence, I knew that trouble had come to York, Maine.

"Anyway, the body was all chewed up," I heard him say. "Headless... or very nearly so. The guys over at the winch house said that they found another

345

body over near York Maine Beach that was in a similar condition." An awful look passed from face to face, as grey beard continued. "Hell, I was walking through Hartley Park about three days ago when I spied a crowd of people standing around gawking at something lying in the grass beside the path. I walked over and saw that it was the clothing of a man — pants, shoes, socks, shirt, everything. They lay in a twisted heap, absolutely soaked in blood, but otherwise perfectly intact. The empty socks were still inside the shoes and the shirt was still buttoned up! Here and there, tiny bone fragments were visible, but there was no trace of the body. It was as if he had suddenly evaporated into a mist of blood. The police arrived shortly after, shoveled the whole mess into a metal cylinder, loaded it into a van, and drove off."

"I heard the body they found on the beach had its face eaten off," said a young Scotsman with a black cap.

"They can't tell yet if it's man or beast, since the injuries leave no obvious clue. The one body had bite marks all over it, bite marks which may or may not be human. The other body had its skull cracked open and emptied of its contents. In some cases, like in Hartley Park, the body appears to have been liquefied, or vaporized."

"Good god!" muttered an older man with white hair, who had been listening intently. "So that's why all these coppers are here."

"Well, no. It's not just because of the bodies," corrected the grey beard. "There's also been several suicides here over the past few weeks. People coming down here and leaping into the sea. Right here off the docks."

"Who is jumping into the sea?" the white-haired man asked, horrified. "What do you mean?"

"I'll tell you later," the grey-bearded man said, glancing over at me. "It looks like we've got company."

By now I was a mere twenty feet from them and, calling out in a friendly way, I asked if they knew any place where I could rent a small skiff or rowboat for a trip around the bay.

"Not from around here, are you, mister?" a bald, heavy set man asked.

"No," I replied, "I've only just arrived actually. Why do you ask?"

"There's no skiffs for rent today," grey beard replied, "Nor any tomorrow. Nor the day after that."

"May I ask why?" I asked.

He seemed on the verge of answering when, suddenly, over on the far side of the dock, our attention was drawn to the sound of someone shouting as several policemen approached. They surrounded a middle-aged man who had been walking along the wharf road; one of the policemen was shouting and the man held up his arms protectively, as if anticipating a blow. The copper continued to lecture him for nearly a minute, while the others stood in a ring around him. To my relief, they moved on, leaving the man badly shaken, but unharmed. Shaking his head, the grey-bearded man turned and looked into my eyes.

Seizing the opportunity, I decided to steer the discussion back to the subject of the strange suicides, which my approach had interrupted. Looking contemptuously over at the policemen on the wharf, I said, "Something fishy is going on around here. The place is crawling with coppers. I just overheard two of them, over by the train station, talking about a rash of suicides happening down here by the docks."

The grey beard looked sideways at the others, and a grave look passed between them. The white-haired man shrugged wordlessly and then nodded.

"We were just talking about that," the grey-bearded man said. "What do you know about it?"

"Not much," I shrugged, "only that, in addition to all the mutilated bodies they have been finding around town, there have also been several suicides down here along the wharf." The men nodded at this and so, extrapolating liberally, I continued, "The coppers suspect that the corpses and the suicides are somehow connected but they don't seem to know how." This, of course, gave the impression that I knew almost as much as they did, possibly more. The effect it had was precisely as I had hoped.

"Hell, it's an epidemic!" the grey-beard said roughly. "We've already had three this week. They are keeping it out of the papers to avoid a panic but there have been numerous sightings of ordinary folks drowning themselves in the sea. That's why we're posted here on lookout. The suicides mostly happen at dawn and dusk."

"Who are these people that are killing themselves?" I asked. "Are they local residents?"

"No. They aren't from here," added an elderly bald man in a pea coat. "They arrive on the train, or on foot. No one knows who they are or where they come from. It's the strangest damned thing! I've been working on these docks for twenty-seven years now and I've never seen anything like it."

"What did these people look like?" I asked, my pulse rising, "Were they remarkable in anyway?"

The others immediately looked at the young Scotsman, who seemed greatly agitated by my question.

"Sure," he blurted, "I saw one of them myself. He was a great big giant of a fellow. He was the first. Arrived here at dawn, alone and on foot. I was standing outside the Red Lion Tavern at about four in the morning when he passed me by without so much as a sideways glance. He was frightfully big and mean-looking, seven, maybe eight feet tall and thick as a house, staggering too, as if he was half in the bag. Several of the patrolling coppers saw him but seemed hesitant to approach. They followed him instead, and then I followed them, at a safe distance, of course."

Hearing this description had made me think immediately of Legion the giant, and I was suddenly, surprisingly, anxious for his safety.

"What happened then?" I asked nervously.

"Well this big, drunk giant, after stumbling straight through the middle of town, headed directly toward the harbor, staggered down to the end of this here pier and dove straight in! He never came up again. The coppers were stunned. They shined their electric torches everywhere, even commandeered a rowboat and searched for his body. They never found nothing. They are guessing he sank and got dragged out by the undertow."

"I overheard as much from the coppers," I lied, "but there were others too, right?"

"Two days later," the young Scotsman continued, "three women were walking along York Beach, right around sunrise, when they saw a young lady with long black hair walk down to the water's edge, take off all her clothes, and walk straight into the surf. She was extremely pale and thin, they said, with unusual scars all over her back. None of them recognized her and all three ladies agreed that she was definitely not a local. They called out to her but she glared at them so fiercely that they stayed back. A minute later, she dove under the waves and did not resurface. Ocean's probably forty degrees this time of year. No human being could survive that!"

Unnerved by the description of the "pale and thin young lady with long black hair" and "unusual scars," I thought instantly of Carmilla, and of her encounter with Howard on the train ride home from Leffert's Corners. Had he told her about his theory of a portal on Boone Island? Had this prompted her to come here as well? And what about the bodies found with semi-human bite marks on them? To whom did they belong?

"There was also that fellow who disappeared last week," added the bald man, lighting up his pipe. "He was an odd sort, they said, strangely proportioned and wearing them old fashioned clothes. He came by here last week. Wanted to rent a rowboat, just like you. He set off, alone, at sunset, rowing due east, toward Boone Island, I reckon. It was late and the water was getting choppy. He never came back. Three days ago, the rowboat he rented washed ashore about three miles south of here, undamaged but empty." He pointed down the coast, squinting at the horizon. "There's been no sign of him since." My heart jumped when I heard this description of Howard, but I kept my face expressionless.

"That is strange," I said, looking from one face to another. "Do you think all those mutilated and decapitated bodies they are finding in the parks and elsewhere are connected with these weird suicides?" A long thoughtful pause followed.

"Whatever it is that's tearing open people's faces and sucking their brains out, certainly ain't human!" said the white-haired man.

There was another pause.

"Well now I don't know why you'd say that," replied the Scottish youth, with a smirk. "They caught that fellow over in Germany a few years back who did precisely that, and a whole lot more besides."

"What's that now?" I asked, suddenly turning towards him.

"Sure, sure, it was all over the papers last year. Fritz Haarman was his name. They called him the Werewolf of Hanover."

"Oh, yes," muttered the bald man in the pea coat, shrinking visibly. "The Wolf Man. I remember reading about him."

"What did he do?" I asked, my mouth suddenly dry.

"What did he do?" mocked the Scotsman. "He killed and butchered a whole bunch of people is what he did! They may never know the full count but some estimate it was around forty. They say he lured his victims back to his apartment in Hanover where he strangled them, or else bit them viciously on the neck, letting them slowly bleed to death. Then he butchered them like cattle. He later confessed to being a cannibal and a blood-drinker. What's more, the portions of human meat he did not eat, he claimed to have sold on the black market, to a wealthy anonymous clientele."

"What?" I asked.

"Sure!" he laughed. "Sorry to be the one to tell you this mister, but the trafficking of human meat has been going on for a long time now! In secret, of course."

"How many did you say this fellow killed?" I asked, eager to redirect the discussion.

"Twenty-seven, that they could prove," replied the grey beard. "Young men mostly, runaways and male prostitutes, or else vagrants and street urchins."

"How on earth did he conceal such activities from his neighbors and co-workers?" I asked, somewhat disingenuously.

"It's amazing the horrors that go on right under people's noses," said the bald man in the pea coat. The others nodded grimly.

"Those poor boys," I said, wincing. "Too bad."

"Yes, it is too bad," groaned the Scottish youth with a strange smile. "It's too bad Fritz Haarman didn't develop a taste for policemen or priests, eh?"

This statement set the others laughing.

"Or landlords!" added one.

"Or politicians!" said another.

"Or judges!" I chimed in with a chuckle. A smile of recognition passed between us. The laughter eventually faded away.

I stood there talking with these gentlemen for nearly two hours. We dwelt, oddly enough, upon the topic of cannibalism for most of this discussion. Most notably, I learned that the Werewolf of Hanover, Fritz Haarman, had commenced his career of murderous cannibalism in September of 1918, continuing in that mode until he was caught in 1924. His period of active cannibalism was, more or less, perfectly framed in between my own two periods of active cannibalism, which spanned roughly from 1915 through 1918, and 1923 through 1926. The second thing I learned was that one of the main reasons Fritz Haarman had been able to get away with his crimes for so long was that, for years, he had been employed by the Hanover Police Department as a professional informer, and therefore enjoyed the protection of the police. Entirely above suspicion, Haarman had even participated in several investigations of the murders he himself had committed, casting aspersions upon numerous innocent persons, giving false leads and, as they later learned, directing the police to his personal enemies, various associates whom he felt had wronged him in some way. Another thing that had enabled him to go on killing so long was that all of his victims were poor, in many cases indigent teenage boys. The revelation of Haarman's horrific murders, and his secret involvement with the Hanover Police Department, had resulted in tremendous feelings of anger and mistrust directed, not just at Haarman, but at the entire law enforcement apparatus that had enabled him to avoid detection. Public outcry had reached a fever pitch and several riots had been narrowly avoided.

From the bald man in the pea coat (a walking encyclopedia of ghastly crimes and murders), I also learned that Haarman wasn't the only one. Two other cannibalistic killers had been apprehended in eastern Europe during this very same period, one by the name of Karl Denke, born in Munsterberg, Silesia, in Prussia. Denke, an organ player in the local church, and well-loved by his neighbors, came under scrutiny when a man, bleeding badly from his head, escaped from his apartment claiming that Denke had tried to kill him with an axe. When they broke down his door they discovered evidence of extensive, ongoing mass murder, flesh curing, and cannibalism. Karl Denke, as it turned out, had been an active cannibal from 1910 till 1924, killing somewhere between forty and sixty persons, mostly travelers and homeless people, and eating them, or else selling their meat to unsuspecting patrons at the nearby market in Breslau.

The second cannibal killer caught in this same period was a sausage-maker by the name of Carl Grossman, a successful businessman who had owned a meat supply company in Berlin, Germany throughout WWI.

Bizarrely, Grossman's cannibalistic killing spree lasted from 1918 to 1921, overlapping almost perfectly with Haarman's killings in Hanover, though apparently the two had never met. He was finally caught when, on August 12th, 1921, the screams of his final victim aroused suspicion throughout the neighborhood. When they forced their way into his apartment, it became clear that Grossman had been murdering, butchering, eating, and selling the bodies of numerous indigent women, mostly prostitutes, whom he met at the train station. Estimates of how many killed are somewhere between fifty and one hundred, though the true number will never be known. Like Denke, Grossman, being a trusted name in the local meat industry, is believed to have served many hundreds of pounds of human meat to unsuspecting customers, telling them that it was pork or beef.

I must admit that, of all the horrors which were described to me on that dock, the one which haunted me most was the fact that two out of three of these men had, not only become cannibals themselves, preying upon the poor and the vulnerable, but had taken it a step further by serving human meat to thousands of unknowing customers. On the one hand, with the vast majority of German people living in dire poverty, the harvesting of human meat had an obvious financial motive. On the other hand, I could not help but to wonder if this ploy was not also, perhaps, a surreptitious way of creating more Encerrados? How many of those unwitting cannibal customers, for example, had, upon tasting human meat, gone on to develop cravings, or prophetic dreams, or enhanced senses of one sort or another, or all three? How many had, knowingly or unknowingly, vomited up offspring? I had a sudden vision of a vast brood of Red Things incubating in the sewer systems of Eastern Europe but I shrugged it off with a shudder.

I added these three European cannibals to the ever-growing list of people I suspected of being Encerrados. I continued to speculate about Fawcett, Carmilla, Mary, Howard, Legion, the entire Galleani Gang, and myself. Just how common was this phenomenon? How many more of us might there be, hidden at every level of society, leading secret lives, awaiting the day when they might come out and show the world who and what they have become.

Repulsed as I was by these men's heartless choice of victims, I had to wonder at the philosophy behind Haarman, Denke, and Grossman's decision to kill the poorest and most vulnerable members of their society. The criteria by which they had selected their victims seemed the very inverse of my own; I felt nothing but revulsion when I thought of them. These were, I felt, without a doubt, the authoritarian Encerrados whose existence I had wondered about for years — the descendants, as it were, of Minski, men whose passengers had, apparently, passed on their generalized loathing for all humanity to their hosts. I was horrified to comprehend at last that, when my own crimes came to light, I, myself, would undoubtedly be placed in the same category as these authoritarian fiends and child-killers. Despite my intense disgust, I also could not help but to feel a certain reluctant sympathy with these poor lost and demented souls.

Near the end of this discussion, I asked the grey-bearded man, "Do you think we've got ourselves a Fritz Haarman, or a Karl Denke, here in York, Maine?"

He looked at me thoughtfully before he replied.

"The word on the street is that the police are looking for a fellow from Southwick. That's all anyone knows. They say he's killed nearly a hundred people... The Law has been trying to hunt him down for years but, officially, they deny his existence."

"I heard he only kills very wealthy men of power and authority," muttered the man in the pea-coat. "That's why they are keeping it out of the papers. They are terrified that others might try to emulate him."

I asked the others what they thought, but I received only shrugs and blank stares in reply.

It was all beginning to hit a little too close for comfort. Shortly hereafter, the wind picked up and, as the cold become unbearable to my companions, I feigned a chill, bid them all a good night, and departed the harbor. Finding an inn that was less than three blocks from the wharf, I rented a room where I slept for the next two days.

*   *   *   *

I AWOKE AT SUNRISE. AFTER PAYING MY TAB, I LEFT THE INN ABOUT 7 a.m., following the smell of freshly baked bread to a bakery, where I purchased several rolls for my breakfast. Already I could feel the strange pull of the sea, a subtle longing to go down to the beach. Instead, I went over to the York public library where I read several documents on the history of Boone Island, and learned of its exact location.

It was here, in a book on famous New England shipwrecks, that I learned of the wreck of the *Nottingham Galley*, a trading ship en route to Boston from Ireland, which had wrecked off Boone Island in the snowy December of 1710. The ship, suddenly immersed in blinding late-night fog, and assailed by contrary winds, had run aground against the rocky shore of the island, instantly splitting the vessel through the middle. Fourteen men made it to the shore, dragging themselves, and each other, onto the barren rock, while their ship was slowly battered to pieces upon the boulders.

Nearly all the food had gone down with the ship, except for a few small hunks of cheese. Exploring the island, the castaways soon discovered that it was little more than a hundred yards in length and fifty in breadth, bereft of soil or vegetation, and void of any shelter. The ground was so rocky and uneven that the men could not even walk around to keep themselves warm. They remained in this pitiful condition for over a month.

It was an uncommonly stormy winter that year and, with no sustenance and no shelter, the wet and freezing men soon sickened. Three days after the wreck, the cook died and, over the next three weeks, several others succumbed to the elements. Simultaneously, hunger set in. One man was able to kill a gull but eventually, when the hunger pains became unbearable, the survivors were left with no other option but to cannibalize the dead. Some were reluctant at first but, with an agonizing death by starvation as the only possible alternative, even the squeamish eventually partook of the fresh meat. Nearly a month later, they were sighted by a passing ship and rescued. They disembarked at the mouth of the Piscataqua River where, coming ashore, their tale of terror soon became known to the world. Eventually, a lighthouse was built on Boone Island.

The only other curious episode I found was a strange, sad tale of an old lighthouse keeper, a fellow by the name of Williams, who had lived there with his young bride, sometime in the late 1800s. Several months after their arrival, there was a terrible storm. Wind, waves, and driving rains pummeled the island savagely for several days. Enormous boulders were tossed across the island like playthings, as colossal waves pounded away at the structures. The couple were trapped inside the lighthouse for a period of several days. One day, the husband had to retrieve supplies from one of the outbuildings. Being outside in this peculiar rain, even for a few minutes, he quickly became ill and died within a few days. His wife managed to keep the beacon lit for the remainder of the storm but, once the bad weather had passed, she ceased to light it. Noted by passing sailors, the unlit beacon was interpreted as a sign of distress; a ship carrying several local mariners went to investigate. Rowing ashore in a small dinghy, they discovered the wife, quite mad, creeping among the boulders near the water's edge and muttering to herself about the strange death of her husband. When the sailors attempted to communicate with her, she cackled at them, vehemently insisting that some of the rocks were not actually rocks, but some kind of monsters cleverly disguised as rocks. Not surprisingly, she claimed to have seen, on numerous occasions, boulders crawling, crabwise, over the surface of the island. Additionally, she told the mariners that, several times, while the storm had been at its worst, she had peered down from the top of the lighthouse and seen a host of nameless horrors, swimming in circles around the island and even, on occasion, rising out of the sea. Committed to a hospital for the insane, the poor woman died soon thereafter.

Most importantly, I learned that Boone Island is located approximately six miles due east of Cape Neddick. It is my plan, barring interruptions or disasters, to swim there tonight, after the writing of this document is complete.

*   *   *   *

WHILE IN THE LIBRARY, I WAS FINALLY ABLE TO PURSUE AN IDEA WOULD which had been haunting me, namely, the notion that sensitive poets like Baudelaire, Artaud, Breton, Longfellow, and Frost may have had enhanced senses and some limited awareness of the Hidden Ones, and of the larger horror unfolding in the world. With this in mind, I selected several recent poetry journals, full of poems from around the world, and was more than a little startled by some of the imagery I encountered. Making my way through this small stack of booklets, I found ample reason to suspect that some of these poets might well be having awakenings and transformations which very much resembled my own, whether or not they were conscious of the fact.

The first one I picked up was a journal called *Caras y Caretas*, where I found a translated version of the following anonymous poem, entitled "Desde los Andes" ("From the Andes") whose vaguely religious mountain imagery immediately conjured up unpleasant recollections of my own nightmares of Machu Picchu. This poem seemed to describe, not just the unforgettable advent of the flapping horror I'd seen in my dream, but even the powers it bestowed upon the nearby worshipers. I will reproduce the relevant passages here.

My immoderate satanic pride
finally trod, beneath its triumphant feet,
The apex of the mountain heights, never before tracked,
Not even by golden eagles...
The sky laments my pain... and everything
Is obliterated by darkness and undone by mire,
And above the ice of the summit, standing tall,

My soul is so frozen that it does not notice,
Snarling over the cadaver of my life,
That gigantic black thing — death!

...the darkness spread and became denser,
Almost palpable, like something alive;
And a convulsive anguish shook

The frozen peace of the immense mountain...

And there was a silence of thoughtful pain
That, thinking, increases its pain...
Life became more sensitive,
And emotion deeper and more intense!

Elsewhere, I came upon a poem by Archibald MacLeish entitled "The End of the World" whose second stanza (like "Desdes los Andes") called to mind my vision of the gigantic airborne Viracocha flying low through the night sky, toward the silent worshipers at Machu Picchu.

And there, there overhead, there, there hung over
Those thousands of white faces, those dazed eyes,
There in the starless dark the poise, the hover,
There with vast wings across the canceled skies,
There in the sudden blackness the black pall
Of nothing, nothing, nothing — nothing at all.

In yet another recent journal I came upon a poem called "Earth Visitors" by Kenneth Slessor, filled with images distressingly reminiscent of the Hidden Ones and whose closing lines seemed to describe a Tree Thing tapping at the window glass. It read, in part, as follows.

There were strange riders once, came gusting down
Cloaked in dark furs, with faces grave and sweet,
And white as air...
It is long now since great daemons walked on earth,
Staining with wild radiance a country bed,
And leaving only a confusion of sharp dreams...
The unpastured Gods have gone,
They are above those fiery-coasted clouds
Floating like fins of stone in the burnt air,
And earth is only a troubled thought to them
That sometimes drifts like wind...

There is one yet comes knocking in the night,
The drums of sweet conspiracy on the pane,
When darkness has arched his hands over the bush
And Springwood steams with dew, and the stars look down
On that one lonely chamber...

355

In a similarly apocalyptic vein, I found a poem entitled "There Will Come Soft Rains" by Sara Teasdale which describes nature reclaiming the earth after the human race has been obliterated in a nameless "war."

There will come soft rains and the smell of the ground,
And swallows circling with their shimmering sound;
And frogs in the pool singing at night,
And wild plum trees in tremulous white;
Robins will wear their feathery fire,
Whistling their whims on a low fence-wire;
And not one will know of the war, not one
Will care at last when it is done.
Not one would mind, neither bird nor tree,
If mankind perished utterly;

And Spring herself when she woke at dawn
Would scarcely know that we were gone.

Finally, in an anthology of Modern Classics I encountered Poe's "Eldorado," published in 1849, which I thought would make an appropriate, if haunting, eulogy for myself and Percy Fawcett and the countless men who had disappeared in the Amazon. Interestingly, this is considered by most scholars to be the very last poem Poe ever wrote.

Gaily bedight,
A gallant knight,
In sunshine and in shadow,
Had journeyed long,
Singing a song,
In search of Eldorado.

But he grew old —
This knight so bold —
And o'er his heart a shadow
Fell as he found
No spot of ground
That looked like Eldorado.

And, as his strength
Failed him at length,

He met a pilgrim shadow —
"Shadow," said he,
"Where can it be —
This land of Eldorado?"

"Over the mountains
Of the Moon,
Down the Valley of the Shadow,
Ride, boldly ride,"
The shade replied —
"If you seek for Eldorado!"

I could go on, dear reader, but I will stop there. I felt my theory of poets with enhanced-senses had received a satisfactory confirmation. I departed the library under a thrill of terror so pervasive that I had to shove my hands in my pockets to stop the uncontrollable shaking.

Seeing that it was still quite early in the day, I purchased several blank notebooks and, selecting a coffeehouse down near the docks, I settled in to write out this final narrative. I began at 9:40 this morning. After eleven hours of furious scribbling, I am finally finished.

EPILOGUE

AT LONG LAST, MY JOURNEY HAS REACHED ITS END. WITH MY departure so near at hand, I cannot help but to reflect on the future of this New England countryside which I have come to know so well over these eleven years. I feel tremendous apprehension for all the countless millions going about their daily lives within the confines of modern civilization. It is all of you whom I wish to address.

Whatever shall we do about the condition of our world? Barring a worldwide revolution, what kind of a future can Humanity reasonably look forward to? The myths of industrial civilization have taken hold of the minds of men, the majority of whom seem only too willing (or else pathetically resigned) to be swept up in its hideous and deadly momentum. When the myth of Progress and fables of Democracy fail to draw them in, then it is the sheer grinding poverty which coerces them to participate, regardless of their hatred. It all has the undeniable appearance of doom and degradation to me now; I can barely recall that I once felt that this place was my home. Now, when I look upon the cities of Man, all I can see are the hallmarks of widespread misery and industrial suicide.

Everywhere men, women, and children toil like beasts for their earthly masters, the new Lords of Profit and Empire. Everywhere men and women founder in their attempts to free themselves from the money system, duped and absorbed at every turn by political charlatans, careerist union organizers, and preachers of Protestant self-hatred and submission. Dangerously large numbers of people are still lost in the fairytales of Modernity, or else passively awaiting the return of the Christ. Human civilization resembles nothing so much as a hostile and ravenous beast, slowly, brutally, subduing and overrunning all as it perpetrates a systematic liquidation and reconfiguration of all life, including its own. It does this, it seems, at the violent insistence of a deranged but profoundly wealthy minority, themselves dangerously possessed by the myths of Civilization and their own eternal glorification. Christianity, Scientism, Capitalism, Communism: all fingers of the same glove; all poisonous; all doomed, sooner or later, to catastrophic failure, and destined to drag the rest of the natural world down with it. The

358

process of industrialization in the urban centers is nearly complete and it has already become difficult to remember that it was ever any other way.

There was a time when I believed that authoritarian societies like America were doomed, their gradual enslavement of the masses inevitably breeding discontent, sowing the seeds of rebellion, inevitably giving rise to revolts. Now I am not so sure. The millionaires who run industrial society have convinced a disturbingly large number of people that humanity could not survive without them, and have derived a kind of bogus loyalty, tinged with the ever-present threat of vilification, police violence, and prison for dissenters. Any antipathy or ambivalence about this system is seen not merely as treasonous, but now (thanks to the psychologists) evidence of some exotic and complex neurosis, a mental disease to be treated with incarceration, behavior modification, drug experimentation, surgery, and sterilization. In the age of psychiatry, the fully assimilated, high-functioning imbecile is held up as the model of mental health.

All over the world, the minds of men are being put to the test. It is now my explicit understanding that, if authoritarianism wins out, then the experiment of human existence shall be deemed a failure, and we shall be exterminated by our makers. Over the last two decades, we have seen increasing rebellions and uprisings, enough to justify the hope that Humanity may be re-ordering itself on a massive scale. Across the globe there have been numerous attempts to overthrow the current global system of domination and exploitation. But the forces of power and privilege have noticed this trend too and have continued to send in the cops and soldiers to suppress these efforts whenever and wherever they occur.

Even so, from Russia to Mexico, from Ireland to Japan, and even here in America, formidable worker and peasant rebellions have shaken the old order. Insurrection has erupted all over Western Europe and, in Belgium, France, and Italy, worker uprisings are becoming increasingly common. The recent General Strike in England, on behalf of the coal miners, lasted for nine days, and the ominous rumblings of their discontent continue to be heard and felt. In Chile, there is also talk of a General Strike, as violent outbreaks continue to occur between police and striking workers from Santiago to Valparaiso. In Mexico, the class war continues to rage between the armed peasantry and the *Federales* who defend the local robber barons. Despite the extreme and often pre-emptive brutality of the police, hired mobs, and military squads, their viciousness is no match for so vast and numerous an opponent as an armed and mobilized underclass. The uprisings in Uruguay, Brazil, England, and elsewhere confirm that the hunger for autonomy is sweeping through the oppressed classes. From the numerous recent assassination attempts against

Mussolini, to the killing of Rogelio Perez, the persecutor of anarchists in Barcelona, I have found many reasons to feel a tentative hope for the future.

Just yesterday I learned of a recent assassination attempt upon Prince Hirohito by members of the Japanese Guillotine Society, a secret group of anarchist assassins who have targeted, among others, the police chief Masataro Fukuda, who murdered two well-known and much loved anarchist agitators. In the chaotic aftermath of the Kanto earthquake of 1923, the Japanese authorities had utilized the civic disruption caused by the earthquake as an opportunity to brutalize and murder numerous political radicals. On September 16, 1923, just two weeks after the earthquake, anarchist propagandists Noe Ito, her lover Sakae Osugi, and their six-year-old nephew, were arrested, clubbed to death, and thrown down a well. Police Chief Masataro Fukuda, it was widely known, took a leading role in these killings. When this brutal triple murder became known, it caused tremendous public outrage, eventually giving rise to the Guillotine Society, comrades of the deceased determined to avenge their friends. Fukuda was shot and had his house blown to bits by a homemade bomb not unlike the one I had used back in Roxbury. The Police Chief, however, was not home at the time. Later, this Guillotine Society made similar assassination attempts against the president of the monopolistic and land-grabbing Kanebo Corporation.

What these events may or may not signal is unknown, and yet I am convinced that if Humanity does not succeed in these revolutionary efforts, if we do not prove ourselves to be imaginative, capable, thinking creatures — dignified beings who will not allow themselves to be bullied and enslaved by a belligerent and deranged minority of our own kind — then we shall be deemed a failure as a species and exterminated. I have seen it many times now in my dreams. The Hidden Ones will emerge and the Earth will be cleared for the next experiment.

So, as you see, all is not lost. It is not too late to destroy this harvester of misery that is sweeping the globe. It is not too late to take apart this nightmare society that we have created and transform the world into the kind of place where all of the earth's inhabitants may live free of authority and develop themselves as they please. To quote a flyer which the Galleanists would hand out at demonstrations, "We were not born to toil as automatons... but to live free, to destroy this world of crime and misery that has been built around us and to rebuild with its freed atoms a new civilization, as yet undreamed of."

I am now almost entirely convinced that our Overlords are trying to create beings comparable to themselves, intellectually and psychically sturdy beings who can behold, and even converse with, a Hidden One and not go instantly insane. They want companions, peers, fellow gods — not livestock. Sadly, the minds of this current human species, when in the presence of these undisguised Beings, seem pitifully volatile and prone to a kind of frenetic instability. This instability is, in fact, the very trait which they had hoped to breed out of us by now. They have need of creatures who can think and build and live in large numbers without forming hierarchies of domination. If we cannot teach ourselves how to do these things — how to expand our minds, our bodies, our selves — then we shall be wiped out (perhaps in a deadly meteor shower, or yet another flood, or by our own catastrophic stupidity) and we shall be no more. If we, as a species, continue to languish within these authoritarian social structures, we must understand that we do so at tremendous peril. How many more idiotic wars and man-made catastrophes will our Overseers permit? A hundred or a hundred million? Who can say?

It is my belief that the hybridized, civilization-hating Encerrados I have described, imperfect though they may be as individuals, represent the next step forward, a new kind of human being. People like Mary Mallon and Carmilla, Luigi Galleani and Bartolo Vanzetti. Perhaps some of my readers know someone with the telltale signs. You shall know them by their strange insistence on living free, their refusal to submit themselves to society's enforced inhibitions. They, too, will have glimpsed the awful future that awaits us, should we continue on this current trajectory, and will express apprehensions along these lines. They will be inclined to denounce, perhaps even flatly reject, any civilized mode of existence. Undoubtedly, they may have abandoned systematized morality, having tasted the fruit of their desires, and thus begun the process of de-civilizing their minds and bodies. But we must be wary. Civilized Humanity continues to kill, banish, or lock away anyone who steps outside the bounds of servility, and the numbskull acquiescence to authoritarian morality that is rapidly becoming the norm. We must learn to listen to these mad individuals, these poets, these paranoiacs, and heed their strange, often coded, wisdom — no matter how unpleasant or disturbing their implications might be.

The time for our self-emancipation is now. If we passively allow ourselves to be policed, governed, and farmed, then we confirm our inferiority and participate in our own enslavement. We cannot behave like livestock anymore. It is time to become like the wolves of the forest. If we are to endure the monstrous conflicts that lie ahead, then we must make monsters of ourselves, just as I myself have done, and countless others before. Civilization has always been a temporary thing, and the wisest among us (men like Rousseau, Fairchild, Whitman, Thoreau, Fourier, and Nordau) have often regarded it as a mistake.

Is it a mistake we are courageous enough to unmake? We must bring back the spirit of the French Terror and the Russian uprisings of 1905 and 1917, the days when arrogant Tsars and spoiled princesses were blown to bits in their carriages, when starry-eyed rebels lunged, with daggers drawn, at the Henry Clay Fricks of the world. We must become what we were always meant to become; something worthy of life, an animal too fierce and too beautiful ever to accept domestication.

New ways of thinking are necessary. The time has come for us to leave our humanity behind us, like discarded clothing, and become something more. We must abandon this ridiculous Humanism which blinds and degrades us by provoking and encouraging our imagined superiority over all other Beings. Man is neither the apex of evolution nor the degraded sinner in need of autocratic governance. A wise man once said, "The most merciful thing... is the mind's inability to correlate its contents." I would modify this and address it to all future generations of Humanity (however few or doomed they may be). The most *insidious and detrimental* thing is the mind's inability to correlate its contents. If we ever expect to endure the nightmare that is coming, we must learn to think in bigger, more complex, ways about everything. We must learn to comprehend these things, or we stand no chance of surviving the coming massacre, and must surely perish in ways too brutal to contemplate.

If nothing else, it is my hope that my tale illustrates how such a change might come about. Take André Breton's suggestion, and permit yourself to go insane, immerse yourself in your dreams, give in to the strange hungers that lurk in the back of your mind, and heed the revelations they inspire. The food of the gods is all around you, you need only avail yourself of its gift. To eat like a god, to live, fight, and dream like a god, is to transform oneself into a god — a god who hunts and eats other gods, and is eaten by them. Human brain meat... ordinary men shun it, and so shall remain ignorant of its transformative powers, but there is no other way I know of.

*   *   *   *

AS I PREPARE TO DEPART FOR BOONE ISLAND, I CANNOT HELP BUT think of the many persons who have gone before me, men like Percy Fawcett, who have disappeared under bizarre and suggestive circumstances over the past few years. How many others (like Legion the Giant, Carmilla, and Howard) have flung themselves into the sea in pursuit of this very same portal, or to join a vast procession of underwater horrors marching down into some unknown oceanic abyss?

What, for example, of the disappearance of Arthur Craven, the Dadaist, anarchist and nephew of the notorious Oscar Wilde? After putting his wife Mina on a boat to Argentina, Craven was last seen departing from Salina Cruz, Mexico in October of 1918, alone in a small sailboat, with a plan to meet up with his wife at their destination. He never arrived and, after several weeks, he was presumed to have drowned at sea. Later, his wife commented that, in the months leading up to his fatal journey, he had been dreaming intensely of the ocean, particularly, of a city beneath the sea, where he heard strange voices calling out to him.

What of the disappearance of writer and journalist Ambrose Bierce, who in December of 1913 had purportedly gone to document (and perhaps join) the Mexican Revolution, only to vanish shortly thereafter? Like Howard, Bierce had been an avid chronicler of unexplainable phenomena and bizarre anecdotes, having a curious knack for tracking down odd folktales about supernatural occurrences and bizarre disappearances. Like Howard, and Arthur Machen before him, Bierce documented them under the guise of fiction. Like certain others, he too seemed to possess a keen, and sadly rare, ability to see through the popular political delusions of his time. In a letter to his niece on the eve of his departure, Bierce confirmed that he was headed to "Mexico and then South America" adding, by way of an explanation, "Civilization is damned! — It's the mountains and the desert for me." Shortly thereafter, he too vanished from the face of the earth.

Were these men headed to Peru? Had they learned of a portal in that region and gone searching for it? Had they learned (or dreamed) of a portal in the Andes and gone to find it? Did Craven and Bierce eventually make their way to Machu Picchu, or the peak which overlooks Machu Picchu? Was it in the desert, as Bierce states in his final note? Perhaps the Nazca Plain? Or was it in the Amazon jungle as Fawcett seemed to think? Had all three vanished men successfully reached their destinations? Had they found and utilized portals which communicated with other worlds? Craven's choice to sail by himself certainly seems curious. Had his dreams led him to a city or portal under the ocean? I thought of the trench off the coast of New York City which I'd floated over, and wondered if Craven had not perhaps joined up with a similar underwater procession off the coast of Peru.

I could speculate endlessly about these things, patient reader, but I must now stop. As you see, it is never-ending. I am only stalling. The coffeehouse is only open for another half hour; it is time for me to go. From where I am sitting, here by the window, I can plainly see the docks, still crawling with coppers and outraged locals. After I quietly make my exit from this coffeehouse, leaving this, my final statement, behind, I will make my way down to York Beach, where I shall undress, enter the water, and begin the long swim to Boone Island.

Will I even reach my destination? Will I be swallowed up by some vast, ocean-going monstrosity? For all I know, I might be swimming straight into the jaws of some unforeseen guardian of the Boone Island portal, perhaps one of those great circling shapes described by the lighthouse keeper's wife. It does not matter. I have no more fear left in me. I must go. York Beach awaits me. It consoles and pleases me greatly to think that I will be following in Carmilla's footprints.

So long, my earthly paradise. Farewell!

Robert Henry Pearce
December 19, 1926

www.ingramcontent.com/pod-product-compliance
Lightning Source LLC
Chambersburg PA
CBHW022206030726
47494CB00021B/1628